# Cha

*Jackie Hall*

mystery

by

# Ken Blaisdell

Copyright © 2022 by Ken Blaisdell
ISBN: 978-1-7344849-3-9

Published by
**Lightkeeper Press**

All rights reserved.
Neither the whole nor any part of this work
may be reproduced in any form without
the written permission of the author.

The following is a work of fiction.
Where the names of real people are used
it is with their permission and they are
acknowledged at the end of this book.

Cover art by Jennifer Deuker

Printed in USA

Chalk Targets					Ken Blaisdell

*When the archer misses the center of the target, he turns and seeks for the cause of his failure in himself, not in the target.*

Confucius
551–479 BC

Chalk Targets                                    Ken Blaisdell

# *Prologue*

She was blindfolded but not gagged. Still, she made no sound; no cry for help as he tied her, fully clothed, to the four corners of her own bed. Only he would have heard her cries and it would only have made him more excited. She refused to give him that satisfaction.

He worked swiftly and silently and she was soon immobilized and helpless. The ropes looped around her wrists and ankles were secure, but not tight. They only dug in if she fought against them, so she didn't fight. She just lay there, willing her breathing to stay even and calm.

She couldn't see him, of course, but she knew that he was standing there looking at her, admiring his work, deciding how he wanted to proceed.

Suddenly, she felt a tug and he ripped open her blouse, sending buttons flying. The suddenness of his action surprised her and she sucked in her breath but still, she did not cry out.

She felt his weight push against the side of the bed. She could hear his breath and she knew he was leaning over her. Then she felt the cold steel of a knife as its flat side slid across her chest and made its way under her bra between her breasts. A sharp tug and the fabric gave way to the blade. He slid the steel slowly over her breasts pushing the cups aside and exposing her flesh to his gaze.

The next excruciating minutes seemed like an hour to her as he moved from one side of the bed to the other and the blade traveled all over her body slitting every article of clothing that she wore. It was obvious that he was in no hurry and she was sure that he was enjoying what he was doing ... maybe even as much as what he was *going* to do.

He took her shredded blouse by the collar and dragged it out from under her. Her bra followed, leaving her naked from the waist up. For several very long seconds, there was nothing. No sound but her own breathing; no touch to her body; no tug at her clothes—what was left of them.

Then she heard a soft click and she knew had taken a picture of her half-naked and tied spread eagle to her own bed.

A moment later he roughly yanked the rag that was her jeans out from under her, taking her panties with them. She now lay completely naked in front of him, save the blindfold tied across her face.

She lay there, helpless, listening to the unmistakable sounds of the man getting out of his own clothes. She felt his weight on the bed, and then she felt his nakedness against hers as he straddled her pelvis. He leaned down and covered her mouth with his.

She returned his kiss with a passionate hunger that she had never known with her husband. Between heavy breaths, in a hoarse whisper, she said into his mouth, "If you don't fuck me pretty quick, baby, I am going to explode!"

He laughed and said, "Your wish is my command, my sweet."

Half an hour later he untied her wrists and ankles from the bedposts and they embraced. They cuddled and kissed lovingly for a long while before getting up and walking hand in hand to the shower.

As he soaped her body, running his hands over every inch of her nakedness, she tried to recall the last time she and her husband—her *late* husband—had taken a shower together. She couldn't.

\*\*\*

"Hey, honey? Are you coming out to eat?" Pamela called down the hallway from the kitchen.

"Yeah!" Harry shouted in reply. "I'm just finishing a chapter. I'll be right out." He hit the save button and looked at the bottom of the screen. Ninety-eight pages; about half done.

As Harry sat down at the table, Pamela asked, "So, is the husband dead, yet? Or did you decide to prolong the agony of him knowing that his wife is cheating?"

"Oh, no, he died in the last chapter," he answered, spearing a couple of green beans with his fork. "The wife is just now getting a taste of how much her co-conspirator lover enjoys total control, but she thinks it's just kinky sex, right now."

"Oh, what a tangled web we weave when we conspire to kill our husband," Pamela joked. "So, does *she* live?"

"I haven't decided, yet," Harry answered. "I've got a couple different directions I'm thinking about taking it."

# *Chapter 1*
**Thursday, July 8, 2021**

"9-1-1. What is your emergency?"

"My wife's unresponsive! I'm doing chest compressions and mouth-to-mouth but she's not breathing! Please get an ambulance here, quick! This is Harry Fletcher at 55 Weldon Farm Road."

"Oh, God, Harry!" Gail said, having known both Harry and his wife, Pamela for years. "Keep working on her; I'll dispatch fire right away. Stay on the line with me. Do you know what happened?"

"I think she fell in the bathtub. She might have downed."

As Gail typed "Drowning; Bathtub" and then pressed a series of buttons to transfer the information and the address to the in-vehicle computers of the fire department vehicles next door and to the two police patrol cars, Gail heard Harry's phone clunk onto the floor, and then the sounds of him grunting as he leaned heavily onto his wife's chest over and over. Between grunts, she heard him plead, "Come on, baby! Come on! Start breathing! Don't leave me, baby! Come on!"

After three minutes of encouraging him over the phone, Gail said, "You're doing good, Harry. Just a little longer; Engine Three just turned onto your street. Is the door open?"

"Shit! No, it's locked!" he answered, and then Gail heard him say to himself, "Where the fuck's my phone?" She heard some shuffling, heard him say, apparently to his phone, "Come on! Come on!" and then to her, "Okay; it's open!"

She heard a thump that she envisioned was Harry dropping his phone again, and then heard him say, "*Shit!* She's still not breathing, Gail!" There was a slight pause, and he added, "And she doesn't have a heartbeat! *Shit! Shit! Shit!*" She then heard the sounds of him resuming the chest compressions.

"Don't give up Harry! They're in your driveway," Gail told him. "Keep up the compressions; that's getting blood to her brain. Thirty compressions and two breaths. You're doing great! Just a couple more minutes!"

A few moments later, Gail faintly heard a door open and then heard Harry shout, "In here! Hurry!" It was followed by rapidly approaching footsteps of people wearing shoes.

"Okay, Harry," Gail heard a woman say, "You did great; we'll take it now."

"All right, I'm going to hang up now," Gail said. But in the confusion and the noise, she didn't hear a reply.

Just before ending the connection, she heard the faint *whoop* of another siren. She hoped it was the ambulance that had responded to her open request.

Knowing she had done all she could for Harry and Pamela, Gail tapped an icon on her screen opening a call to Chief Hall's cell phone.

A few moments later the call was answered over the car speaker by Susan Belle, the swing-shift dispatcher. Susan's father, Bob Hardy, had been Rowley's first Chief of Police, and at that time her mother, Hilda, was the *only* dispatcher.

"Rowley Police ... oh, hi, Chief," Susan said with Jackie's name on her screen. "Did they tell you about Pamela Fletcher?"

"Scott got there right after the EMTs," she replied. "He said they took her in the ambulance, but she didn't look good. They were still bagging her and doing chest compressions."

"Did he say if Harry went with them to the hospital?" Jackie asked.

"He said he did," Susan answered. "I told Scott that Gail had called you, and he said he was going to wait there to hear from you."

"Okay, thanks, Susan ," Jackie said. "I'll call Scott, right now, but I think I'm going to head to the hospital. If you hear anything from the hospital or the EMTs or anybody, call me right away."

Half a minute later, she was talking to Scott through the Jeep's speakers.

"Hi, Chief. Are you on the way here?" he asked her.

"I was planning to drive over to the hospital unless you need me there," she replied. "What does the scene look like? Did you take pictures?"

"It looks like someone was pulled out of the bathtub and was lying on the floor. There's water everywhere," he answered. "She has a good size gash over her right eye, and there's blood on the edge of the tub where she hit. I have pictures of everything."

"How much water is in the tub?" she asked.

"About half full, maybe," he said. "But it's going down. The drain doesn't seal very well, apparently."

"Go to the kitchen and find a Tupperware container or something and save a sample of the water before it's gone," she told him.

"You suspect foul play?" he asked, the surprise obvious in his voice.

"Not in the least," Jackie said. "But insurance company investigators get paid to suspect that. I just want everything documented. In fact, shoot the whole house while you're there.

Bedrooms, other bathrooms, kitchen, wastebaskets; pretend it *is* a crime scene."

"Okay. Will do," he said. "I was going to wipe up the water on the floor since I already have pictures of it. Is that okay? If it gets under the tile it's not going to be good for their floor."

Jackie thought for a moment, and then said, "Is there any blood on the floor or in the water on the floor?"

There was a pause while Jackie assumed he was looking, and then he answered, "I don't see anything."

"Okay," she said. "Go ahead and wipe up the water. Good work, Scott. Thanks. I'll talk to you later."

She disconnected the phone and as she drove north toward Newburyport, she thought about the exchange she just had with her patrolman. Not only had he done good police work at the scene, considering he was a relative rooky, but he showed personal concern for Harry and Pamela by wanting to clean up their bathroom so the floor wouldn't warp. She really did like living in a small town.

## Chapter 3
**Thursday, July 8, 2021**

When Jackie walked into the emergency room entrance at the Anna Jaques Hospital in Newburyport, she saw Harry standing and talking with a woman whom she took to be a doctor. They both looked very solemn, and a knot grew in her stomach.

As she approached, the doctor walked away leaving Harry standing there staring at the floor.

"Harry," Jackie said softly. "Are you okay?"

He turned, looked at her vacantly, and then after a couple of focusing blinks, he said, "She's dead."

"Oh, God, Harry, I'm so sorry," Jackie said opening her arms to embrace him.

He closed his arms across her back, not really in an embrace but more as a perfunctory reaction to her hugging him.

"Thanks," he said then opened his arms indicating the embrace was over. He looked at her, and added, "I wasn't there for her. She drowned in her own fucking bathtub because I wanted to watch a movie I've seen a dozen times. Shit!"

"Don't blame yourself, Harry; it was an accident," she said knowing how cliché the words sounded even as they left her mouth. "From what I was told, you did everything right. Everything anyone *could* have done."

"But it was all too late," he said. "The doctor just told me that things were probably irreversible before I started CPR on her ... as if *that* was going to make me feel better somehow." He looked Jackie in the eyes with a hard stare, and said, "She died in her bathtub while I was watching James-fucking-Bond!"

Just then a man in casual office attire rather than scrubs approached, and said, "Are you the next of kin for Pamela Fletcher?"

Harry looked at him and answered, "I'm her husband, Harold."

"On behalf of the hospital and the staff, please accept my deepest sympathies on your loss, Mr. Fletcher," the man said. "My name is Robert Thomas. I'm a grief counselor and I just wanted you to know that there's somebody here to talk to if you feel the need. I can see that you're not alone, and that's a good thing, but if either of you needs me, here is my card."

As he handed each of them a business card with the hospital's logo, he added, "I'm aware that it's a hard time, so if you'd like me to call someone to make arrangements to have your wife transported, I can do that for you, too."

"Oh, God," Harry exhaled wearily. "I hadn't even thought about that. Yes, if you wouldn't mind, could you call Robert's Funeral Home in Rowley? Tell them I'll call them tomorrow to talk about her, um ... her services."

"Absolutely, Mr. Fletcher. I'll take care of it, right away," Thomas said. "Again, I know how traumatic a loss like this can be, so if you feel the need to talk at any time, please give me a call."

"Thank you," Harry said as he extended his hand. "I appreciate your condolences and your help, Mr. Thomas."

After shaking with Harry, Thomas extended his hand to Jackie, and said, "Are you a friend or family member?"

"I'm Jacquelyn Hall. Rowley Chief of Police," she said.

"Oh!" he said in surprised reaction.

"But I'm a friend of the family," she added. "Thank you for your sympathy and your help, Mr. Thomas."

As Thomas walked away, Harry said, "I guess I should get back home. There's a mess in the bathroom that needs to be cleaned up, and I've got a bunch of phone calls to dread making."

"I told Scott Lain to mop up the water in the bathroom before he left your house," Jackie said. "I'd volunteer to make some of those phone calls for you, but I know that's something that only you can do."

"But, you know, I can see how it might be ... uncomfortable to spend the night at home tonight," she went on, "so you're welcome to stay at my place if you'd like. I've got a guest room with its own bath." She immediately regretted mentioning the bath.

"Thanks. I appreciate that," he said, "but I think I'll be okay."

"Well, if you think of anything else at all that you need, just call me."

"I will, thanks," he said and gave her a more meaningful hug than the first.

"Are you okay to drive home?" she asked. "I can give you a lift and come back tomorrow for your car."

"No, really, I'm fine," he said. "I'll need the time alone to figure out what the hell I'm going to tell people when I call them."

In the parking lot Jackie walked with Harry to his car, they hugged once more, and then she walked back to her Jeep.

She started it, and as she took the Rowley Police placard out of the windshield, she looked at her gas gauge. The tank was nearly empty. She had planned on getting gas on the way to the station in the morning, but now she was concerned that she might not make it home. A detour to a nearby gas station was about to make a long night a little longer.

# *Chapter 4*
### Thursday, July 8, 2021

As Jackie approached her house she could see Jeff's car still in her driveway. Closer still, and she could make him out sitting behind the wheel. She groaned out loud. She really didn't need to deal with him, right now.

When she pulled into her driveway, she realized that it wasn't Jeff's car, nor was it Jeff behind the wheel. It was Harry in his identical generic Toyota.

They both got out at the same time and met in front of Jackie's Jeep.

"Are you okay, Harry?" she asked.

"Not as okay as I thought I was," he said. "I had quite an attack of guilt on the drive home and I envisioned putting my .357 in my mouth when I got there and joining Pamela. I thought it might be better if I took you up on that offer of a spare bedroom."

"Of course, Harry," she said. "You're welcome to stay as long as you need; as long as you want."

Inside the house, she motioned for Harry to sit at the kitchen table, and asked, "Do you want me to put on a pot of coffee? I have real or decaf."

"Do you have anything stronger? Like ninety-proof, or so?" he replied.

"You just told me that you thought about sticking your gun in your mouth," she replied. "I don't think alcohol is an advisable course of action."

"Good point," he said. "I knew I could count on you to be the straight and narrow voice of reason. I'll do decaf on the off, off chance that I might actually be able to fall asleep later."

As the coffee dripped through the filter, Jackie sat at the table, and said, "I'm here if you want to talk, Harry, but I also have the names of a couple of grief counselors in my phone if you'd like someone more professional."

"What the Christ am I going to tell her mother?" he said as though he hadn't heard her speak. She's still alive but it'll probably kill her when I tell her I let her only daughter drown."

Having delivered tragic news to families as part of her job Jackie knew how hard finding the right words could be. Doing it if she felt guilty about the death was beyond comprehension.

"I wish I could give you some advice on that, Harry, but that's way above my training. Those people that I mentioned could probably help you through it, though." She took out her phone, and said, "I'll text you their information. It'll be there if you want it. What's your number?"

She was glad when he recited the number, feeling that he was at least open to the idea of counseling.

"Oh, yeah. I need to call Roberts, too, and make all of the *arrangements*," he said wearily. "I've never done this before. Pamela handled all that when my mother died. God, she was organized."

"I'm sorry, Harry," she said. "I won't pretend that I know how hard this is for you; the pain and the anguish is unimaginable for me. But if it'll make you feel better in any way, I'm ready to sit here and talk all night if you want. And if you feel like crying, I'll probably join you in that, too."

"You want to take my statement?" he said.

"That's not what I'm talking about," she replied. "I mean if you just …"

"You have to have an official statement from me sooner or later, right?" he said.

"Yes, but it doesn't have to be tonight. You can come into the station whenever you're …"

"I'd feel more comfortable here," he interrupted her. "Maybe it will help to unravel the tangle in my head if I talk it all out. Maybe the objective logic can quell my emotional guilt."

"Okay, if that's what you want," she said and picked up her phone. She swiped to the page with her recorder app, and said, "Are you sure you want to do this, now? Because this will be official once we start. You can wait and do it in the morning if you want."

"I'm sure," he said. "It's not like I'm trying to hide anything."

Jackie got up and went to the coffee maker. Although it wasn't finished brewing there was enough for two partial cups.

"Cream or sugar?" she asked as she went to the fridge for half-and-half for herself.

"Black," he replied, "Thanks."

When she returned, she also brought a yellow legal pad and a pen.

"Ready?" she asked after he sipped his coffee.

"Yup," he answered, and she tapped the record button on her phone.

"This is Chief of the Rowley Police, Inspector Jacquelyn Hall," she began. "I am in the kitchen of my residence with Harold Fletcher, husband of the recently deceased Pamela Armstrong Fletcher. It is 11:34 on the evening of July 8, 2021.

"Mr. Fletcher has requested that an official statement regarding the death of his wife be taken and is aware that this conversation is being recorded.

"It is my obligation to inform you before you start, Mr. Fletcher, that you have the right to have an attorney present during this statement, and that anything you say can and will be used in legal proceedings if they should come to pass.

"If the preceding statements are correct, if you understand your rights as I've explained them, and if you have declined to have an attorney present, please state your full name and acknowledge those facts."

"My name is Harold Eldred Fletcher," he began. "I live at 55 Weldon Farm Road, in Rowley, Mass. Zip code is 01969.

"I am aware that this is being recorded and I am giving this statement of my own free will without an attorney present. I understand that anything I say can be used against me in court."

"Thank you, Mr. Fletcher," Jackie said. "How would you like to proceed? Would you like me to ask you questions or would you prefer to simply state the facts as you recall and understand them?"

"I think I'd like to just tell you all that happened tonight, and then, if you feel there are any blanks, you can ask questions," he replied.

"Understood," she said. "Please begin whenever you're ready."

"Pamela and I sat down to dinner about 6:30 or so," he began. "It was pot-roast. That took maybe a half-hour. We watched the news while we were eating; we always do that.

"After we finished eating we cleaned up the kitchen. Pamela's a great cook, but certainly not the neatest. Pots, pans, and dishes everywhere. That was probably another half hour or so."

Jackie found it interesting that Harry referred to his wife in the present tense, not the past tense. Had the reality—the finality—that she was gone not sunken in, yet?

He went on, "She went into the den to check her email and Facebook and stuff, and I went into the living room to watch a movie.

"Last night I'd gotten done with a couple of chapters in the book I'm working on, so I wanted to get away from it—kind of purge my mind of the story before I went back and did a read-through and edit.

"I decided to watch *From Russia with Love*, which I've probably seen a dozen times. Sean Connery is the only true James Bond in my opinion, and the movie has what I think is the best fight scene ever filmed when he and Robert Shaw go at it on the train.

"Sorry. I'm sure that's irrelevant," Harry said with a little shake of his head as if to get his thoughts back into alignment. "Anyway, Pamela came in about a half-hour later and said she was going upstairs to take a bath. While I had the movie paused I went to take a potty break in the downstairs bath. I heard the water in the tub running upstairs when I got back, but once I started the movie again it drowned out everything else. I had taken my hearing aids out and I had the volume turned up a bit.

"It wasn't until a little after 9:30, I think, that I turned off the TV. I was going to go in and check my email and things, but I heard the water still running. Actually, I thought it was running, again, and she was warming up the water, but then it occurred to me that that would have put her in the water for an hour and a half. She likes long baths, but that would be extreme, even for her. Something told me to go up and see if everything was all right."

He stopped talking and just looked down at the table while fidgeting with his coffee cup but not drinking.

"Would you like to stop for a few minutes?" Jackie asked.

He blew out a long breath, and said, "No. Let's get this done.

"When I went into the bathroom, she was facedown in the tub," he said. "It was full up to the overflow and the water was still running. I yelled her name and I grabbed her and lifted her head up out of the water, but she didn't move at all; she was just limp. It scared the shit out of me.

"I held her head up and I got my hand under her arm and I rolled her out of the tub and onto the floor. She wasn't breathing and I listened to her heart and there was nothing. I thought I was going to throw up.

"We had taken a CPR class at the fire department once, a few years ago, so I gave her some chest compressions and then a couple of rescue breaths, but she didn't react at all. Nothing. That's when I ran and got my phone to call 911.

"I kept the compressions and breaths going until the EMTs got there. Well, actually I had to stop and use my phone to unlock the front door, but I went right back to working on her—trying to get her to breathe—trying to get her heart to beat until they told me to back away.

"While they were working on her, Rowley Police Officer Scott Lain showed up. I remember him talking to me but I have no recollection of what he said. When they took her away in the ambulance, he said I could follow them if I wanted and that he'd lock up the house.

"Ten or fifteen minutes later—after I got to the hospital—they told me that she hadn't made it. She never regained consciousness.

"That's about the time that you showed up, so I guess that's the end of my statement unless you have any questions."

"Thank you, Mr. Fletcher," Jackie said. "I do have a few questions." Looking at the notes she'd taken as he spoke, she asked, "Did you or Pamela consume any alcohol prior to the accident?"

"We each had a glass of wine with dinner," he answered. "We almost always do."

"Just one?"

"One each, yes."

"About how large of a glass?"

"Oh, probably a six once pour, I'd guess," he replied. "About what you'd get in a restaurant."

"Any more alcohol after dinner?" Jackie asked.

"No. Neither of us. We almost never do. We're not heavy drinkers."

"From what you said you would have started watching the movie about 7:30, is that correct?" she asked.

"About that, I'd say," he answered. "I don't recall looking at a clock. I'm kind of guessing at how long we were eating and cleaning up."

"That's fine," she said. "Do you recall where you paused the movie when Pamela went upstairs and you went to the bathroom? I'm just trying to establish a timeline."

"Good point," he said. "It was during the shootout at the gypsy camp. Are you familiar with the movie?"

"I've seen it maybe twice over the years," she said. "I do remember the gypsy-camp scene."

She wrote, "Gypsy camp" next to the note on her sheet, and then asked, "When did you notice that she was bleeding? Was there blood in the water when you found her?"

He didn't reply right away, and Jackie watched him as he thought about it. Finally, he answered, "I don't remember seeing any blood. When I lifted her head I recall being surprised by the cut above her eye, but thinking back on it, now, it wasn't bleeding." He looked at Jackie, and said, "It should have been, shouldn't it?" He blinked a couple of times, processing that information, and then said, "She was already dead, wasn't she?" He let out a sad sigh, and added, "I never had a chance to bring her back, did I? Shit! How long had I left her lying in the water?"

"There's no way you could have known she'd had an accident, and you did exactly the right things when you discovered her," Jackie said. "If she could have been brought back, what you just told me that you did was how to do it."

"Christ," he said with a sorrowful shake of his head. "Can we be done with this now?"

"Sure, Harry," she said. "I just have one other question here. When did you turn off the water in the tub?"

Again, he thought, and after a few moments, he said, "I don't remember doing it exactly. It's one of those single-handle fixtures, so I might have just reached over and hit it off when I first went to her. Maybe when I left her to go get my cell phone. I really don't remember."

"It's okay," Jackie said. "It's not critical. I was just curious." She then added, "If you feel this is a complete and accurate statement, and there's nothing you'd like to add, Mr. Fletcher, please acknowledge that, and I'll end the recording."

"This has been a true and accurate statement to the best of my recollection," Harry stated.

Jackie tapped the button on her phone ending the recording, and then said, "Thank you, Harry. That was good—very detailed. Are you okay?"

"I guess so," he answered, "I hoped that would be ... I don't know ... *cathartic*, somehow. It really wasn't. I still feel that it was my fault; that I should have been able to do something else. Heard the water running; gone and checked on her; something."

"I think it's natural for you to feel that way, Harry," she said. "I think that would be anyone's reaction under the circumstances. Please don't forget about those counselors; I really think it would be helpful to talk to one of them. It helped *me* after the Jerome Carlton serial killer thing a few years ago."

"Thanks," he replied. "I'll probably do that. Right now, though, I think I'd like to turn in. I probably won't sleep, but I'm *sure* I won't if I sit here."

She showed him to the guest bedroom, pointed out the clean towels in the connected bath, and gave him a packet containing a toothbrush, a roll of floss, and a tiny tube of toothpaste.

When he looked at the packet quizzically, she explained, "My dentist gives me a little care package every time I go, but I use an electric and a different brand of floss; I've got a whole drawer full of those."

Jackie looked at her clock when she got into bed; it was just after 11:30, and although she felt physically tired her mind was churning. She didn't give sleep much of a chance.

# Chapter 5

**Friday, July 9, 2021**

Jackie had been right about the sleep; it had been more than an hour before she managed to finally drift off. And now, at 5:30, her mind has back in high gear, and she knew better than to lie there and try to force another hour.

She got up, pulled on a robe, and quietly went to the kitchen to start a pot of coffee. She was surprised when she looked out the window and saw only her Jeep in the driveway. Then she noticed a note written on her legal pad on the table.

> Thanks for everything, Jackie.
>
> It helped a lot to have someone to talk to, but after lying awake until about 3:00, I finally gave up. Don't worry about me wanting to "join Pamela." Of all the things jumbling my mind right now, that isn't one of them.
>
> As soon as I have funeral arrangements made I'll let you know what's going on.
>
> Again, thank you for being a friend when I needed one more than I thought.
>
> Harry

Jackie picked up her phone to give Harry a call but then thought better of it. If he had managed to drift off to sleep in the familiar surroundings of his own home she didn't want to wake him. After talking with him last night, she did not have the sense that he was suicidal.

With her phone in hand, she saw that she had several new emails—not unusual—and three new texts. Middle-of-the-night texts were a lot less common.

One was from Scott Lain and was sent about the time that his shift ended. He asked if there was any news on Pamela.

The second was from Susan on the station switchboard, also asking about Pamela at about the time her shift ended.

The third was from a number that Jackie didn't recognize. It read:

Hello, Chief Hall.

This is Bob Thomas with the Anna Jaques Hospital. We met earlier this evening. I thought you would want to know that I wasn't able to arrange for the funeral home to pick up Mrs. Fletcher this evening as Dr. Madden has recommended that the state ME perform an autopsy on the deceased.

I expect that you will have questions about this and can probably get them answered best by calling and asking to speak with Dr. Madden, directly. Her shift ends at 6 AM.

Respectfully, Robert Thomas.

*An autopsy?* Jackie said to herself. *What the hell for?*

"Seri, call the Anna Jaques Hospital," she said to her phone. Fifteen minutes later, after two transfers and a long wait, she was finally talking with Dr. Madden.

"Good morning, doctor," she said. "This is Chief Jacquelyn Hall with the Rowley Police. Thank you for taking my call."

"What can I do for you, Chief Hall?" the doctor replied.

"I understand that you've requested an autopsy on Pamela Fletcher—a middle-aged Caucasian woman who died in your ER tonight—and I was wondering if you could tell me why."

"It shall be the duty of any person," the doctor began to recite, "having knowledge of a death which occurs under suspicious or unusual circumstances to immediately notify the office of the chief medical examiner and the police authorities having jurisdiction over …"

"Um, yes, Doctor," Jackie interjected, "Mass. General Laws Chapter 38, Section 3. I'm aware of the statute. What I meant was could you explain the circumstances that made you feel the need to invoke it."

"Due to patients' rights I can't discuss the details of the examination over the phone, Chief Hall," Madden replied. "I believe you're probably who you say you are, but I have no means of officially verifying your identity. I'm sure you understand."

"Of course," Jackie said resignedly, ever-frustrated by bureaucracy. "I get it. No problem. I'll go through official channels when I get to the station."

"Oh! You're not at the station," Madden said. "Now, your call makes more sense. Since the death occurred in your jurisdiction, a copy of the report that we sent to the ME was forwarded to your department. I assumed you'd read it and wanted to take exception to it."

"No. When I left the hospital last night I was under the impression that the death was the result of an accidental drowning," Jackie said, "so I was curious about what had changed."

"I'm going off shift in a little while, Chief Hall," the doctor said, "but I'll give you my cell number, and after you read the report if you have any questions, call me."

"Thank you, doctor. I appreciate that," Jackie said. "Go ahead; I've got a pen."

After hanging up with Dr. Madden, Jackie headed for the shower. She had just turned the water on when her phone rang with the department ring-tone.

"Hall here," she said standing naked in the bathroom.

"Hi, Jackie. I hope I didn't wake you, but I thought you'd want to know this right away," said Sharon Ford, the department's first-shift admin-volunteer.

Jackie's gut went into a knot as an image flashed into her head of Harry on his bathroom floor in a pool of blood with his .357 still in his hand.

"I was up. What is it, Sharon?" Jackie asked uneasily.

"We got an email in the department mailbox from the Anna Jaques with the subject, *'Notification of Suspicious Death Re: Fletcher, Pamela A.'*" Sharon answered. "Scott said it was an accident, so I thought this is something you'd want to know."

Relieved that it wasn't about Harry, Jackie said, "Thanks for letting me know; I did actually know that was coming. I spoke with somebody at the hospital already this morning. Have you read the email?"

"No. It's addressed to you," she replied. "Do you want me to open it?"

"No, that's okay," Jackie said. "I'm going to be there shortly. And let's not say anything about this to anyone until I know what it's all about, okay?"

Twenty-five minutes later, Jackie was heading out the door.

## Chapter 6

**Friday, July 9, 2021**

When Jackie got to the station, the first thing she did—after getting a cup of coffee—was to read the email requesting an autopsy on Pamela.

As required, the email was addressed to the Office of the Chief Medical Examiner, the Essex County District Attorney's Office, and to the Rowley Police.

Technically, the email *didn't* ask for an autopsy of the body, but rather an investigation into the cause of death, but the effect was the same. Only the ME or the District Attorney's office could order an autopsy if they deemed it necessary after an investigation, but that was almost always the result after such a request.

Jackie read through the report in its medical/legal officialese and then scrolled down to the attached "exhibit" photos.

When she got to the end, she picked up her desk phone and called Dr. Madden.

After hellos, the doctor asked Jackie to read her the report number in the first line of the report's text. After she did so, Madden said, "I apologize for the almost cloak and dagger stuff, Chief Hall, but you'd be surprised at the calls I've gotten from people pretending to be relatives or police or what have you when they're really reporters or insurance investigators or something, trying to get private information."

"Oh, no, I wouldn't be surprised, at all," Jackie replied with a little laugh. "We've had our share of run-ins with unscrupulous reporters and even had our phones tapped. I understand the need for caution, completely."

"I'm glad," the doctor said. "Now, what questions can I answer for you?"

"The petechial hemorrhaging is probably the standout," Jackie said. "I'm assuming that's rare in a case of accidental drowning?"

"If *I've never seen it in my career* qualifies as rare, then yes," the doctor answered. "In cases where it's present when a patient has died of asphyxiation it's most often an indication of restriction of the airways during manual strangulation."

"I've read that it can also be induced by straining during something like weightlifting," Jackie offered, "but also that a violent coughing or vomiting spell—like one might experience during drowning—can cause it."

"I never say never," the doctor replied, "but again, in my experience, I haven't seen it in a passive drowning, which this would be if the report that came in from the EMTs is accurate."

"You mean that she was unconscious when she drowned," Jackie said, "as opposed to an *active* drowning where she was struggling ... perhaps against an assailant."

"That's another scenario, yes," the doctor answered. "The exertion and trauma of a life or death struggle could possibly cause the hemorrhaging, I expect."

"You didn't mention in your report whether or not you found water in her lungs," Jackie said. "I would have thought that that would be significant—especially if there was none."

"A thoracic dissection is really the only way to know if the lungs ever contained enough water to be incompatible with life," the doctor answered. "And it's not always the case with a drowning, anyway."

"There's a thing they call dry drowning in which the victim experiences a laryngospasm which occurs if the trachea below the vocal cords detects the entry of water. It's a reflex action common in most mammals that involuntarily constricts the laryngeal cords to shut out the water. The result can be death by hypoxia—lack of oxygen—even though the lungs are dry. It's essentially involuntarily holding your breath until you die."

"Your report mentions the laceration over the right eye," Jackie moved on. "Is there a reason that you're suspicious that the cut might not have been the result of an accidental fall?"

"There's nothing suspicious about the cut, specifically, and it could certainly have been the result of a fall against a hard, sharp object as I understand the husband stated," Madden replied. "But it could also be the result of being struck *by* a hard, sharp object."

"One of my officers at the scene saw her blood on the edge of the bathtub where she hit it," Jackie said.

"Or where her head was pushed into it," the doctor countered. "And I'm not saying that's what *did* happen, only that it *could* have happened, which together with the hemorrhaging of the eyes adds up to enough probable cause for me to recommend an investigation under state law. And I know I'm preaching to the choir, here; you were able to cite chapter and verse of the law when we spoke earlier."

"No. I understand where you're coming from," Jackie replied. "You've done exactly what you're supposed to do. So, have they said when they're going to pick up the body?"

The doctor laughed, and said, "The coroner's office hasn't even acknowledged the request, yet. Those wheels grind slowly."

"Yeah, I've been on that sluggish road," Jackie replied. "I'm going to open an investigation file—as opposed to accidental death—and I'll give the ME's office a call a little later.

"Thanks, Doctor, I appreciate your patience with my questions," Jackie added.

"No problem, Chief. If there's anything else you want to know, give me a call."

Jackie opened a case file on her computer in the department's "Open Investigations" directory, transferred the request-for-investigation email and its attachments, and then made notes regarding the conversation she had just had with Dr. Madden. She then linked her phone to the computer and copied the recording she had made of Harry's statement last night.

With "foul play" being inconceivable, Jackie found it relatively easy to put logical explanations to what the doctor had just told her, but she had to admit that if she didn't know Harry Fletcher personally, she would probably agree with the doctor; there was probable cause for an investigation. The question then was, how would the ME see it?

She opened Google and did a search on the pathology of drowning. After skimming several articles, including two regarding autopsy findings on drowning victims, she concluded that the lack of water in the lungs would be inconclusive to a finding of death by drowning.

According to what she read, 10 to 20 percent of cases were considered to be "dry drownings," as Dr. Madden had explained.

Encouraged that a lack of water in Pamela's lungs could still be consistent with an accidental drowning, she did a search for petechial hemorrhaging. Cutting right to the chase, she typed, "Can drowning cause petechial hemorrhaging?"

The top answer of the 356-thousand results returned in less than a second read:

"Petechial hemorrhages involving the periorbital region and the conjunctiva have been described in many causes of death, but are thought to be exceedingly uncommon in cases of drowning."

Her heart sank, and she went through a number of the other articles. Some supported the same conclusion, others were vague, but none that she read answered her question with anything approaching a definitive yes.

As she tried to think of what else could possibly have occurred to cause the ruptured capillaries, her intercom buzzed and Sharon said, "Harry Fletcher is on the phone for you, Chief."

She had a pretty good idea why he was calling, and she was right.

After brief hellos, Harry said, "I called Roberts this morning to start making arrangements, and they told me the hospital wouldn't release Pamela's body to them. They wouldn't say why; they said I needed to call the hospital. And then the hospital told me I needed to call the Rowley Police or the County District Attorney. Jackie, what the hell is going on?"

"Apparently, the ER doctors noticed some things that they considered unusual in an accidental drowning, and ..."

"What things?" he interrupted her.

"The primary flag apparently is that there's petechial hemorrhaging in her eyes. That's when the tiny capillaries burst from excessive pressure in ..."

"I know what it is; I've described it in some of my books. But *that* usually only happens when ..." Suddenly the light went on, and he said, "Wait! They think I strangled Pamela!? Are you shitting me?"

"Nobody's made any kind of accusation, Harry," Jackie said calmly. "But it's an unusual enough occurrence under the reported circumstances to warrant a closer look."

"Who's going to be doing the looking?" he said.

"Since the death occurred in Rowley, we will be," she answered. "But the state medical examiner and the Essex County DA will also be involved."

"The medical examiner?" he repeated. "They're going to do an autopsy?"

"Most likely," Jackie answered. "Unless there's some obvious and logical explanation for the hemorrhaging that you're aware of."

"So, am I a suspect now?" he asked.

"At the moment, Pamela's death is still considered an accidental drowning by us, so no," she replied. "I *would* like you to come in so we can talk a little more, though."

"So you can drag a confession out of me?" he said.

"Come on, Harry," she replied. "You know how all this works; like you said, you've written about it. I'm sure there's an explanation, and I think if we walk through the events of last night in detail we'll find it."

"You're right. I'm sorry," he said. "I guess I'm just wondering if I'm ever going to wake up from this nightmare."

"I've got a department meeting at 8:00," Jackie said. "Do you think you can come in at 9:00?"

"Yeah. I can be there at 9:00," he said resignedly. "Should I wear heavy socks in case you need to put an ankle monitor on me?"

She knew that sarcasm was Harry's brand of joking, so she replied in kind. "We're fresh out of monitors," she said. "So you might want to bring a toothbrush in case we have to throw you in the slammer. Otherwise, you'll have to share one with Gertrude."

He gave a little laugh, and said, "Gross! Okay, I'll see you at 9:00. Thanks, Jackie."

"We'll get it figured out, Harry," she replied. "See you in a while."

Jackie thought for a moment about this investigation. She was going to have to take the lead on it because her next-in-charge—the department's only other accredited detective—left last week for what she saw as greener, or at least more interesting, pastures with the city of Lynn's police department.

Carolyn was a good officer and a bright investigator, but she could be abrupt. Jackie was a little glad that she wasn't here to take this on. With her desire to sink her teeth into some kind of real investigation—as opposed to automobile collisions and a minor burglary or two—she was concerned that she would have looked at it as a homicide-until-proven-otherwise. Carolyn didn't know Harry—or Pamela—the way that she did.

But that brought up another thought. Because she knew both Harry and the deceased, would her objectivity be called into question by anyone? *She* knew it wouldn't be an issue, but she also knew how people's minds worked. She was going to have to run this, even more, by-the-book than she normally would.

She looked at the file on her computer that contained the recording of Harry's statement last night. In light of today's development, inviting him to her house and taking his statement there was an obvious mistake from an investigation standpoint. But last night it made perfect sense both personally and professionally. He was a grieving friend whose wife had just died in an accident and who was experiencing suicidal thoughts.

Jackie picked up her nearly-empty coffee cup and headed toward the break room for a refill before the meeting. She detoured on the way and spoke to Sharon in the dispatch room.

"Thanks for the call, this morning," Jackie said to her. "It looks like we're going to have to do an investigation into Pamela's death. I opened a ..."

"An investigation? Why?" Sharon interrupted her.

"The doctors at Anna Jaques found some things they considered unusual in an accidental drowning, so they ..."

"Really? What kind of things?" she interrupted again.

"I've created a new folder in the Open Investigations directory," Jackie went on with her original thought. "The email from the hospital is in there; you can read that. Also, there is a copy of Harry's statement that I recorded on my phone last night. I'd like you to transcribe that, please. I'll need that by 9:00 this morning. And remember that all of this is department-confidential. No sharing with anyone else who doesn't have badge-status." That meant none of the other support volunteers although Sharon was one herself. "I'm going to tell everyone at the meeting this morning that there *is* an investigation, but details will go out on a need-to-know basis."

"Got it," Sharon said. "Nine o'clock and mum's the word."

As Jackie continued on to the break room, Sharon opened a voice-to-text program and navigated to the audio file. After it was done converting she would put on her headphones and listen to the recording while reading the text that the program created, making corrections and notations as required. She could hardly wait.

## Chapter 7

**Friday, July 9, 2021**

At the podium at the front of the meeting room, Jackie began, "Good morning. I expect that you've all heard about Pamela Fletcher's death last night. She apparently fell in her bathtub, was knocked unconscious, and drowned before Harry discovered her. Resuscitation efforts by Harry and then by Rowley Fire were unsuccessful, and she was pronounced dead at Anna Jaques at around ten p.m.. I was there with Harry at the time, and because of his despondent state he opted to spend the evening at my house rather than going home."

Jackie wanted to get that last part out there before the inevitable rumors started floating around and she was forced to answer questions from a defensive footing. She intentionally used the phrase *evening at my house* rather than *night at my house* for its more benign connotation.

"As a matter of hospital policy in this type of case," Jackie went on trying to sidestep any details, "the attending ER doctor has requested that the Office of Chief Medical Examiner make the determination as to cause of death. Pursuant to that request, Rowley PD will be conducting a supportive investigation."

As expected, the last sentence was met with surprised looks, low murmuring, and quiet echoes of, "*Investigation?*"

"Let's not read more into that than there is," she went on. "There've been no suggestions of foul play, and Harry had already provided a statement about the evenings' events prior to the hospital issuing their request. I'm confident that any questions they have will be resolved in a timely manner."

Although everyone in the room probably had at least one question of their own, in keeping with Jackie's meeting rules, no one interrupted with any of them.

"Moving on," Jackie said after a swallow of coffee. "Benton Brothers are doing some construction off the side of Wethersfield St. just east of where Bradford joins it. They've asked for traffic control between nine this morning and probably three this afternoon. Jim, can you work that?"

"Will do," Jim—one of the town's "unbadged" civilian volunteers—answered.

"Thank you," Jackie said as she scrolled down the screen of her laptop. "Mr. MacDougal out on Haverhill St. has been in his front yard with his radar gun, again," Jackie went on and then waited a moment for the groans and chuckles. "He's reported twenty-two ten-over violations, seven fifteen-overs, and two vehicles going more than thirty-over in front of his house in the past three days.

"Bill, will you set up out there for a while this afternoon? Maybe official presence will slow people down more than an elderly man with a sign that reads *Smile! You're On Candid Radar.*"

For the next twenty minutes, the meeting went on much the same way with the mundane and sometimes humorous business that was the life of a small-town police chief.

## Chapter 8
**Friday, July 9, 2021**

Sitting at her desk, Jackie's intercom buzzed, and then Sharon said, "Harry Fletcher is on the phone for you, Chief."

She looked at her clock; it was five minutes to nine.

"Hi, Harry, "she answered, hoping he wasn't canceling.

"Hi, Jackie," he said. "Hey, I'm in the parking lot. Can you come out so we can talk for a minute before everything gets all official?"

She looked out the window and saw his now-familiar Toyota. She didn't like the sound of his request, but she agreed and went outside.

As she walked up to the driver's window, Harry said, "Thanks, Jackie. Why don't you come around and get in?"

"No thanks," she said. "This is weird enough. What's going on Harry?"

He blew out a long sigh, and said, "Can we talk off the record for a few minutes?"

"Actually, no, Harry," she replied. "I'm not a priest or an attorney; I can't hear something and pretend I didn't, especially since I'm heading an investigation in which you're a subject. What's going on?"

"I guess asking you for a do-over of my statement last night is out of the question then, huh?"

"For many reasons," she said. "Harry, what's the matter?"

He blew out another sigh, and said, "Well, since we can't do it off the record, we might as well go inside and put it all *on* the record."

Jackie showed Harry to the interview room, went to her office to get the case folder and a pad, and then joined him.

"So you're aware, Harry, everything we say in here is being recorded in video and audio," she told him. "As always, you have the right to have an attorney present if you'd like."

"No. That's not necessary," he replied.

She opened her folder and took out three sheets of paper. Sliding them across the table, she said, "This is a transcript of the statement you gave me last night. Would you take a few minutes to read it, and if you agree that those are your words and mine, would you sign and date it, please?"

"What if part of it is a lie?" he asked.

"Which part?" Jackie replied.

He sighed once more, and answered, "I wasn't at home watching a movie last night when Pamela drowned."

"Where were you?"

"I had gone out to look at a car," he replied.

Puzzled, Jackie asked, "Why would you lie about *that*?"

"I ... I guess I felt even more ashamed that I wasn't even in the house when she had her accident. I didn't feel I could tell people I was out indulging my vanity and looking to recapture my youth by buying a sports car. If I'd been there, maybe I'd have heard a thud or a splash and I'd have gotten to her in time.

"The thought of having other people—her friends and her family—heaping their guilt on me on top of what I was already feeling would have been too much. It was those thoughts that put the idea of sucking on the barrel of my .357 into my head."

"I guess I can see that," Jackie said, understanding that people didn't always make the wisest or most logical choices in traumatic situations. "What made you decide to tell me this, now?"

"When I told you about watching the movie, I figured that if the whole thing was seen by everyone as a horrible accident—which it certainly was—then my penance would be to carry the guilt of not being there for her for the rest of my life.

"When you told me that there was going to be an investigation, I got nervous about having lied; it's not something that I usually do, so I knew that if you—or somebody else—started grilling me I'd fall apart. I figured it was better to come clean up front. Well, almost up front."

"Okay," Jackie said. "Well, I'm glad you told me. I'm going to ask you to write out that amendment, and sign and date it." She tore a sheet of paper from her pad and then slid the rest over to him, along with a pen. "Where did you go to see this car?" she asked with her own pen poised. "Do you remember the person's name?"

"I don't actually," Harry answered. "I'm terrible with names. It was an ad on Car-Lister. The car was out in Saugus. I met the guy in the parking lot of a McDonald's. Having driven all that way, I took it for a test ride, but the condition was way too rough for what I wanted, so I just came home."

"What time would that have been? When you got home?" Jackie asked as she wrote a note.

"Well, just before I found Pamela, so I'm guessing 9:30-ish?" he answered.

"What kind of car was it you went to see?" Jackie asked.

"An MGB," Harry answered. "A '68. Red with wire wheels. I had one during my senior year in high school." He gave a little laugh, and added, "It was a fun car on twisty back roads, but not much good on lover's lane."

"I can imagine," Jackie replied. "Hey, sorry. I asked you to write an amendment and then keep interrupting you with questions. I'll be quiet until you're done."

When he finished writing, Harry signed the paper with a flourish, and then said, "I'm sorry about the lie in the first place, Jackie, but I do feel better having it off my chest."

"So, let's go over what happened last night after you got home," she said.

"Yeah, the petechial hemorrhaging," he said. "I've been trying to think what might have caused that."

With some thoughts of her own, Jackie said, "You said that when you discovered Pamela she was face down in the water, and you lifted her head up out of it."

"Yeah."

"How did you lift her? Was it by the sides of her face? A hand under the chin? Both hands around her neck?"

He thought for a moment, and then answered, "I think I grabbed her under the chin, but maybe by the throat ... I just grabbed her to pull her up, I wasn't thinking about how."

"You said you held her head up for a while trying to get her to respond," Jackie went on. "How long do you think that might have been before you tried to get her out of the tub?"

"Oh, God, I have no idea, Jackie," he said. "It could have been ten seconds or sixty. I really don't remember."

"When you did try to pull her out of the tub, you said you got your arm under hers and kind of rolled her out," Jackie said.

"That's right," he said, "but I was keeping her head up, too."

"I'm wondering if, without thinking and in the panic of the moment, you could have been actually squeezing her throat while you were lifting her," Jackie said. "I wonder if while you were trying to keep her face out of the water, you were unintentionally holding her too tight."

"Oh, god!" he said. "I was doing more harm than good!"

"Well, certainly not intentionally," Jackie said, "And that's just a wild-ass theory to try to explain the hemorrhaging in her eyes. Unfortunately, the overload that your brain was under didn't allow for much of what was happening to be committed to memory."

"Do you think the EMTs could have done something?" Harry asked. "I think they put a cervical collar on her before they transported her. Could that have compressed her neck, do you think?"

"It would seem unlikely," Jackie said, "but then we know that *something* unlikely happened. I'll look into it."

"So, getting into the customary death-of-a-spouse investigation questions," Jackie said, "how would you categorize your marriage?"

"Probably pretty average, I'd say. Maybe a little better," he answered. "We don't have any real money issues; no big credit card debts or anything like that. We're comfortable enough that I was going to be able to buy that MG just as a toy, not a second car."

"Was Pamela okay with you getting a sports car?" Jackie asked. "That often shows up on a midlife-crisis checklist."

He laughed, and said, "Yeah, she was on board with it. When I first started dating her I was driving a Mazda Miata. She loved that car."

"When was that?"

"1999 when we started dating."

"How long were you married?"

"It was twenty-one years on New Year's Day," Harry answered. "We promised each other that if the world didn't collapse at midnight because of the Y2K thing we'd get married the next day."

"Was there any infidelity along the way?" Jackie asked.

Harry just looked at her for several moments, and then said, "Yes, I'm ashamed to say. I had a brief fling with a woman where I worked."

"When was that?"

He thought for another moment, and then answered, "About eight years ago, I think. I honestly hadn't thought about that—about *her*—in years."

"What was her name?"

"Does that matter?"

"Probably not," Jackie replied, "but it will leave a pretty obvious hole in my report if her name's not there."

"Janet McClelland," Harry said. "I haven't a clue where she is or how to get in touch with her."

"Did Pamela know about the affair?" Jackie asked.

"Yes. And she had one of her own as payback," he answered.

"And did that straighten things out?" Jackie asked, not imagining how it could.

"That and several thousand dollars worth of counseling over the next couple years," he replied. "But we were doing fine, now. All that was behind us."

"Did Pamela have a life insurance policy?" Jackie asked.

"Several, actually," he answered. "One from before we were married, one that she got through her employer, and another one that we got when we married. We took out matching policies on each other so if anything happened the other could pay off the house and not have to worry about life on one income."

"Are you the sole beneficiary on the policies?" she asked.

"Yes."

"How much are the policies worth, in total?"

"A little under half a million," he replied.

Jackie tried not to look surprised as she wrote the figure down.

"Motive, means, and opportunity, huh?" he said. "If I was a character in one of my books I think I'd be nervous."

"Are you nervous?" she asked.

"It's cliché and probably naive, but I'm counting on the truth to set me free," he answered. "Pamela's death was an accident. I'm hoping the county DA will be able to see that when they look at the findings from her autopsy and your investigation report."

"I hope you're right Harry," Jackie said. "That's the way the system is supposed to work."

"So, how long until you have the results of the autopsy?" Harry asked.

"Assuming she was picked up last night or this morning, and assuming that the county DA has ordered the autopsy, it should be performed today or tomorrow. If they're really backed up it could go another day or even two, possibly.

"The DA and I will probably see a report the day after the autopsy was done, but some tox reports could lag that by a week or more."

He blew out yet another long sigh, and said, "Well, let me know as soon as you can, okay? And thanks, Jackie. I appreciate you being a friend and not just a cop. I'm thinking that maybe your assistant who left—Carolyn?—she might have been a lot more bad-cop. She always seemed to have a chip."

After Harry left, Jackie went into her office and began typing the notes she'd taken into the case file. There was something that bothered her about the interview, but she couldn't put her finger on it.

When she was done transcribing and adding notations, she brought up the recording that had been made of the interview. She switched the audio to go to her earbuds and sat back to watch and hopefully zero in on her feeling.

A little more than halfway through, Jackie finally figured it out. And it turned out to be nothing, really. She noticed that Harry was still referring to his wife in the present tense—as if she were still alive—just as he had last night. As far as the investigation went it didn't mean anything, but obviously, it sent some kind of incongruity signal into

Jackie's mind. A psychoanalyst might have a field day with it, but to Jackie, it only meant that Harry hadn't quite come to grips with the actuality of Pamela's death.

Jackie took Harry's handwritten statement-amendment out to Sharon and asked her to transcribe it into the case file. She then continued on to the break room to refill her coffee cup.

Scott Lain was just leaving the room when she got there, and she looked at him a little surprised, and she looked at her watch. His shift ended at 1:00 in the morning, and although he always showed up for the 8:00 a.m. meeting, he generally left right afterward.

"Hey, Chief," he greeted her. Noting her glance at her watch, he added, "Had to come back to get my lunch cooler out of the fridge." As he spoke, he held up the small, insulated, zipper-top container.

"Boy, that really sucks about Pamela," he went on. "How's Harry taking it? I saw him leaving when I pulled in. He was really shaken up last night when he left to follow the ambulance."

"He's doing okay," Jackie replied. "It's certainly a lot to process; losing your wife one night and then being investigated for it the next morning. Thanks for uploading the photos, and well done. I put them into the case file. Where is the water sample from the tub, by the way?"

"It's in the evidence fridge," he replied. "Sorry. I meant to send you a note on that when I uploaded the pictures; I guess I forgot."

"No problem. It's marked, dated, and signed?" she said.

"Yup," he replied. "I put the Tupperware container in an evidence bag, and the whole thing's in the fridge."

"Perfect," she said. "I don't expect it will come into play, but with there being an official investigation, all the ducks need to be in a row. Thanks."

"Right. Hey, I've got a dentist appointment I need to get to, so I'll see you tonight at shift-start," he said.

"Okay. Good luck at the dentist," Jackie said as he left.

After filling her coffee cup, Jackie went into the evidence storage room and looked in the refrigerator. On the top shelf was a paper evidence bag marked, "Pamela Fletcher drowning. Bathtub water sample. 10:01 p.m." It was then dated and signed by Scott.

Jackie took the plastic sandwich-size container from the bag and held it up in front of a light. She was curious to see if it might have a red tint from Pamela's blood in the water. She wasn't surprised that she couldn't see any, however.

Harry had said that the water was running and going out the tub's overflow drain when he found his wife, so if there had been much blood in the water initially, it would be pretty diluted by the time Scott took the sample. She was also looking through the less-than-clear plastic of the container. It would take a microscope to tell for sure.

As she was putting the container back in the bag, something occurred to her; it wasn't very cold. She opened the fridge and touched a couple of other articles, and they were the expected temperature; the fridge was certainly working.

Had Scott forgotten to put the sample in the refrigerator when he brought it in last night, and that was the reason he had come back? She couldn't see that as a problem as far as the integrity of the water sample was concerned, or even as an honest mistake. The only thing that bothered her was that Scott felt it necessary to lie to her about it. She would have to talk to him about *that*.

Back in her office, Jackie went about the routine chief-of-police stuff that occupied most of her days, but for some reason, Scott Lain kept pulling at her mind. There was something disquieting there rolling around in her subconscious, although aside from fibbing about forgetting to put the tub-water in the refrigerator, she couldn't get a focus on it.

Pushing Scott back to the incubation part of her brain, Jackie began reading the Town Council's reply notes to her proposed budget for the next year.

About 3:30 in the afternoon, Jackie's intercom buzzed, and Sharon announced, "There's a Marcia Grieves here to see you, Chief. She says you probably weren't expecting her, but she's with the Essex County DA's office."

Marcia was right; Jackie hadn't expected anyone at the DA's office to get involved until at least Monday. Typically, anything that showed up for them on Friday fell into the weekend vortex.

"Could you bring her back, please?" Jackie asked Sharon and then set about straightening up her desk.

When Sharon and the woman appeared in her doorway, Jackie was surprised at how young the woman looked. Seeing her on the street Jackie would have put her at twenty, tops. She did notice the engagement ring and wedding band on her left hand ... not that that said anything about age, necessarily.

Jackie extended her hand, and said, "Jacquelyn Hall. Pleased to meet you, Mrs. Grieves. I have to say that you did catch me by surprise; I wasn't expecting anyone from the DA's office until probably Monday."

"And put off meeting the legendary Inspector Hall for a whole weekend?" Marcia replied as she enthusiastically pumped Jackie's hand. She then added with a little laugh, "No chance!"

Jackie reacted with a surprised look, and repeated, "*Legendary?*"

"On, my gosh, yes!" Marcia said. "Solving the Holly McCray murder and bringing down a fifteen-time serial killer almost all by yourself? Hell yes, legendary!"

"Um, thank you, but I was hardly by myself," Jackie replied. "There were an awful lot of other ..."

"Oh, I know," Marcia said. "Even my Dad, but it was you who pulled together all the seemingly unrelated clues to zero in on Carlton."

"Who's your father?" Jackie asked.

"Dick Santori, the Attorney General," Marcia answered. "He was an assistant AG then, but being in charge of the task force, he told me all about the whole case. There's no question in my mind that you were the star, Chief Hall!"

Jackie found it had to believe that when Santori related the details of what the newspaper had dubbed the Nightmare Murders, that *he* wasn't the star of the story. She wondered if Marcia had developed the gift of reading between the lines of her father's self-aggrandizing tales.

"Well, I'm flattered, Marcia," Jackie said. "Please, come in and have a seat. And please call me Jackie."

"Oh, thank you!" Marcia said as she took a seat in front of Jackie's desk. "I've only been with the county DA's office for a little over a year, so getting assigned to work a murder case with you is beyond my wildest hopes."

*Oh, my God!* Jackie said to herself. *I have a groupie!*

To Marcia, she said, "Again, I'm flattered, but at this early point in the investigation, we're still calling it an accidental drowning."

"Oh, sure, *officially*," Marcia replied with a knowing nod. "But the petechial hemorrhaging that the hospital reported, the life insurance policies on the wife, the husband's affair. It's just kind of a formality to wait for the autopsy results, right? I mean, it all seems pretty obvious where it's going to go, right?"

"How do you know about the insurance policies and the affair?" Jackie asked.

Marcia looked a Jackie a bit confused, and answered, "It's all in the report you shared with us earlier this morning."

Not that she was trying to withhold or hide anything, but Jackie had not told Sharon to open the file link to the DA's office, yet.

"Oh, of course. I guess Sharon was on that faster than I thought," Jackie said. "Well, I'd like to think there'll be a lot more to an investigation than that," she went on. "Even if the ME were to come back with a finding of homicide, Pamela's husband would be only one person we'd need to look at."

"Oh, sure, of course," Marcia said. "I'm actually looking forward to working with you on that part. So, what would you like me to follow up on?"

"Um, well ..." Jackie stumbled. She had not put any thought into assigning someone to actively follow anything up. She had intended to wait for the ME's report before planning the next moves.

"I could try to find Janet McClelland," Marcia offered.

"Janet McClelland?" Jackie repeated just as it clicked for her. "Oh, yes. The woman that Harry said he had an affair with. Well, I'm not sure how relevant she would be; that was a long time ago, according to him, but it certainly can't hurt."

Jackie saw the task as busy-work, but she got the impression that Marcia had nothing else other than this case to be working on, so it would at least give her something to focus on.

"Perfect!" Marcia said. "Where would you like me to set up?"

"Um, well ..." Jackie began, once again caught off guard. She had not expected help from the county this quickly, and certainly not live-in help.

Misreading Jackie's hesitation, Marcia said, "Oh, I don't need a department computer or anything," Marcia said. "I have a county laptop; all I need is a secured Internet connection."

"Um, okay. I guess you can set up in Detective Bellner's office. She took another job last week," Jackie replied, wondering how long it might be before having a groupie would get old. "Carol Soucy, our IT person is going to be in this afternoon," Jackie continued. "I'll have her get you set up."

"Perfect!" Marcia repeated. "I'll get my stuff out of the car."

A few minutes later, she returned pulling a wheeled travel case that would have a hard time fitting under an airline seat. Jackie was a little surprised; she'd expected a simple over-the-shoulder laptop case. She had to wonder how much of her office Marcia had brought with her.

An hour later, Marcia rapped on Jackie's open door, and said, "Can I buy you lunch?"

Jackie looked at the watch, and answered, "Yeah, sure."

"Is that little dining-car place on the corner any good?" Marcia asked.

"The Agawam? Yes. It's where I was going to suggest," Jackie said as she logged out of her computer.

With the typical lunch crowd, the two had to wait for a pair of stools to open at the counter—they didn't have time to wait for a booth. Even then, an older man in coveralls generously shifted his seat so that the two women could sit together.

"So, what's good?" Marcia asked as she looked at the menu.

"The simple answer is, nothing's *not* good," Jackie replied. "So the real question is what are you in the mood for? I'm going to do the hot turkey sandwich with cranberry sauce, which is really more like a pot pie."

"How's the seafood?" Marcia asked.

"In my humble opinion, you won't find any better on the whole North Shore," Jackie said.

"How big's the clam roll?"

"About like so," Jackie answered, holding her hands in a generous circle.

"Sold!" Marcia said.

After ordering, Jackie asked, "So, what got you into the legal field? Do you want to follow in your father's footsteps?"

"Oh, Lord no!" Marcia replied. "That's politics. Sure, he's a lawyer, but that's always been more of a means to an end for him. All those games and wheeling and dealing are in his blood, but thankfully it seems to have skipped a generation for me."

"There's easier ways to make money with a law degree than working for the county," Jackie said.

"Oh, trust me, I know!" Marcia said. "In school, I was all ready to take the Clarence Darrow, F. Lee Bailey, Perry Mason route into defense law. I knew I'd probably start out as a public defender to cut my teeth, but everybody has to pay their dues."

She turned and looked Jackie in the eyes, and went on, "And then you and Holly McCray came along."

"Ah! I imagine with your father leading the task force you were able to follow all that pretty closely," Jackie said.

"I was," she replied. "I even sat silently off to the side for a few of the tele-meetings. But I became a card-carrying Inspector Jacquelyn Hall fan when I read the brief that you sent my Dad to get a warrant to go after Carlton. It was freaking brilliant! The research, the detail, the legal arguments. I couldn't believe my Dad didn't jump all over that. But that's the politics part. He's always been so afraid of offending anyone who might hinder his climb up the ladder."

"I'll admit to a certain frustration when he wouldn't act on it," Jackie said.

Marcia laughed, and said, "To the point where you went rogue."

"Yeah. Don't emulate *that* part," Jackie said. "That was stupid. I believe the phrase they used in my reprimand was *impetuous and impatient*."

Marcia laughed again, and then went on, "But the other part of that whole McCray case that made me switch sides was the thought that if I was in the public defender's office I could have been assigned to defend Jerome Carlton. After reading the final report on the case I knew that was something I just couldn't do.

"As a prosecutor, I think I'd have a little more respect for the truth, and only go after people who could be proven to be guilty. As a defense attorney, the job is to use any trick in the book to get your client off in *spite* of his guilt. I just don't think my conscience would let me do that."

"I'm glad to hear that, Marcia," Jackie said. "I understand and agree with a person's constitutional right to a vigorous defense, but I sometimes think it needs qualifiers."

As the two women talked, the long-time waitress, Mary Alice Timmons, set their sodas on the counter. "Thanks, Mary Alice," Jackie said. She then lifted her glass, and said to Marcia, "To truth, justice, and the American way!"

They clinked, and each took a sip.

\*\*\*

When they got back to the station, Carol was there and was just starting to configure the department's new laser printer so it could be networked to everyone's computer and the department-issued phones.

"Carol Soucy, this is Marcia Grieves," Jackie introduced. "Marcia is with the Essex County DA's office, but she's going to be with us here in Rowley for a little while. She has a county-issued laptop; can you set her up with a secure Internet connection? Nothing to the department network; just the Internet."

"Connection to the printer?" Carol asked crooking a thumb in its direction.

"Nope," Jackie said. "There's an inkjet in Carolyn's office. Can you hook her up directly to that?"

"No problem," Carol replied. "Put in the usual hacks so you can monitor her private emails and personal Internet searches, and stuff?"

Marcia blinked in surprise, and said, "Excuse me?"

"She's joking," Jackie said. "She does that ... sometimes inappropriately."

"You should be around when I've had a couple glasses of wine," Carol said. "I can get *really* inappropriate!"

Turning to Marcia, Jackie said, "We put up with this because she's one of the best IT people I've ever met."

"Also, because I know everyone's password and where on their hard drives the skeletons are hidden," Carol responded.

"And for future reference, she will always get in the last word," Jackie added.

"Darn right!" Carol said.

"See?" Jackie said to Marcia as she led her away.

At ten minutes to five, Marcia rapped on Jackie's door. "What's up?" Jackie asked. "Carol get you set up okay?"

"Yup. Everything works fine," Marcia answered. "Carol's kind of a hoot, isn't she?"

"She can be," Jackie answered. "It kind of belies how good she is with computers and tech stuff." Looking at her watch, she added, "You heading out?"

"Actually, I'd like to sit in on your second-shift meeting, if you don't mind," Marcia replied.

Jackie shrugged, and said, "There won't be anything about the Fletcher case. I won't be giving assignments on that until we have the autopsy report."

"Oh, no, that's fine," Marcia said. "This is actually my first time in the field aside from in a city jail or a courthouse. I just want to get a feel for how small-town police departments operate."

"My former boss here, Chief Booker, would probably tell you to watch reruns of the *Andy Griffith Show*," Jackie replied. "But no, I have no objections as long as you don't snore too loudly."

During the meeting, Jackie briefed the second-shift officers and staff on what had gone on during the day and gave out a few routine assignments. She then introduced Marcia.

"Marcia Grieves is with the Essex County DA's Office, and will be spending a little time bivouacked in Inspector Bellner's office," Jackie said. "She's here to participate in Pamela Fletcher's investigation."

That perked everyone up, but Jackie stuck a pin in the rising balloon by adding, "We haven't gotten anything back from the ME, yet—and won't until Monday, most likely. So, for now, that's pretty much on hold. Do give Marcia your cooperation, however."

After the meeting, Jackie was putting things away to close up her office and go home when she looked out to see Scott Lain talking with Marcia. She looked at her watch, and then called out Scott's name. He and Marcia both looked, and Jackie raised her left arm and tapped her watch.

"Crap! Sorry, Chief!" Scott called back and then turned and headed out the door.

As Marcia walked back to her temporary office next to Jackie's, she said, "Sorry, Jackie. That was on me. I was just talking to him about the crime scene ... the *accident* scene. He was the only sworn officer there that night."

"No problem with that, but he needs to be handling traffic for a gathering at the Pine Grove School about four minutes ago."

"Sorry," Marcia repeated. "It won't happen again."

Jackie waited for Marcia to gather up her things, shut down her laptop, and repack her case. Outside, Jackie said, "Have a good weekend, Marcia. You'll be back Monday, right?"

"Eight o'clock?" she replied.

"If you'd like," Jackie said. "I can't imagine the ME's report on Pamela showing up until late afternoon, if then. But you're welcome to camp here until it does."

"Thanks," Marcia said. "I already like it better here than my cubical in Salem."

As Jackie went through the intersection of Rt.-1 and 133, her cell phone rang through the Jeep's speakers.

"Hall here," she answered.

"Hi Jackie, it's Jeff. You on your way home?"

"Just left the station," she answered.

"Actually, I knew that," he replied. "I'm right behind you."

She looked in her mirror, saw him waving, and returned it. "What's up? You get that battery, yet?"

"Yeah, I had them put one in at Knowlesies," he answered.

He was referring to the corner gas station that had been owned by the Knowles family since the '30s. She inwardly grimaced that he was not able to replace a battery in his car by himself.

"Good," she said. "Well, that should hold you for a while."

"So, are you doing anything for dinner tomorrow night?" Jeff asked. "I've had a hankering for Kowloon for a week or two. You interested?"

"Oh, man! I haven't been to the Kowloon in a couple years," Jackie said. "Pu Pu platter with teriyaki beef! What time?"

"Pick you up about 5:30?" he replied.

"I'll be at the door, salivating!" she answered.

"Oh, that'll be an attractive look," he replied with a laugh.

# Chapter 9

**Saturday, July 10, 2021**

Temporarily without an Assistant Chief, Jackie would be on call all weekend and spent a few hours in the station Saturday afternoon.

She was waiting outside her house when Jeff pulled up at 5:40.

As she climbed into his car, she leaned over to give him a kiss, but he pulled back and stared at her face.

"What?" she said.

"I just wanted to make sure you didn't have drool running down your chin," he said.

She laughed, and said, "If you'd been much later, I would have." They exchanged a quick kiss, and she buckled her seatbelt as he pulled out.

"So, how was your day?" Jeff asked as he drove.

"Productive, actually," she said. "Without the typical daily minutia, I was able to get a couple of reports done that had been sitting on Carolyn's desk but were now on mine. You?"

"Played a round of golf this morning, and some softball this afternoon," he replied. "You should really take up golf. I think it would help you to unwind; take your mind off work."

"I'm glad that you're able to do that," she said, "but my work actually invigorates me ... well, most of the time. There is that minutia. Besides, about the last thing I need in my life is a *game* that I know I'd obsess over."

Driving south on I-95, when they went under a freeway sign announcing that Saugus was ten miles ahead, it tickled life into a sleeping thought.

When Harry had confessed to lying about being home when Pamela drowned, he said he had gone to look at a car in Saugus. Aside from the fact that he was fessing up to a lie when he told her, she really had no reason to not believe him. But even subconsciously, the cop in her knew it needed to be checked out and stuck the question away for revival when her mind was more free of all that minutia.

"How'd you like to take a ride and go look at a car after dinner?" Jackie said as she navigated to the Car-List website on her phone.

"Where?" he asked.

"Saugus is all I know so far," she said. "I'm working on narrowing that down."

She typed "1968 MGB" into the search window and waited a few seconds. The first car displayed was a pretty powder blue and was located in Amesbury—thirty miles in the other direction.

She scrolled down to the others, but there were none. Below the description of the blue car was a box that read, "Expand your search?"

A small knot began to form in Jackie's stomach as she reduced the search criteria to just "MGB."

Three additional cars showed up, but none were in Saugus, none were red, and none were 1968. Jackie was sure that she had those details right. She had gone to high school with a girl whose father bought her a red '68 MGB, and she was always envious of it ... until she heard that second gear had gone out and she sold it because she couldn't afford to fix it.

Then a thought occurred to her. What if the guy had sold the car between when Harry drove it and now? She knew that eBay had a page where you could go and look at items that had previously sold to get an idea of what your stuff might be worth; could Car-Lister have something similar?

Working on the small screen of her phone, it took a while, but she finally managed to find the "Closed Listings" page. She typed in simply "MG" this time and clicked on the "within 30 days" tab. Two cars showed up. One was a black '72 B sold in Danvers, and the other was a nicely restored '51 TD that sold up in Seabrook, NH.

The knot in Jackie's stomach tightened a bit as she tried to come up with another explanation for the missing car. Unfortunately, all she had was *another lie*. But why? Where had Harry really been? As cliché as it was, and as unfair as it was to leap to that conclusion, Jackie's mind still settled on *another woman*.

It would have been hard to completely ruin the shared meal of the assorted fried foods on the Pu Pu Platter, the pork fried rice, the sweet & sour chicken, the Mai Tai cocktail (her), the Manhattan (him), and the orange sherbet dessert, but thinking about Harry's lies all evening did put a dent in it.

On the drive home, Jeff asked Jackie, "So you want to go back to my place and watch a movie? I put my TV on a table with wheels so I can turn it to face out the window and we can watch from the hot tub."

"Innovative," she said with a little laugh. "But I think I'm going to pass. I don't think I'd be very good company tonight. I've kind of got something stuck in my mind. Besides, I didn't think to bring a swimsuit."

"I was going to loan you one of my old t-shirts," he said with a smile. "You did seem a bit off all night, though. I didn't have to arm-wrestle you for the last butterfly shrimp. Is it the thing with the car?"

"Yeah," she said. When she couldn't find it, she had told him that it must have been sold. "It's connected with something at work," she added. "I have a feeling that somebody is lying to me but I'm not sure why."

He knew better than to press her for work-related details, and he could also see that she was deep in thought about it, so he let the topic drop and they drove in silence for a while.

After several miles, she turned to him, and said, "You know what, Jeff? I think I'm going to take you up on the hot tub and t-shirt. I really need to get my work/life balance tipping a little more to the life side. What did you have in mind for a movie?"

"Your call," he said. "What's going to help you to unwind and get your mind off work? Probably not a murder-mystery cop-drama. Blow-'em-up action-adventure? Rom-com? Tear-jerker love story? I've got HBO, Netflix, Hulu, Amazon ... I'm sure you'll be able to find something to escape with."

"Did you ever see *An American President*? Michael Douglas, Annette Bening?" she replied.

"Yeah, I think so. A long time ago, if it's the one I'm thinking of," he said. "Wasn't Richard Dreyfuss in it, too?"

"Yeah. Also Martin Sheen and Michael J. Fox," she said. "Mid 90's."

"I'm sure somebody has it," he said.

She reached over, patted his leg, and said, "Thanks, Jeff. Thanks for leading the horse to the water but letting me drink on my own. I really do appreciate your not being pushy with this relationship."

"Hey, as long as you categorize it *as* a relationship, I'm okay," he replied. "I've heard that patience is a virtue."

The movie, which she had seen a dozen times or more—and which was predictable even the *first* time—was simple, feel-good entertainment for Jackie. That, plus Jeff's patient company—refraining from making comments about the obvious plot and restraining himself from trying to capitalize on the wet t-shirt effect—coupled with a glass or two of a very nice chardonnay, all conspired to put Harry Fletcher and the phantom MG into a deep recess of Jackie's mind, and she enjoyed the evening completely.

\*\*\*

As Jackie stepped out of the shower the next morning, she smelled coffee and frying bacon. When she had gotten in, Jeff was still asleep in bed.

She dried off, got dressed, and went out into the kitchen with still-wet hair.

Jeff was at the stove wearing pajama bottoms and a t-shirt that he had not had on last night. He turned, and said, "Hey, good morning! You look wonderful!"

"Didn't put your contacts in, yet, huh?" she replied. "Wet hair, no make-up, my walk-of-shame clothes. I'm a real supermodel."

"Beauty's in the eye of the beholder," he said. "Your timing's perfect; what kind of eggs do you want? Fried? Scrambled? Poached? Oh, and don't choose poached if you like poached eggs; you won't be impressed."

"Full disclosure," she laughed. "Scrambled. Wet but not runny."

"Got it," he said opening the fridge for the eggs.

"Can I do anything?" she asked as she walked toward the coffee pot.

"Choose between English muffins and wheat toast, and drop whichever in the toaster," he answered.

As they ate at the high-top island, Jeff said, "You know, I don't remember being out with you when you've seemed as relaxed as you were last night. Well, not in bed—that was actually kind of aggressive ... which is not a complaint, mind you."

She laughed, and a little color came up in her cheeks ... which Jeff found adorable.

"Thank you for that," she said. "For everything last night. Dinner, the invitation back here, politely watching a chick-flick without a running commentary on its predictability, allowing me to sleep over. I needed that shake-out. I needed to be reminded to have a life."

He leaned over, gave her a light kiss, and said, "To tell you that it was my pleasure would define the word *understatement*."

"So, do you want to do something, today? I've got a friend with a boat down at Perley's Marina; I could borrow it and we could go out to Plum Island."

"I appreciate that Jeff, but I'm going to pass," she said. "I'm afraid my respite from reality hasn't lasted very long, and my mind is already back on that missing MG.

"I'm wondering now if I even have the sales website correct. I *think* he said Car-Lister, but what if he said Craigslist and I misheard him? I'm going to go back into the station and verify it. I'll feel like a real doofus if I was mentally accusing this guy of lying when I just needed my hearing checked."

"I know better than to ask you who or what you're talking about," he said, "but I find it admirable that you're trying to find a way to blame yourself rather than believe whoever it is has lied to you. A little naïve perhaps, but admirable."

"I know," she said, "It's a curse and a gift, but I'm still a big benefit-of-the-doubt person."

At home, after changing into fresh clothes, Jackie booted up her laptop and went to the Craigslist site.

She was disappointed, but not particularly surprised, to not find any MGBs for sale locally. When she couldn't find a "previously sold" page on the site she let that fact fan the flickering ember of hope that Harry wasn't lying to her, but the faint glow was fading quickly.

With no remote connection capabilities into the department's computer network, Jackie headed out the door for the station.

Although Carol had told her that it would be *wicked easy* to do, Jackie had decided not to have her set up any kind of remote login capabilities for anyone including herself. After having had the department's phone system tapped and conversations recorded in the Holly McCray case a couple of years earlier she was a bit paranoid. And since there was always someone on duty at the station, anything that needed to be accessed in an emergency could be sent out through a secure email.

When Jackie got to the station, she was surprised to see Marcia's car in the parking lot. Inside she found her in her new temporary office across the hall from her own.

"You're in early," Jackie said from the doorway. "Like by a day."

Marcia laughed, and said, "I told you I like it here. Actually, my husband invited some buddies over to the house and they're watching the Red Sox game on the big screen. The noise was a little distracting." She turned her laptop, and said, "I found Janet McClelland; Mr. Fletcher's mistress."

Jackie bridled slightly at the term *mistress*; it denoted something long-term in her head, and she believed that it was just a brief affair, possibly even a one-time fling. When she thought about it, though, she realized that Harry had not gone into any detail on the subject, so it was only a benefit-of-the-doubt reaction she was having to mentally protect a friend. She didn't say anything about Marcia's choice of words.

"Where'd you find her?" Jackie asked looking at the face filling Marcia's screen. She was a reasonably attractive woman; not as pretty as Pamela, but comely in her own way.

"FaceBook," Marcia answered in an *of-course* tone.

"Where would we be without it," Jackie said. "But I meant *geographically* where."

"Orleans, out on the Cape," Marcia said.

"So, *almost* local," Jackie replied. "Have you contacted her, yet?"

"No. I'm putting together a list of questions for her, now," she replied.

"How do you know it's her?" Jackie asked.

"I don't, actually, hence the questions. But her age being close to that of Mr. Fletcher, and her proximity lead me to believe it," Marcia said. "I listened to the recording of Mr. Fletcher's statement, and he didn't say much about her."

Jackie was about to ask how she had gotten into the case file on the department's computer when she remembered that the directory had been linked to the Essex County DA's office.

"Let me know when you call her," Jackie said. "I'd like to listen in."

"Will do. Maybe a half-hour or so," she replied. "So, what brings you in on Sunday morning? Is this usual for you?"

Gesturing to the office that Marcia was borrowing, Jackie said, "It is since Carolyn left. Fewer people but no less work. I'm actually here to listen to that recording, too. I was following up on something that Harry said, and I need to check whether I heard a word correctly."

Behind her desk, as she waited for her computer to boot up, she thought about Marcia making a list of questions. It was something she would have done herself in her early days, but not now. Now, she might scribble one or two salient questions on her pad, but otherwise, she'd play it by ear, letting the conversation guide the interview.

That thought triggered a memory from a few years ago.

She was remembering a conversation with one of the Somerville detectives who had worked the Jill Kelly murder, and he had said that they had been helped out by what he called *a human polygraph*. She was a blind woman who could supposedly pick up on the tiny fluctuations and stress tremors in a person's voice when they were telling a lie. She thought about getting her to listen to Harry's recorded statement.

As she logged into the network and navigated to Pamela's case file, she told herself that that wasn't a very benefit-of-the-doubt thing, and she dismissed the idea ... mostly.

First, she pulled up the transcript of Harry's statement and did a search for "Car-Lister." A box popped up that said the search item was not found.

*Well, well! Maybe I do have it wrong,* Jackie said to herself as her dying benefit-of-the-doubt ember received a reviving fan of air.

Just as quickly, though, the fanning stopped as she realized that Sharon might not have spelled the name of the website with a hyphen. She could have typed it like *Craigslist*, as one word, or as two words separated by a space.

A revised search proved that she was right and as she stared at the highlighted words *Car Lister*, the hopeful ember all but died. She was getting more sure all the time that Harry was lying.

Ever optimistic, she pulled up the recording, and with her earbuds in, she scrolled to the right part of his statement, and was able to hear, quite clearly, "*I don't actually. I'm terrible with names. It was an ad on Car-Lister. The car was out in Saugus. I met the guy in the parking lot of a McDonald's.*"

A tiny wisp of smoke rose from the dead ember.

Jackie pulled the buds from her ears and sat back, dejected. She was trying to decide whether she wanted to call Harry and ask him what was going on, or to get him to come in and do it more formally in the interview room.

She hadn't reached a decision when Marcia leaned in her doorway and said, "I'm ready to call McClelland; you still want to listen in?"

"Your list of questions all done?" she replied.

"Actually, I only came up with a few key ones," Marcia said. "I figure others will present themselves as we talk."

Jackie grinned at her answer. As she got up, she said, "Your office?"

Marcia smiled and replied, "You know, I like the sound of that. Are you taking applications?"

"Yes," Jackie said. "The question is whether or not working this case with me is going to look good on your resume."

Having used the DA office's resources to get Janet's cell phone number, Marcia dialed as Jackie picked up the extension with its switch to turn off the mouthpiece.

Not surprisingly, since she wouldn't recognize the Rowley Police number, Janet let the call ring until it went into voicemail, where most spammers quit.

"Hello, Ms. McClelland," Marcia said. "This is Marcia Grieves. I'm working with the town of Rowley up on the North Shore. I wonder if you could give me a call back when you get a chance. It's in regards to …"

Halfway through the word *regards* Marcia pressed the button to end the call.

Jackie looked at her for a moment, then said, "Nicely played. Official sounding, no misleading information, and an *accidental* disconnect before you quite got to the subject matter. If she listens to her voicemail that should get you a callback if anything would."

"Thanks," she said. "So, how did your search go?"

"Swing and a miss for what I was hoping," Jackie answered. She then explained her online search for the phantom MG; her thought that maybe she had the website wrong; and her final conclusion that Harry was lying about it for some reason.

"Another woman?" Marcia suggested.

"That would be the safe bet," Jackie said disappointedly. "But we do need to give him the chance to explain. I'm going to call and ask him to come in."

"You mind if I sit in?" Marcia asked.

"Of course not. This is as much your case as mine," Jackie said.

"But it's obvious that you're friends. I understand that you …"

"I'm actually sorry that it *is* that obvious," Jackie interrupted her. "I've been thinking that I was being pretty objective and professional; apparently not. I've known the Fletchers since I moved to town eight years ago. Pamela was on the town council at the time and interviewed me for the job of deputy chief, and Harry did a lot of work to help get our humble little station, here, rebuilt and expanded a few years ago. It's a major shock that she's dead, and an even bigger one to think that he could have had something to do with it. From all outward appearances, they had a solid, loving marriage."

"There is the possibility that the ME will find that it really was an accident and that Mr. Fletcher *didn't* have anything to do with it aside from trying to save her," Marcia offered.

Jackie smiled, and said, "Thanks for the positive thought, and I hope you're right, but the longer this goes, the more I think it's going to be more of an investigation than I originally imagined."

Marcia didn't say anything, of course, but she was actually glad that it was turning into more of a real investigation. It gave her a chance to spread her professional wings a bit, got her out of her Salem cubical, and she got to work alongside *the* Jacquelyn Hall. If things transpired so that the case went to trial and she was able to prosecute it ... well, that was probably too much to be hoping for, right now.

Jackie began to leave to go back to her own office when a thought struck her. "Oh, I meant to ask you; when you were talking to Scott Lain yesterday after the shift meeting, was he able to shed any more light on your understanding of what went on in the Fletcher's bathroom?"

"Actually, I asked him if he remembered his initial reaction when he walked into the room," Marcia said. "Did he think he'd stepped into a crime scene or an accident scene?"

"And?"

Marcia hesitated a moment, and then answered, "Crime scene. But he qualified that reaction by saying that the first thing he remembered seeing when he looked around was the blood on the edge of the bathtub. Nothing else really reinforced that knee-jerk thought, he said."

"Well, it's not what you'd call evidence, but write it up and put it in the case folder," Jackie said.

"I asked the first-responders next door at the fire station the same question," Marcia went on. "Both of them said accident. I asked if they noticed the blood on the bathtub, and one said yes, the other no. Again, not evidence, just observations, but you never know what those will trigger."

"Nice work," Jackie said. "Good follow-through."

"Can I quote you on my job application?" Marcia replied with a smile.

In her office, Jackie tapped Harry's number into the office phone. It rang a number of times, and as she anticipated the call going into voicemail, she began to formulate what she wanted to leave as a message. Halfway through the seventh ring, the phone was answered.

"Hello," he said noncommittally, not recognizing the number.

"Hi, Harry. It's Jackie. I thought I was going to be listening to a recording in a couple seconds."

"Forgot where I left my phone," he replied. "I could hear it but I couldn't find it. What's up? Did the autopsy report come back?"

"No," she said. "I don't expect to see that until late tomorrow at the earliest. I was wondering if you could come in to the station sometime. Could be today, if you're free; or tomorrow's fine."

"What's up?" he repeated, with a hint of wariness in his tone.

"There's somebody I'd like you to meet," she said. "Her name is Marcia Grieves; she's an investigator with the Essex County DA's office. She's been assigned to Pamela's case, and she's here at the station temporarily."

"You called for reinforcements?" he said.

"No," she said with a little chuckle, although she wasn't sure he was kidding. "Standard procedure. When the hospital asked for an investigation, the agency where the incident occurred—that is, the state medical examiner, and the county DA where it occurred—that's Essex—are all notified and become involved."

"Okay. Yeah, I guess I can come in this afternoon," he said. "One-ish?"

"Great! Thanks, Harry. I appreciate your cooperation."

A few moments later, Marcia appeared in Jackie's doorway, and said, "I couldn't help but overhear; am I going to be the bad cop?"

"God, I hope it doesn't come down to playing games," Jackie said. "No, I just used you because I didn't want to tip my hand about the missing MG. If he needs to make up another lie, I want him doing it in front of me."

"Makes sense," Marcia replied. "So, he's coming in?"

"One-ish," Jackie said. "We'll take lunch about eleven-thirty, okay?"

"Sure." Then crooking her thumb back toward the other office, she said, "I just tried Janet, again; I hung up before it went into voicemail. It would be interesting to talk to her before Mr. Fletcher got here."

"You think he's lying about her?" Jackie asked.

"No reason to, specifically," Marcia said, "but if a guy will lie about a used car, lying about another woman isn't exactly a stretch."

To avoid leaving a string of hang-up calls on Janet's phone, all from the same number, Marcia refrained from calling her again until quarter to one. This time, Janet picked up.

Marcia could see Jackie outside in the parking lot talking to someone, so she went ahead on her own.

"Hi, Ms. McClelland, my name is Marcia Grieves. I left you a voicemail a few hours ago; did you happen to get it?"

"I'm afraid I'm pretty bad at checking my voicemail," she replied. "What was it about?"

"Well, I'm with the Essex County DA's office, but I'm on temporary assignment with the Rowley Police, up on the North Shore."

"And what would you like to talk to *me* about?" Janet asked. "You said the county DA's office?"

"Essex county, yes," Marcia replied. "Do you know a man by the name of Harold Fletcher? He lives in Rowley."

"Yes. We worked together, but that was several years ago," she said. "Is he all right?"

"Yes, but his wife, Pamela, passed away Thursday night," Marcia answered, "and there's an inquiry into her death. I was …"

"An *inquiry*? How did she die?"

"A drowning after an apparent fall in a bathtub," Marcia replied.

"Oh, my! I'm sorry to hear that," Janet said. "I didn't know her very well; I think we met at an office party or two."

"How well did you know *Mr.* Fletcher?"

"We worked for the same company for, I think, three years or so," she answered. "Oh, and I proofread a couple of his manuscripts for him."

"Manuscripts?" Marcia asked.

"He's an author on the side," she replied. "Self-published, I think … or he was then, anyway. I know he was always looking for an agent and publisher; hoping for the big break."

"What kinds of books?" Marcia asked.

"Murder mysteries," she answered. "At least the couple that I read were. And I have to say, they were pretty good. Interesting characters, good plots, really well written. Better than some best sellers I've read."

"That's interesting," Marcia said. "I didn't know that."

"I think you can buy them on Amazon," Janet said.

"I'll have to check that out," Marcia said. "So, um, it was only through work and the proofreading that you knew Mr. Fletcher? You weren't … closer than that?"

"Are you asking me if we had an affair?" Janet asked, obviously surprised.

"I didn't mean any offense, Ms. McClelland," Marcia said. "The subject came up and I need to follow up on it."

"*Who* brought the subject up?" she asked with some indignity. "Did Harry say that?"

"It was in a statement he gave shortly after his wife's death."

"Well, why the hell would he say *that*?" Janet asked rhetorically. "No, we never had an affair!" she added definitively. "And it's *Mrs.* McClelland, which it's been for twenty-six monogamous years!"

"I apologize for the insinuation, Mrs. McClelland," Marcia said. "But thank you for setting the record straight. Can you think of a reason that Mr. Fletcher would fabricate something like that?"

"No! I thought we were friends!" she said, her ire obviously piqued. "I have no idea *why* he would say such a thing!"

"Well, again, I apologize, Mrs. McClelland," Marcia said.

"It's not *you* who needs to be apologizing," she said. "It's *Harry*."

"I think he needs to be apologizing *and* explaining," Marcia replied. "So, in the time that you worked with him, do you recall him ever being caught in any lies around the office? Taking credit for other people's work; denying responsibility that was obviously his; that sort of thing? Maybe saying something about someone that was untrue ... like this."

"Not really," she answered. "That's why it's such a shock that he'd say this about *me*."

"Well, I'm certainly going to try to find out," Marcia said, "but my guess is that he's covering for someone else, and he didn't think we'd contact you. Thinking back on your time at work with him, do you recall ever wondering if there might be anything going on between Mr. Fletcher and anyone else in the office?"

There was a pause, and then she said, "No. Not really. He was pretty friendly with everyone, but no one leaps out that he was *overly* friendly with."

"How many other women were in the office, besides you?"

"Three when I started there, and four when I left," she answered.

"Do you happen to recall their names?"

"Oh, my! Now you're really going to give my brain cells a workout," she replied. There was another pause as Janet dredged them up, and then she gave Marcia three names. "I can't recall the last one; I wasn't there very long after she started."

"Mrs. McClelland, I can't thank you enough for talking with me. This has been very helpful," Marcia said. "And once again, I apologize for the attack on your character. Believe me; I'm going to talk to Mr. Fletcher about that."

Just as she was hanging up with Janet, Jackie walked into the station with Harry.

A few moments later, Jackie appeared in Marcia's doorway, alone.

"Where's Mr. Fletcher?" Marcia asked.

"I left him in the interview room," Jackie answered. "You ready?"

"Can he hear us?" Marcia asked.

"No," Jackie replied. "Why?"

Marcia then recapped her conversation with Mrs. McClelland. "Shit!" Jackie said when she was done.

# Chapter 10

**Sunday, July 11, 2021**

When Jackie and Marcia entered the interview room, Harry stood up for introductions, but Jackie caught both of them off guard when she said, forcefully, "What the hell's going on, Harry? First, you lie to me about being home, then you lie about going to look at an MG, and now I find out you lied about having an affair with Janet McClelland! I'm trying to be on your side here, but Jesus, you're making it damned hard!"

Both Harry and Marcia blinked at the abrupt assault. Marcia wasn't sure if this was a bad-cop play on Jackie's part or if she was really pissed.

"I, um ..." Harry stammered.

"Sit down, Harry!" Jackie commanded as she closed the door. "This is Marcia Grieves," she went on in a tone only slightly less aggressive. "She's with the Essex County DA's office. She's been sent up here from Salem to make sure that my friendship with you doesn't get in the way of a complete and impartial investigation into Pamela's death."

That was certainly not how Marcia would have characterized her assignment, but she didn't say anything.

Jackie sat down heavily in the metal chair next to Marcia. With Harry now seated across from them, she leaned over the table, and as she fixed her eyes on Harry's, she said, "Tell me what's going on, Harry! I don't even have an autopsy report back, yet, and you've already told me three fucking lies about what happened ... *that I'm aware of*! You better have a damned good explanation or I'm going to recuse myself from the case and you can deal with Ms. Grieves. And trust me; *I'm* the good-cop in the room!"

Jackie almost never used the f-bomb, so when someone who knew her heard it, they knew she was fuming. Marcia didn't know her that well, but she had the feeling that what she was seeing and hearing wasn't acting.

Harry lowered his eyes, sat back in his chair, and blew out a long breath.

"I'm sorry, Jackie; you're right," he said. He looked at Marcia, and added, "Ms. Grieves, I apologize to you, as well.

"I swear to God that Pamela's death was an accident, so I never thought there'd be an investigation into anything. Yes, I lied, but only to make things ... well, simple, I guess. I'm sorry."

"Tell me about the car," Jackie said, softening her tone only a fraction. "I tried to find a red '68 MGB on Car-Lister and even on Craigslist and none exists anywhere in the state, nor have they in the last month."

"I *was* out of the house when Pamela had her accident, but no, I was not looking at a car." He paused for a deep breath, blew it out, and finished, "I was with another woman."

"Janet McClelland?" Jackie asked.

"No. I really haven't seen or talked with her in years," Harry said meekly.

Under the table, Jackie gave Marcia's foot a nudge with her own, handing her the baton.

"I just got off the phone with Mrs. McClelland," Marcia said, "and she was quite adamant that she *never* had an affair with you ... or anyone for that matter. Why did you say you had?"

"Obviously, Ms. Grieves, to protect the *actual* person," he replied in a patronizing manner. "A long-past indiscretion didn't seem very relevant to Pamela's accident, so I didn't think anyone would check. Janet's was simply the first name that popped into my head when Chief Hall was pressing me."

"You might want to watch the condescending tone, Harry," Jackie said. "You're not in that position, here. Who was the *actual person*?"

He looked back and forth between the two women, and then said, "First, I think I need to explain that Pamela and I had an open marriage."

"Did your wife know that?" Marcia said sarcastically.

Harry met her eyes, and replied, "Let's *both* not be condescending, okay?"

He looked at Jackie, and said, "Yes, she knew, but I'm sure it's not what you're thinking."

"Is it ever?" Marcia quipped.

Harry shot her a look, and Jackie interceded with a simple, "Okay! Both of you!" To Harry, she said, "Tell us about it."

Harry leaned back, interlaced his fingers atop his head, and began, "Pamela and I honest-to-God did love each other. And we were happy and compatible in every aspect of our marriage except sex."

Marcia made a *Hmm* sound that easily carried the thought *like you weren't getting enough so you decided to cheat.*

Harry gave her an exasperated glance, and Jackie said, "Stop it," to her.

The reactions were exactly what Marcia was going for; she wanted to give Jackie the opportunity to show that she really was on Harry's side. The good cop.

Suspecting that that was Marcia's motivation for her comments, Jackie turned to her, and said, "Seriously; stop it."

To Harry, she said, "Go on."

"Well, after our mutually-destructive affairs, our marriage counselor eventually zeroed in on the fact that the reason that our sex lives had faltered, was because we were each looking for something different in that regard."

Marcia had to almost bite her lip to stifle a reaction to that statement. She wasn't able to disguise her body language, however.

Jackie ignored it, but Harry turned to her, and went on, "And contrary to what I'm sure you're thinking, Ms. Grieves, Pamela was the one to jump on board the open-marriage concept as soon as our counselor mentioned it." Turning to Jackie, he said, "Are you familiar with the concept of an open marriage? Clinically, it's referred to as *consensual non-monogamy* or CNM."

Jackie put her foot lightly on top of Marcia's to keep her from saying anything, and answered, "Only very generally."

"Well, it's different for every couple, of course, but it's rarely just about promiscuity," Harry explained. "It almost always has something to do with one of the partners having different tastes or desires when it comes to sex. In almost all other areas of the relationship, they're in harmony. And they do love each other; it's just that one, single aspect that keeps a pebble in the shoe of the marriage."

Marcia shifted in her chair, and Jackie pressed her foot again to head off the glib comment she was sure was brewing.

"And it wasn't as simple as our counselor saying *'Go out and screw other people; I'll see you next week.'* There was a lot of ground that we covered; some hurt; some resentment; the lies; the betrayals.

"Before she would even tell us about how to engage with other CNM-compatible people we ended up being far better communicators than we had ever been before. We were able to talk about anything. Things that we would have just kept hidden under the carpet before, stepping around the lump whenever we walked across the room. That made our marriage a hundred percent stronger and allowed the CNM to work.

"The way our counselor explained it, most marriages seem to have sex as the keystone; that one critical block in the top of the marital stone-arch that keeps the whole thing from falling down. The problem with some relationships is that the keystone doesn't fit the same way on both sides of the arch. Each partner expects and wants something different from that block—from sex.

"One partner may be under-the-sheets, lights-off, meek and demure, while the other one is an extrovert-bordering-on-exhibitionist. One might be in the mood every night while the other is ready once a week if that.

"But the thing is that everything else in the relationship works fine. How to rear the kids, spending habits, where to go on vacation, even what to eat. The rest of the stones in the arch all fit beautifully. So, to allow the misfit of that sexual keystone to bring down the whole arch— the whole marriage—is a total shame.

"So, her theory is that communication, not sex, becomes the keystone, and sex gets moved to some non-critical spot in the structure where it's almost more decorative than functional. It fills out the framework and makes the whole thing complete, but it's not the be-all-end-all."

He looked at Marcia, and said, "And since you're probably guessing wrong and I know you're dying to ask, Pamela was the first one to move on the CNM thing.

"Pamela's appetite with regards to sex was more ... *assertive* than mine," he went on. "She liked being kinky. She found dirty-talk to be erotic; I find it crude and demeaning. She could somehow get pleasure from pain; a concept that completely baffles me. For me, pain is pain and an instant turn-off. She found bondage to be exciting; that *never* aroused me—being the binder *or* the bound. Again, I never got how being tied up and helpless—even in make-believe—should be anything but terrifying.

"For years, I tried to up my game to please her, and she backed off on hers to meet me in the middle. The result was a compromise that didn't satisfy either of us. CNM fixed that."

"How long had you been practicing CNM?" Marcia asked in a more curious rather than patronizing tone.

Jackie had her shoe on top of Marcia's, but happily didn't feel the need to press down.

"Five years or so, probably," he answered, also surprised at the benign question from Marcia.

"And having sex with other people *saved* your marriage, in your opinion?" she asked.

It wasn't an argumentative question; she was genuinely perplexed. So was Jackie.

"Yes. Absolutely," he replied. "You're probably imagining that we *only* had sex with other people," he went on, guessing correctly. "No, the whole point of CNM—for us anyway—was to have a way that we ... mostly Pamela, could have our unfulfilled desires met. We probably only went outside once a month or so. The rest of the time our sex together was wonderful. It was true love-making without any pressure. We probably had sex once a week-ish, and it was better than it had been in years."

"Did you have some ... *itch* that your wife couldn't or wouldn't scratch?" Marcia asked. "You've made it sound like she was the only one who needed the CNM release."

He shifted in his chair uncomfortably and averted their eyes for a few moments, but then answered, "Feet. I have a foot fetish."

Jackie had to fight to suppress a laugh.

"And Pamela could not *stand* to have her feet played with," Harry went on. "She was super ticklish there." He paused for a moment and added, "Strange; pain was pleasure for her, but even giving her a foot massage was like torture."

"So, you realize that we have to ask you who you were with Thursday night," Marcia said, getting back on track.

"Yeah," he said resignedly but didn't offer the name.

"Is she married?" Jackie asked.

"No. That's one of the boundaries we set—at our counselor's suggestion," he answered. "We could only go out with someone in another CNM relationship, or a single person who understood it. The idea of doing something to save your marriage while possibly ruining someone else's is a bit hypocritical."

Marcia and Jackie just looked at him, waiting for him to go on.

Finally, looking at Marcia, he said, "This won't mean anything to *you*, but it was Megan Hope." Turning to Jackie, he added, "We'd been seeing each other for eight months or so."

Jackie nodded, hoping she had suppressed any outward manifestation of her surprise. Megan was an attractive woman and probably young enough to be Harry's daughter provided he was sexually active in his teens, but the surprise she tried to hide was that she was one of the two EMTs who responded to his 911 call that night.

"Well, that will make it easy to verify," Jackie said. She turned to Marcia, and added, "Megan works next door at the fire station."

"Yes, I talked with her on Friday, but I only asked her about the crime scene," Megan said. To Harry, she went on, "That must have been pretty awkward having her show up at your house right after you'd been with her."

"More than a little," he replied. "She was supposed to be off duty. They asked her to be on call while we were still together. Somebody had called in sick, I think."

"Did Pamela know that Megan was your CNM partner?" Jackie asked.

"Very tactful," Harry said with a smile. "A lot of people would have called her my mistress or my lover. I appreciate your respect. In answer, though, no, she didn't. We decided to go with a kind of don't ask, don't tell thing—which was *against* our counselor's advice. That way if we crossed paths with each other's partners it wouldn't be so uncomfortable."

"So, you don't know hers, either?" Marcia asked.

"Only her first," he answered. "Following our counselor's advice, Pamela introduced us so that everything was all aboveboard. Apparently, the guy didn't grasp the whole CNM concept, and he saw me as a loser and a cuckold and started talking trash to me. Pamela almost punched him in the face she was so pissed. That's when we switched to don't ask, don't tell."

"Do you remember his name?" Marcia asked.

Harry thought for a moment and then shook his head. "Nothing," he said. "I could maybe pick him out of a line-up, but I don't think I'd recognize his name if you told it to me."

"Well, thank you, Harry," Jackie said as she pushed her chair back. "That clears up a lot. Please don't do it in the future, but I understand why you lied." She turned to Marcia, and asked, "You have anything else?"

"Janet McClelland," she said. "You never told us who you actually had that long-ago affair with."

He looked at Jackie, let out a resigned breath, and said, "Helen Booker."

Jackie didn't stand a chance of suppressing her surprise this time. "*Chief Booker's wife?*" she said.

"Sorry. I know how you respect him. I do too. It was a monumental screw-up for both of us. Please don't ask me for any details, because I won't tell you. It really is completely irrelevant. She's dead, and now, so is Pamela."

"Jesus," Jackie said shaking her head and looking at nothing as the information processed. Then she looked at Harry again, and asked, "Did Roy find out?"

"I don't think so," Harry said in an almost pathetically sad tone. "It was a guilt-ridden secret we were going to take to the grave with us."

"But your wife knew?" Marcia said.

"About *an* affair, but I told *her* it was with Janet McClelland, too," he said. "I guess I owe her a hell of an apology, don't I?"

After Harry left, Jackie explained, "Roy Booker was the Chief of Police here during the whole Holly McCray thing. I was Acting Chief because he was in the hospital with a smashed-up leg. I didn't know Helen real well, but I looked up to him like a second father. It's kind of a kick in the guts to find out your mother was cheating on your father."

"Tell me about it," Marcia said.

"Oh, shit!" Jackie said. "I'm sorry. That was stupid."

Marcia shrugged and said, "Life in the big city. You couldn't have known."

"Sorry," she said, again. She looked at her watch, and said, "I think we've accomplished more than either of us expected to, today. I say we head home."

As she packed her laptop, Marcia leaned out of the doorway and said to Jackie, "I'm going to send you the bill for my shoeshine, by the way."

Jackie laughed, and said, "I'll pony up for half; I was only stepping on one shoe."

## Chapter 11

**Monday, July 12, 2021**

When Jackie arrived at the station Monday morning, she was surprised that she didn't see Marcia's car already there.

Inside, she had just sat down at her desk with her first cup of coffee when Sharon buzzed and announced, "Marcia is on the line for you."

"Good morning," Jackie said. "Is everything okay? I was a little surprised that you didn't beat me in."

"Hi, Jackie. Yeah, everything's fine," she replied. "I got called into the home office for a big meeting this morning. I should be in after lunch."

"Great. Thanks for calling and letting me know. Should I save a blueberry muffin for you?"

"Oh, God, yes! Even two days old that was so good!" Marcia answered referring to the one they shared on Sunday. "But you know what *else* should be in after lunch besides me? Pamela Fletcher's autopsy report ... well, the preliminary report, anyway."

"Really? Did they have a slow weekend in the morgue? Death took a holiday?" Jackie said.

"No, but it turns out that if your Dad's the Attorney General, you can get strings pulled by association," Marcia said.

"Awesome!" Jackie said remembering how hard it had been to get her father off the dime four years ago. "I'll tell you what," she went on, "if it shows up before you get here, I won't open the email so we can go through it together."

"Thanks!" Marcia said.

The morning went by in a busy blur after the morning meeting, with three traffic collisions—one of which included an extreme DUI at 9:00 in the morning, a shoplifting from the CVS, and a domestic disturbance that was settled by the time the officer arrived.

When Jackie got back from lunch there was a note on her desk that said that Marcia had called and to call her back.

When Marcia picked up, Jackie said, "I have a cell phone, you know; you didn't need to leave a message at the station."

"I know; I didn't want to disturb your lunch," she replied. "It wasn't that important."

"Well, thank you, I appreciate that. What's up?"

"The ME's office called, and said they're not going to release the autopsy report today," Marcia said. "They want the results of the tox testing to come back from the lab, first. Apparently, my strings aren't all that strong."

"Did they say how long that would be?"

"They said that with the backlog in the labs, we're looking at probably a week."

"Crud!" Jackie said. "And things were going so smoothly."

"But all is not lost," Marcia said. "He told me that if we come in to his office at the end of the day, he'd go over the *unofficial* findings he has so far."

"Good news offset by the bad news of rush-hour traffic in Boston," Jackie said.

"I can go alone and maybe put you on a speakerphone call," Marcia suggested.

"I was hoping there'd be photos to go with the report," Jackie said. "If he's doing this unofficially because of your strings, he may not want you sending me snapshots of them. But here's a thought: I'll come to your place in Salem and we can go from there, together. Misery loves company."

"Perfect! Can you be here about 3:30? The ME's office closes at 4:30."

"An hour from downtown Salem to downtown Boston at rush-hour?" Jackie said.

"I'm looking at the map," Marcia replied, "and it shows it taking forty-six minutes if we take 114 to Rt. 1."

Having gone through the better-a-lot-early-than-even-a-little-bit-late debate many times before, Jackie simply countered, "How about 3:15? Humor me; I'll owe you one."

Jackie and Marcia were shown into the office of Deputy Chief Medical Examiner, Dr. Karl West at 4: 25. "Please, have a seat; Dr. West will be with you shortly," the young woman said.

As they sat, Jackie made a show of looking at her watch.

"Yeah, yeah," Marcia said dismissively. "Like Google-maps is supposed to anticipate a fender-bender that closed a lane on the Tobin Bridge."

Jackie just smiled at her.

When the doctor still had not shown up at nearly 5:00, Marcia made a show of looking at *her* watch, and said to Jackie, "Good thing we left early."

"Yeah, yeah," Jackie said with a little laugh.

Five minutes later, Dr. West came in carrying a stack of eight or ten manila folders. He set them on his desk as he dropped heavily into his chair, and said, "Fletcher, right? Pamela?"

"Yes, Doctor," Marcia replied. "I'm Marcia Grieves with the Essex County DA's office, and this is Chief Hall with the Rowley Police. Thank you for seeing us."

"Glad to do it," he said. "Be sure to say hi to your father for me."

*Always get a receipt when doing a favor*, Jackie said to herself sarcastically.

West ran his finger over the tabs of the folders and then pulled one from near the bottom. He flipped it open, scanned it quickly, and then said, "Reported accidental drowning." He looked up at the two women, and added, "Except that she didn't drown at all, accidental or otherwise."

"Oh!" Jackie responded.

"Really?" Marcia said.

"So, there was no water in her lungs?" Jackie said.

"About enough to result in a severe coughing spell," West replied. "Not enough to cause unconsciousness and far too little to cause death."

"I've heard of dry-drowning where the throat constricts when it senses water," Jackie said. "Could that have happened here?"

"I found no evidence of laryngospasm," he answered. "I believe the water entered her lungs post-mortem."

"Then what was the cause of death?" Marcia asked.

"The *mechanism* of death was acute cerebral anoxia; absence of oxygen in the brain," he went on. "Which would be the same if she *had* drowned, but I found evidence that the *cause* of death was manual strangulation."

"What kind of evidence?" Jackie asked.

The doctor flipped a couple of pages in the folder and then turned it around so they could see the photo he had exposed. "A faint subcutaneous hematoma located on either side of the neck aligning with the carotid arteries. Someone pinched off the supply of blood to her brain, resulting in unconsciousness and then death."

"Holy crap!" Jackie said.

"Then she was murdered?" Marcia said.

"I'm certain that the manner of death is not suicide because the victim could not have continued to apply pressure to her own neck after she passed out.

"Likewise, natural and accidental deaths can be logically ruled out," he continued, "which leaves homicide."

"Wow," Jackie said as she looked at the photo. "Not what I was expecting."

"What about the cut over the right eye?" Marcia asked. "Could you tell if that was pre- or post-mortem?"

"Ah! I'm glad you brought that up," the doctor said. He flipped to another photo showing Pamela's brain after it was exposed by peeling back her scalp and sawing off the top of her skull—the calvaria.

"As you can see," he said as he pointed, "the right frontal lobe, here—located directly behind the laceration—looks perfectly normal, as does the left occipital lobe, here at the back. If there had been a fall or a strike hard enough to cause unconsciousness, the brain would have surged back and forth within the cranial cavity and there would be swelling of the brain tissue in these two areas. Because there is none, there is no doubt that the injury occurred after she was already deceased."

"Wow!" Jackie repeated.

After a few moments of processing this new and surprising information, Jackie said, "Her husband reported that when he found her he pulled her head up out of the water so she could breathe. If he was gripping too tightly in his panic could that account for these bruises? They're certainly pretty faint."

"I would consider that highly unlikely," Dr. West replied. "Their locations align precisely—on *both* sides—with the carotid arteries. It would seem a pretty bizarre coincidence for that to happen by accident. And it would take a fair amount of prolonged pressure to create even these faint bruises."

"Wow," Jackie said, yet again, still in disbelief and trying to picture Harry Fletcher as a murderer. But then, she could never have pictured him having an affair with Chief Booker's wife, either.

"There is other evidence of foul play, as well," the doctor went on as he flipped to another photo; this one a close-up of Pamela's right hand. "There is a light abrasion at the base of the opponens pollicis muscle—where the wrist transitions to the thumb. The left hand has one as well. Both would be consistent with a ligature used to bind her wrists together.

"Additionally," he went on, "I found skin cells under the fingernails of her right hand, and evidence of recent vaginal penetration. Some trace amounts of a foreign lubricant on the vaginal walls would tend to explain why there was no seminal fluid present; whoever penetrated her was most likely wearing a condom. The cells from under her nails have been sent out for DNA testing." Looking at Marcia, he said, "I believe that you may be looking at a rape as well as a homicide."

The tone with which he delivered the last sentence made Jackie almost expect him to add, "*Congratulations!*" as if he felt they should be happy about there being a rape on top of a murder.

Jackie asked, "So, the toxicological tests that you're having performed; are you looking for anything specific there?"

"Yes," he answered. "I asked them to screen for the usual suspects; alcohol, cannabis, common recreational drugs, but also any of the date-rape drugs; Rohypnol, GHB, ketamine."

Again looking at Marcia, he said, "Your father put in a few good words for me here and there to help put me behind this desk, so if I can help you get your first conviction with the county DA's office, it's the least I can do. So, whatever this office can do to help you to frame a stronger case, you just let me know."

Jackie cringed inwardly at the doctor's statement, but she didn't say anything. In her mind the purpose of the autopsy was to uncover the facts, not to get a conviction or repay a favor. She had to wonder if maybe Dr. West was skewing findings that might correctly lean more in the *undetermined* direction toward *homicide* for Marcia's benefit.

"You said the tox and DNA tests would take a week?" Marcia said.

"I've put a rush on them," the doctor replied, "but the labs are pretty independent folks. That's probably *best* case."

"Now, if you'll excuse me," he went on as he withdrew and closed the folder, "I have a dinner engagement."

"Well, thank you, Dr. West," Jackie said pushing back her chair. "This has been very helpful. We appreciate you giving us a chance to go over this with you before it's actually complete. This is going to help us direct our efforts."

"As was my intention," he said as he stood up. "It's a pleasure to meet you, Chief Hall," he added, shaking her hand. "And certainly you, Marcia," he went on giving her a shake. "Again, please say hello to your father for me when you see him. And, as I said, if there's anything you need, just call."

"Oh, where is Dr. Shannon?" Jackie asked, turning back as she reached the office door. "I hoped I'd get a chance to see her again; we worked on that big serial-killer task force a few years ago along with Marcia's father."

"Oh, yes. What did they call those? The Nightmare Murders, wasn't it?" he replied. "Pretty creepy having the guy working right here in the morgue helping to dissect his own victims. Anyway, Dr. Shannon is attending a medical examiner's conference ... on a cruise ship in the Caribbean. One of the many perks of not having *deputy* in front of your title."

As they left the building, Marcia said to Jackie, "I'm really sorry about that; that's got to be pretty hard to accept that a guy you've known for a bunch of years could have killed his wife ... whom you've known just as long."

"It is," Jackie replied flatly. "To the point where I don't."

"What? You don't think it's a homicide after all the evidence Dr. West just showed us?" Marcia asked as they walked across Concord St. to the parking garage.

"I'm not disputing the physical evidence that he found," Jackie said. "I'm disputing the conclusions that he drew from them."

They reached the car, and Jackie leaned on the roof, looking across at Marcia. "I promise not to do this all the time," she said, "but I'm going to tell you a story that Chief Booker told me ... and he did that a lot.

"Anyway, this local guy and his out-of-town buddy are walking down a back road, and they come across an old barn. On the door of the barn are half a dozen targets drawn in chalk. The buddy looks closely, and he sees that there's a bullet hole right in the middle of every single target.

'Wow!' he says to the local guy. 'That is some impressive shooting!'

'Not really,' the guy says. 'That's Tommy Birch; he shoots first and then draws the target around the hole.'"

Marcia chuckled, and said, "Cute."

"Whenever the Chief thought someone was looking at things backwards—trying to make the evidence fit the conclusion they wanted, he'd say, *'You shootin' or drawin' targets?'*"

"You think Dr. West is drawing targets?" Marcia asked as she opened her door.

"I do," Jackie said. Inside the car, she went on, "When he used the word *frame* in talking about getting a conviction it was like jamming an EpiPen in my leg; first I was hit by the shock of the jab and now I'm wired with adrenalin because of it."

"I'm sure that's not what he meant," Marcia said.

"Probably not overtly, but I'm not ruling out a Freudian slip."

"So, again, you don't think it was a homicide?"

"Assuming his finding of strangulation is correct—and it seems hard to disagree with unless he's a complete incompetent," Jackie said, "then by definition, because one human being caused the death of another human being, it has to be homicide. But that doesn't mean that it was intentional, and certainly not that only one person could have done it."

"Who else could it have been?" Marcia responded. "There were no signs of forced entry, and Mr. Fletcher said himself that the front door was deadbolted until he unlocked it with his phone. Your patrolman reported that all of the other doors were locked, too."

"Maybe while Harry was out giving Megan a foot massage," Jackie suggested, "Pamela was entertaining *her* CNM partner."

"Why wouldn't he have told us that?" Marcia replied.

"Maybe he didn't know," Jackie answered. "Maybe the don't-ask-don't-tell thing extended to when as well as who."

"Okay," Marcia replied with a slightly dubious tone. "Present your case."

"All right," Jackie began as Marcia pulled out of the garage, "after dinner Harry says, 'I'm going out; don't wait up.' Pamela knows where he's going even if she doesn't know with whom. She calls her kinky friend and tells him to come over and bring the ropes.

"The play gets hot and heavy and he's got his hands on her neck, squeezing, to get her right on the edge of passing out to intensify her orgasm."

"That works?" Marcia said.

"No first-hand knowledge—thank you very much—but that's what I've read. The actor David Carradine accidentally hung himself doing it. A lot of others too.

"Anyway—like Carradine—the erotic-strangulation goes too far. Maybe she was having such an intense orgasm that she blacked out from the combination. In his own ejaculatory enthusiasm—and maybe inexperience—he didn't let go and she didn't wake up. He panicked and put her in the tub to make it look like an accident. Maybe he's a little guy and couldn't carry her easily and he *dropped* her putting her in and that's when she hit her head. Or, for that matter, maybe he *intentionally* whacked her head against the tub to make her being unconscious and drowning more believable."

"What about the skin cells under her fingernails?" Marcia asked. "Hard to do if you're tied to a bed."

"Maybe the scratching happened *prior* to her being trussed up," Jackie offered. "Or maybe she wasn't tied to the bed. Maybe it was more of a handcuff style of restraint but with rope to give her some participatory freedom of movement."

Stopped at a light, Marcia looked at Jackie for a moment, and then said, "Have you read Mr. Fletcher's books? Because that sounds like a plot he could have written. You do know he writes murder mysteries, right?"

"I did know that, but I've never read one. I'm more non-fiction," Jackie answered. "So, are you telling me that this accidental-drowning-murder is the plot in one of his books?"

"No. Well, I don't know, really; I've only read one," she replied, "but that's his style. I downloaded one onto my Kindle after I got home yesterday and I was up 'til 1:00 finishing it. He's actually quite good for somebody who's self-published."

"I guess I should give one a try," Jackie said.

"You need to," Marcia replied, "because he is really good at weaving an intricate plot. And I'm not suggesting that he could be dumb enough to write a plot and then act it out. What I'm saying is that he has a mind that could conceive of something like this and work out the details to the nth degree."

"Wow!" Jackie said, running that idea around in her head.

"Somebody once referred to fiction writers as professional tellers of lies," Marcia said. "It seems that that would make his lying in his statement easy and almost natural."

Jackie was silent for a little while, then she said, "As the spouse of the deceased he automatically goes to the top of the suspect list. He had the means; she was apparently strangled by hand, and he has two. Opportunity is still in question until we talk to Megan Hope to check his alibi. And he *could* have motive if that's how you want to look at her life insurance policies. We need to find out when those were issued, and verify his assertion that there's no huge debt that he's fighting to get out from under."

Marcia glanced over at Jackie, and said, "I am impressed. You just went from Mr. Fletcher's defense attorney to a witness for the prosecution in about thirty seconds."

"Yeah, objectivity over loyalty," Jackie said with a hint of resignation. "Cop first; friend second. I saw myself drawing a target there."

"So, what's next?" Marcia asked.

"I'm a little embarrassed to put it this way," Jackie said, "but now we treat this like a real homicide investigation."

"You want me to get a warrant going for Mr. Fetcher's arrest?" Marcia asked.

"I'd be very surprised if you could get one," Jackie said having lectured on the subject of getting warrants. "You're not going to be able to attach an autopsy report listing that the death even *is* a homicide, so coming up with enough probable cause to convince a judge that he likely *committed* it will be tough ... as well it should be."

She went on, "Getting warrants to search the house and to look at his and Pamela's computers as part of an investigation into a *possible* homicide should be straightforward, though."

"Also getting permission to look into his finances and those insurance policies, I should think," Marcia added.

"But I want to hold off on serving them," Jackie said. "First and foremost I want to talk to Megan Hope. Depending on how that goes, I might simply ask Harry if he'll give us permission to look at their computers. His answer to that might tell us a lot."

"You can tell him we're looking for who his wife's partners were ... which won't be a lie," Marcia added.

"Yeah. And you should start warrants for their email and phone records, too," Jackie said.

With a plan of attack laid out, Jackie said, "So, tell me about Harry's book. Were you able to figure out who-dun-it before the last chapter?"

"I *thought* I had it figured out in chapter two," she replied. "By chapter five I was doubting myself; in the middle of the story I was absolutely *sure* I had the killer nailed; and by the next to last chapter, I was back to guessing. The short answer is no; I didn't figure it out. Like I said, he's a good writer."

"So, one has to wonder," Jackie mused, "if he could script *reality* equally well."

## *Chapter 12*
**Monday, July 12, 2021**

Back at the station, Jackie called next door to the fire department and asked to speak with Megan Hope.

"Hi, Megan, Jackie Hall, here," she said when she picked up. "I wonder if I could get you to step over here to the station for a few minutes. I have a couple of questions I'd like to ask you about Pamela Fletcher. You were one of the EMTs on that call, right?"

"Yeah, I was. God, that was a tough one," she replied. "I'm actually on duty right now, so I'm not supposed to leave in case a call comes in. Can we do it over the phone?"

"I'd rather not," Jackie said, always preferring face-to-face interviews to phone chats. "What time do you get off? Can you come over then? It should only take a few minutes."

"I actually have something right after work," Megan answered. "Let me ask the chief if I can run over there if I take a radio. If it squawks, I'm outa there, though."

"Agreed," Jackie replied. "See you in a few."

In the interview room, Jackie said, "I understand that you've talked to Marcia Grieves with the county DA's office, so you're aware that there's an inquiry into Pamela's death, right?"

"She said it was initiated by the hospital."

"Correct. Now *we* have the task of following it up," Jackie said. "So, I heard that you weren't even supposed to be on duty that night," Jackie went on. "Is that right?"

"Yes. I'd already worked the day shift, but Travis Lind called in sick, so they asked if I could cover for him."

"When you talked with Marcia," Jackie continued, "you told her that your first impression when you got there was that you were walking into an accident scene as opposed to a crime scene. Was there anything specific that made you feel that way?"

She thought for a moment and then said, "I think maybe it's the other way around. Not so much that it looked like an accident scene as it *didn't* look like a crime scene. You know, no signs of struggle, no blood splatter, no broken mirror. Maybe it looked like an accident scene to me because we'd been dispatched to an accidental drowning so that's what I was expecting."

Jackie paused for a moment, and then said, "I apologize in advance for the personal nature of this next question, but it has to be asked to form a complete timeline of the night's events."

Megan looked at her warily.

"Were you with Harry the night Pamela died? Before you were asked to be on call?"

Megan held Jackie's eyes for a second or two, then turned away. After a few moments and a deep breath or two, she replied, "Yes. And I feel like complete shit about that." She quickly added, "But he wasn't cheating on her. They had an open marriage. They were both allowed to date other people. That's the truth!"

"I know," Jackie said. "He referred to it as consensual non-monogamy; CNM. I'm not judging you, them, or anyone; I just need to gather all the facts surrounding the case." She waited a moment, then asked, "I'm just curious, but had you ever talked to *Pamela* about the CNM thing?"

"No. One of the rules he said they had was that neither should know who the other was seeing, so it wouldn't be awkward if they met at the grocery store or something." She met Jackie's eyes, and added, "It was sure as hell awkward Thursday night."

"I can imagine," Jackie said. "And while we're on the subject of awkward," she went on, "is Harry into bondage?"

"*Bondage*?" Megan repeated in surprise. "No. Harry is into feet. He said that *Pamela* liked being tied up. According to him, she liked to get her butt smacked but couldn't stand to have her feet touched."

"And are *you* into foot-play?" Jackie asked.

Megan held Jackie's eyes for a second or two, and said, "I'm beginning to dislike this conversation."

"I'm sorry. It's no fun for me, either; I'm finding things out about people that I can never un-know. But if the ME should come back with a finding of homicide, Harry could be in pretty big trouble without an airtight alibi for the time that Pamela had her accident. He's already lied to me a couple times about it. Understandably, as it turns out to protect both you and Pamela, but lies, nonetheless."

"Well, I will swear on any Bible you have in any court you want that Harry was with me Thursday night between about quarter of eight to nine o'clock."

"Can I ask how you happen to remember those times?" Jackie asked.

"I had expected him at seven-thirty, so I was kind of watching the clock," Megan answered. "Nine o'clock is when I got the call from the station and he was just getting ready to leave."

"You were at your house?"

"My apartment, yes," Megan said.

"Where is that?"

"Up the street at Millwood Apartments," she answered. "I usually bike to work."

"Handy," Jackie said. "It looks like a nice place."

Megan shrugged, and said, "It'll do until I can afford to buy a house. The American dream; thirty years of debt."

Sliding her chair back, Jackie said, "Thank you, Megan. I really do appreciate your candor in all of this." As she stood up, she added, "I'd like to ask one more favor. I know it will be natural to do so, but please don't tell Harry about this conversation if you can possibly avoid it."

"Why?" Megan asked as she got up.

"Well, like I said, the ME's report hasn't even come back yet," Jackie said, "and I don't want him to have to worry about this inquiry on top of everything else he has to deal with. If we're all lucky, they'll determine it was only a tragic accident, and the whole thing will be done pretty soon."

In her office, Jackie pulled up the case file and looked at the transcript of the 911 call Harry had made. The call was received at 9:34. If Megan was accurate about when she got called in and when Harry left, then Harry would still have had enough time to get home, strangle Pamela, and stage the bathtub accident.

*Crap!* Jackie said to herself. *No help*. And that was the real reason that she had asked Megan not to tell Harry about their conversation.

She was concerned that if he knew there was a time-gap in his alibi he might concoct some new story to fill it in. She felt bad about it, but she had to treat Harry with the same suspicious distrust as she would any other suspect.

She made notes in the file, made sure the recording of her conversation with Megan was attached and closed out of the directory. She then set about addressing her regular chief-of-police duties.

As Jackie was clearing her desk to leave for the night, Sharon buzzed her, and said, "Marcia is on the line for you."

Jackie smiled that the people in the station were already taking to calling Marcia by her first name. She was an easy person to get comfortable with. "Put it through," she said.

"Hey, Jackie!" she said cheerily when Jackie answered. "I already have the warrant for both of the Fletchers' phone and text records!"

"Wow! Nice going. More string-pulling?" she replied.

"Nope. Well-written warrant request, thanks in part to your lecture," Marcia answered.

"Oh, yes! You were that person who managed to stay awake," Jackie joked.

"Well, through enough of it, apparently," Marcia replied. "Anyway, I'm pushing the paperwork through to her provider as we speak, so we should have something to look at tomorrow morning, I hope."

"Excellent! Well done!"

"Thanks! So, did you get a chance to talk to Megan Hope?" Marcia asked.

"I did," Jackie answered. "And the short version is that she was with Harry at her apartment for most of the time in question."

"*Most*?" Marcia repeated.

"Yeah. She says he left at nine o'clock right when she got called into the station," Jackie said. "Unfortunately, that leaves about a half-hour window before Harry called 911."

"Crap!" Marcia said. "That's no help, at all."

Jackie laughed, and said, "Two minds with a single thought."

## Chapter 13

**Tuesday, July 13, 2021**

Jackie managed to beat Marcia to the station the next morning, but not by much. Marcia stopped in Jackie's doorway before even setting her backpack down, and said, "I have an email from their provider with a link to their records. I haven't clicked it, yet. You want me to forward it to you so you can save it to the case folder?"

"Absolutely!" Jackie said as she got up. She looked in her cup to check the level of coffee—three-quarters full—and then said, "I'll go get us a muffin to split while you do that."

It took a few minutes to finally get to the list of numbers from which Pamela had received texts and phone calls. The list also included her outgoing calls and their numbers. Marcia had requested that data going back two years.

Jackie downloaded the file onto the department computer, but when she tried to open it, she got a message that it was an unrecognized file type and could not be opened.

She went back to the link through the provider, opened it there, and happily found that the format of the list was interactive, so they could sort the list by incoming or outgoing items, the date, the phone number, the length of the call, whether it was text or voice, etc.

She scrolled to the end of the two-year-long list and saw that there were over one and a half thousand entries. There appeared to be few, if any, days that Pamela was not on her phone swapping texts or phone calls with someone.

"Yipes!" Marcia said. "This is going to take a while!"

The list was arranged with the last item received at the top and went backward in time. That last item was a text at 9:24 p.m. on the night she died.

One of the columns in the list was headed "MSG" and under it were apparently the first three or four words of the text message if that's what the call was. For this call, the box read, "OTW."

"On the way," Marcia translated. "That could be Harry. Do you know his phone number?"

"Not off the top of my head," Jackie said. "Write it down and we'll look it up."

As Marcia began writing, she got an idea. "Click on the phone number," she told Jackie.

When she did, the box expanded, and it showed the caller's name, address, and service provider.

"Well, that's handy!" Jackie said. The number was Harry's.

She clicked again, and the box shrunk back to the single line. Taking a hopeful chance, she clicked on the few words in one of the MSG boxes, and it expanded to show the entire text message. "Nice!" she said happily as she clicked to make it shrink, again.

The next message—an outing text sent at 6:23—read: ALT **128077** in the little box of the MSG column.

Neither knew what that could mean, but when Jackie clicked the box it expanded to add, (Thumbs up).

"Ah! The code for the emoji, apparently," Jackie said. "And just who was she thumbs-upping?" she asked hopefully as she went down the list to the message that Pamela was replying to. It was another acronym, "SYS."

"That's *see you soon*," Marcia said.

Jackie glanced at her, and said, "I'm not *that* old. I didn't think it meant *system*."

"Sorry," Marcia said with a little laugh. "My mother never gets these."

"Well, just so you know, *Missy*," Jackie replied with theatrical indignation, "I'd had to have gotten busy on like the day I hit puberty to be your mother."

"Sorry," Marcia repeated but with an equally-theatrical grimace.

"Moving on," Jackie said.

The timestamp for the text showed that Pamela received it at 6:21 p.m. Jackie thought for a moment, and then said, "I'm pretty sure that's around the time that Harry said they were eating supper." She clicked on the sender's number, and it expanded to show the name Aaron Delaney and his address in next-door Georgetown.

"Ooo!" Jackie said excitedly. "Could it really be this easy? Could we have hit on her partner just like that?"

"No," Marcia said. "Not unless it's also really *weird*. That's her son from a previous marriage. I saw that on her Facebook page."

"Crud!" Jackie said. "You're right. I remember that now. I met him once."

"I wonder how soon *soon* is," Marcia said. "If she had her kinky lover planning to drop by, a visit from her son could get awkward."

Jackie laughed, and said, "To say the least!"

At 7:36 there was a phone call to Aaron's number, but of course, there was no way to know what had been said between them. They wondered if she had suddenly remembered her "date" that evening and called him to postpone his visit. The call had lasted three minutes and twelve seconds.

They continued down the page, going back in time, noting phone calls and reading Pamela's texts, but found nothing suspicious or helpful. Just run-of-the-mill chit-chat. Jackie recognized many of the names—mostly women—but Marcia wrote down those she didn't for a follow-up search.

There were several more exchanges back and forth with Aaron, but only one from Jessica Fletcher, whom Jackie knew to be Harry's daughter, also from a first marriage.

On the seventh day—the Thursday before she died—there was a text from Pamela to a number they hadn't seen before. It read:

It has! Next week looks good I think. I'll get back to you.

Jackie clicked the phone number and they saw that the text went to a man named Steven Collins, with an address in nearby Newburyport. "I don't recognize the name," Jackie said with a hint of caution-tempered excitement in her voice. "But she's obviously answering a text from him."

Six lines down the list—earlier the same morning—was an incoming message from Collins' number.

Hey, Pam! It's been a while since we've "tied one on." Are you in the mood? If so, how does next week look?

"Well, that's intriguing," Marcia said. "I'm guessing he's not talking about binge-drinking when he says *tied one on*."

"No," Jackie chuckled. "But if we didn't know what we know about Pamela, I'd never have suspected it might refer to bondage." Running her mouse slowly back up the list of phone numbers, Jackie said, "But she doesn't appear to have gotten back to him like she said. No other texts or phone calls to him after that Thursday before she died."

"Maybe they met up in person," Marcia suggested. She then added, "Are there any exchanges prior to that?"

They did a sort-by-phone-number of the list and it grouped a dozen or more calls and texts together that Pamela either received from or made to Collins.

The texts could all be seen as a bit suggestive—like the *tie-one-on* reference—but were never explicit about bondage or even sex. They deduced that there had been three previous hook-ups between Pamela and Steven—not including the night she died.

Then Marcia noticed something. "Look at the dates of all of her other see-you-tonight replies to him; it looks like they always got together on Friday night."

"Interesting," Jackie said. "Which would explain why he didn't get the usual Friday text after their exchange earlier in the week; she died on Thursday."

With an I-think-we've-stumbled-onto-something lilt to her voice, Marcia suggested, "Yeah, but when he *didn't* get one on Friday, why wouldn't he have texted her to see if everything was okay? When she bailed on their planned hook-up back in April, she texted to explain why. Could it be that he wasn't surprised to not get a text *Friday* because he had killed her on *Thursday*?"

"Possible, I guess," Jackie said, "But what the heck would his motive be? And if they had a planned rendezvous for Friday, why go there and kill her Thursday? Maybe he just heard about her death sometime Friday; that news seems to have traveled pretty fast."

"Should I give him a call?" Marcia asked.

"Can't think of a reason not to," Jackie replied.

Marcia used Jackie's desk phone so the call would be logged through the department's network and could be recorded.

The phone rang several times before going into voicemail. After the beep, Marcia said, "Hi, this is Marcia Grieves. I'm working with the Rowley Police Department. I wonder if you'd be good enough to give me a call back when you get a chance." She then recited the number, repeated her name, and added a thank you.

After Marcia hung up, Jackie said, "Collins' first text to her—which reads as an obvious introduction—is about four months ago, but Harry said they'd been doing the CNM thing for what? Five *years*? She must have had a previous partner ... maybe even more than one over time."

Jackie clicked the top of the Date column to go back to the chronological order, but when she did, Marcia noticed something else change.

"Go back to the number-sort for a second," she said.

When Jackie did, Marcia pointed and said, "All of the texts and calls to his number have an X in this "DFD" column." She scanned down, and said, "So do a bunch of others. What is DFD?"

"You're the millennial," Jackie said. "You don't know?"

"No," she replied, "but *as* a millennial, I have the technology to find out." She typed the question into her phone, and after a few obviously wrong answers, she found that it stood for "Deleted From Device." But although the text was gone from a person's phone, its record remained with the provider, which was why they were seeing them.

"Oh, thank you, Pamela!" Jackie said as she clicked the DFD heading to sort the list by deleted calls and texts. "That is going to make this *so* much easier!"

All of the deleted items were now collected together and arranged by date, which neatly sorted them into groups of identical phone numbers that made it apparent that Pamela had had six other partners over the two-year period that the list covered.

With Marcia listening in on the extension, Jackie picked up her desk phone and dialed the next most current partner.

That person was Gary Wilmot. When he answered Jackie said, "Hi, my name is Jackie Hall; I'm with the Rowley Police Department. Is this Gary Wilmot?"

"Yes," he answered with a hint of understandable apprehension.

"Do you happen to know a Pamela Fletcher from here in Rowley?" Jackie asked.

"Pamela Fletcher? I know her, yes," he replied, "but I haven't seen her in months. Is she all right?"

"I'm sorry to say that she passed away this past Thursday," Jackie answered.

"Oh, my God! What happened?" he asked with genuine-sounding surprise.

"An apparent home accident," Jackie replied. "But the hospital has asked that it be looked into, so that's why I've contacted you."

"Oh. Well, I don't know how I can help," he replied, "Like I said, I haven't seen her in months."

"I understand that she and her husband shared what they called a consensual non-monogamous relationship," Jackie said. "Were you aware of that?"

There was a short pause as the reason for the call probably became apparent to him, and then he answered, "Yes. My wife and I were into the CNM lifestyle for a while, as well. We've gone back to the traditional form of marriage, though. That's why I stopped seeing Pamela."

"Do you remember the last time you saw her?" Jackie asked.

"The last time I *saw* her was probably two months ago; sometime in May," he answered. "We bumped into each other coming out of a movie theater. We were each with our spouses so we just exchanged looks and went on our ways. Her husband didn't know who I was and my wife didn't know who Pamela was. My wife noticed the looks, however, and asked me about her. I explained, and that was that."

Cynthia had CNM partners that I didn't know, too. I don't know if Pamela's husband might have asked the same questions or not."

"When was the last time you saw her as a CNM partner?" Jackie asked, looking at the dates of their text exchanges followed by a single phone call.

"February 10th," he replied. "I remember because the following day my wife and I had a long discussion and decided to go back to our monogamous marriage. We consider the 11th to be our anniversary, now. I called Pamela the following day and told her I wouldn't be seeing her anymore."

"How did she take that?" Jackie asked.

"Pretty well; maybe even relieved," he answered. "The novelty of our time together was beginning to wear off so it was time to move on for both of us, I think. For me, it meant going back to Cynthia. I can't say what she did next. I believe she had other CNM partners, but we never talked about that."

"The novelty you mentioned was BDSM?" Jackie asked.

"It was," he replied. "It was an interesting diversion at first, but I'm really not a dominating kind of person, so it was hard for me to give her the kind of pleasure she seemed to derive from the control and from the pain ... or for me to get much pleasure *from* giving them. As I said, the novelty wore off pretty quickly, at least for me." Suddenly, something apparently occurred to him, and he said, "Oh, my God! Is that how she died? Is that why you're calling me?"

"The autopsy report hasn't come back, yet," Jackie said, "so we're not a hundred percent sure. How many times had you been with Pamela as a CNM partner?" she went on.

"Three," he replied. "I don't have the specific dates off the top of my head, but I can probably figure them out from our text messages back and forth."

"That won't be necessary," she said, looking at that same data on her computer screen herself. "Can I ask how the two of you met up?" she asked.

"A website," he replied. "It's called The CNM Life—all one word—dot com."

"Was Pamela your only CNM partner?" Jackie asked.

"No. Cynthia and I had been in the lifestyle for about a year and a half," he answered, "but she was the only one who was into bondage and pain and stuff like that."

"Did you know that when you arranged your first meeting?" Jackie asked. "Was that in her profile?"

"Yes. As I said, I thought it would be an interesting diversion," he replied.

"Would you have some way of verifying your whereabouts on this past Thursday night between 6:30 and 10:00?" Jackie asked.

"Am I a suspect or something?" he said.

"Because of your past relationship with the deceased," she replied, "you're on the list as a person of interest." She then repeated, "So, can you verify your whereabouts on that night?"

"I was here at home all night," he said. "After supper, I worked on a proposal that I brought home from the office, and then Cynthia and I watched TV. We probably went to bed around 10:00 or 10:30. Cynthia will verify all that."

"Is she there, now?" Jackie asked.

"No. But I can give you her phone number," he said. He recited it and then added, "I really am sorry to hear about Pamela, but if there was any funny business involved in her death, I assure you I had nothing to do with it."

"One last question, Mr. Wilmot," Jackie said. "Do you happen to know any of Pamela's other CNM partners? I don't know how close of a group the CNM community is."

"I don't," he replied. "There are some couples who are into swinging and group sex and that sort of thing, but we never were. I don't believe that Pamela was either. Certainly, she never mentioned it."

"Okay. Well, thank you, Mr. Wilmot. I appreciate you talking with me," Jackie said. "If anything should happen to pop into your head that you think could be helpful, please give me a call."

"I can give his wife a call later," Marcia said after Jackie hung up. "You want to keep going down the list of Pamela's partners?"

"Yeah. You want to take the next one?" Jackie replied.

"Sure," Marcia said. As she picked up the phone, she added, "Is this part of my interview?"

"Anything you say can and will be used ..." Jackie said with a grin.

Clicking on the next phone number, the name Mark Plant opened up with an address in Lynn. After introducing herself Marcia asked him, "Are you acquainted with a Pamela Fletcher from Rowley?"

"Acquainted?" the guy laughed. "If tying her to her own bed and screwing her brains out counts as acquainted, then yes."

The blunt, crude reply took Marcia aback for a moment, but she regrouped quickly, and asked, "Were you part of her CNM community?"

"*CNM*?" Mark repeated. "Oh! Oh, yeah. That open-marriage bullshit. A fancy acronym for cuckolding her old man. No. I didn't belong to any club or anything; I just took advantage of the opportunity when it presented itself."

"How did it present itself?" Marcia asked.

"She was at a porn store checking out the bondage shit, so I walked up and told her I could show her how to use it like it was meant to be used," he said. "We exchanged numbers and we hooked up a couple days later. Why? What's this all about?"

"Mrs. Fletcher passed away this past week," Marcia said. "We're looking into her death."

"No shit?" he said. "She get snuffed or something?"

"Would that surprise you?" Marcia asked.

He laughed, and said, "Not really, I guess. She liked it rough. I probably left my fingerprints imprinted in her ass I was slapping it so hard. Maybe she picked up a guy who took things even further than I did. That how she died; tied to her bed?"

"No," Marcia answered and offered nothing more. "How many times did you have sex with Mrs. Fletcher?" She was looking at the text list and it appeared to be only once.

"Just the one hook-up," he said. "Oh, but that included multiple orgasms for both of us if that's what you meant."

"It wasn't," Marcia replied. "Why didn't you see her again?"

"I like to play the field," he answered. "It's usually one-and-done for me. I don't want to get all involved in a long-term thing."

"When was it that you had your one meet-up with Mrs. Fletcher?" she asked, looking at the dates in the list.

"Oh, jeez, I don't know. There's so many," he replied. "No! No, wait! It was November. I remember because it was around Thanksgiving and she was plenty thankful."

The two women looked at each other and rolled their eyes.

"Do you happen to remember where you were this past Thursday night, between 6:00 and 10:00 p.m.? Mr. Plant?" Marcia asked.

"Am I under suspicion?" he said.

"Would that surprise you?" she asked again.

Again he laughed, and said, "I guess not; I just got done telling you I tied her up and smacked her ass raw. But to answer your question, I was at supper with my mother. It's a regular Thursday night thing with us since my dad passed away."

"Would you mind giving me a number where I could reach her?" Marcia asked.

There was a pause and then he said, "Um, you're not going to say anything about the sex stuff, right? She's ... well, kind of prudish, you know?"

"I can be discreet," Marcia said.

He gave her the number, and added, "Her name is Marion. She's a little hard of hearing, so speak up."

"Thank you, Mr. Plant," Marcia said. "We'll be in touch if we have any more questions, but I think we're good for now. Enjoy the rest of your day. Good-bye."

"Well done," Jackie said.

"Thanks," Marcia replied. "He seems a bit creepy and very egotistical, and he sure wasn't evasive. I don't think he sounded particularly dangerous." Looking at Jackie's computer screen, she pointed and said, "It look's like there's an attachment with one of his texts there. Click on it."

"Oh, man!" Jackie groaned when a photo opened up. "There's an image I'm never going to be able to un-see!"

Looking at them was a thickly set, mostly-naked man about five feet tall wearing a black leather hood and mask that resembled something an executioner would wear. His only other article of clothing was a black leather Speedo. One fist was on his hip and was holding a long-tasseled whip. His other arm was crooked at the elbow and a pair of fur-lined handcuffs dangled from an extended finger. His body was covered with hair, and he had a pot belly protruding over the waist of the Speedo.

"Oh, Lord!" Marcia said with a laugh. "The way he talked about himself I was half picturing an Adonis; that comes up a little short."

"He must have looked better in clothes when they first met at the porn store," Jackie said. "The single meet-up is making more sense." She then closed the attachment, and they moved on.

The next set of texts—eight in all—ended with an apparent brush-off. The guy had written to her:

Come on, one more time. Please?

To which she replied simply:

No means no.

The earlier six were pretty obviously arranging a pair of hook-ups; one at his place and one at hers. Prior to that were three phone calls from him to her and two from her to him.

As Jackie moved the cursor over the phone number to get it to expand, she got the feeling that she'd seen the number before. She clicked it and then seeing the name, she said, "Holy crap!"

Marcia looked at it and said, "Oh, wow!"

The box on the screen read, "Scott Lain, 404 Wethersfield St, Rowley, MA."

"Why wouldn't he have told me he was involved with her?" Jackie asked rhetorically.

"Based on the dates of their last texts, and her '*No means no*' reply to his plea, it doesn't look to me like they *were* involved for almost a year," Marcia said.

"But still, when I announced that there was an investigation into her death, he should have said something," Jackie replied.

"Maybe he didn't want to cause unnecessary embarrassment for the family if it turned out to be just an accident," Marcia offered. "Or embarrassment for himself, either. Is he married?"

"No," Jackie answered. "But he told you himself that the bathroom looked like a crime scene when he walked in. That he knew she was seeing other men should have been important enough for him to tell me regardless of who it might embarrass."

As she spoke she recalled his screw-up with the sample of the tub water, and she wondered if she had been giving him too much credit as a rooky officer.

"Are you going to call him?" Marcia asked.

Jackie looked at her watch, and said, "He's nightshift; he may be sleeping. I think I'll wait until he comes in later on and talk to him in person."

Shaking off her exasperation, Jackie turned back to her computer screen and said, "Who else have we got?"

Going backward through to the end of the list they found three more sets of exchanges that made it pretty obvious that they were arrangements for hookups.

Marcia called the next most recent number—for a man named Craig Davenport from Ipswich. The call went into voicemail, but a recording said the mailbox was full.

Jackie took the next one, which was listed as R. Ford with an address in Gloucester. She was a little surprised when the call was answered by a woman. With Marcia on the extension, they looked at each other, wondering if Pamela also had female CNM partners. The question was shortly answered, however.

"Hi, my name is Jackie Hall. I'm with the Rowley Police. Can I ask who I'm talking to?"

"This about that Fletcher woman?" the woman asked in reply.

"Um, yes it is," Jackie said. "Why would you have thought that?"

"I told him it was going to happen," the woman said, not answering the question. "I told him she was going to be trouble."

"How do you mean trouble?" Jackie asked.

"Well, like this!" the woman answered. "She's married; he screws around with her; she ends up dead; and here you are looking for him."

"How did you know about Mrs. Fletcher's death?" Jackie asked.

"I got a sister who lives up in Rowley. She told me all about it. How the hospital thinks it was murder."

"You almost seemed to be expecting this call," Jackie said. "Is there a reason for that?"

"All that ropes and handcuffs and whips bullshit that he's into," she said with obvious disgust. "Sick!"

"Are we talking about your husband here, *Mrs*. Ford?" Jackie asked making what seemed a logical assumption.

"What? No! Chuck's been dead for ten years," she said. "I'm talking about Chuck's son, Roger."

"Is this Roger's phone?" Jackie asked.

"No, but he uses it when he can't find his ... which is half the time," she replied. "That how you found him? Phone records?"

"It is," Jackie answered. "Is he there?"

"No."

"Do you think he might have his own phone with him?" Jackie asked.

"Probably, since he doesn't have mine. You want his number?"

"That would be great."

The woman recited it and Marcia wrote it down, then Jackie asked, "Who am I talking to, by the way?"

"I'm Roberta. Roberta Ford."

"Well, thank you, Mrs. Ford. I appreciate your help. I'll give Roger a call. Bye, now."

As Jackie hung up, Marcia pointed to the computer screen, and said, "There's *Roger's* number. Apparently, he used both phones to text Mrs. Fletcher."

Jackie clicked the number and "Roger Ford" popped up with the same Gloucester address as the R. Ford number.

Marcia dialed the number and after several rings, a computer-generated voice recited the number and added that it was not available to take the call but to leave a message. After the beep, Marcia began her intro, but right after she said that she was with the Rowley Police, the call was picked up.

"This is Roger," the man said.

"Oh, hi. Yes, this is Marcia Grieves. I'm with the ..."

"Yes, I heard that," he said. "What do you want?" he interrupted.

"Can I ask who I'm talking with?" Marcia responded.

"You called me," he said. "Who do *you* think it is?"

Jackie rolled her eyes, but Marcia replied, "Well unless you've stolen his phone, the court records I'm looking at say that you should be Roger Ford. Is that right? Or do I need to get yet another warrant?"

Jackie almost laughed at Marcia's quick and aggressive pushback.

"Yeah. Yeah, okay, I'm Roger," he answered far more cooperatively. "What is it you want?"

"Do you know a woman in Rowley named Pamela Fletcher?" Marcia asked.

There was a heavy sigh and he replied, "Yeah. I did know her. But I haven't seen her in more than a year. I had nothing to do with her dying, if that's what this is about."

"Why would you think that's why I called?" Marcia asked, pushing back, again.

"Well, it's not about a traffic ticket," he replied sharply. "I haven't even driven *through* Rowley in a year."

"Your mother seemed to think you might be involved, somehow," Marcia said.

"*What!?* Are you shitting me? She told you that?"

"Maybe she was upset that you were using her phone to set up your kinky dates with Mrs. Fletcher, and now *she* ends up on my list here, too."

"You've got to be shitting me!" he reiterated. "Look, I don't know what BS she fed you, but I swear to God, I had nothing to do with Pamela's death."

"Can you establish your whereabouts for last Thursday night between 6:00 and 10:00?"

There was a pause, and then he said, "Oh, wait! Yes, as a matter of fact, I can!" The confident tone had returned to his voice. "I was with my girlfriend and another couple at Hampton Beach. You can call and ask any of them. Oh! And I used my credit card to buy food and stuff there!" he added triumphantly. "You can check on that, right?"

"Is *your* name on the card or your *mother's*?" she asked poking back a little bit. "Visa? MasterCard? What?"

"Yes, it's *mine*!" he snapped back. "And it's a Visa! You want the number?"

"Just the last four will do," Marcia replied. "And your friends' phone numbers, too, please."

When Marcia hung up with Roger, Jackie said with a little chuckle, "You can be downright nasty when you turn off the charm."

"It's a gift," Marcia said with a shrug. She gave her boobs a little lift, and added, "I developed early; I had to learn to deal with guys who were jerks."

"So, what do you think about Roger?" Jackie asked. "Truth or BS?"

"We should call his friends, but it sure *sounds* like he's telling the truth," Marcia said. "No ums and ahs; no hesitation. No nervousness in his voice."

"Oh! That reminds me!" Jackie said excitedly. "When I was on that task force looking for our serial killer, Carlton, one of the detectives in Somerville told me about this woman they used as a consultant who was like a human polygraph. Apparently, she's blind but has extraordinary hearing and has learned to pick up on those little voice-stress cues that give people away when they lie. I wonder if I could get her to listen to these recordings and give her opinion."

"Um ... you know that that wouldn't be admissible in court, right?" Marcia said.

"No. No. It wouldn't be for court. It would just be to give us an idea whose stories might need more looking into," Jackie said.

"You know her name?"

"If he ever mentioned it, I don't remember it," Jackie answered. She then made a note on her pad to call the Somerville Police.

"So, with Roger Ford using two of the numbers we thought were separate CNM partners with Pamela," Jackie said, "that brings us to our last one in the two-year list."

Jackie tapped the number and the box expanded to show, "Rev. Richard M. Fairfield Jr." of Peabody.

"A reverend," Marcia said. "You think he was trying to save the wayward Mrs. Fletcher from her wicked ways?"

Jackie scrolled down to what would have been his first text to Pamela, dated Aug 2, 2019, and expanded the abbreviated snippet. It read:

Hi Pamela! My name is Richard but many call me BD for "Big Dick" (The attached photo will explain.) I'm new to this CNM site, but I saw your profile and it appears we have much in common, including a spouse who doesn't get us. I'd love to get together with you sometime to explore our mutual appreciation of the finer points of BDSM. Looking forward to your reply!
BD

Jackie moved the arrow over the box indicating there was an attachment, but hesitated. "Do we dare?" she said.

"Can it be worse than the Marquis?" Marcia replied.

Jackie clicked, and the image enlarged to fill half the screen.

"Yipes!" Jackie said.

"Whoa!" Marcia said. "I guess that's a fitting nickname!"

The man was full-frontal and nude from his feet up to his neck where the photo ended. He had a bodybuilder physique and was endowed like a porn star ... would like to be.

Jackie quickly reduced the image back to its icon size.

The two women laughed, and then Jackie clicked on Pamela's reply to see how she reacted to the Big Dick's introductory message.

> Hello, Richard. That was probably a little more information than required for an introduction. Frankly, I'd have preferred a photo showing your face, and let the rest be a surprise, rather than the other way around. Size may matter to some women, but I find technique—especially with regard to the finer points of BDSM, as you put it—to be far more erotic.
>
> Perhaps you should try Tinder.
>
> Warm regards,
>
> S.

"Gently but firmly putting him in his place," Marcia commented with a chuckle.

"But he still replied six minutes later," Jackie said as she clicked his next text—which they noticed also included an attachment.

> My most honest and abject apologies, Pamela. You are absolutely correct; that was crude, egotistical, and even childish. Attached is a photo of my face, which I hope begins to convey my sincerity.

He then went on to describe—in almost clinical detail—some of the "finer points of BDSM" that he apparently hoped she would recognize and be impressed by.

He signed off by saying:

> If I don't hear back from you I completely understand, and that will be both my loss and my fault.

But I do respectfully beg your forgiveness and dearly hope to hear back from you.

I remain sincerely yours,

R.

As Jackie moved the arrow to the attachment icon, she said, "A guy once confided in me that the way to a woman's heart was to apologize to her about something. It didn't even matter what, as long as he was admitting he was wrong about it."

"I hope you didn't date him very long," Marcia said with a laugh.

"Only long enough to figure out he was a player—which was not too long," she replied. "He actually told me that a couple years later. We're friends even now. I like him but he's not dating material."

She opened the attachment, and they were looking at a very handsome, serious-looking man in his mid-fifties, probably.

"There's your Adonis," Jackie said. "That's a good-looking guy!"

"Mrs. Fletcher was right," Marcia said. "The other picture was ... *amusing*, but this one would have gotten my attention better. I'd meet this guy, but I'd have passed on the other one, just like she did."

"Let's see if she's fallen into his apology trap," Jackie said closing the photo and lining up with Pamela's reply of a full day later.

"*That's* cynical," Marcia said, but not too seriously. "He *could* actually be sorry."

"His opening volley was with a naked, headless photo of himself with a partial erection, and you read humility into that?" Jackie said.

Marcia laughed, and said, "Point taken."

Pamela's reply read:

Hello, Richard. Let's meet for coffee. I am a firm believer in second chances. Plus, your apparent physiological knowledge (and appreciation) of the pain/pleasure paradox has me intrigued.

She added the name of a coffee shop in Ipswich and a day and time, then concluded,

I've attached a photo of myself so you'll recognize me.
Yours,
S.

As Jackie hovered the arrow over the attachment icon, she said, "I sure hope she didn't try to one-up his first picture with *her* photo."

They were both relieved when it was a tasteful, smiling headshot.

On the day of the meeting there were texts to verify that they were both still planning to show up at the coffee shop, and then a week after that there was one from him that read simply:

Still good for 7?

Her reply was a thumbs-up and a smiley face.

"Obviously, she reacted better to the coffeehouse meeting than his first text," Marcia said.

Following that, there were a number of texts similar to his *Still good for 7?* message that made it apparent that they had met up at least four other times. The second was four weeks after the first, then it went to three weeks, then two, then back-to-back weeks. Interspersed with those texts were phone calls back and forth that also increased in frequency and number over time.

"Apparently, she became a fan of his technique and his *physiological knowledge*," Jackie commented with a little laugh.

"Maybe she decided that sized *does* matter," Marcia suggested.

Looking at the notes she had been taking on her pad, Marcia said, "It's interesting that none of her hook-ups with anyone else are closer than about four weeks apart; just with the reverend. And he's the only one she met more than four times. And it looks like a lot more."

"Remember we're looking backward in time here," Jackie pointed out. "I wonder if Harry saw Pamela's increasingly frequent meet-ups with the reverend as more like dating than the purely sexual release the CNM arrangement was supposed to be."

"Good point," Marcia said and added, "I believe it's your turn to make the call."

The phone rang several times before a man answered simply, "Yes?"

Both women had expected a more formal answering from the reverend, stating his name or his church or something. They looked at each other, both guessing—correctly—that the phone number might belong to a private, non-church-provided phone.

"Hello. This is Jacquelyn Hall. I'm with the Rowley Police Department. Am I speaking with Rev. Fairfield?"

"You are," he answered with just a bit of hesitation. "What can I do for you?"

"Are you acquainted with a Mrs. Pamela Fletcher from here in Rowley?"

A bit longer hesitation, and then, "Yes?"

"We're investigating her possible murder, Reverend, and I'd like to ask you a few questions about your relationship with her."

"Mur ...?" he began to repeat but caught himself. "Oh! I, um, I see. Well, yes, of course, I'd like to talk with you about that. Can I give you a call back in say, ten minutes?"

"That'll be fine, Reverend," Jackie said. She then recited his address, and asked, "That's still your primary residence, correct?"

"It is, yes," he answered with a hint of curiosity behind the words.

"Okay, thank you, Reverend Fairfield. Ten minutes."

Jackie hung up, and Marcia chuckled, "*Now* who's the bad cop? You probably have him thinking the SWAT team is waiting around the corner in case he doesn't call back. Why the murder reference this time?"

"I don't know," Jackie said. "That popped into my head when he answered with the one word. Maybe I thought he needed some motivation."

"You think he was with someone?" Marcia speculated.

"That's my guess from his responses," Jackie replied. "Also, I'll bet that if we look up his church we're not going to find that phone number associated with it. I'm thinking that's personal and private, which is why he sounded almost perplexed when he answered; he didn't recognize the number."

Jackie looked into her coffee cup, and said, "Want to stretch your legs? I need a refill."

When they got back to Jackie's office, Marcia looked at the notes she'd been taking about Pamela's CNM partners, and said, "Assuming their alibi's check out, I'm not seeing any smoking guns here. Definitely people of interest—some more interesting than others—but I don't know that I'd call any of them *suspects*. I certainly didn't hear any *motives* for killing her pop out. No rage or even animosity."

"Unless—as we've discussed—it was accidental and then staged in the tub as a cover-up," Jackie replied.

"Agreed," Marcia said. "But why would one of these partners from her past suddenly reappear without any apparent communication? No texts or even phone calls in months, and they just happen to knock on her door the same night that Mr. Fletcher is out with *his* CNM partner."

"I see your point," Jackie said, "but playing devil's advocate here, they *could* have bumped into each other in the grocery store or Wal-Mart and set something up face to face."

"They all live in different towns," Marcia replied. "Bumping into one another by accident would be a stretch, I think."

Just then, Jackie's desk phone rang. She picked it up and Sharon told her that a Rev. Fairfield was on the line for her.

"Hello, Reverend," she answered. "Thank you for calling me back."

"Now, what is this about Pamela Fletcher being murdered?" he said in a barely veiled demanding tone.

But Jackie wasn't about to let him control the conversation, and replied, "If you don't mind, Reverend, I'll ask the questions first, then you can have your turn." Without waiting for an acknowledgment, she went on, "Were you in a sexual relationship with Pamela Fletcher?"

Marcia grinned and pantomimed being shot between the eyes.

Jackie grinned back and winked at her.

"I, um ... we, ah," he stammered, probably caught off guard by both Jackie's assertiveness and her blunt—and well-informed—question. He quickly collected himself, though, and answered, "Mrs. Fletcher and I met on several occasions, but not in any sexual sense. She and her husband were having some marital problems—which centered around *their own* conjugal relationship—and having been introduced by a mutual friend, I was offering her some spiritual guidance and counseling. I believe it was helping."

"So, when you introduced yourself in a text to Mrs. Fletcher as *Big Dick* with a headless photo to explain the nickname, and then suggested exploring the finer points of BDSM, was that spiritual guidance or marriage counseling?" Jackie asked.

Marcia almost burst out laughing.

After just half a second of surprised pause, he snapped, "That ... that is clergy-penitent privileged communication!"

"No it's not," Jackie replied calmly. "Since you initiated the communication with Mrs. Fletcher; and since Mrs. Fletcher had never even heard of you prior to that, you cannot claim clergy-penitent privilege. That's settled law, Reverend, and it means that that text and the photo can be used to obtain a warrant to seize your phone and your computer and to search your office, and your premises in this homicide investigation.

"Now, why don't we cut the BS and you tell me what your relationship with Mrs. Fletcher was."

In fact, Jackie had no idea if what she has just told him would really strike down the clergy-penitent privilege, but it sounded logical enough to be a good bluff. The *settled law* bit was just icing.

There was a several-second pause and then the reverend said, "First and foremost, and certainly most importantly, what that relationship was is *over*. I have not seen Pamela in probably a year and a half."

"My records put it at a year and two months," Jackie said. "What caused the relationship to sour?"

"It didn't," he replied. "It kept getting better. To the point where Pamela was forced to choose between me and her husband. He's the jealous type in case your investigation hasn't ferreted that out, yet."

"Your text mentions being new to a CNM website," Jackie said. "What is that? CNM?"

"It stands for consensual non-monogamous," he answered. "It's what they call an open marriage, these days."

"I see," Jackie said. "Are you married, Reverend?"

"I am," he replied in a resigned tone, no doubt knowing where the questioning was going.

"So, then I suppose that you and your wife are in one of these CNM relationships, too, right?" she asked.

"No," he replied. "She is unaware of that particular shortcoming of mine."

"That you cheat on her or that you're into whips and chains?" Jackie asked.

Again, Marcia had to stifle a laugh.

There was another pause, and then he answered, "Both. And now that you've sufficiently humbled me, Ms. Hall, how about if *you* stop the BS? If you have any questions directly relating to Pamela's death, please ask them, or else I'm going to hang up after which you can talk to my lawyer."

"Where were you on the night of Thursday, July 8th, between 6:00 and 10:00?" Jackie asked.

"Calling BINGO," he replied with a satisfied tone. "It's something I've done every Thursday night for years, and I can give you a couple dozen very reliable witnesses who can testify that I was in our parish hall doing just that this past Thursday."

"Two," Jackie said.

"Two?" he repeated. "What's that supposed to mean?"

"Names," she replied. "I don't need a couple dozen. Just give me two names and their phone numbers. Not family members, though. Oh, and don't worry; I'll be discreet. I won't mention why I'm checking up on you."

"Do I have your word that after you've verified my whereabouts, that you'll leave me the hell alone?" he said.

"You have my word," she answered. "I'll be happy if I can eliminate you from my list of suspects; the warrant process is frankly a pain in the butt."

After taking a short while to look them up, he gave her two names and phone numbers, and then said, "May I ask how you're going to *be discreet*?"

"I'll tell them I'm with the Massachusetts Gaming Commission calling to verify that the Thursday night games are being conducted fairly," Jackie said. "I'll only mention you offhandedly."

"Okay," he said. "I want you to know, Ms. Hall, that I am deeply saddened to hear of Pamela's passing, and I sincerely wish you the best of luck in finding her killer. And, no offense, but I hope we never speak again. Good-bye."

"Me, too, Reverend," she said. "Just one more question, though. How many times had you been with Mrs. Fletcher in the nine months between August of 2019 and May of 2020?"

"A dozen; maybe more," he replied. "I didn't keep count."

"Thank you, Reverend. You've been very helpful," Jackie said. "Goodbye, now."

"Kind of sleazy," Jackie said after she hung up, "but, again, no obvious motive for killing her."

"Unless maybe she threatened to expose him to his wife and congregation," Marcia suggested.

"Possible, but why do that after more than a year since their last contact?" Jackie replied. "And I'd expect to find a recent phone call to him in here where she made the threat. I don't think that's something anyone would do in a text."

"Good point," Marcia agreed. "I guess we'll have a better idea after we call his BINGO players."

Now at the end of Pamela's text and phone records for the two years, Jackie said, "Should we jump into Harry's, now?"

"I've got no place to be," Marcia replied.

Unlike Pamela's phone record that ended with Harry's "OTW" text on the night she died, Harry's list continued until midnight on Monday when his provider compiled the list that Marcia had requested.

Beginning late Thursday night and continuing Friday morning there were understandably calls to the kids, Aaron and Jessica, as well as to a Mrs. John Whitherspoon, whom they learned was Pamela's mother. There were also a total of six calls to, and four from Megan Hope between Friday morning and midnight on Monday. There was also one call to Megan early on Thursday and another to her at 7:21 p.m.

"The first call—the one in the morning—was probably an are-you-free-tonight call, and the one in the evening would likely be his I'll-be-right-over call," Marcia speculated.

"I sure wish they had texted rather than calling each other," Jackie said. "Given their relationship and the whole situation, the calls aren't surprising, but it would be nice to know what they talked about.

"Apparently, Harry's not a big texter, at all," Jackie went on. She scrolled down the two-year-long list—which was a third the length of Pamela's—and found only twenty or thirty text exchanges. None of them discussed anything sexual or appeared to have anything to do with arranging hook-ups.

"Kind of a dead end, isn't it?" Marcia said.

"Probably," Jackie agreed, "but let's do our due diligence and put names and associations to all these phone numbers like we did with Pamela's."

Some of the names Jackie recognized as townsfolk, but the others Marcia wrote down for follow-up.

When they reached the end of the list, Jackie looked at her watch, and said, "It's a bit early, but you want to break for lunch? When we come back, I have chief-of-police stuff I need to do, and you can work on your list of follow-ups."

Twenty minutes later, while sitting at a table in Phillip's Roast Beef & Pizza, Marcia got a text from her office in Salem.

"Rats," she said after reading it. "It seems that the out-of-sight-out-of-mind thing isn't working. I'm being called back to Salem this afternoon for a meeting about that fishing boat scam in Marblehead."

"Oh! I hope you don't get reassigned," Jackie said after a swallow of her Coke. "I'm getting used to having you on my team."

"I hope not," she replied. "I'm really getting into this case. I think I'm going to make some of those follow-up calls tonight, from home. There's probably a better chance of catching people while *they're* home."

After Marcia left, and before Jackie settled into her chiefly duties, she pulled up her notes from the Holly McCray case of four years before. She did a search for "Somerville" and eventually found the name she was looking for; Lt. Hays. He was one of the detectives who had worked on the Jill Kelly murder, also committed by the man who had killed Holly, Jerome Carlton.

After a brief conversation with Hays, Jackie had the name and number of the "human polygraph" that they had used to put the lie to the false tip that Carlton, had phoned in about Kelly.

"Suzan Engles," the woman answered on the second ring.

"Hi, Ms. Engles. This is Chief Jacquelyn Hall with the Rowley Police. How are you?"

"I'm doing well, Chief," she replied. "And please call me Suzan. What can I do for you?"

"Thank you. Please call me Jackie," she responded. "I got your number from Lt. Hays at the Somerville Police. He had told me about your unique ability to detect if people are lying by listening to their voice. I wonder if I can enlist your help in that regard."

"Well, let's do the full disclosure thing, first," Suzan said. "Nothing I tell you can be used in court or even as probable cause to get a search warrant. What I tell you is to be viewed as only my opinion; there is nothing about what I do that can be scientifically proven ... or disproven, either. I will not always be able to *give* an opinion; some voices are so neutral that it's like listening to someone mumbling in their sleep. All that said, however, I have a ninety-plus-percent accuracy rate in those cases that were subsequently verified by other means."

"Fair enough," Jackie said. "Now, full disclosure on my side. I did a little Google research on computer voice stress analysis—CVSA—and it apparently shows no better than about fifty-percent accuracy. I can do that by flipping a coin. On the other hand, Lt. Hays swears by *you*."

"That's because some programmer is sitting at a desk somewhere pecking at his keyboard trying to create an algorithm to mimic human emotions," Suzan replied. "Artificial intelligence isn't there, yet ... if it ever will be."

"Your analysis is based on *emotion*?" Jackie said.

"In the end, yes," Suzan answered. "It's backed up by years and years of honing my listening skills to pick up on subtle cues and fluctuations and nuances, but that all gets boiled down to give me a *feeling* for whether or not the subject is lying. There's no absolute yea or nay; no specific litmus test. I don't recommend you go out and buy a rope to hang someone based on what I say, but it's usually a good indicator that you should be asking more questions and digging deeper. Or sometimes, looking somewhere else."

"So, do you have a better success rate listening to someone in person, as opposed to their recorded voice?" Jackie asked. "Because what I'd like you to analyze is all recorded."

"As long as the recordings are good quality and clear—and especially if the subject didn't know the recording was being made—those are usually better," Suzan replied. "There's a certain amount of nervous stress that seeps into the voice if the person knows what they're saying is going to be scrutinized."

"There was no undercover stuff or phone taps," Jackie said. "There are some recordings from here at the station in our interview room, but there's a big sign that says that everything is being taped. Others are phone calls where we clearly stated that it was the police who was calling."

"Do you have a timeframe when you need this done?" Suzan asked. "I have a couple of hours tomorrow afternoon, and then I'm in Colorado for two weeks." She then told Jackie her hourly rate and added, "Plus cab fare, to and from. I don't do the rideshare thing. Being blind, I've been using cabs virtually all my life and I think they've gotten the royal shaft by that whole thing."

"Put me down for those couple hours," Jackie said. "What time can I expect you?"

"Let's say two o'clock," she replied. "That'll give me time to get home and finish packing."

## Chapter 14

**Tuesday, July 13, 2021**

After talking with Suzan, Jackie had just begun going through the items that had collected in her in-basket when Sharon called her.

"Hi, Chief. You want me to call Fred Hardy and see when he can come by and look at the cruiser?"

"What's wrong with the cruiser? Which one?" she asked. Fred Hardy owned a local auto-body and paint shop.

"Car fourteen," Sharon answered. "I thought you'd seen the report. I put it in your basket."

Jackie flipped down through a dozen sheets of paper and found the accident report. It had been filled out and submitted by Scott Lain. Jackie groaned inwardly, and told Sharon, "I found it; let me read it and I'll get back to you."

Jackie looked at the photo that was printed on the bottom of the report, and saw that the damage was thankfully minor. It looked like the left front fender had struck something, creasing the plastic molding around the wheel opening, scraping the paint off the adjacent metal, and tearing the police department decal that ran most of the length of the car.

Reading the report she found that Scott had maneuvered too close to the pumps at Knowles' gas station, and had brushed one of the heavy steel guard posts at the end of the island. No big deal, really, but it just added to the growing list of *Scott-isms*.

Jackie called Sharon back and told her to see if she could get either Fred or his son Brice to come out during shift-change when the cars would be at the station. She then added, "And when Scott shows up, will you have him come see me?"

Nearing the bottom of her inbox pile, Jackie was looking over Mr. MacDougal's latest speeder-report—less than half the incidents compared to last week—when Sharon called and told her that car fourteen had just pulled in if she wanted to go out and look at it.

The damage wasn't too extensive. She guessed that the plastic trim around the wheel opening would need to be replaced because it was split, but that the scratches could probably be smoothed with a little body filler, sanded, and repainted.

Jackie had just gotten back to her desk when Sharon called to tell her that Scott had pulled in. She met him in the hallway and motioned him into the interview room.

As she closed the door, he said nervously, "I'm really sorry about the car, Chief. I'll pay to have it fixed myself."

"That's not necessary," she replied. "That's why we have insurance." She pointed to a chair as she took her own, and said, "But let's start there. Tell me what happened."

"Well, I needed to fill up at the start of my shift," he began, "but there were three cars already at the pumps and the drivers were apparently inside the station. So, I had to jockey the car in close enough to the pump to stretch the hose over to the filler on the other side, and I made one of the turns too close. I'm really sorry."

"It's okay; those things happen," Jackie said. "The other thing I wanted to talk to you about is the sexual relationship you had with Pamela Fletcher. I've read the text exchanges that you and she had, and although the relationship seems to have ended nine months ago, you should have told me about it when you found out her death was being investigated."

The color drained from his face, and Jackie was a little afraid he might pass out.

"I ... ah ... I ... oh, shit," he stammered. "I am really, really sorry about that. I thought about telling you, honest, but I figured it was so long ago that it couldn't really make any difference, now. All it would do is embarrass her ... and Harry, too."

"Did you engage in bondage with her?" Jackie asked flatly.

He swallowed hard, and then answered simply, "Yes."

"How many times?" she asked. She knew the answer from Pamela's phone records, of course, but she wanted to see how forthcoming he would be.

Another swallow, and he replied, "Two."

"When was the last time you were with her?"

"October of last year," he answered. "Honest, Chief, I hadn't even *seen* her—except maybe driving past—in probably six months. That's why I didn't think it was important. I'm really sorry. I should have told you."

Jackie already knew that October was their last apparent hook-up from Pamela's text messages, and she was happy that he was being honest and accurate.

"How did you know she and Harry were in an open marriage?" she asked skipping past the *if he knew* part, making him believe that she knew more than she actually did.

He took a long breath, looked up at the ceiling, and exhaled with a resigned, "Oh, Christ."

Jackie just looked at him and waited for him to go on by himself.

"I, um ... I found her on the Internet," he finally said and added nothing more.

"Tell me about it, Scott," she said calmly. "Don't make me drag every answer out of you. Please?"

Another deep breath and then he sat up straighter in his chair, apparently ready to *man-up*. "Okay. I cruise the Internet for sex," he stated. "I mostly use Tinder, but somebody told me about this site where couples in open marriages advertise."

"Do you remember the name of the site?" Jackie asked.

He thought for a few moments, and then answered, "The open lifestyle dot com, or something like that."

"Could it have been the CNM lifestyle?" she asked.

"Yeah! Yeah, that's it! Something non-monogamy," he said.

"Consensual non-monogamous," she corrected. "Why did you stop seeing one another?"

"She said that Harry didn't like that she was ... you know, doing their CNM thing with me."

"Harry knew you were Pamela's CNM partner?" Jackie asked wondering what happened to the don't-ask-don't-tell rule. It also meant that Harry had lied—again—when he said he only knew who one of her partners was.

"Yeah. He was just leaving when I showed up at their house the second time," Scott said. "That was really awkward. I think maybe he told her to stop with me because I was local and he didn't want that getting around about them. You know, that they were swingers ... and the kind of stuff she was into. I promised her I'd never tell anyone, but she said Harry insisted." With a shrug, he added, "That's why I didn't tell you before. Like I said, I didn't think it would make a difference it was so long ago, and I wanted to keep my word ... especially since she was dead and couldn't defend herself or anything."

"Well, it does make a difference," she said.

"So, am I fired?" he asked.

"No," she answered. Using a lesson she had learned from Chief Booker, she went on, "I want you to write this up, though. When you come in tomorrow, I want a detailed report on your failure to report pertinent information regarding an ongoing investigation. I also want you to include a recommendation for disciplinary action if you believe any should be taken." She then stood up, signifying the meeting was over.

"Thanks, Chief," he said as he stood. "Again, I'm sorry. For not telling you about Pamela and me, *and* about the car."

When the second-shift meeting was over Fred Hardy was waiting for Jackie, and she led him back to her office.

"Thanks for coming out, Fred," she said as they walked. "So, what'll it cost us to fix the cruiser, and how long will it be out of service?"

In her office, he handed her an estimate sheet, and told her, "We'll have to order the trim piece, and the decal—hopefully just the front-fender piece, but once they come in, I think we can turn the car around for you in twenty-four hours. We'll need to paint the whole fender, of course. We'll do three shifts if we need to, though. The clear-coat won't be fully cured, but you'll be able to drive it. After a week or so, if you drop it off for a few hours we'll color-sand it, buff it, and apply the new piece of decal."

"All right," she said, signing the estimate. "Let me know when the trim comes in, and we'll coordinate giving you the car for a day."

As he took the paperwork back, he asked, "How'd it happen, anyway?"

"One of the officers was trying to squeeze in too close to the pumps at Knowlesies, and rubbed one of the posts that guard them."

"Ah, yes," he said. "Well, I guess that's why they put them there, huh? Crashing into the pump would be a lot worse."

## Chapter 15

### Wednesday, July 14, 2021

Before getting into the shower, and while her all-important first-cup-of-the-day coffee brewed through the maker, Jackie checked her email. Among other things, there was a notice by Roberts Funeral Home regarding the services for Pamela scheduled for Friday at 1:00 p.m. There was also a personal invitation from Harry to attend the services.

The most recent email was from Marcia. It read:

> Good morning, Jackie. Good news/bad news. The good is that they're going to release the autopsy report this afternoon. The bad is that I'm stuck at the office in Salem again today. Call me when you get in. MG

After filling her office coffee cup and refraining from taking one of the donuts in the break room, Jackie called Marcia.

"Hi Jackie," Marcia answered halfway through the second ring. "I've got to be quick; the boss has the troops gathering here in five minutes."

"Got it," Jackie said. "So, how did the tox and DNA tests get back so quickly?"

"Turns out that my father can pull strings that are far longer and stronger than any of my strings-by-association," Marcia answered. "He got the tox testing pushed to the top of the list and done overnight, and then he talked with Dr. West and convinced him to release the report with the DNA results listed as *pending* since who the DNA belongs to doesn't change the manner of death from being homicide."

"It's good to have connections in high places," Jackie replied. "How did you make out with your follow-ups?"

"I was able to verify most of the alibis to an eighty or ninety percent satisfaction level. The only two that I couldn't get any contact with were Steven Collins, the guy she appeared to be planning to hook up with the week that she died, and Craig Davenport, the guy from Ipswich with the full voicemail box."

"Of the two," Jackie said, "I think I'd like to talk to Mr. Collins the most since he was her most recent contact."

"I left him another voicemail, and tried to impress the importance of getting back to us," Marcia said. "And now that we have the autopsy report ... or *will* have, I'm going to polish up the warrant request for both Mr. and Mrs. Fletcher's computers, if that's all right with you."

"Go ahead," Jackie agreed. "But while the paperwork makes its way through the system, I think I'm going to ask him if I can look at them. I'm curious how forthcoming he'll be. Will he let me look or will he want to call a lawyer?"

"You really think that's a good idea?" Marcia replied. "I mean if he lawyers-up, what's to keep him from deleting anything incriminating while we wait for the warrant?"

"My guess is that if there's anything incriminating on his computer he's already deleted it," Jackie said. "It's sure as heck what *I'd* do if I was responsible for my spouse's death and knew it was being investigated."

"Hey, I have to go," Marcia said, "the bugler just sounded assembly. I'll talk to you later. Good luck."

"You, too," Jackie said. "Keep your head down if arrows start flying ... or assignments, too."

Jackie hung up the phone for a moment, and then picked it back up and called Carol Soucy.

"Hi, Carol. Jackie Hall, here. How are you today?"

"I smacked my knee into a dresser drawer that some idiot left open this morning, so I'm sitting here with a bag of frozen peas draped over it trying to figure out if I was more stupid for leaving it open or for walking into it two minutes later." She then added, "Sorry. Your question was probably rhetorical, wasn't it? You probably didn't call to hear about my knee ... or my stupidity."

"Well, I *am* sorry to hear about your knee, but no, that's not why I called," Jackie answered, amused at Carol's ability to talk at length about almost anything ... and sometimes nothing. "I was wondering if you were available for some computer tech work today. That is if you're ambulatory."

"Fortunately, I still have my cane from when I bruised my hip last year," she replied. "Like Betty Davis said, *Old age ain't no place for sissies*. What have you got?"

"I want to clone a hard drive," Jackie answered. "Is that very hard?"

"There at the station?" Carol asked.

"No. A private computer."

"Yours?"

"No."

"Harry Fletcher's?" Carol asked.

"Why in the world would you say that?" Jackie replied.

"Sorry. Never mind. I'm speaking out of school, here."

"No. seriously," Jackie said. "What makes you think this is about Harry?"

"Well, his wife died in their house a few days ago; the death is being investigated by you and the county DA; and Harry writes murder mysteries that read like how-to manuals. *I'd* sure as heck want to see what's on his hard drive!"

"Okay, you're right," Jackie said. "But that's classified. Just like anything you do here at the station. Even the fact that you're *doing* it is private and confidential."

"Mum's the word," Carol agreed. "When and where?"

"Hopefully, at Harry's," Jackie answered, "but I haven't coordinated with him, yet, so I'll have to get back to you. Are you available all day?"

"Pretty much," Carol replied. "My roller derby tryout is going to have to be rescheduled because of the knee, so yeah, whenever. Do you have a second drive to clone to?"

"Oh, shoot! I forgot about that part," Jackie said.

"Well, Carol to the rescue, again!" she said. "I happen to have an eight-terabyte solid-state drive—SSD—here that's scheduled to go into another client's system next week. Do you know how big Harry's computer is? It's hard to imagine it's bigger than that. The client has a couple of engineering programs running on his machine; Harry only writes books and text doesn't take up a lot of space. Unless he's a gamer, of course; then all bets are off; those people just go nuts."

"No idea," Jackie replied. "But you're probably right; I don't see him as the gamer type. Anyway, so plan on bringing your SSD, and I'll call you as soon as I have a time. Thanks, Carol, I really appreciate it." She then hung up before Carol could get started on some other subject. As well as being an invaluable tech resource, Jackie really liked Carol as a friend ... but Lord, could that woman talk!

With Carol lined up, Jackie called Harry.

"Hi, Harry. It's Jackie. How are you doing?"

"Okay, I guess," he answered. "I'm just leaving Roberts after talking about the arrangements for Friday. That was tough. So, you're going to be there, right? You got my email."

"Absolutely, I'll be there," she said.

"So, what's up?" he asked. Then a reason for the call occurred to him, and he added, "Oh, did the autopsy report come back?"

"No, I'm afraid not," Jackie answered, technically telling the truth. "There's still some lab work they're waiting for."

"Damn," he said.

"So, the reason I called," she went on, "is that I'd like to come out to the house sometime when you have a little while. We've gone through Pamela's phone records and managed to get in contact with some of her CNM partners, and I'd like to talk to you about a couple of them. Is this evening or tomorrow morning good for you?"

"Um, yeah," he answered. "Tonight works. Six o'clock? As I said, though, I don't really know them; I don't know what help I can be."

"Even if it's nothing, I'll have done my due diligence and asked the questions," Jackie replied. "I'll see you tonight. Thanks."

When she hung up, she texted Carol to see if six o'clock worked for her, and offered to pick her up.

Her reply was:

> Six works fine, but I don't think I can climb up into your Jeep, right now. How about I meet you there?

Jackie responded:

> How about if I pick you up in one of the cruisers?

Carol answered:

> Oh! Can we use the lights and siren?

Jackie laughed, and typed back:

> Only if there's heavy traffic. See you at 5:45.

## Chapter 16
**Wednesday, July 14, 2021**

Jackie had just opened Pamela's autopsy report on her computer when Sharon called to say that Suzan Engles was there to see her. It crossed her mind to respond *Probably not since she's blind*, but she let it go. Sharon usually didn't get her glib comments; it would have worked better with Carol. She closed the report, and said, "Show her back here, would you please?"

Jackie was standing when Suzan stepped into her office, and she extended her hand, and said, "It's a pleasure to meet you, Suzan." Even as she spoke it awkwardly occurred to her that her guest couldn't see her hand sticking waiting to be shaken. As she tried to decide whether to mention that it was there or to retract it, Suzan reached out and gave her a firm shake.

"It's a pleasure to meet you, too, Jackie. Very impressive work on the Jerome Carlton case." She then added, "Are you wondering how I knew to shake your hand?"

"Um, actually, yes," Jackie answered.

"I could hear the blood pulsing through the veins in your wrist," Suzan said, "so I could tell exactly where your hand was and that it was open, not clenched in a fist."

"Really?" Jackie said thoroughly impressed.

"No, I'm messing with you," she said with a little laugh. "Almost everyone extends their hand to shake when they meet—well, not including last year with all the fist-bumping—but I heard your shirt rustle on your right side, so I took a shot that your hand would be there. Worst case, you'd have seen my hand hanging out in midair and relieved my awkwardness."

Jackie laughed, and said, "Oh, I think I'm going to like you!"

"So, what have you got for me?" Suzan said. "You said some recorded interviews?"

"Phone conversations," Jackie replied. Then, as they stepped into the interview room where it would be quieter, she explained the case and the calls that she and Marcia had made to Pamela's CNM partners.

As they sat down, Jackie asked if Suzan needed a set of headphones.

"I shouldn't" she answered. "The acoustics are pretty good in here." Lifting her purse, she added, "I brought my own if I do."

Jackie brought up the recording of the first conversation on the computer, skipping Steven Collins for whom Marcia had left a message. She hit the Play button and Suzan listened intently.

Jackie: *"Hi, my name is Jackie Hall; I'm with the Rowley Police Department. Is this Gary Wilmot?"*

Gary: *"Yes."*

Jackie: *"Do you happen to know a Pamela Fletcher from here in Rowley?"*

Gary: *"Pamela Fletcher? I know her, yes. But I haven't seen her in months. Is she all right?"*

Jackie: *"I'm sorry to say that she passed away this past Thursday."*

Gary: *"Oh, my God! What happened?"*

Jackie: *"An apparent home accident. But the hospital has asked that it be looked into, so that's why I've contacted you."*

Gary: *"Oh. Well, I don't know how I can help. Like I said, I haven't seen her in months."*

Jackie: *"I understand that she and her husband shared what they called a consensual non-monogamous relationship. Were you aware of that?"*

The recording played on until the end and stopped by itself.

"Your Gary Wilmot seems to be a pretty straight shooter," Suzan said. "He was genuinely surprised when you said that Pamela was dead, and I didn't hear any deception cues in the rest of it, either. I'd scratch him off your list. Who's next?"

Jackie looked at the file title, and said, "This is Mark Plant. My counterpart, Marcia Grieves, with the county DA's office, is the other voice."

Marcia: *"Hello. This is Marcia Grieves working with the Rowley Police. Is this Mark Plant?"*

Mark: *"It is."*

Marcia: *"Are you acquainted with a Pamela Fletcher from Rowley?"*

Mark: *"Acquainted? If tying her to her own bed and screwing her brains out counts as acquainted, then yes."*

Marcia: *"Were you part of her CNM community?"*

Mark: *"CNM? Oh! Oh, yeah. That open-marriage bullshit. A fancy acronym for cuckolding her old man. No. I didn't belong to any club or anything; I just took advantage of the opportunity when it presented itself."*

When the recording played out, Suzan said with a chuckle, "Well, he's a piece of work, isn't he? But I doubt he's a killer. In the first part, he's not being completely honest, but not so much to deceive as to impress. There's a lot of hubris in his voice."

"When Marcia told him Mrs. Fletcher was dead, he really was surprised," Suzan went on. "And when she asked about calling his mother, there was near-panic in his voice. I think he fears her probably more than the police."

"That's pretty much what we got out of it, too," Jackie said. "He attached a photo of himself to one of his texts to Pamela that you might be thankful you can't see."

Suzan laughed, and said, "Let me guess. I'm picturing full-frontal nudity; not very tall; overweight; probably balding; and mediocre in the manhood department?"

"He was wearing a hood and a mask so I don't know about the hair," Jackie said. "And he had on a Speedo but without much of a bulge, so I'd say otherwise you're spot-on. You got all that from his voice? Or is this another trick like the handshake thing?"

"No trick, just lots of experience," she said. "The tone of his voice told me he was probably short and stocky. His choice of words and the inflection on certain of them told me he was compensating for something."

"I'm impressed!" Jackie said. "Do you mind if I ask how long you've been blind? You mentioned *picturing* him; I'm guessing not since birth."

"Industrial accident when I was twenty-two," she replied, "so I have half a lifetime of mental images to call on. I always had great hearing—even absolute pitch—and when I lost my sight it seemed to get exponentially better. I can walk through a strange room and locate the furniture by making clicks with my mouth and hearing the echoes. I'm bat-woman without the sexy outfit."

"When did you realize you could hear when people were lying?" Jackie asked.

"Oh, long before I lost my sight," Suzan answered. "It used to piss off my brothers when I'd blackmail them with telling our folks they were lying about something. My mother would ask them, '*Were you smoking,*' or something, and then she'd look at me when they answered." She laughed, and added, "I got a pretty good supplement to my allowance, but they got away with a lot of shit, too."

Suzan felt her watch, and said, "I have a cab scheduled to be here at 4:00, so if you have many more of these, we should get back at it."

The next recording was the call that Jackie made to "R. Ford," who turned out to be Roberta, the mother of Pamela's CNM partner.

When the recording ended, Suzan commented, "Interesting family dynamic there."

The next one was Marcia talking with Roger Ford, the son who had used his mother's phone to set up his meetings with Pamela.

Suzan laughed when the recording was over, and said, "Marcia's a pistol, isn't she? All full of bluff and bluster. But she got him on the ropes right where she wanted him. He started out like he was going to lay down a bunch of lies—probably like he usually did when confronted about anything—but she turned him around nicely. I'm pretty sure he's telling you the truth about where he was that night."

"Oh, this last one is interesting," Jackie said. "It's a ..."

But Suzan cut her off. "Don't tell me about it," she said. "Let me draw my own conclusions."

"Good point," Jackie said and hit the Play button.

They heard the phone ring several times, and then a man's voice. Fairfield: "*Yes?*"

Jackie: *"Hello. This is Jacquelyn Hall. I'm with the Rowley Police Department. Am I speaking with Rev. Fairfield?"*

Fairfield: *"You are. What can I do for you?"*

Jackie: *"Are you acquainted with a Mrs. Pamela Fletcher from here in Rowley?"*

Fairfield: *"Yes?"*

Jackie: *"We're investigating her possible murder, Reverend, and I'd like to ask you a few questions about your relationship with her."*

Fairfield: *"Mur ...? Oh! I, um, I see. Well, yes, of course, I'd like to talk with you about that. Can I give you a call back in say, ten minutes?"*

Jackie: *"That'll be fine, Reverend. 2154 South Jackson St. in Topsfield. That's still your primary residence, correct?"*

Fairfield: *"It is, yes."*

Jackie: *"Okay, thank you, Reverend Fairfield. Ten minutes."*

The recording ended, and Suzan asked, "Did he call back?"

"Yes. That's the next recording," Jackie answered.

"Well, the good reverend is nervous as a cat, so far," Suzan said. "You really caught him off guard. I think that was probably a private phone you reached him on. I could almost hear him scrambling to figure out how the hell you got the number while he was talking."

"That was our guess, too," Jackie said. "But I'll let you hear the rest of our conversation before we talk about it."

"I'm ready," Suzan said. "Go ahead."

Jackie: *"Hello, Reverend. Thank you for calling me back."*

Fairfield: *"Now, what is this about Pamela Fletcher being murdered?"*

Jackie: *"If you don't mind, Reverend, I'll ask the questions first, then you can have your turn. Were you in a sexual relationship with Pamela Fletcher?"*

Fairfield: *"I, um ... we, ah ... Mrs. Fletcher and I met on several occasions, but not in any sexual sense. She and her husband were having some marital problems—which centered around their own conjugal relationship—and having been introduced by a mutual friend,*

*I was offering her some spiritual guidance and counseling. I believe it was helping."*

Jackie: *"So, when you introduced yourself in a text to Mrs. Fletcher as Big Dick with a headless photo to explain the nickname, and then suggested exploring the finer points of BDSM, was that spiritual guidance or marriage counseling?"*

Suzan let out a small laugh.

Fairfield: *"That ... that is clergy-penitent privileged communication!"*

Jackie: *"No it's not. Since you initiated the communication with Mrs. Fletcher; and since Mrs. Fletcher had never even heard of you prior to that, you cannot claim clergy-penitent privilege. That's settled law, Reverend, and it means that that text and the photo can be used to obtain a warrant to seize your phone and your computer and to search your office, and your premises in this homicide investigation. Now, why don't we cut the BS and you tell me what your relationship with Mrs. Fletcher was."*

When the conversation between Jackie and Fairfield ended, Suzan said, "The good reverend is also a good liar ... at least a practiced one. When he started in with the marriage-counseling bit I could barely pick up on it. I think that ten-minute lag gave him time to work out what he saw as a good story in his head. You kicked his feet right out from under him with the photo and text description. He obviously had no idea where you had gotten his private phone number."

"You think he could have had something to do with Pamela's death?" Jackie asked.

"No. Not really," Suzan answered. "He's a scumbag to the core, but once you had him in your stranglehold, he started telling the truth ... more or less. I doubt seriously that he's your killer."

"Pretty much the consensus that Marcia and I came up with," Jackie said. "Which leaves only two of her partners—who we're aware of—that we haven't talked to yet." Then she noticed Scott Lain's name on the screen, and she added, "Actually, that's not true. Let's listen to one more." Not wanting to bias Suzan's opinion, she didn't mention that this subject was one of her officers.

With the arrow over the Play button of the interview recording, Jackie said, "The first part is just about a minor incident with a car. The bit about Pamela comes after."

Scott: *"I'm really sorry about the car, Chief. I'll pay to have it fixed myself."*

Jackie: *"That's not necessary. That's why we have insurance. But let's start there. Tell me what happened."*

The recording played on, but after a while, Suzan said, "Wait! Pause it for a minute."

"What's the matter?" Jackie asked as she clicked the button.

"I take it from the car incident that this guy is one of your officers," Suzan said. "Is that right?"

"Yeah. I didn't want to mention that for fear of skewing your analysis."

"He is all over the place!" Suzan said. "Half truth, half lies."

"Really? What is he lying about?"

"Back it up a little ways," Suzan said.

When she started it again, Jackie was saying, *"... seems to have ended nine months ago, you should have told me about it when you found out her death was being investigated."*

Scott: *"I ... ah ... I ... oh, shit. I am really, really sorry about that. I thought about telling you, honest, but I figured it was so long ago that it couldn't really make any difference, now. All it would do is embarrass her ... and Harry, too."*

"Lie," Suzan interjected.

Jackie: *"Did you engage in bondage with her?"*

Scott: *"Yes."*

"Truth."

Jackie: *"How many times?"*

Scott: *"Two."*

"Lie."

Jackie: *"When was the last time you were with her?"*

Scott: *"I think it was October of last year. I hadn't even seen her, except maybe driving past, in probably six months."*

"Big lie."

The recording played on until its end with Suzan flagging each answer as a truth or lie.

When it was over, Jackie said, "So, you're sure he was lying about those things?"

"Pretty sure, yeah," Suzan said. "If it wasn't for the truths in there, I might have chalked some of it up to nervousness over being called on the carpet by the boss. But there was a big swing in his voice with almost every other answer."

"Well, I guess I'm going to have to do a little more digging into my officer, huh?" Jackie said. Looking at her watch, she added, "We've got time for a few more if that's all right with you."

"I'm all ears," Suzan quipped.

Jackie found the recording of the first interview she did with Harry there at the station, and clicked Play.

Jackie: *"So you're aware, Harry, everything we say in here is being recorded in video and audio. As always, you have the right to have an attorney present if you'd like."*

Harry: *"No. That's not necessary."*

Jackie: *"This is a transcript of the statement you gave me last night. Would you take a few minutes to read it, and if you agree that those are your words and mine, would you sign and date it, please?"*

Harry: *"What if part of it is a lie?"*

Jackie: *"Which part?"*

Harry: *"(sigh) I wasn't at home watching a movie last night when Pamela drowned."*

Jackie: *"Where were you?"*

Harry: *"I had gone out to look at a car."*

Jackie: *"Why would you lie about that?"*

Harry: *"I ... I guess I felt even more ashamed that I wasn't even in the house when she had her accident. I didn't feel I could tell people I was out indulging my vanity and looking to recapture my youth by* buying a sports car. If I'd been there, maybe I'd have heard a thud or a splash and I'd have gotten to her in time.

"The thought of having other people—her friends and her family—heaping their guilt on me on top of what I was already feeling would have been too much. It was those thoughts that put the idea of sucking on the barrel of my .357 into my head."

"Can you stop it there?" Suzan said.

Jackie did, and asked, "You hear something peculiar?"

She replied, "I've listened to a lot of voices doing this lie detector thing—most of them criminals—and you begin to see a pattern. I think he told you what he saw as a minor lie so that when he confessed to it later on, your estimation of his veracity would go up and you'd be less likely to question other things ... like looking for a car and thoughts of suicide. I think both of those are lies. But they're different kinds of lies from what most criminals tell while being interrogated. This isn't something he's trying to hide; it's something he wants you to know ... but it's just as untrue. Does he happen to be an actor, by chance? Even amateur theater?"

"Not that I know of," Jackie said. "But he is an author. He writes murder mysteries."

"Oh! Well, there it is!" Suzan replied. "See, there's a slightly different cadence, a different flow to the voice when people are describing thoughts that are coming into their head as they speak, than when they're reading a script or reciting something they've memorized and probably rehearsed. That's what I'm getting from Harry, here. He's thought long and hard about what he's telling you; this isn't spontaneous. It's even more pronounced than it was with the reverend's call-back."

"That's interesting," Jackie said. "I happened to know that the bit about the car was a lie—I caught him in it later—but I hadn't guessed it about the suicide thing."

"Let's keep going," Suzan said. "This guy fascinates me."

Jackie restarted the recording. Hers was the first voice.

Jackie: *"I guess I can see that. What made you decide to tell me this, now?"*

Harry: *"When I told you about watching the movie, I figured that if the whole thing was seen by everyone as a horrible accident—which it certainly was—then my penance would be to carry the guilt of not being there for her for the rest of my life."*

For the next several minutes, the recording played and Suzan listened closely.

Harry: *"It's cliché and probably naive, but I'm counting on the truth to set me free. Pamela's death was an accident. I'm hoping the county DA will be able to see that when they look at the findings from her autopsy and your investigation report."*

Jackie: *"I hope you're right Harry. That's the way the system is supposed to work."*

Harry: *"So, how long until you have the results of the autopsy?"*

Jackie: *"Assuming she was picked up last night or this morning, and assuming that the county DA has ordered the autopsy, it should be performed today or tomorrow. If they're really backed up it could go another day.*

*"The DA and I will probably see a report the day after the autopsy was done, but some tox reports could lag that by a week or more."*

Harry: *(sigh) "Well, let me know as soon as you can, okay? And Thanks, Jackie. I appreciate you being a friend and not just a cop. I'm thinking that maybe your assistant who left—Carolyn?—she might have been a lot more bad-cop. She always seemed to have a chip."*

"Boy, he's hard to peg," Suzan said. "I often try to establish a baseline for things I know the subject is telling the truth about compared with things I know they're lying about, but this guy just doesn't fluctuate.

"For instance, you said you knew that what he told you about going to look at a car was a lie, but he stated that with the same flat, emotionless tone as he did everything else he said. I'm not a psychologist, so this is just experience talking, but based on just his speech pattern, I'd say that Harry might be classified with anti-social personality disorder if he did talk to a shrink. There's a lot of *deliberateness* in his speech; the words and patterns are very controlled; there's little emotion."

"Anti-social personality as in sociopathy?" Jackie said.

"I was actually thinking psychopathy since he's high on your suspect-radar," Suzan replied.

"Interesting," Jackie responded. "I've known Harry for several years, and I've also known a couple of first-class psychopaths. I don't think Harry fits that mold, at least not altogether. He's certainly not egocentric; in fact, he tends to be pretty reserved, almost shy until you get to know him. He's always been supportive of community causes, donating his time even without being asked. I've never perceived him to be manipulative, and he's never had any issues with the law since *I've* known him."

"Well, again, I'm not a psychologist," Suzan said, "and I certainly can't speak to any of the other classic psycho traits, but his voice is a red flag for me. I'd try to find a way to verify anything he told me."

"You're right on that count," Jackie replied. "At least half of what you just heard I now know to be untrue."

"You said he's an author of murder mysteries, right?" Suzan said. "I think it would be very interesting to get a look at his computer. His flat speech pattern *could* be heard as being scripted, rehearsed. I wonder if he wrote what he was planning to tell you like he was outlining a story. That way he could make edits and tweaks to it until he got the story to sound exactly right. Writing something out also commits it to a different place in your memory, so he actually would be recalling something when he was answering your questions. That could explain why I wasn't hearing the usual cues when someone is making something up on the spot."

"Interesting that you should mention looking at his computer," Jackie said. "I have that scheduled for this evening."

As Jackie scrolled to the recording with Harry where she confronted him with lying about the car, a light on the desk phone began to blink. Jackie said to Suzan, "I have to interrupt for a second. Sharon's putting a call into the room and she wouldn't do that if it wasn't important."

"Sorry to interrupt you in there, Chief," Sharon said, "but I have a caller who won't give her name, but says she has information about Pamela's death, and that she'll only talk to you."

"Make sure Gail gets the incoming phone number, give me twenty seconds, and then put her through," Jackie said.

She hung up and then said to Suzan, "Perfect timing; there's an anonymous caller with a tip about Pamela's death on the line." She handed Suzan the extension handset and added, "I'll be very interested in your analysis."

When the light blinked again, Jackie picked up, put it on speaker, and said, "Hello, this is Chief Hall. What can I do for you?"

In a thick southern drawl, the woman said, "I have some information about Pamela Fletcher's murder that you need to look into."

Suzan pantomimed writing something down, and Jackie gave her a pen and a pad as she answered the caller, "May I ask who's calling, please?"

"I'd prefer not to say. I want to be anonymous," she replied. "I have my reasons."

"That's fine," Jackie said. "I appreciate you calling. Do you mind if I ask why you believe Mrs. Fletcher's death was a homicide?"

As she spoke, she looked over at the pad and saw that Suzan had written, "Fake accent!" in remarkably pretty cursive that lay perfectly between the lines on the paper.

Jackie nodded her agreement, thinking the same thing ... forgetting that Suzan couldn't see her nod.

"Well, wasn't it?" the woman said. "That's what the hospital said. That's what was in the paper."

"It's being investigated as a *possible* homicide," Jackie said. "To my knowledge, the ME hasn't made that determination, however." That was the truth, but just barely, only because she had not actually read the autopsy report, yet.

Jackie went on, "Do you have some information that makes you believe that there was foul play?"

There was a slight pause, and the woman answered, "No, I guess not." She then quickly added, "But if it was foul play I know who did it! It was those two kids."

Jackie turned and looked at Suzan with a surprised expression expecting a similar look in return. She immediately realized, though, that that was not something Suzan would be likely to do. Instead, she cocked her head slightly, as if trying to hear more intently.

"Do you mean Mrs. Fletcher's kids?" Jackie asked the woman.

"Her son and step-daughter, yes," she answered.

"You have to admit, ma'am, that that's a pretty extraordinary accusation," Jackie said. "What would make you think that? Do you have some close association with them?"

"School," she answered.

"Were you a teacher of theirs?" Jackie asked. "Or a fellow student?"

There was another pause, and then the woman said, "Let's just leave it that I know them from school ... for several years."

"Okay," Jackie said. "Is there something specific that makes you suspect that one or both of them could have had a hand in Mrs. Fletcher's death?"

"Oh, it would be both!" she replied. "Those two are more like twins than step-kids. If one got into trouble the other was there to bail them out, making excuses, covering up, lying, whatever it took. They always had each other's backs.

"She was really smart in some subjects, and him in others, and I know they used to do one another's homework and reports—basically any assignment that didn't have to be done in class."

Jackie replied, "Well, being close is hardly an indication that they could have had something to do with Mrs. Fletcher's death. Do you have some evidence? Are you aware of a motive for why they'd want her dead?"

"The three oldest motives," the woman answered. "Love, hate, and money. Neither one of them liked Pamela—not even her own son. And Jessica never called her Mom; she always used her first name. But they both adore Harry. He's like a god to them.

"I think they arranged her *accident* to get her out of the picture and so that Harry could collect on her life insurance policy and they'd all live happily ever after. Accidents pay double indemnity, right? So there'd be plenty to go around."

"What insurance policy are you talking about?" Jackie asked.

"I don't know, but I'll bet a dime to a dollar that there is one," she replied.

"That's an interesting theory," Jackie said, "but without some evidence—even an overheard conversation—again, there's nothing to indicate foul play on their part. Did you ever hear ..."

"Look, getting the evidence is supposed to be *your* job!" the woman cut her off. "I've told you where to look; the rest is up to you if you want to see justice done for Pamela." With that, the call ended.

Suzan asked, "Could you recognize the voice? She's from around here. Despite the Memphis Belle routine, she was still dropping the occasional R."

"I was actually concentrating more on what she was saying than on her voice," Jackie said. "Maybe if I listen to the recording a couple of times. But I'm sure Gail has her number so we can get back to her if we need to. Do you think she was telling the truth?"

"Whether it was true or not I'd have no way of knowing, but *she* believed it," Suzan said. "I didn't get any deception there, at all aside for the accent. That wasn't a smokescreen; she really thinks those kids killed your Mrs. Fletcher. But what do *you* think about what she was saying? Do you see the kids as suspects?"

"I think what she said is pretty far-fetched, but far-fetched isn't the same as impossible. We'll do our homework and check them out. Whereabouts, phone records, emails, that kind of thing."

"Will you interview them?"

"Probably," Jackie answered. "If just for the sake of checking off all the investigation boxes."

"Well, let me know if you want me to listen to their recordings. You can send me the files in Colorado and I'll check them out in the evening."

## Chapter 17

**Wednesday, July 14, 2021**

Jackie finally got back to Pamela's autopsy report, and as expected, found nothing new. The manner of her death was now officially homicide, with the mechanism being acute cerebral anoxia, and the cause being manual strangulation—all as Dr. West had told them.

The tox report showed a small amount of alcohol in the blood, but well below the intoxication level. No other drugs were found.

She saved the report to the case file, and as she looked over her notes for the second-shift briefing coming up in an hour or so, Sharon called her to say that Marcia was on the line.

After hellos, Marcia said, "During lunch, I called the guy in Ipswich whose mailbox was full, and his sister answered the phone. It turns out that he died Saturday morning."

"Oh, no! What happened?"

"Apparently, he hung himself," Marcia replied.

"Suicide?" Jackie asked, murder/suicide leaping to her mind.

"Accidental was the impression I got, but she wasn't very talkative … understandably," Marcia said. "I was thinking that maybe you could call the Ipswich Police and see what they know. I'm still pretty much sequestered in the big meeting. Can you tell from the hollow sound where I'm calling from?"

"Lady's room," Jackie answered with a chuckle, having picked up on the echo. She looked at her watch and said, "I'll give them a call, now. You think you'll be excused tomorrow?"

"Lord, I hope so!" she replied.

"Okay, real quickly," Jackie said. "I just got a tip from an anonymous caller who is convinced that Pamela's kids faked her accident to collect the double-indemnity insurance money and free Harry from the burden of being married to her."

"Holy crap!" Marcia said. "And the caller was serious … and believable?"

"I happened to have Suzan Engles, the human polygraph I told you about, sitting with me when the call came in, and she feels that the *caller* believed what she was telling us. Which, of course, is not the same as being believable to the rest of the world. So, when you break free, can you see if you can get warrants for the kids' phone records and emails? I think it's a dead-end, but we have to check it out."

"Will do," Marcia said. "Okay, I really have to go, now ... leave, that is. I'll talk to you later. Bye."

"Hi, Charlie," Jackie said when she was connected with her counterpart at the Ipswich Police. "How is Sarah? Did she get the cast off her leg, yet?"

"Oh, yes. She's been out on the bay water skiing," he answered. "So, what's up?"

"I heard that you had an apparent accidental hanging over there by the name of Craig Davenport," she said. "What do you know about the death, so far? I'm asking because his name popped up in connection with our Pamela Fletcher who died over here last Thursday, and whose death has just officially been listed as a homicide."

"The ME has it, right now," he replied. "The wife says it was an accident; my first-on-the-scene said it could have been a suicide; and of course, there's always murder. How does he figure into your case?"

"He had a sexual relationship with the deceased about a year ago," Jackie said. "A one-time thing as far as we can tell, so it's not a real strong connection, but I want to cross all the T's and dot all the I's.

She went on, "So, if your guy sees it as a suicide, how does the wife see it as an accident? What did he hang himself with?"

"His belt," Charlie answered. "According to the wife, he was into kinky sexual stuff, including choking himself with a belt while he got off. She says she's seen him pass out from it, but he always set himself up so if he fell the belt would release itself. She says he'd loop the belt around his neck and then pass the loose end over a hook. But then he'd hold the loose end in his free hand as his safety device. If he passed out, he'd fall down, the loop around his neck would go slack, and then he'd wake up in a bit."

"Weird what people will do in the name of pleasure," Jackie commented, seeing how he and Pamela would get along well.

"Not to mention stupid," Charlie said. "This time, the prong of the buckle popped through one of the holes, so even though the belt released from its hook when he fell, it stayed tight around his neck while he was lying on the floor. Hence the possibility of accident, suicide, or homicide. Needless to say, we're looking into motive and opportunity for the wife. If she knew he did this kind of thing she could have used it and staged it to look like an accident."

"Speaking of opportunity, can you do me a favor, and see if you can find out where Mr. Davenport was last Thursday night?" Jackie asked. "It turns out that my victim, Mrs. Fletcher, was into kinky stuff, too, and that's almost certainly how they knew each other. The ME says that accidental erotic-strangulation could have been the cause of her death. What if they got back together, he accidentally killed her in the throes of kinky passion, and became so guilt-ridden that he killed himself ... in a similar and fitting manner?"

"Interesting," Charlie said. "Yeah, I'll see what we can dig up on him for last Thursday."

As Jackie headed to the break room for the shift briefing, Sharon flagged her down, and said, "Scott Lain phoned in sick. I called Kyle to fill in for him. He's on his way, but might be a couple minutes late for the briefing."

"Oh, okay," Jackie said. That disappointed her because she was planning to talk to Scott more about his relationship with Pamela based on Suzan's analysis of their previous interview.

## *Chapter 18*

**Wednesday, July 14, 2021**

When Jackie left the station to pick up Carol she borrowed the shift commander's cruiser and left him with the keys to her Jeep. With a sore knee, Carol would have an easier time getting into the sedan.

In Carol's driveway, her husband Neil put her backpack of tech stuff in the backseat, and then kissed her goodbye.

"Don't wait up," Carol said to him. "We'll probably go out to I-95 and cruise for speeders when I'm done with the boring work." She rolled up the window, turned to Jackie, and asked, "Where's the switch for the flashing lights ... just in case?"

"Over here where you can't reach it," Jackie replied as she backed out of the driveway.

"Party pooper," Carol sulked.

As Jackie and Carol walked up to Harry's door—Jackie carrying the briefcase and Carol limping with her cane—Harry opened the front door.

"Hi, Harry," Carol said. "I am so, so sorry about Pamela. Please accept our whole family's condolences. She was such a sweetheart."

"Thank you, Carol," Harry said and then gave Jackie a questioning look.

"I'll explain inside," she said.

In the kitchen, Jackie excused herself and Harry and stepped into his den. "The autopsy report came in this afternoon. There's still a couple of tests he's waiting on, but the ME has ruled Pamela's death a homicide."

"Ah, fuck!" he groaned, quickly adding, "Pardon my French." He put his hands together in front of him, and asked, "So, are you here to arrest me? Is that why you came in the cruiser?"

"The cruiser is because Carol hurt her knee and couldn't get in my Jeep," she answered. "And no, you're not under arrest; you're under investigation. As you said yourself, you had motive, means, and opportunity, so that puts you at the top of the suspect list."

"But still innocent until proven guilty," he said.

"I'd *prefer* to prove you *innocent*," she replied. "Please help me do that."

"So, what's Carol doing here?" he asked, crooking a thumb toward the kitchen.

"I'd like you to give me permission to make a copy of your computer's hard drive," she answered. "With the issuing of the report, the county DA will have a warrant for it in a day or two, and when they seize it, it will go to the State Police lab and there's no telling when you might see it again.

"You probably have a lot of stuff on your system that you'd rather not lose access to; I know that's true for myself. So, if you'll let Carol make a clone of the drive tonight, then you can copy whatever files you might need onto a laptop or something, and we'll have a date-stamped backup that will prove that you didn't *delete* anything before the Staties took your computer."

He looked at her skeptically, and said, "That sounds like you're playing fast and loose with the rules of evidence."

"I haven't seen a warrant, yet, so I have some flexibility," she said. "I'm trying to be the *good* cop, here."

"So, after you make this clone, you're going to lock it in the Rowley Police vault and only bring it out if the State Police suspect I deleted files?" he asked, calling her bluff.

She looked him in the eyes, and with a small conceding grin, she said, "No. I intend to look at it myself. As far as I'm concerned this is a Rowley investigation, and when the county takes your computer and turns it over to the Staties I'll lose access to it, just like you will."

"Thanks for your honesty," he said. "What exactly do you expect to find on my computer?"

"You're a writer of murder mysteries, Harry," she replied. "And although nothing resembling Pamela's death shows up in any of them that I'm aware of, more than one person has pointed out that you have the *capability* to create such a plot."

"And *these people* think I'd be dumb enough to leave it on my system if I did write such a plot?"

"They probably hope so," she answered. "No criminal was ever caught because the police *overestimated* his intelligence or his self-confidence.

"As a cop, I have to be impartial and objective, but on a personal level, I hope there's nothing there. But either way, it does have to be looked at."

"Well, you're going to find plenty there," Harry said. "I've researched so many ways to kill people that I wouldn't even guess at a number. There's poisoning, suffocation, and strangulation. There's stabbing, gunshots, bludgeoning, and yes, even drowning. There's ways to fake suicide and to fake an accident. There's ways to create a new identity and switch identities. And there's ways to dispose of a body so no one will ever, ever find it.

"Pamela and I used to joke that the research I had on my computer was the best life insurance policy she could ever have, because if anything suspicious ever happened to her I'd be in a world of shit." He looked at Jackie, and said, "The joke's not so funny anymore."

Twenty minutes later, Carol had her cloning software installed on Harry's computer, had its case opened up, and had all of the necessary hardware connected. She started the process and as she watched the progress bar begin its long creep from left to right, she said, "There's time for at least one glass of wine while this grinds away."

"We're on duty," Jackie said.

"We? I've been deputized?" Carol said excitedly and only half joking.

"Yes, Barney," Jackie kidded. "Tomorrow we'll look into getting you a bullet."

"To heck with tomorrow!" Carol said, "I call dibs on driving the cruiser home tonight! *I'll* find that light switch!"

While the cloning software ran, Jackie and Harry went back to the den, leaving Carol in Harry's office. She took a copy of one of his books from a shelf, and as she sat in front of the computer and read it, she glanced up occasionally to see if the progress bar was still moving. The time-remaining counter said six hours and eleven minutes but she knew that would start dropping rapidly when the process was about a quarter of the way done. She expected the transfer to take about an hour.

In the den, Harry went to the wet-bar, took a rocks glass from a shelf, and said, "You may be on duty, but I'm not." He got a large ice cube from the mini-fridge, dropped it in the glass, and poured scotch over it from a crystal decanter. Holding the fridge open, he said, "Can I offer you anything? Water, Coke, Dr. Pepper? I think I have some diet versions in there."

"DP on the rocks, please," she answered. "Thanks."

They sat down opposite each other in comfortable, cloth-upholstered wingback chairs. Jackie took out her phone, swiped to its recorder app, and said, "This is official business, so I'm going to record it."

"That's fine," he said although she wasn't asking for his permission. She was only putting it on tape that she had told him.

Harry took a sip of his drink, and said, "So when you called me earlier today and said you wanted to talk to me about Pamela's partners, that was just a ruse to get in my door before I could sabotage my computer, right?"

"It started out that way," she said. "Cop first, friend second."

"Which one doesn't trust me?" he asked.

"Both," she answered. "By your own admission, you've lied to me about this."

He sighed, and said, "That's fair, I guess. I am sorry about it and can only hope to regain your trust.

"You said, *It started out that way*," he went on. "I assume that means something's changed?"

"You said you didn't know Pamela's partners," Jackie said, "but you knew Scott Lain was one and, in fact, told her to break it off with him. Why didn't you tell me that?"

"It happened almost a year ago, I think," Harry said, "so it was water under the bridge as far as I was concerned. I didn't see any need to drag him into it."

"It's a homicide investigation, Harry. There's no such thing as water under the bridge. I need you to tell me everything; I need to be able to trust you."

"Can I ask how you found out that Lain was a partner?" Harry asked.

"Pamela's text messages," Jackie answered.

He frowned, and said, "She always deleted those texts in case she ever needed to let one of the kids or somebody use her phone."

"That doesn't delete them from the server," Jackie replied.

"Ah!" he said and took a swallow of his drink. "Then you probably know about Reverend Fairfield, too."

"We've spoken to him, but why don't *you* tell me about him," she said.

"Again, it was a long time ago; even before Lain," Harry said. "He was an asshole, but apparently he was pretty good with the kinky stuff that Pamela was into, which she liked at first. She finally figured out that he wasn't actually into the CNM thing, but was just cheating on his wife. And when he started to put me down, apparently so she'd like him more than me, she told him to get lost."

"That's a slight variation on the story I got from him," Jackie said. "But I agree that he's an ass, so I tend to believe your version more. Anyone else you can tell me about?"

"I never met him, but she told me about some guy who came on to her in one of those adult superstores. Neither of us ever even thought about picking up a partner that way. But she had just come from lunch with a friend, which included a couple glasses of wine, and apparently, she was feeling pretty *frisky* at the moment and he talked a good story about knowing what a kinky woman wants. Anyway, she gave him her phone number.

"Later—I think the next day," he went on, "he sent her a text with a naked photo of himself. She showed it to me and she wondered aloud how the hell much she had had to drink at lunch. She called him and told him that I had found the picture and had threatened to kill both of them if he ever came around. To my knowledge, she never heard another thing from him."

"Again, a variation on how he seems to remember things, but your version probably fits better," Jackie said. She wondered silently if Pamela's change-of-heart rejection could have enraged him to a point where he decided to kill her. Based on their conversation, she doubted that was in his personality, though. "I've seen the picture that the adult superstore guy sent her," Jackie went on. "Did she ever show you the one the Reverend sent her?"

"No."

"It's at the other end of the spectrum," she said. "And I suspect he sent it to a lot of other women, as well."

"That sounds about right based on my opinion of him," Harry said and took another sip of his scotch.

"Any others that you remember?" she asked.

"There was a guy that she just called Gary," he answered. "We bumped into him coming out of a movie theater. He was with a woman I assume was his wife. This was back in January of this year, I think. We didn't stop and talk, but Pamela told me later that he had quit the CNM thing, so she hadn't seen him in four or five months."

Jackie was feeling a little better about Harry telling the truth now because most of what he said she already knew from hers and Marcia's phone calls to those partners.

"Any thoughts on who might have wanted Pamela dead?" Jackie asked.

"*Wanted her dead?* Nobody. Literally," he said. He took a sip of his drink, and then went on, "I think it was probably an accident by whoever was with her Thursday night. If the ME ruled her death a homicide based on the petechial hemorrhaging, that indicates strangulation. I don't have the slightest problem believing that she was into erotic-asphyxiation along with everything else, so *my* theory is that she died from an overdose of sexual-stupidity at the hands of someone who wouldn't have the balls to own up to it. He panicked and put her in the tub where I found her."

"Is there evidence that someone was in the house with her while you were gone?" Jackie asked.

"Evidence? No. Except that there's no other explanation," he said.

"But no idea who that might be?" she asked.

"You're the one with her list of partners," he replied. "You know more about her sex life than I do."

"Other times when you've come home after Pamela had had a partner here, did you ever notice any evidence of them being here? Unmade bed? Wine glass in the sink? Strange hair in the shower drain?"

He swirled a sip of scotch around in his mouth while he thought about that, then swallowed and said, "I see where you're going with that. You're right; the house was almost *too* clean. We each knew what was going on when it was our turn to use the house, so neither of us was obsessive about cleaning things up. I'd found a rope still tied around the bedpost one time, and she found a sock that may have had stains of seminal fluid once. We just looked the other way."

"Did Pamela always take a bath after she'd been with a partner?" Jackie asked.

Harry looked at her as he rested his glass against his lip, mid-sip. Finally, he said, "You're good at this, aren't you? I completely missed that. No. Pamela rarely took baths, at all, except if she was down with a cold or something. If she was going to slip and fall and crack her head, it should have been in the shower. Except that that couldn't have been staged to look like she'd drowned."

From the doorway, Carol announced, "Congratulations! Your computer just gave birth to a three-ounce identical clone!" In her hand, she held a black and silver item that could have been mistaken for a cell phone at a distance.

Jackie looked at her watch, and said, "That was fast."

"First time I ever cloned to a solid-state-drive," Carol said. "It was wicked fast!"

"Is there room on your baby there to clone Pamela's computer?" Jackie asked Carol. She then turned to Harry, and said, "If that's okay with you."

"If it'll help figure this out, go for it," he answered and drained his glass.

With far less on her system, it took less than twenty minutes to duplicate Pamela's hard drive. As the software ran, Harry autographed the copy of the book Carol had been reading and gifted it to her.

Ten minutes after the second clone was complete, Carol and Jackie were getting back in the cruiser ... with Carol reluctantly in the passenger seat. As they drove, Jackie told Carol, "I'll need to take the drive and keep it in the station, but can you come by tomorrow and install it in one of our computers so we can see what's on it?"

"Wicked easy," she answered. "Do you need someone to do the searching, too?"

"I know both clones are on one drive, but can you set it up so each one shows up on a different computer?" Jackie asked.

"I can put it on one and designate it as a server, then connect another and make it a client," she answered. "You could network as many as you want."

"Okay. Marcia is supposed to be back tomorrow, and I'm sure she'll want to dig into Harry's hard drive," Jackie said, "so it will probably make sense for you to go through Pamela's. But I was serious about you being deputized, Carol. While you're working on this you're part of the Rowley PD and need to abide by our rules."

"Okay, so no drinking on the job," Carol said. "What else?"

"No talking to anyone about what you're doing," Jackie answered. "And that means *anyone*; not even Neil."

"He really doesn't listen to me anyway, so no problem," Carol said.

"It also means *ever*," Jackie said. "You're going to be looking at personal and private information that you can never share with anyone outside of this case. Anything you read on her hard drive you take to the grave with you."

"Not talking on *top* of not drinking?" Carol said.

Jackie knew she was joking, and replied, "The latter should make the former a little easier, I'd think. But I'm serious. I need your solemn word on this."

"I know you are, Jackie, and you have my word," Carol said. "Believe me; I know how to keep a secret. I've seen stuff on people's computers when I did repairs for them that I don't even want to remember, much less repeat."

## Chapter 19
**Thursday, July 15, 2021**

As Jackie pulled into the station parking lot the next morning, she noticed Jeff's car already there, and him standing next to it, talking with another man. Driving farther, she saw that the other man was Dave Price.

She parked, and as she walked up to them, she said, "Good morning." Then to Jeff, she went on, "What brings you around so early?"

Dave spoke first, and said, "We were just discussing which position you liked the best. I say missionary, but Jeff insists it's reverse cowgirl."

"What!" Jeff blurted. "We were not!" Turning to Jackie, he said, "We were talking about Harry Fletcher! Honest!"

She gave a little wave of dismissal, and said, "Don't worry about it; I know he's just trying to rattle your cage." Then, with her backpack in the other hand, she gave Jeff a one-armed hug and a quick kiss.

"None for me?" Dave asked with a theatrical pout.

Jackie was sure that Jeff knew who Dave was from his connection with the McCray case, and she was pretty sure she had mentioned that they had dated previous to that. She didn't think they had ever met, however.

"In case you haven't been properly introduced, Jeff Holder, meet Dave Price. Dave, Jeff." The two shook hands.

"I just swung in to see if you might be free for lunch," Jeff said to Jackie.

"Sorry, I've got a chiefs-of-police meeting in Boston in a couple of hours," she answered. "I'll be there all day."

"Tonight, maybe?" he asked.

"It'll probably be getting late by the time I get back," she said. "But I'll call you when I'm out of Boston, okay?"

"Sounds good," he said. He shook Dave's hand, again, said, "Nice to meet you, Dave," and then got into his car.

As Jeff backed out, Jackie said to Dave, "That was pretty rude, even for you."

"Sorry," he said. "I was only joking. It was just such an easy set-up I couldn't resist."

"Some detective," she said as they walked toward the station door. "Not only have you never figured out my favorite author, you don't know any of my other favorite things, either."

"So, give me a hint," he said. "Facing or not facing your partner?"

"*That* favorite is even more moot as far as you're concerned than my reading habits," she replied.

In her office, she asked him, "So, aside from harassing my friend, Jeff, what brings you to our fair little town?"

"Your Pamela Fletcher case," he answered. "I'm here to offer my services."

"Did you know her?" she asked. Given Dave's penchant for female companionship that would only have surprised her a little bit.

"No. I never met her," he said. "That's why I dropped by; I thought an unbiased third-party might be helpful."

"Well, thanks for thinking of us, but I already have a person in that role," Jackie replied. "An investigator and lawyer with the county DA's office."

"Not Bill Healy, I hope," Dave replied.

"Would that be a problem?" Jackie asked as she shooed him out of her doorway so she could go to the break room to get her coffee.

"Only because he couldn't cut it with the State Police, so he downgraded to the county," Dave answered as he followed. "He couldn't investigate his way out of one of those escape rooms."

"Well, fortunately for me then, it's not Bill," she replied.

"Okay if I have a muffin?" Dave asked as Jackie poured her coffee.

"If you take it to go," she replied. "I have a lot to do this morning."

Just then, Marcia appeared in the doorway, still carrying her laptop case. "Morning, Jackie," she said. "Hi, Dave. What are you doing here?"

"Leaving," Jackie said. Then she added, "You know each other?"

"We worked together on Marcia's first case with the county," Dave answered. "Excellent legal groundwork and brilliant detective work got Ms. Grieves her first conviction."

"*Your* first conviction as a detective, too," Marcia added, feeling he was trying to one-up her in Jackie's eyes.

"Well, congratulations to both of you on that," Jackie said. "Now, Dave must really be leaving because we have work to do."

"I'll go put my case down," Marcia said. "Hey, good to see you, again," she said to Dave.

As Marcia turned away, Sharon stepped up and said to Jackie, "There's a Steven Collins here to see you, Chief. He says you're not expecting him, but that it's about the Pamela Fletcher case."

"Well, that's interesting," Jackie said. "Have him wait out there for a few minutes," she told Sharon. To Dave, she said, "And so my morning gets even busier. It's been nice chatting, but ..."

"Steven Collins from Newburyport?" Dave interrupted her. Turning to Sharon, he asked, "About six-foot, hundred and eighty pounds, mostly-gray short hair, close-cut beard?"

"That's him," Sharon said.

"You know *him*, too?" Jackie asked.

"I worked an insurance fraud case against him about three years ago," he answered. "He got five years. If he's in your lobby, he must be out on parole."

"Okay," Jackie said, switching gears quickly. To Sharon, she said, "Bring him into the interview room and close the door. Tell him we'll be just a few minutes." To Dave, she said, "I don't want him to know you're here, but I'd like you to look in on our interview."

"He's a suspect in your Fletcher case?" Dave said.

"A person of interest," Jackie replied. "I'll explain in my office." To Marcia, she said, "Go put your stuff down, and wait for me."

As Jackie did a brief explanation of Pamela and Harry's CNM arrangement and of Collins' connection to her through it, she brought up the audio and video feed from the interview room on her computer. Collins, wearing a short-sleeve dress shirt, and a necktie, sat at the table with his hands together in front of him, but with the fingers of one drumming lightly on the other.

"Is that *your* Steven Collins?" Jackie asked.

"Yup." He then added, "So, you didn't know he had a record?"

It was an obvious jab at what she was sure he was thinking was poor police work, but before she could make a reply, Marcia said from her doorway, "I found that out yesterday during one of the lulls between meetings. He's out on parole for the remainder of his sentence or until he completes restitution, pays all of his court costs, and does his community service, whichever is longer."

"Nicely done," Jackie said, referring to both the police work and setting Dave back on his heels. "Do you have his parole officer's name?" she asked her.

"It's in my notes," she replied.

"Have it when we sit down with him, in case we need to make a point," Jackie said. Marcia went back into the other office, and Jackie said to Dave, "Text me if you see or hear anything I need to know while I'm in there. Also if you come up with any pertinent questions that we don't."

When Jackie and Marcia entered the interview room, Collins stood up to greet them.

"Hi, Mr. Collins," Jackie said. "I'm Jacquelyn Hall, Chief of Police here in Rowley, and this is Marcia Grieves with the Essex County DA's office."

He extended his hand, and said, "Pleased to meet you; both of you," as they shook.

"Please, have a seat," Jackie said as she and Marcia took theirs opposite him. "Thank you for coming in, but can I ask why you did that, rather than just returning Ms. Grieves' phone calls?"

Perplexed, he looked between them, and then said, "There were phone calls?"

"I left you several messages," Marcia said. "The first was on Tuesday."

"Really?" he said and took out his phone. He swiped to the screen with his voicemail box, and said, "I'm not showing any new messages."

He turned the phone so they could see it, and added, "There would be a little number next to the icon showing how many I have."

"Well, it was definitely your voice I heard on the recording," Marcia said. "Is that a new phone, by any chance?"

He stared at her for a moment, and then said, "Yes. How did you know?"

The same thing just happened to my mother. We upgraded her phone for her, but she never activated the voicemail account during the setup." She reached out and tapped the icon, the app opened up, and showed that he had eleven messages.

"Oh, shit!" he said, then quickly added, "Sorry; pardon my language. Three of those are from my parole officer. Crap! She is going to be pissed!"

"You can call her when we're done here," Jackie said. "If she needs corroboration of why you didn't call her back, I'll talk to her."

"Oh, thank you! I really do apologize for that," he said. "I lost my phone Monday afternoon—well, technically, I know where it is; it's at the bottom of the Merrimac River—but that's why I have a new one."

"We understand, "Jackie said, "But if it wasn't in response to Marcia's call, why are you here, today?"

"It's in regard to your Pamela Fletcher investigation. I, um ... I have a history with Pamela," he said uncomfortably.

"*History*?" Jackie repeated, hoping to get more without having to ask specific and direct questions.

He blew out a long breath, and said, "Have you ever heard the term *consensual non-monogamous relationship*?"

"The politically-correct term for an open marriage," Jackie replied.

"Exactly," he said. "Well, Pamela and her husband had such a relationship, and I happened to be one of her extra-marital partners.

"When I heard that Pamela had died, I was stunned," he went on. "We had been planning to get together Friday, the night after she passed away. But then when I read, yesterday, that her death was being looked into as a possible murder, I figured that sooner or later you'd come across my name, somehow, and I knew I needed to contact you and should do it before you contacted me ... or more importantly, before you contacted my parole officer. She hates surprises."

"Is there any reason that being with Mrs. Fletcher would have violated the terms of your parole?" Marcia asked. "Did you do drugs with her or anything like that?"

"No," he answered quickly. "It's just that, well, being involved with a married woman who ended up murdered the night before we were supposed to meet I think would get Ms. Hartley's shorts in a knot if you called her before I spoke to you and explained things."

Jackie asked him, "You're on parole for insurance fraud, is that correct?"

"Yes." There was a slight questioning tone behind his answer.

"Well, there happen to be a number of life insurance policies connected with this case, totaling several hundred thousand dollars," Jackie said, "which would pay double in the event of accidental death ... which Pamela's was staged to look like. That seems a curious coincidence."

"*What?* Oh, my God, no! No!" he blurted with wide eyes. "Mine was a phony car crash and injury deal. I didn't even know she *had* insurance! I swear! I swear! God, please don't tell Hartley that! She'll want me back inside until somebody else is convicted just so she can say she knows where I am."

"Can you establish where you were last Thursday night, Mr. Collins?" Marcia asked. "Between six and ten."

"I was home alone, so no, not really, I guess."

"What were you doing?"

"Watching TV, mostly," he said.

"Were you on your computer or your phone at all during the time I mentioned?" she asked.

He thought for a moment, and then said, excitedly, "Yes! Yes, I was! That would prove I was at home, wouldn't it? I was watching the movie *Patton*, and I used my phone to look up when George C. Scott died. You can verify that, right?"

"We can," Marcia replied.

"Thank you!" he said with another sigh, but one of relief this time.

Jackie nudged Marcia and nodded toward the door then stood up. "Give us a few minutes, Mr. Collins," she said. "Can I get you some water? Coffee?"

"Water would be great, Chief Hall, thank you."

Conveniently, Jackie almost walked into Gail as they came out of the room, and she asked, "Would you get Mr. Collins a bottle of water, please? Thanks."

In her office, Jackie closed the door, and said to the other two, "Put one hand behind your backs. When I count three bring it out. One finger means you think he's being honest with us, two means you think he's blowing smoke."

Dave laughed, and said, "Consensus by rock, paper, scissors."

Jackie counted, and they all produced one finger.

"So, no inconsistencies with what you know about him?" she asked Dave.

"Nope. Same squirrelly little guy. And there's no way he could be involved in a double-indemnity life insurance conspiracy. He botched getting a few grand out of a simple car crash."

"You're okay with his answers?" she asked Marcia.

"Yeah, I think he's being straight with us. I'll check the search history on his phone just to be sure, though. And I'll have him call his PO and talk to her on his behalf."

When she opened her office door, Jackie saw that Carol had just gotten there. To Marcia, she said, "Can you wrap things up with Mr. Collins? I want to get Carol going." Then, motioning him out of her office, she said, "Thanks, Dave, I appreciate your help with this. If anything else comes up, I'll give you a call."

"She said, giving him the bum's rush," he replied with a little laugh.

At the door, she introduced Carol and Dave but made sure that Dave kept moving.

"That's the guy who worked with you on the McCray case, right?" Carol asked as they went to Marcia's temporary office. "Is he on this one, too?"

"Only by very strange coincidence," Jackie answered.

Inside the interview room, Marcia borrowed Collins' phone, navigated to the "Manage History" page on his Google account, and scrolled until she found July 8. At 9:04 p.m. he had asked, "When did George C. Scott die?"

She knew that it was conceivable that he could have been standing in Pamela's bathroom when he made the search to establish an alibi, and that finding out what cell towers the phone was linked to at the time was the only way to know for sure, but she really didn't see him as being that clever. On the other hand, it was part of proper due diligence, so she wrote down his phone number, his service provider, and the exact time of the call.

Handing the phone back, she said, "Why don't you call Ms. Hartley while I'm here with you? Put it on speaker."

"Where the hell have you been, Steven?" a woman answered. "I left three messages for you!"

"I'm sorry Ms. Hartley," he said. "I have a new phone and my voicemail didn't get set up right, so I didn't see your calls."

"Which is just one step removed from *the dog ate my homework*," she replied.

"It's true, Ms. Hartley," Marcia said. "This is Marcia Grieves with the Essex County DA's office. How are you?"

"Wonderful," she replied sarcastically. "What has Steven done to be in your company?"

"Nothing more nefarious than giving us some background information on a woman who passed away last Thursday," Marcia said. "I left him a message, as well, and when I looked at his phone a little while ago, I could see that his voicemail was, in fact, not alerting him to new calls. I helped him fix it and it's when he saw your calls. I asked him to call you so I could vouch for him."

"Thank you, Ms. Grieves," Hartley said. "Steven, are you still there?"

"Yes?"

"I want to see you in my office in thirty minutes."

"I, um I don't think I can get there that fast," he replied.

"We're not in the Salem office, Ms. Hartley," Marcia interjected. "We're in Rowley at the moment. Where is *your* office?"

"Lynn," she replied, which would have been about a fifteen-minute drive from Salem. "I'll give you forty-five, Steven."

"Again, Ms. Grieves, thank you," she went on. "I really need to be going, now. Goodbye."

Marcia and Collins both said, "Goodbye," at the same time, but the call disconnected before the second syllable.

"She seems charming," Marcia said mockingly as Collins picked up his phone.

"There's a reason that her clients call her Ms. Heartless."

Marcia chuckled, and said, "On the other hand, she gets paid to get lied to by people who are only not in prison by the grace of God, the parole board, and an overcrowded system. I'd probably leave my heart at home, too."

Collins nodded, and said, "Sorry; you're right. But thank you for bringing *your* heart today. I appreciate you being on that call with me."

"You're welcome," Marcia replied. "So, why do you think she wants to see you?"

"Drug and alcohol test," he answered. "She pops those on us from time to time. I had a prior DUI, so the judge imposed an alcohol ban as one of my conditions."

"Are you clean?" she asked.

"Yup. I'll happily pee in any cup you care to hand me," he replied. "I actually feel a lot better now that I'm not drinking, and Lord knows I need the money it saves me."

# Chapter 20

**Thursday, July 15, 2021**

After showing Collins to the door, Marcia went to Jackie's office, where Carol was just finishing the setup to have Jackie's computer on the three-system network that could see the two cloned hard drives.

Sitting in Jackie's chair, Carol went to the root directory, which showed her internal "C" drive, her backup "D" drive, and all of the other virtual drives that resided on the department's server. At the bottom of the list were two that had not been there before.

Hovering the cursor over the drives, Carol explained, "XH is the cloned drive from Harry's computer, and XP is Pamela's. They're installed in Marcia's computer and networked only to this one and to my laptop. Nobody else can access them, plus they're passworded." She then told them the password.

Marcia gave Jackie a questioning look, which she acknowledged with a simple nod, but didn't say anything.

"That's perfect, Carol. Exactly what I was looking for," Jackie said.

"I can also install an app that will create a log of when anyone does access either of them, if you want," Carol offered.

"That could be handy," Jackie said. "Is that something you can do on Marcia's computer? I need to talk to her alone for a few minutes."

"Well, if you don't want me around, just tell me to leave," Carol said with mock indignity.

"Leave," Jackie said but followed it with a smile.

She closed the door on her way out, and then Marcia said to Jackie, "You're giving a civilian access to evidence in an ongoing homicide investigation?"

"I deputized her when she cloned the drives last night," Jackie replied as she sat down.

"Oh, well that changes everything," Marcia said sarcastically.

Jackie just laughed, and said, "Carol has had her fingers in the department's computers longer than I have. If she ever wanted to copy anything, or set up a hack, or install a virus, she could have done it long ago, and nobody here would ever know.

"I have her confidentiality agreement as well as a nondisclosure agreement on file, and she has my absolute trust. Yes, technically, she's a civilian, but with special circumstances.

"Plus, you and I need the help," she went on acknowledging that this was Marcia's case, too. "I wish I could pull some strings to get you dedicated to this case, but yesterday proved your part-time status with the county holding sway. I want Carol to work under you on Pamela and Harry's computers. That's going to be a lot of grunt work that I don't have the personnel to take on. You tell her what to look for and turn her loose; I think you'll be impressed."

"Sorry. I guess I didn't look at it like that," Marcia said. "I was concerned about compromising evidence if we find anything. I can see a defense attorney claiming the drives were tampered with by unauthorized or unqualified personnel."

"A valid concern," Jackie said. "But Carol is both authorized and qualified, and she won't be looking at anything that will ever be entered as evidence, anyway. That's why I wanted the clones. We can do whatever we want to them, and then if-and-when the originals get seized as evidence we can tell the folks at the State Police lab exactly what to look for."

Marcia nodded, and said, "I guess that's why you're a chief."

Jackie laughed, and replied, "I used to say that exact thing to Chief Booker." She then said, "Will you call Carol in here, please?"

Marcia opened the door, leaned across the hall to the other doorway, and said to Carol, "The boss wants to see you, and is she pissed!"

"Oh, you two are going to get along well!" Jackie laughed.

Addressing both of them, Jackie said, "I'm going to be gone for most of the day at a Northshore chiefs meeting with the attorney general. Carol, please take your direction from Marcia."

Carol pantomimed hooking a leash to an imaginary collar around her neck and handing the other end to Marcia.

"I want to do a follow-up call on Steven Collins," Marcia said to Jackie. "Is it okay if I use your office for that?"

"Sure," she answered. "Remember to hit the record button."

Back in the other office, Carol asked Marcia, "So, what would you like me to do, boss?"

"First of all, you'll call me Ms. Grieves," Marcia told her sternly.

Carol blinked in surprise, but then Marcia smiled, and said, "Kidding ... *ma'am* will suffice."

Carol laughed, clicked her heels, and snapped a salute. "Yes, ma'am! Ready for my assignment, ma'am!" she barked.

"At ease," Marcia said as she sat down. Then seriously, she said, "I'd like you to go through Pamela's emails. I have a list of people we need to see correspondence with. I'll email it to you."

Pointing to Marcia's monitor, Carol said, "You can just go to my computer in your network, there, and drop it on my desktop. So, what will I be looking for in these emails?"

"For now, just collect them all into a single folder," Marcia said. "Then we can go through and see if they're pertinent."

A few moments later, Carol opened the file of names, addresses, and phone numbers on her computer. "So, this is your suspect list?"

"They're people of interest for the moment," Marcia replied. "Graduation to suspect may depend on their emails."

"Scott Lain?" Carol said as she read down the list. "*Our* Scott Lain?" When she read his address, she answered her own question. "It is! Oh, is that because he was first on the scene? No, what would that have to do with emails? I don't get it; why is his name here?"

"If there are any emails between him and Mrs. Fletcher, that might tell us," Marcia replied in a non-answer.

Carol also recognized Aaron and Jessica's names, of course, but none of the others.

Just then, Jackie stepped into the doorway, and said, "I'm off to Boston. Good luck with your searches." To Marcia, she added, "The office is all yours."

Marcia first called Steven Collins' service provider. After several holds and hand-offs, she was finally connected with someone who could apparently help her.

"Hi, my name is Marcia Grieves. I'm with the Essex County District Attorney's Office in Massachusetts," she began, yet again. "I'm working on a homicide investigation, and I'm trying to verify where a cell phone call was made a week ago. Is that something you can help me with?"

"It is," the man answered. "Do you have a warrant?"

"The subject is on parole, so none is necessary," Marcia replied. "I have his information here."

"That works," he said, "but I'll need the request in writing—an email will do. Please send it directly to me under your county DA email address, and include your county-issued phone number." He then gave her his email address, and went on, "Along with his parole information, please include all the particulars for the search, of course; name, cell number, date, time, everything you have."

"It was actually a Google search that he made," Marcia said.

"That's fine. Just include whatever details you have."

"About how long do these searches take?" Marcia asked. "This is my first one."

"The search itself, about thirty seconds," he answered. "But I have to get verification on your subject's parole status, first. So, my guess is anywhere from one to forty-eight hours, depending on how busy the department of corrections is and how motivated they are to get back with me."

"I get that," Marcia said. She thought about dropping her father's name but realized that it would only have an effect once the request had made it through to the DOC so she decided to hold it in reserve. "Okay, thank you. I'll have the email off to you in a few minutes."

She went back to her own computer, and as she sat down, Carol said, "All done. What's next?"

"Really? Weren't there very many emails?" Marcia asked.

"Oh, scads of them," Carol answered. "But I wrote a little DOS batch routine that did a search against all of the names for me. You don't have to work hard if you work smart."

Marcia nodded, and said, "I have an uncle who spins that differently, saying that if you give a lazy person a hard job, they'll find an easy way to do it."

"That works, too," Carol said with a chuckle.

"So, did you find many?" Marcia asked.

"No, not really. A dozen or so back and forth between her and the kids. Well, actually mostly with Aaron; there was only one with Jessica. But none for any of the names on your list."

"Really? Did you check her deleted folder?"

"Yup. But it gets automatically emptied every thirty days, so there wasn't much there but obvious junk." Carol answered. "You'd probably have to go back to her provider to get any more."

Marcia thought for a moment, and then said, "Aside from the two kids, I'd be surprised to find any of the other names from the list on *Mr. Fletcher's* computer, but why don't you run your program through his emails, too? Oh, and add the name Megan Hope."

"The EMT Megan Hope?" Carol asked, pointing toward the fire station next door.

"Yup," Marcia answered and offered nothing more.

"Fine; don't tell me. I'll be your mushroom and just work in a cold, dark, little cave," Carol said feigning indignity.

"I'd rather let Jackie explain what's going on if you find anything," Marcia replied. "And you didn't find any emails to or from Scott on Mrs. Fletcher's drive?"

"Nope."

"Okay. I need to get an email out," Marcia said. "Then I'd like you to show me how to use that batch routine. Can it find deleted files?"

"If the disk space they used hasn't been totally overwritten it will find what's left of them," she answered. "You know that's how it works, right? Only the address to the file gets deleted; the body stays there but is marked as available memory space."

"I did know that," Marcia said. "That's why I'm going to search for specific words, not whole files."

Carol put her hands together, fingertips to fingertips, and as she drummed them together, she said, "Ooo! Cloak and dagger secret-code-breaking!"

"That might be overstating it," Marcia replied with a smile. "Maybe hoodie and pen-knife obvious-word-search."

By the time Marcia had finished her request to Collins' service provider, Carol was done with her search of Harry's emails.

"Nothing to or from anyone on the list," Carol told Marcia. "What words do you want to look for, first?" she asked, excited to get started.

"Let's start with the obvious," Marcia answered. "Let's try *drown*, *bathtub*, and *stage*. I want to see if he might ever have written a plot—or even outlined one—that is similar to what happened to Mrs. Fletcher. I've read a couple of his books now, and there's nothing in those, but this kind of search through the manuscript files for *all* of his books will be much faster. Plus it will find matches in unpublished writings, as well as deleted files."

"Ah! Like if he wrote out the idea for a book, but then decided he could put the plan into actual practice," Carol said. "Wow! That would be cold! ... and dumb. So, you really think Harry killed his wife, then?"

"Well, we know that somebody did," Marcia answered. "And Mr. Fletcher had motive, means, and opportunity, so he's pretty high up the suspect list. If we were to find an unused or deleted file that described how his wife died, he'd certainly have some explaining to do."

"Life imitating art," Carol said. "Or *death* imitating it, rather."

Half an hour later, they had found seven instances of *drown*, *drowned*, or *drowning*; three of *bathtub*; and twenty-two of *stage*, *staged*, or *stages*. Reading the words in the context of their surrounding text, however, they could easily see that none of them were in reference to a death or situation even remotely resembling Pamela's.

"Swing and a miss," Carol said when they eliminated their last hit on *staged*. "What's next, Holmes?"

"Can we look through his Internet-search history with your batch routine?" Marcia asked.

"Never tried it," Carol said. "But if I can find the history file on the drive it *should* work."

"Okay. Can we do phrases," Marcia asked. "Like petechial hemorrhaging, drowning death, erotic asphyxiation. I want to see if he felt the need to know more about those subjects."

"Erotic asphyxiation?" Carol repeated.

Marcia mentally bit her lip having forgotten that Carol wasn't privy to all of the details of the case. "Humor me," she said. "I'll let Jackie explain when she gets back."

"Oh, so like when I asked my Dad where babies come from, and he said my Mom would explain it," Carol said.

Marcia laughed, and said, "Exactly!"

Ten minutes later, Carol announced that she had found hits on all three phrases.

"Interesting!" Marcia said.

"That's the good news," Carol replied. "The bad news is that those searches aren't very recent. Petechial hemorrhaging was almost six years ago. Erotic asphyxiation was a little over four, and searches about drowning go back three and a half."

"Hmm. That would be pretty long-range planning, wouldn't it?" Marcia said. "Send me the dates. I'm going to see if the searches line up with when books containing the subjects would have been written."

With chronological alignment making it obvious that the searches were done for books that Harry was working on at the time, Carol and Marcia broke for lunch and walked down to the Agawam.

As they walked, Carol said, "So, I've noticed that you always call Harry *Mr. Fletcher*, and Pamela *Mrs. Fletcher*. Why is that? You use everybody else's first name, even Jackie. Me I get; I'm a civilian peon, but Jackie's the Chief."

"I had a professor in law school who told us to never get on a first-name basis with anyone we were investigating," Marcia answered. "She said it helps to keep things impartial and objective. *Mrs.* Fletcher is just out of respect for the dead, I guess.

"And I hardly see you as a peon, by the way" she went on, "and I know that Jackie doesn't, either. She respects the hell out of you, and I'm quickly learning why."

They arrived at the Agawam, but before taking a seat at the counter next to Marcia, Carol talked with all of the waitresses, said hello to the cooks, and said at least *hi* to half the customers.

"So, is there anyone in this town that you're not on a first-name basis with?" Marcia asked after Carol finally sat down and Mary Alice had taken their order.

"Oh, sure," she replied with a smile, "but I'm working on it."

"So, you know Mr. Fletcher and you knew Mrs. Fletcher?"

"Oh, yes. I did some IT work for them, but Pamela and I were on a couple of volunteer committees in town, too. Wicked nice person!"

"So, could you conceive of Mr. Fletcher murdering her?" Marcia asked.

"Not a chance," Carol answered.

"You don't think he could have done it, huh?"

"*Could have done it?*" Carol repeated. "Sure. You've read his books; he could have worked it all out. I just can't *conceive* of him doing it. That would take ice water for blood, and I don't see him like that."

"Is there anyone you *do* see like that?" Marcia asked. "Anyone from the list we've been working with?"

Carol thought for a moment before answering and then said, "Not really. Of course, I only actually know a few of the people on the list, and those not all that well. Megan Hope never struck me as warm and fuzzy. Of course, that's a far cry from ice-cold, and even further from a murderer. Scott Lain always seemed a little flaky to me, bordering on creepy. The two kids, Jessica and Aaron, I only know because my kids went to school with them. They seemed to think Aaron was okay, but Jessica could be kind of a bully. They never came around the house after school or anything."

Mary Alice appeared behind the counter with their lunch orders—a tuna roll for Carol, and a turkey club for Marcia—and as she set the plates down, she said, "No Jackie today?" having recognized Marcia from previous visits.

"Duty called her away to Boston," Marcia answered.

"I've been deputized to take her place," Carol said proudly. From her shirt pocket, she retrieved a small item, and showing it to Mary Alice, she added, "See? I even have my own bullet!"

"Deputized?" Mary Alice repeated, familiar with Carol's joking manner.

"She's helping with some IT work," Marcia said, wanting to keep Carol's involvement low-profile.

"About Pamela?" Mary Alice asked.

"Why would you think that?" Marcia asked.

"Well, *you're* here on the case, right? And I saw Jackie and Carol going into Harry's house last night, and now she's here with you, so ..."

"She lives across the street for the Fletchers over on Weldon Farm Road," Carol told Marcia. Then to Mary Alice, she said with a finger to her lips, "Shh! I'm undercover. That's why they didn't give me a badge. Heck, I had to buy my own bullet!"

Mary Alice stretched to look over the counter, and said, "You have a gun?"

"Just the one bullet, so far," Carol answered. "We'll see how things go."

Having seen reruns of *Bewitched* on TV, an image of nosy-neighbor Gladys Kravitz popped into Marcia's head, followed immediately by a serendipitous thought.

"Did you happen to see anyone coming or going from the Fletcher's last Thursday night? The night that Mrs. Fletcher died?" she asked. "I mean other than Mr. Fletcher and then the police and ambulance."

"We weren't home," Mary Alice replied. "That's spaghetti night with our daughter and her family."

*Pop!* went Marcia's serendipity bubble.

"But there could be something on our doorbell camera," Mary Alice went on. "It sometimes goes off when it sees headlights driving by or across the street. Michael's tried to adjust it but I don't think he has it working right, yet."

The bubble began to re-inflate as Marcia asked excitedly, "Would you still have the videos from that night on your phone?" She knew that most doorbell camera apps could be set to save the recordings for various periods or—perish the thought—not at all.

"Oh, I wouldn't know," she said. "That's all on Michael's phone."

The bubble shrank a bit, but it didn't pop.

"Would Michael be home now?" Marcia asked with crossed fingers.

"Oh, no. Michael still works," she answered. "Almost thirty years with UPS. But he's usually home by about six. No, wait. What day is this? Oh, never mind; it's Monday. He bowls on Tuesday nights. So, yeah, six o'clock."

"Could you give me his phone number?" Marcia asked. "I'll call him before I drop by."

As she recited it, Marcia tapped the number into her phone. Mary Alice then asked, "Will you two want any dessert?"

"We're splitting a piece of coconut cream pie," Carol answered immediately and for both of them.

Back at the station, Marcia sent Jackie a text that read:

Hi, Jackie. Hope you're having fun! The search of the Fletchers' drives was pretty much a bust, but I stumbled onto a potentially promising lead at lunch. When do you expect to be back in Rowley? MG

Unexpectedly, she got a reply almost immediately.

Just heading back after lunch break. Supposed to wrap about 5. Rush hour in Boston!! My favorite! So, maybe 6 or so. Will you still be there?

She replied:

I'll wait up for you.

For the next two hours, Marcia went through Harry's computer drive, and Carol went through Pamela's. They soon ran out of specific words and phrases to look for and began just scanning directory, folder, and file names hoping to hit on something pertinent. They found nothing they could connect to the case.

At a few minutes to three, Carol told Marcia, "I need to be heading home. We have some company coming over tonight, and Neil is not so good at making appetizers. Well, he is, but he's even better at sampling them to make sure they taste good. Will you be needing my services tomorrow?"

"I'm guessing no," Marcia answered, "but I'll let Jackie make that call. She may have something other than sifting through bits and bytes that she wants you to do."

Carol patted her pocket, and said, "I'll hang onto the bullet, then."

At 4:35 Marcia received an email from Steven Collins' service provider. It read:

To Marcia Grieves; Essex County District Attorney's Office. Pursuant to your request of 7/15/2021 for triangulation data regarding the cell phone number and time-of-call shown, please find the attached file. Accuracy of location within approx. 500 to 700-foot radius."

Marcia opened the file and was looking at a map of an area that straddled the Massachusetts, New Hampshire border. A number of red dots indicated cell phone towers, each with an eight-digit identifying number. Three just south of the New Hampshire border were circled, also in red. A more detailed blown-up map of the area around those towers showed a star with a line reaching out to each of the three towers, and a leader that connected to a box that showed Collins' phone number, the time of day the call started and stopped—each down to the second—and longitude and latitude coordinates of the phone during the call. Around that point was drawn a yellow circle indicating the radius of accuracy for the location.

Marcia remembered that Collins lived in Newburyport, and although she couldn't recall his exact address she decided this was close enough. He obviously wasn't in Rowley at the time that Mrs. Fletcher died.

## *Chapter 21*

**Thursday, July 15, 2021**

Jackie called Jeff as she drove home, and made her apologies for not being able to make dinner. When she pulled into the station parking lot at quarter past six, Fred Hardy was just pulling out, and they stopped side by side and rolled down their windows.

"Hi, Jackie. I was just here double-checking the VIN number on your scratched cruiser," he said. "My parts supplier said that model didn't have a fender flair. Turns out I transposed two letters so he's probably right."

"Well, at least you're big enough to admit you made a mistake," Jackie said.

"Only to you," he replied. "I'm going to blame a poor-quality fax when I call him back."

She laughed, and said, "It's good to have an escape plan."

"Oh, and I don't know if this matters to you, at all," he added, "but that scrape didn't happen at Knowles gas station. I looked, and his pumps have upside-down U-shaped guard posts at the ends. They don't reach high enough to have scraped the fender. If somebody turned into one of them right where the scrape is it would have gone into the wheel-well and the tire would have rubbed it. Maybe scraped the wheel, but not the fender."

"Oh," she said. "Maybe I misunderstood. Maybe it happened at the Richdale store when he was getting gas there."

"Nope," he said. "I thought about the same thing. They have the same guards as Knowlesies; big inverted steel U-shaped things."

"Interesting," she said. "Well, I guess it really doesn't matter too much where it happened, as long as you can fix it."

"No problem, now that I've cleaned that darned fax machine," he said with a laugh.

She parked, and as she walked to the door, it occurred to her that she wasn't mistaken about where Scott said he scraped the cruiser; it was in the written report.

Inside, she stopped at Sharon's desk, and asked, "Did Paul take care of the shift meeting, okay?"

"Oh, sure," she replied. "Scott didn't come in, so he called Mark to fill in for him."

"He's still sick?"

"Don't know; I assume so," she answered. "He didn't call in."

"Have you tried calling him?"

"When he was about five minutes late, Paul had me call," she said. "But there was no answer."

Jackie looked at her watch, and said, "Why don't you give him another try."

As Jackie set her briefcase on her desk, Marcia stepped into her office, and said, "Welcome home, Chief. Fun day at the office?"

"It certainly reminded me why I like being chief *here*," she answered. "So, what's your potentially promising lead?"

"You probably already know this, but Mary Alice, the waitress at the Agawam, lives across the street from the Fletchers."

"I actually didn't know that," Jackie said, her interest quickly piqued.

"Well, she says she has a doorbell camera that sometimes triggers by cars going by on the street, but also going in and out of the Fletcher's driveway."

"Interesting!" Jackie said. "And ..."

"And that's the end of it, so far," Marcia answered. "Hence the *potentially promising* label. She said that the videos go to her husband Michael's phone, and he wasn't home then. So, I thought you might want to go over there with me, now."

"Hell, yes!" Jackie said.

"I'll call, and let them know we're on the way," Marcia said as they headed out of Jackie's office.

On the way by, Jackie poked her head into the communications room, and asked Sharon, "Any answer from Scott?"

"Still no answer," she replied.

Jackie thought for a moment, and then turned and said to Gail at the dispatch station, "Gail, will you see who's on patrol out near where Scott Lain lives? Have them do a well-check on him, and then give me a call. Thanks."

In the Jeep, Marcia asked, "Is something wrong with Scott?"

"I don't know," Jackie answered. "I wanted to talk to him about a fender-bender he had in one of the cruisers, but he called in sick last night and tonight he's a no-show *without* a call-in, and doesn't answer his phone. That's not like him. I hope he's not lying on his bathroom floor too sick to get up or hurt or something."

"Does he have enemies?" Marcia asked, voicing the more sinister train of thought that had certainly crossed Jackie's mind.

"Well, he's a cop, so there are bound to be people who automatically don't like him," Jackie answered. "But it's not like he's ever busted up a drug ring, or sent anyone away for ten to twenty. And retribution for giving a speeding ticket seems like quite a stretch."

"We know he was sleeping with the wife of at least one other man," Marcia offered. "Could he have hooked up with the spouse of the wrong guy?"

"It wouldn't be the first time a love triangle ended up with a bullet hole in the middle of it," Jackie said. "But I'm still hoping for stomach flu. I *was* concerned about his lying, now I'm concerned about him in general. I hope he's okay."

When they got to Mary Alice and Michael's house, they saw that it was not directly across from the Fletcher's, but diagonally across. Both Marcia and Jackie had been wishfully imagining a doorbell video straight into the Fletcher's driveway, clear enough to read a car's license plate.

Mary Alice welcomed them inside, and Jackie introduced Marcia and Michael. After hellos and handshakes, he said, "So, Mary Alice told me you wanted to see if we caught any videos of Harry and Pamela's the night she died. I knew the camera went off a number of times when we were eating over at Linda's, but I never thought to look at them before. But they do show all of the comings and goings, all right."

They sat down at the kitchen table, with Marcia and Jackie side by side and Michael's phone between them. Jackie scrolled down the history list watching the date-stamps until she reached the previous Thursday. She continued until she found one marked 7:11 p.m., remembering that Harry had told her that he left the house about 7:30 that night. The video was of a truck passing by.

The next seven clips were of passing cars and trucks as people were likely heading home from work. It occurred to Jackie that Michael needed to adjust the sensitivity of the motion detector to keep it from going off with every passing car. On the other hand, she was happy that he hadn't done it before last Thursday.

She tapped the next clip, marked 7:27, which began when the backup lights of Harry's car came into view as he backed out of his driveway and cleared the hedges that lined both sides of the driveway.

Marcia commented, "That would be him going to ..."

"To the store," Jackie interrupted her, assuming she was going to say *to meet up with Megan Hope*. Jackie didn't want to share that with any of the townspeople, and especially not Mary Alice who was not known for being tight-lipped.

Marcia immediately got why Jackie had cut her off, and just said, "Yup."

To Mary Alice and Michael, Jackie said, "So, it looks like your doorbell did capture the activity over there Thursday night. Naturally, I'll need to put this into my report, so do I have your permission to copy all these files to the police database?"

"Oh, sure! Sure!" Michael said. "Do whatever you need."

"Can you do that, please?" Jackie asked Marcia. "Send them to the department's Dropbox account. You've used that, right? We'll download them to the file at the station."

Marcia selected all of the Thursday night recordings, and then tapped all of Friday's as well with the adage about the criminal returning to the scene of the crime in mind.

As Marcia was selecting, Michael said to Jackie, "I'm probably talking out of school here, but if you ask me my opinion, I'd tell you that Harry's daughter had something to do with Pamela's death."

"What makes you say that?" Jackie asked.

"Oh, he watches too many of those forensic shows," Mary Alice said dismissively. "He's always trying to figure out who did it before the police do."

"And I usually have it right!" he said to his wife. Turning back to Jackie, and pointing at his phone he went on, "I looked through all those videos for Thursday night and who do you think should pull up just a little while after Harry left? Jessica! And she pulled right into the garage to make sure nobody saw her car parked there!"

"I'm not sure I'd read anything too sinister into that, Michael," Jackie said indulging what she saw as an overactive imagination fueled by too much "reality" TV. "She *is* Harry's daughter, so dropping in to visit wouldn't be too unusual I don't think." Trying to recall the few clips she had just seen on Michael's phone, she wasn't sure that he could even have known that she pulled into the garage with the bushes that obscured the view.

"But not if her father's not home," he replied. "She and Pamela hated each other."

Mary Alice interjected, "Oh, I think *hate* is a strong word."

"Maybe she didn't know he had left," Jackie offered.

"She pulled into the garage where his car should have been," Michael replied. "She *had* to know."

"Well, we certainly will check that out," Jackie said. "But aside from not liking each other very much and being there Thursday night, is there anything that would make you believe that Jessica could have had anything to do with Pamela's death? Had you ever overheard threats or anything?"

"Not recently, but when she was younger we heard a couple of good rows over there," Michael answered.

Mary Alice said, "She was a teenager, for God's sake! They're all like that."

"She has a temper, that one," Michael said to Jackie. "And no respect for elders. She and her brother and their friends were having a party in the front yard one time—I don't know where Harry and Pamela were. I asked her if they could turn down the music, and she said, 'If it bothers you, old man, get some earplugs; it's a free country.' Then she gave me the finger.

"I called Chief Booker—this was before your time," he went on. "He came out and got them to quiet it down, but ten minutes later it was back up and louder than before. She hated me after that. I'm pretty sure she keyed the side of my car."

"Interesting," Jackie said. "Well, as I said, we'll definitely look into her some more. Thank you for sharing that." She pointed to his phone, and added, "And for sharing that."

"All done, by the way," Marcia said as she slid the phone across the table to Michael. "Thank you."

In the Jeep on the way back to the station, Marcia asked, "So, what do you think of Mr. Timmons' theory on Jessica?"

"Normally, I might think that Michael was being a bit vindictive considering his history with Jessica, but given the anonymous phone tip I got about the two kids, it certainly warrants a closer look. It'll be interesting to see what the doorbell videos show."

At the station, Jackie opened Dropbox, and as Marcia transferred the videos into the case file, Jackie logged into the state's Registry of Motor Vehicles—RMV—database to find out what kind of car Jessica drove.

At her desk with Marcia beside her, Jackie opened the first of the saved videos. Its thirty-two-character file name—apparently randomly generated—gave no clue to when it was recorded so she had to open and close several until they got to the one showing Harry backing out of his driveway at the far left of the screen. She renamed it in the case folder as "Harry Leaving 7-27p" She had to use the dash in the time because it wouldn't accept a colon as part of the file name.

They opened and closed four more passing cars before they came to the clip that Michael was apparently talking about with Jessica pulling into the driveway. It had been triggered by a passing truck, but then twenty seconds into its one-minute and three-second length, another vehicle's headlights appeared at the left of the screen, moving slowly. Then, three cars in close succession passed by from right to left, blocking the view of the vehicle as it turned into the Fletcher's driveway. Because it was taller than the passing cars, however, Jackie and Marcia could see its roof make the turn. Then, just as Michael had said, they could see the light from the garage through the bushes, and then the roof of the car was gone. Seconds later, the door came down and blocked the light.

"It looks like Michael was right," Jackie said. "Jessica's car is a black 2018 Ford Explorer; I recognized the roofline."

"You memorize automotive rooflines?" Marcia asked. "Is that a hobby or was it preparation for this specific, completely random moment?"

Jackie laughed, and as she saved the clip as "Jessica Arrival 7-41p" she said, "No. The department owns five of them, so I've seen them a lot."

There were three more drive-bys, and then as the last car exited the image to the left, the backup lights on Jessica's truck appeared in the driveway. She backed out and drove off to the left. Jackie saved the video as "Jessica Leaving 8-07p"

After two more passing-car clips, at 8:38 Harry's car triggered the camera as it entered the view from the right. It turned into the driveway and stopped in front of the garage door, but the door didn't open. About thirty seconds later, the interior light came on as the car door opened, and Harry got out.

As Jackie was typing the new file name, "Harry Returns 8-38p," it occurred to her that that was much earlier than Harry had told her he had gotten home. She would need to check her notes and her recording, but she was almost sure he had said it was around 9:30.

Just as Jackie hit the save button, Marcia said, "I didn't think he got home until around 9:30; just a little before he called 911. This is about an hour before that, if I'm remembering the timeline right."

"I noticed the same thing," Jackie said.

The next video, at 8:59, was triggered by Harry's backup lights. He backed out into the road, and then drove off to the right, where he had come from.

Marcia and Jackie looked at one another with mutual *what-the-hell-is-going-on?* looks.

"Methinks we need to havith another talk with Harry," Jackie said.

"We concur," Marcia said. "Something seemith amiss."

Getting later in the evening, there was only one drive-by on the small back road, and then, at 9:30, Harry's car appeared again, crossed the screen, and turned into his driveway. They then watched the light come on and go out from the garage opening and closing.

Nine minutes later, a Rowley unmarked cruiser, with its hidden lights flashing from inside, pulled into the driveway and came to a stop.

"That would be Scott Lain," Jackie said, as she typed a new file name. With the lights flashing and washing out the image they couldn't see him go to the front door.

Four minutes after Scott arrived, the ambulance pulled in behind the cruiser. Six minutes after that, they could see the EMTs putting the gurney with Pamela strapped to it into the back.

In the next video, beginning at 9:53, they could make out the light from the garage when the door opened, and then watched the glow from Harry's taillights, backup lights, and headlights sweep back and forth as he maneuvered his car around the cruiser, finally backing onto the street and driving away.

There was another passing-car clip, where the vehicle slowed way down when they saw the still-flashing lights of the cruiser. Then, at 10:22, the lights stopped flashing, and they watched as Scott backed out onto the road and drove away.

Three minutes later, a car entered from the left, slowed to a near stop and pulled into Mary Alice and Michael's driveway as they got home from their daughter's.

There were two more drive-bys, and then at 10:59, they watched Harry's car pull into the driveway, but the garage didn't open and the car's lights never went off. After two minutes, the car backed out and drove off.

"That must have been when he was thinking about getting his .357," Marcia said.

"Probably," Jackie agreed. "I got home about ten past eleven, I think, and his car was in my driveway."

They kept going into Friday's videos with only one passing car until 4:41 a.m. when they watched Harry's car pull into the driveway and go into the garage. About six o'clock the drive-bys picked up as the morning commute began, but there was no more activity at the Fletcher house.

Looking down the list of video files that Jackie had created, Marcia said, "So, what does all that tell us?"

"That we need to talk to Jessica, and see what she was doing there," Jackie answered, "and to Harry to find out why he went home and then left, but didn't mention that to us."

"Tasks for tomorrow?" Marcia said as she looked at her watch. "I need to be heading home."

"Yeah. It'll give us time to digest this a little," Jackie said. "Plus, they've got the funeral tomorrow; I think we should leave them alone until after that."

After Marcia had left and as Jackie was closing her office door to leave, as well, her desk phone chirped with a call from Susan at the dispatch desk. Rather than go back in, she walked down the hall and into the communications room.

"I was just leaving," Jackie said to Susan, "What's up?"

"Kyle just called in," she said. "He went to Scott Lain's for the well-check, but he's not there."

"Did he say if he went inside?" Jackie asked.

"He said he did. Everything looks fine in the house and his truck's not in the garage. I've been calling his cell, but it goes right into voicemail like he has it turned off."

"Hmm," Jackie said. "Do we know if he has family or a girlfriend or anything where he might be?" Being relatively new to both the town and the force, Jackie didn't know him that well, yet.

"I don't offhand," Susan answered. "Would there be anything in his personnel file? Emergency contacts or something?"

"I'll take a look," Jackie said and headed back to her office.

She found numbers for his mother in Waltham and his sister in Derry, New Hampshire. His sister hadn't seen or heard from him in a year and seemed perfectly happy with that. His mother was a different story.

"I've been trying to reach him, too," she had said when Jackie explained why she was calling. There was obvious concern in her voice, and she went on, "We talk at least every other day. I'm ... I'm worried he might have tried to hurt himself, again."

*Hurt himself, again!* Jackie repeated to herself. "Scott tried to take his own life before?" she asked.

"When he was in his teens," his mother answered. "It was with pills; it was really just an overreaction to everything; the hospital only kept him overnight. We got him psychiatric care and he was fine after that."

*Psychiatric care!* Jesus, what else didn't she know about Scott? She scanned through his folder, and as she expected, nothing about a psych problem showed up anywhere.

"Why did Scott try to take his own life?" Jackie asked. "What was it an overreaction to?"

There was a slight pause, and then his mother said, "I'm a little surprised you don't know about this. I thought they did a background check of criminal records before someone could join the police."

*Criminal records?* Jackie said to herself. Then it clicked, and she said, "We do, but if he was underage at the time of the incident his case file could have been sealed by juvenile court when he turned eighteen. If he completed some court-ordered program, it could have been expunged altogether. Do you mind telling me what the incident was?"

"The girl next door accused him of watching her through her bedroom window, and of him standing in *his* window and masturbating when he knew she was looking," she answered. "The little tramp used to parade around in her room getting dressed with the shades open, so in his hormonally-charged pubescent mind, he thought she was coming on to him; he believed she wanted to have sex with him; wanted to be his girlfriend.

"Anyway, he admitted what he'd done and apologized, and his father and I said we'd get him counseling, but the girl and her parents refused to drop the matter and he was arrested. He was released into our custody after his booking, and when he got home is when he took the pills. We moved shortly after that. He was in therapy and on probation until he was eighteen. And now that you mention it, the judge did say that his record would be sealed after that."

"Do you know if he continued seeing a therapist after that?" Jackie asked.

"Yes. We paid for his sessions all the while that he lived with us," she said. "He moved out when he was twenty-one, but I think he continued, at least for a while."

"Okay. Thank you for sharing that with me, Mrs. Lain," Jackie said. "If you should hear from him, please give me a call."

"Is Scott in trouble over something?" his mother asked.

"He missed his shift and we haven't been able to reach him," Jackie answered honestly although incompletely. "We want to make sure he's okay; hasn't been in an accident or anything."

After hanging up, Jackie leaned back in her chair and thought about the conversation she had had with Scott over him not telling her about his relationship with Pamela. Withholding that information made much more sense, now. But now she was concerned that it might have triggered some drastic PTSD overreaction.

She left her office again and went back to the communications room.

"Any luck?" Susan asked.

"Not really," Jackie answered. "Would you put out a be-on-the-lookout request for his truck? Send it to our cruisers, of course, but the surrounding towns, too. Get its description and tag number from RMV."

"Okay," Susan said, obviously surprised by the request. "How far out do you want to go?"

Jackie thought for a moment, and answered, "Let's go out to Derry; he has a sister who lives there. Sweep a radius of the towns that far out." She knew a circle that size would include where his mother lived in Waltham, cover Boston, and reach up into southern Maine.

"Is there something wrong?" Susan asked.

"I hope not," Jackie said. "I hope it's just my motherly instinct overreacting."

# Chapter 22

**Friday, July 16, 2021**

Jackie was awakened a little before five by a crash of thunder that sounded like it was right above her house.

She got up and checked her phone to see if she had gotten any messages on the search for Scott's truck. There were none.

By the time she got out of the shower, twenty minutes later, the deluge that had followed the thunder had tapered off to merely a downpour. She turned on the TV news to see what the weather for Pamela's funeral in the afternoon was supposed to be. The cheery, twenty-something, stand-in meteorologist assured her viewers that the storm was passing through, and they could plan for a day of sunshine after about eight.

At the station, as much as she wanted to talk to Jessica and Harry about what she and Marcia had seen on Mary Alice and Michael's doorbell camera, she knew that the morning of Pamela's funeral was not the time to do it, so she immersed herself in the day to day business that had been backing up.

She was halfway through her first cup of coffee and her third file folder of paperwork when Carol rapped on her open door. "You got a minute, Chief?" she said.

"Sure," she answered as she initialed a comment on a complaint about an "unfair" traffic stop. "What's up?"

Carol stepped in and closed the door behind her.

"Should I be concerned?" Jackie asked.

"Well, I think I might have done a bad thing," Carol said a bit sheepishly. She quickly added, "But I did it for a good reason!"

Jackie motioned to her guest chair, and with a solemn expression, said, "I'm listening."

"Well, it seems that I might have made a second copy of Pamela's drive, and I might have taken it home to continue searching through," Carol said.

"You *might* have?" Jackie said.

"Actually, I'm pretty sure it was me," Carol replied. "Well, positive if you come right down to it. But I *did* find what I think is a clue!" she added quickly, "so that makes it kind of all right, right?"

Jackie gave a theatrical sigh, held out her hand, and said, "Give me your bullet, Barney."

Carol pouted, and as she fished into her shirt pocket, she said, "So, I'm fired?"

Jackie took the bullet, stood it on its end in the middle of her desk, and answered, "Probation. Tell me what *clue* you found and we'll see where it goes."

"I'm pretty sure that Pamela had narcolepsy," Carol said. "You know, where you just fall asleep while you're doing something?"

"Are you being serious, Carol?"

"Swear to God!" Carol said holding up her hand. "So, I thought maybe that could have something to do with her drowning in her tub, right? Maybe she had an attack and slid under the water."

"That wouldn't explain ..." Jackie caught herself realizing that Carol wasn't privy to the autopsy findings or even the circumstances of how Pamela was found. "... some of the coroner's findings," she finished. "But how did you find that out?"

"Well, I remembered one of those forensic shows where a computer tech ran a program against a suspect's computer looking anywhere for repeated words," Carol began feeling a little less on the carpet. "Naturally, he got like a zillion hits on words like *the, and, but,* and those kinds of things, but when he filtered through to the less common words he found that words like *hypodermic, cannula,* and *subcutaneous* had been searched a number of times shortly before the victim's death. They looked at the body again and managed to find needle marks inside a gash on the head that was caused by a fall, but that shouldn't have resulted in death. Another word that he found further down the list was *succinylcholine.* That's a paralyzing drug that can make it look like a person had a heart attack and ..."

"I know what it is," Jackie interrupted. "Extremely difficult to trace. You're not telling me that you think it was used to kill Pamela, are you?"

"No! No! That was in the forensic show," she answered. "Anyway, to make a long story short ..."

"Too late for *that*," Jackie interjected with a grin.

Carol laughed, and said, "Sorry. No one ever accused me of being a woman of few words." She pulled a slip of paper from her pocket and reading it, she went on, "Anyway, I found the words *narcolepsy*, *solriamfetol*—a.k.a *Sunosi*, and *pitolisant*—a.k.a. *Wakix* several times. When I searched them out, it looks like Pamela was trying to get into a clinical study of those drugs to treat narcolepsy."

"May I?" Jackie asked as she held out her hand for the slip. "I'm not seeing how narcolepsy would play into Pamela's death, but I'll send this to the ME to see if it was in her blood and if he thinks it could be a factor."

"So ... can I have my bullet back, Andy?" Carol asked attempting to lighten the severity of her *faux pas*.

Jackie picked it up and held it out, but before letting Carol take it, she said, "First, erase the second copy of her drive. I don't want anything to do with the case outside of the control of this department."

"Got it, Chief. Sorry," she said. "As soon as I get home."

"Second," Jackie went on, still holding the bullet, "No more doing things without asking permission and then begging for forgiveness afterward. I applaud your initiative, but if you have any more clever ideas, run them past me *first*."

"So you think I was clever?" Carol said.

"Don't push it, Barney," Jackie answered as she dropped the bullet into her hand.

After Carol left, Jackie called Dr. West at the ME's office and told him about the discovery that Pamela had narcolepsy, and what medications she was likely on for it. Like her, he didn't see how the disorder could play into the cause, manner, or mechanism of her death, but agreed to take a look at the drugs to see if an overdose or combined reaction with any other drug in her system could have been a possible contributor.

Before she left to go home and change for Pamela's funeral, Jackie checked with communications to see if there had been any word on

Scott. Nothing had come in, and the uneasy feeling she had gotten earlier became more disquieting.

## Chapter 23
### Friday, July 16, 2021

The service for Pamela was held in the First Congregational church in the center of Rowley, after which the mourners followed the hearse the half-mile to the cemetery. As best she could without openly staring, Jackie had tried to observe Harry, Aaron, and Jessica during the church service and at the graveside.

Both Harry and Aaron spoke about Pamela—wife, and mother respectively—and their remarks and demeanor were reverent and appropriate. Jessica did not get up to speak about her late stepmother, and in fact, seemed bored with the whole affair.

Following the interment, a reception was held back at the meeting hall of the church. When Jackie expressed her condolences in the receiving line, Aaron gave her a warm thank you, but Jessica barely acknowledged her words. Jackie was itching to ask her about being at Pamela's the night she died, but she held off out of respect for the situation.

Later, passing a small knot of women, Jackie overheard one of them comment, "… he let her go, but she was still wicked pissed at him for some reason. She had to have been DUI after the wine she put away that night."

The comment might barely have registered if Jackie hadn't just been reviewing a complaint against Scott Lain regarding an "irregular" traffic stop he had allegedly made. She hadn't heard Scott's name, but that the incident apparently took place at night, possibly during his overnight shift gave her good reason to want to find out more.

Jackie turned to see who was speaking, but as she did, a tap on her shoulder interrupted her and she turned to face an unsmiling Jessica.

"I hear you copied my dad's computer," she said without preamble. "What were you looking for? Did you think he'd be stupid enough to have acted out a murder plot that he wrote for one of his books?"

"It's due diligence, Jessica," Jackie replied evenly. "As the husband of the deceased and the person who found her, your father is automatically on the suspect list until he can be eliminated."

"Am I on your list?" Jessica asked.

"Yes, you are. As is Aaron and a number of others your stepmother was acquainted with," Jackie answered. "And since you've brought it up, I'd like to ask you some questions about the night that Pamela died. Would you mind coming in to the station sometime tomorrow?"

"Do I have a choice?"

"Yes. It's strictly voluntary," Jackie answered. In her mind, she added, "*For now.*"

"I'll think about it," Jessica said, and walked away.

Jackie stared at the retreating Jessica for a few moments, and when she turned she found Harry walking toward her. He was motioning that they step outside.

"So, did you find anything incriminating on my computer?" he asked once alone. "Aside from a dozen different ways to kill a person and either make it look like an accident or how to dispose of the body?"

"Yes, but none involving a bathtub and strangulation," Jackie answered with a smile. "No, probably the most curious thing I found out was that Pamela had narcolepsy. Not that I could see how it might be a factor in her death, it's just curious that you never mentioned it."

He looked at her peculiarly for a moment, and then said, "I never mentioned it because Pamela didn't *have* narcolepsy; I do. What made you think Pamela did?"

"All of the searches about medications and treatments on her drive," Jackie answered. "Was she looking things up for you? Was she trying to get you into a clinical trial of a couple of new drugs?"

"You found that on *Pamela's* computer?" he said, obviously perplexed. "*I* made those searches and contacts with the drug companies." Then the answer occurred to him. "That was back in February, right?" he said. "My computer was having some motherboard problem, and I was using Pamela's while Carol fixed mine. I'm sure you can confirm that with her if you need to."

It hadn't occurred to Jackie to ask Carol when the searches had taken place, but Harry's explanation seemed perfectly logical.

"Well, the medication must be working," Jackie said. "I'd never have guessed that about you."

"The drugs help, but a lot of it is lifestyle management," he replied. "If I stay focused and busy I'm fine. And, naturally, I try to avoid known triggers."

"You've never had a problem driving?" she asked, imagining him falling asleep at the wheel.

"Never. As I said, I just need to stay focused. And some researchers say that for some people there seems to be a survival component where your subconscious or something blocks an attack if you're in a life-and-death situation like walking down stairs or driving.

"I have what's called secondary narcolepsy," he went on. "It was caused by a brain injury from a motorcycle accident in my twenties, rather than being congenital. I don't exhibit all of the classical symptoms, and have a few atypical ones."

Shifting subjects, Harry then said, "I saw you talking with Jessica. She went ballistic when I told her you had made copies of our computer drives."

"Yeah, I got that," Jackie said. "I've also heard that she and Pamela were not very close. Was that always the case being the step-daughter? Or did something specific trigger it along the way?"

"I guess it was always there to some extent," he said. "She resented someone trying to take the place of her real mother, which is probably natural, but wasn't really the case at all. Pamela never tried to assume that role. She was okay with Jessica calling her Pamela rather than Mom, and any discipline was left strictly up to me. I tried to get her to warm up to her, but the older she got—especially in her early teens—the worse it got. Jessica is a bit of a rebel by nature."

"Would you say that Jessica hated Pamela?" Jackie asked.

Harry let out a sigh, and answered, "By the time she moved out, probably yes. Enough to kill her?—if that's where you're going—no. She was out of the house; they had very little contact."

"It doesn't sound like Jessica would just drop by to visit Pamela, then," Jackie said.

"She rarely drops by to see *me*, and she *likes* me," he replied.

"How about Aaron? How did he get along with her?" Jackie asked.

"With Jessica or his mother?"

"Both, I guess."

"Aaron and Jessica are quite close considering they're not actually brother and sister," Harry said. "I thought it was great when they were young, but when they both entered puberty with all of its mysteries and curiosities I thought maybe they were *too* close. Not being blood-related, I was concerned that they might end up as boyfriend and girlfriend on some level if you know what I mean. I don't think anything ever happened in that regard, though. But Jessica sure did give Aaron some tips on how to attract *other* girls. I think she set him up with nearly every one of her girlfriends at one point or another. It seems like she got as much thrill from him cutting notches in his bedpost as he did."

"Is Jessica misogynistic?" Jackie asked. "That seems an odd way to treat your friends, pimping them to your step-brother."

"Does she hate women? Oh, no, it was nothing like that. She just likes to be manipulative. It gives her a thrill to get someone to do something they said they didn't want to do. And she's quite good at it."

"And how did Aaron get along with his mother?" Jackie asked.

"I would have to call that relationship about average," he answered. "It had its ups and downs over the years as Aaron went through his different growing-up phases, but they had a pretty good bond in the end."

"Did that bother Jessica, at all?" Jackie asked. "She being so close to her step-brother while he was close to someone she hated?"

He thought for a moment, and then said, "Not that I ever picked up on."

"How do you and Aaron get along as step-father and step-son?" Jackie asked.

"Good," he replied. "I don't think it would have been any different if we shared DNA. He always called me Dad, and I always referred to him as my son. Neither of us ever threw the *step* in there. Jessica, on the other hand, referred to Pamela as *my father's second wife*."

"When you and Pamela married," Jackie asked, "did you legally adopt one another's kids?"

"Actually, no," he said. "There's a trust that Aaron will get access to when his real father passes away, but it has a proviso that if he was to be adopted by any other man and took that person's name, he loses it. Being his only son, apparently he wanted to protect his lineage.

"Our lawyer said that the way it was written—because of the placement of a semicolon—that I *could* adopt Aaron and as long as he didn't also take my name the proviso didn't kick in. But we decided not to take that legal-technicality risk. And it didn't seem to make much sense to adopt Jessica but not Aaron. Pamela and I always treated them—or at least tried to—like we were all one natural family. *Brady Bunch* on a micro-scale."

Another guest approached to talk to Harry, and Jackie excused herself to go in search of Brenda Sloan, the woman who had been telling the story about Pamela getting stopped and let go.

She found her filling a cup from the coffee urn and when she approached, Brenda said, "Oh, hi, Jackie. That was a lovely service, wasn't it? And there's so many people here to pay their respects. She certainly was loved, wasn't she?" Without letting Jackie respond to any of those statements, she asked in a more hushed tone, "So, how is the investigation going? Do you have any suspects?" It was how one had a conversation with Brenda; you did a lot of listening.

"Well, I really can't talk about the investigation. I'm sure you understand," Jackie answered. "But, yes, this is a wonderful turnout for her, and I was really moved by Harry's and Aaron's words. I was a little surprised that Jessica didn't say anything, though."

"Harry probably made sure she didn't!" Brenda said. "She and Pamela did *not* get along very well." She suddenly put her hand to her mouth, and said, "Oh, my! Is *Jessica* a suspect?"

"Would you think she should be?" Jackie asked in reply.

"Well, I saw you talking to her earlier, and as I said, they didn't get along," she answered. "Pamela said they'd had some pretty heated arguments."

"Did she ever mention any physical altercations? Did Jessica ever strike her that you're aware of? Or threaten her?"

"No. I don't recall her ever saying anything like that," Brenda said.

Seeing a segue to get to the subject of the traffic stop, Jackie said, "I happened to overhear you a little while ago, saying that Pamela was really angry about something," Jackie said leaving out much of what she'd heard. "What was that all about? Was that something that Jessica did?"

"Oh, no," Brenda answered. "That was about ..." She stopped, thought for a moment, and then went on, "I probably wouldn't say anything about this normally, but since she's passed, I guess it doesn't really matter, now, does it?"

"Whatever it is, probably not," Jackie said.

In a quieter, conspiratorial tone, Brenda continued, "Well, Scott Lain pulled her over on her way home from a book club meeting at my house, and she *had* to be under the influence; I think she had finished almost a whole bottle of cab all by herself in the course of the night. Most of the others drink white—chardonnay usually—except Joyce; she always has a martini. But, anyway, then he just let her go without even a warning."

"What the heck would have made her angry about *that*?" Jackie asked.

"Right?" Brenda agreed. "Hell, I'd have kissed him, and I think he's creepy!"

"So, you don't know what she was upset about? She never mentioned that?" Jackie asked.

"Nope. Maybe she was just angered that he pulled her over, at all," Brenda offered. "She said she was driving perfectly when his lights started flashing behind her. She wasn't speeding, she wasn't swerving. There was no way he could have known she'd been drinking."

Jackie just nodded at that suggestion, knowing that drunk drivers rarely realized how badly they were driving, and some even claimed to drive better while drinking *because they were more relaxed*.

"When did you say this took place?" Jackie asked.

"The first Thursday of the month," Brenda answered. "That's always when our meetings are. So, that would be ..."

"*This* month?" Jackie said allowing more surprise in her voice than she intended. Scott had told her that he hadn't had any contact with Pamela in *six* months.

If Jackie's surprise registered with Brenda she didn't react to it. "Yeah," she said. "So, that would be the first, right?"

"Yes. July first," Jackie agreed. "Do you know about what time it would have been?"

"We usually break up just about ten," Brenda answered, "so probably about quarter past?"

Jackie's mind raced to put meaning to this new information. Had Scott let Pamela go because of their past relationship? If he had stopped her for a DUI that would certainly be unacceptable. She needed to check to see if he had logged the stop as he was supposed to even if the result was a verbal warning, but she somehow doubted it. She was beginning to see, more and more, that her confidence in Scott had been misplaced. When he eventually came back to work, there was a whole shopping list of things they needed to talk about. Lying about his criminal history, alone, could be cause for immediate dismissal.

"So, is Scott going to be in trouble over that?" Brenda asked.

"Well, I certainly need to talk to him about it," Jackie said. "From what you've told me it's irregular and I need to know his side of things since Pamela can't tell us."

Set to silent, Jackie's phone vibrated in her pocket, and as she took it out she excused herself from Brenda. The call was junk, but she checked her messages and seeing nothing new from the station, she called in and asked if there was any news on Scott. There was none. Jackie was becoming as much concerned *for* him as *about* him at this point.

From across the room, Jackie watched Aaron talking with a small group of family members and friends. She wanted to talk to him, as well, but knew that this wasn't the time or place. She decided to leave, and she found Harry and said her goodbyes, but didn't see Jessica anywhere. When she looked, Aaron was not with his group any longer, either.

As she headed across the parking lot Aaron appeared from beside a car, tossed his cigarette away, and fell in beside her. "You want to talk to me, too?" he asked. From his phrasing, she guessed that he had probably talked to his sister about her earlier conversation with Jackie.

"I would, yes," she said. "When it's convenient. I know this isn't a good time."

"Jessica said that she and I and my Dad are all suspects. Is that true?" he asked.

Jackie stopped and answered, "People of interest. But you're hardly alone on that list. We've eliminated probably half the people that we started with because they had solid alibis. That's why I'd like to talk to you and Jessica. I'd just as soon scratch you from the list, too. I'm not trying to harass anyone, but somebody murdered your stepmother, and it's my job to find out who. I assume you want to know that, too."

"Do you want me to come to the station tomorrow, too?" he asked.

"Can I give you a call tomorrow with a good time?" Jackie replied.

"You don't want me and Jessica there at the same time, huh?"

"We only have one interview room," she answered. "One of you would have to cool your heels in the lobby. I'm trying to make it as convenient for you as I can."

"You have my number?" he asked.

"I do," she said. "Thanks for your cooperation, Aaron."

"I'll talk to Jessica," he said. "I'll make sure she comes in to talk with you."

"I appreciate that," Jackie said, wondering if the two of them were playing good-sibling, bad-sibling for some reason.

# Chapter 24

**Friday, July 16, 2021**

Jackie went home and changed out of her funeral attire and back into her uniform. She then went back to the station.

She opened up Scott's shift log for the night of July 1 and the morning of July 2. He had not logged any traffic stops between one for excessive speed on Rt. 1 near the Rowley/Newbury town line at 9:35 and a failure-to-stop at 11:08 at the intersection of 133 and 1A. The stops were at opposite ends of the town, but left plenty of time to have stopped Pamela between Brenda's house on Bennett Hill Rd. and Pamela's on Weldon Farm Rd.

If she had heard the story a couple of weeks ago—before Scott's spate of lying—she'd have been more inclined to believe that it was a gossip-exaggerated rendition of something relatively innocent. She would still have talked to Scott about it, but she'd have started out giving him the benefit of the doubt. That had certainly turned around, now.

She called the dispatch desk and asked one more time if anything had come in on Scott. In her gut, she knew it was a waste of time because they would certainly have called *her* if it had.

Forcing Scott's puzzling behavior out of her mind for a while, Jackie switched her focus to Pamela's investigation.

She ran an internal search for any police reports regarding Jessica or Aaron. The only reference to Aaron was in 2013 when Chief Booker had taken away his two-month-old driver's license because he pushed the yellow light in front of the Agawam just a little too far and entered the intersection on the red. In typical Booker fashion, he didn't cite him and didn't report the incident to the Mass. RMV. Instead, he held his license for two weeks during which time he had Aaron write a report on the dangers of red-light running. When he and his step-father came to the station with the report, Booker gave Aaron an impromptu verbal quiz from the RMV license-test book. Only then did he give him his license back.

Jessica was another matter.

Her name showed up first in Booker's report on the noise incident that Michael Timmons had described, but then in several other minor-disturbance calls, which were all to other residences where Jackie assumed the kids she hung out with probably lived. But there was also one at the Richdale convenience store when the clerk accused the group of shoplifting. No formal charges were filed in that case.

From the time she got her license, Jessica's name popped up more frequently. When she was stopped for traveling fifty-three in a thirty-five zone, she laughingly brushed it off by saying that she had dyslexia and thought the speed limit *was* fifty-three. Booker nonetheless had tried the same unofficial-license-suspension tactic that had worked on Aaron, but with much poorer results. The report she had turned in on the dangers of excessive speed consisted of one paragraph, and Booker noted in her file that he knew for a fact that she had continued to drive without her license.

Because he had decided to take the unofficial path, Booker didn't try to reinstate the original speeding charge even though she had not complied with his conditions. He didn't need to; he knew she was going to be committing plenty of new infractions.

There followed a virtual shopping list of citations including speeding, red-light running, passing in a no-passing zone, excessive speed in a school zone, illegal lane change, failure to yield to oncoming traffic, failure to stop at a stop sign, and aggressive driving.

Considering that Massachusetts didn't have a traffic-school-alternative to avoid insurance increases and penalties on your license as many states did, Jackie wondered how Jessica still had her license ... and what her insurance premium must be.

Although all of the traffic violations certainly told Jackie something about Jessica's don't-give-a-damn attitude toward authority, they said nothing about her personality regarding confrontations and possible violent behavior. But she had an idea who might know more about that side of her.

From her contacts list, Jackie put in a call to Lori Keller, the Principal's Administrative Assistant at Triton Regional High School.

Triton was a regional public high school that served the small towns of Newbury, Rowley, and Salisbury. At Lori's invitation, Jackie had spoken at the school several times on drug and alcohol awareness, among other things.

"Hi, Lori," Jackie said when she picked up. "Jackie Hall here. Do you have a few minutes to talk?"

"Oh, hi Jackie! Sure, just let me send this email; give me ten seconds," she replied. Jackie heard some keyboard clicking, and then, "Okay, done! So, how have you been? What's up?"

"I'm well. Busy, but well. How about you?"

"Aches and pains I'm sure you didn't call to talk about," Lori answered. "What's on your mind?"

"I'm wondering if you can tell me something about Jessica Fletcher," Jackie said. "What kind of student she was; did she ever get into trouble; how did she get along with others; that sort of thing."

"On or off the record?" Lori said. "I'm assuming this has to do with her stepmother's death."

"Off," Jackie replied. "I'm just trying to get my head around everyone close to her. Trying to fill in background detail, you know?"

"Well, if I had to come up with a list of ten students that I wish went to some other school, she'd be on it," Lori said. "Her grades were very good—which I think involved some amount of cheating—but she was a troublemaker."

"How so?" Jackie asked. "Was she disruptive? Prone to fighting? You mentioned cheating; did she get caught doing that?"

"Often suspected; never proven as far as cheating went," Lori said. "She was prone to being *around* fights," she went on. "She was an instigator. She seemed to like to egg others on to get into some altercation—verbal or physical—that she could watch from the sidelines. I think she got some perverse thrill seeing other people going at it or getting into trouble."

"I've heard the word *manipulative* used," Jackie said.

"Oh, yes!" Lori agreed. "That girl could talk others into just as much trouble as she could talk her own way out of."

"How about her step-brother, Aaron?" Jackie asked.

"Almost no trouble at all in his four years. About as opposite to her as you could get, at least on the surface," Lori answered.

"On the surface?"

"A couple of teachers assumed that Aaron was involved in Jessica's suspected cheating—oddly similar answers; getting the same questions wrong in the same way. But they couldn't even prove that she *was* cheating, much less that he was part of it," Lori said. "Their math teacher mentioned the coincidences to Jessica one time, and she just said, 'We study together; what do you expect?'"

"Do you think Jessica was controlling Aaron, too? Manipulating him like she did others?"

"Hmm. Interesting question," Lori said. "I can't say that it ever crossed my mind that that might be the case. I never noticed anything that would suggest that, but I wasn't around them as much as their teachers. Do you want me to ask around?"

"No. Let's keep this between you and me, okay?" Jackie answered. "I'm just trying to get a feel for her personality for when I talk to her."

After goodbyes with Lori, Jackie opened the folder of doorbell video files and played them through, trying to imagine a scenario that would make all of the pieces fit.

She watched all the way from when Harry first left the house at 7:27 until he left again, following the ambulance to the hospital at 9:49. Returning to the first clip, she took out her legal pad, and made notes as she watched them, again.

> Harry leaves 7:27: Pamela alive as she made call to Aaron (verify).
>
> Jessica arrives 7:41: Tipped off by Aaron that Harry was gone? Could he be with her?
>
> Jessica leaves 8:07: 26 minutes to kill Pamela and stage scene in tub; easier with two.
>
> Harry returns 8:38: Bizarre! Harry involved in conspiracy with kids?
>
> Harry leaves 8:59: What did he do for 21 minutes?
>
> Harry returns 9:30: Harry "discovers" Pamela; calls 911.

Scott arrives in cruiser 9:39: Received call from dispatch at 9:35; 4-min response.

EMTs arrive 9:43: 8-min response.

EMTs leave 9:49: 6-min turnaround.

Harry leaves for hospital 9:53: 4-min behind Pamela.

Scott leaves 10:22: 29 minutes to take photos and clean up.

Harry arrives 10:59; leaves at 11:02: Enough time to go inside?

Harry arrives 4:41 a.m. Fri: After spending night at my house.

She looked at her coffee cup, which was three-quarters empty, and then at her watch. 3:15; one more cup. She wanted to step away from her notes and the videos for a few minutes, anyway, to let her thoughts incubate a little bit.

Ten minutes later, with a full coffee cup and after a conversation with Kyle Hopkins—the officer who had done the well-check on Scott, she got back to her desk.

As she sipped and read through her notes a couple of times to get a flow of events going in her head, a question popped up, and on her computer, she opened the file of notes that she and Marcia had put together from Pamela's cell phone records. There was one time-stamped call in particular that she was looking for, and when she found it, it fit perfectly with the scenario she was evolving in her mind.

Interrupting her train of thought, her desk phone rang with a call from Sharon. Hopeful that it was news about Scott, she picked it up, answering simply, "Yes?"

"Marcia Grieves is on the line," Sharon said. "Would you like me to put her through?"

"Yes. Thank you." The phone clicked, and then Jackie said, "Hi, Marcia. What's up?"

"I'm curious how the funeral went," she said. "I wanted to be there, but we had a big meeting here right after lunch."

"Well-attended, that's for sure," Jackie answered. "Pamela had a lot of friends."

"Did any of her CNM partners show up?"

"I wondered the same thing," Jackie said. "I only know what a few of them look like and I know *they* weren't there. But there *were* a couple of men that I didn't recognize, but they could easily have just been out-of-town family. I wanted to ask how they knew the deceased, but I got tied up in conversations and they were gone by the time I broke free."

"Bummer," Marcia said. "I don't suppose you were taking pictures."

Jackie chuckled, and said, "That might have been more acceptable if it had been a wedding and not a funeral. But let me tell you about those conversations." She then outlined the confrontational exchange she had had with Jessica, her talk with Harry about how the kids got along with Pamela, the curious and concerning discourse with Brenda about Scott, and the conciliatory chat with Aaron.

Jackie then told Marcia about Jessica's Rowley police record and the conversation she had with Lori Keller about her high school days.

"Wow!" Marcia said. "Personality-wise, it sounds like Jessica is edging her way up the person-of-interest list."

"Exactly," Jackie replied. "So, I've been going through the videos from the Timmons' doorbell cam, and I have a scenario. Do you have a few minutes that I can run it by you?"

"Sure! Go ahead!"

Using the notes on her pad to trigger the events as she imagined them unfolding, Jackie began, "So, just about 7:30 Harry leaves the house. A few minutes later, Pamela makes a call to Aaron's cell phone, presumably to tell him not to drop by."

"Okay. I remember talking about that," Marcia agreed.

"But what if Pamela didn't make that call?" Jackie said. "What if Harry took her phone and called Aaron to tell him the coast was clear?"

"You have Harry conspiring with the kids to kill Pamela?" Marcia asked, her shock obvious.

"I know," Jackie said. "But hear me out; there's a lot of pieces to the puzzle. And I'd like to get cell tower locations on Pamela's and Aaron's phones to verify this of course."

"I can do that," Marcia said. "I just went through it with Steven Collins."

"Oh, good. Thank you. So, anyway, about twenty minutes later, Jessica arrives and pulls right into the garage. There's no way to know, of course, but I'm guessing that Aaron is with her. If Pamela heard the garage door, she would probably have thought it was Harry coming back for some reason. Even if she went to look, it was just the two kids. A surprise maybe, but nothing to put her on any kind of alert, so overpowering her would be easy. I'm envisioning Aaron holding her while Jessica administers the neck pinch to knock her out and kill her."

"Wow! That's cold-blooded," Marcia said.

"Well, *somebody* has ice-water in their veins, we *know* that much," Jackie said. "The task is figuring out who." She went on, "Jessica doesn't pull back out of the driveway for twenty-six minutes so there's plenty of time for them to kill Pamela and stage the bathtub scene. And it would be so much easier with two people."

"Maybe even *too much* time," Marcia said. "If I was going to do something like that I think I'd want to get in and get out."

"Maybe they had to have some conversation with her before they could get the drop on her," Jackie suggested. "Maybe there was a confrontation; she *did* scratch somebody."

"Maybe she was in the shower when they showed up and they waited for her to come out," Marcia suggested, getting more onboard.

"If she was expecting a partner to show up, that would make sense," Jackie replied. "Which is a serious black hole in all of this. Who was he, and why *didn't* he show up?"

"Or maybe he did!" Marcia suggested. "Isn't the next video of Mr. Fletcher returning home?"

"Yeah, at 8:38," Jackie answered looking at her notes.

"And didn't you tell me that your boyfriend Jeff and Mr. Fletcher have the same type of car and that you mistook one for the other one time?" Marcia asked.

"You think *Jeff* killed Pamela?" Jackie asked in disbelief.

"No, no, no!" Marcia replied. "I'm saying that Mr. Fletcher's car is common enough that maybe it wasn't him that pulled in at 8:38."

"That would be a pretty bizarre coincidence," Jackie said, "but certainly not impossible, I guess. The fact is that I don't have anything to explain why Harry came back. I was thinking that maybe he wanted to bring her cell phone back so it was in the house when she was discovered, but if *he* was going to discover her later on, why not wait until then?"

"Maybe her partner was supposed to discover her," Marcia offered. "Maybe he drove up just as Mr. Fletcher was pulling in and he decided to pass on by and pass on his evening with Mrs. Fletcher."

"Possible," Jackie said. "But why would Harry have been in the house for twenty-one minutes just to bring a phone back? And if he knew—or expected—that Pamela's partner was coming by, wasn't his timing a little precarious? I mean why wait more than half an hour after Jessica pulled away before going back?"

"He was supposedly with Megan Hope, right?" Marcia said. "Maybe he was in the middle of playing footsies with her and couldn't break away."

"That's interesting," Jackie said. "I'd forgotten about that. Megan said he was with her until nine o'clock, I think. Was she lying to back up his alibi? Could she be part of the whole thing?"

"Wow! We're getting quite a cast of characters here," Marcia said.

"Yeah," Jackie agreed. "It's almost getting too complex to be plausible. The number of people involved; the precise—or the incredibly lucky—timing. It's like an Agatha Christy novel."

"You know what else it's like?" Marcia said. "It's like drawing targets all over a barn door with bullet holes already in it."

Jackie laughed, and said, "You're right. There's no actual evidence to support *any* of that except video clips that show cars coming and going whose license plates we can't read and whose occupants we can't see."

"It would be hard to call that even *circumstantial* evidence," Marcia agreed. "But as long as we're playing make-believe here, how about this? Jessica shows up at the house a short time after her father leaves. Maybe that's planned or maybe it's a coincidence; it probably doesn't matter. Anyway, Jessica and her step-mom get into an argument that escalates and she strangles her in a fit of rage.

"When she realizes what she's done," Marcia went on, "she calls her father. Blood being thicker than marriage vows, he tells her to take off and establish an alibi for herself somewhere. He then goes home and stages the bathtub accident. Then he leaves to establish *his* alibi with Megan."

"You've been thinking about this, haven't you?" Jackie said with a laugh.

"More than a little," Marcia answered. "I think those videos are etched into my retinas."

"That's ice-cold for Harry, and once again, it puts Megan in the middle of it," Jackie said. "I just went in and checked my notes, and Megan swears that Harry was with her from quarter to eight until nine o'clock."

"What if that's not a lie?" Megan asked. "What if she went with him to stage the scene? Like you said, that would be a lot easier with two people."

"So, now we need to check the alibi's alibi," Jackie said. "And I sure hope that Jessica and Aaron aren't each other's only alibis."

"You said they're both coming to the station to talk tomorrow?" Marcia said.

"Aaron said *he* was and that he'd try to get his sister to," Jackie replied.

"Well, being Saturday, I won't be tied to the office here," Marcia said. "I'd really like to be there for those interviews. I have a family dinner later on, but aside from that, I'm free."

"I'll make sure to save you a muffin," Jackie replied. "See you in the morning."

After hanging up, Jackie opened Harry's cell phone record—which they had not gone through in the same detail as Pamela's—and found one incoming call at 7:36—inside the timeframe between when he had left the house and when Jessica had arrived. But it wasn't from Jessica; it was from Aaron.

To refresh her memory, she then opened Pamela's phone records. She had sent the thumbs-up emoji to Aaron at 6:23—an hour before Harry left. Then, at 7:32, five minutes after Harry pulled away,

Pamela—or someone using her phone—made a call to Aaron. Four minutes later Harry received a call from Aaron.

As flimsy a piece of evidence as it was, it tended to support her hypothesis that Harry had tipped the kids off that he was gone and that they were all acting together. It would have been so much better if they had been text messages so she'd know what was said.

She texted Marcia and asked her to get Aaron and Jessica's phone records. Even without texts, phone communication between all three in the right timeframe could imply some kind of mutual involvement. It would not be enough to make an arrest, of course—or even a serious accusation—but it would be a direction to follow.

# *Chapter 25*

**Saturday, July 17, 2021**

Jackie pulled into the station parking lot heading west on Haverhill St. and Marcia pulled in right behind her coming from the opposite direction.

Inside, they went to the break room, and as Jackie filled her coffee cup Marcia split a blueberry muffin down the middle. On the way to her office, Jackie poked her head into the dispatch room, and asked simply, "Anything?"

"Sorry, Chief," Gail replied. "Nothing."

As they sat down on opposite sides of Jackie's desk, Marcia's cell phone chirped its new-mail sound. She looked, and then said, "Well, that was fast. It's the kids' phone records."

"Apparently, you know how the system works, now," Jackie said.

"Apparently. So, you want to open my email and download this to the server?"

"On it," Jackie said after she set her cup down on its warmer.

A few minutes later they were on the same side of the desk and looking at the familiar format of phone records. They started with Aaron's call logs and their search was greatly simplified this time as they were only looking at a few-hour time span, not two years,

They quickly found the emoji text from Pamela at 6:23, then the call from her phone at 7:32. The next item was the call to Harry's number at 7:36. Then things began to go sideways for the three-way conspiracy theory.

At 7:51 Aaron called Jessica. The call lasted thirty-one seconds. Three minutes later, Jessica called Aaron. That conversation lasted two minutes and eleven seconds.

"Why would they be calling each other if they were in the house together?" Marcia asked.

"My thought exactly," Jackie said.

Forty-eight seconds later Aaron made a call to a new number. Jackie clicked it and saw the recipient was George Sweeny, from Rowley.

"George is a guy about the kid's age," Jackie said. "Little bit of a troublemaker, but no criminal record that I'm aware of."

Aaron's next call was to Diane Short. "Again, about their age," Jackie told Marcia. "I know her parents, but have never had the occasion to even talk to her."

After four more similar calls in ten minutes, Marcia said, "It sounds like he's trying to get a party together. You think he's trying to set up an alibi?"

Jackie clicked the box to shrink Aaron's phone records, and said, "Let's look at his sister's activity." She opened Jessica's log and arranged hers and Aaron's side by side.

They found the two calls between them, then, like Aaron, Jessica seemed to be calling friends one after the other. A few of the calls had the siblings on their respective phones at the same time.

"Kind of odd behavior if you're in the middle of murdering your mother," Marcia observed.

"If it's setting up an alibi, that would require cold-blooded planning to the n-th degree," Jackie agreed as she sat back and looked at her computer screen hoping for something like a pattern to pop out.

"When did you say they were coming in?" Marcia asked.

"I didn't; I don't know," Jackie answered. "I don't even know *if*."

Just then, Jackie's desk phone chirped. She pressed a button, and said, "Yes?" hoping it was news about Scott.

"Chief, Jessica Fletcher is here to see you," Sharon replied. She then added, "Nothing on Scott."

"Could you bring her into the interview room, please? And thanks for the update on Scott," she told Sharon. She turned to Marcia, and said, "Speak of angels and hear wings flapping."

Marcia laughed, and said, "You're giving her the benefit of the doubt there. I might have gone with *Speak of the devil*."

"Open mind! Open mind!" Jackie said as she got up.

"Should I sit in?" Marcia asked getting to her feet.

"How about if you watch and listen from here?" Jackie said as she switched her monitor to the camera in the interview room. "I think she's already going to be a bit contrary. I'm afraid she might get downright antagonistic if she thinks she's being ganged up on. If you need to interject anything, text my phone."

They watched on the screen as Sharon ushered Jessica into the interview room, then heard her say, "Chief Hall will be in in just a minute. Can I get you anything? Water? Coffee? Soda?"

"You have a Diet Coke?" Jessica asked.

"Is diet Pepsi okay?" Sharon replied.

"Hardly!" she scoffed. "Water, thanks."

Sharon left the room and Jessica looked around at her surroundings. She found the three cameras, looking into each of them for a few moments before sitting back in her chair, seemingly bored.

"Oh, this'll be fun," Jackie said sarcastically. "Little Miss Attitude." She picked up her tablet and headed out the door.

Half a minute later, Marcia watched her enter the interview room carrying a bottle of water.

Jackie put the bottle on the table and slid it in front of Jessica as she took her seat opposite her.

"Thank you for coming in, Jessica," Jackie said. "I'm sure that you …"

"Let's just get on with it, okay?" she interrupted. "Skip the pleasantries, because this isn't pleasant. What do you want to know?" She unscrewed the top from the bottle and took a long drink.

"Okay," Jackie said. "What were you doing at your father's house the night that Pamela was murdered?"

"Really, Hall? That's the best you've got?" Jessica replied with a slight laugh. "You're running your big-bluff on the very first hand? I *wasn't* there and I can prove it."

Jackie flipped open her tablet, and as she brought it up on the screen, she said, "I have video of you arriving at your father's house at 7:41 that evening, and pulling right into the garage. You stayed for twenty-six minutes, and then left." She turned the tablet for Jessica to see and started the clip. She watched her face closely for the expected shocked expression. She was disappointed.

"That's from old man Timmons', isn't it?" Jessica said calmly. "It figures the paranoid old bastard would have a spy camera."

Both Jackie and Marcia found it telling that Jessica didn't deny that the video showed her pulling into the garage, but skirted the question by bringing up Mr. Timmons. Their satisfaction didn't last long, however.

"And that's not my car, Hall," Jessica went on. "I do have a black Explorer, but it has a roof-rack for all my camping shit. It won't even fit in my father's garage. It's right out front if you'd care to check."

This time Jessica watched Jackie for a reaction. When she blinked in surprise, Jessica said, "Brilliant detective work, Hall. While you've got your head up your ass the real killer could be *walking* to fucking Canada!"

Quickly recovering, Jackie said, "I will check. If it's an add-on rack, that makes it a removable rack, doesn't it?"

"Jesus!" Jessica said, rolling her eyes. "Well, lucky for me, I don't wash the beast very often. You'll find a nice, undisturbed layer of crap around all of the mounting brackets."

"So, if you weren't at your father's house that night, where were you?"

Jessica laughed, and said, "That was a quick end to your opening volley. I was at a party at Aaron's with eight or ten witnesses who can attest to me being there all night."

Jackie took a pad and a pen from the drawer of the table and slid them across to Jessica. "Write down the names for me, please."

She pushed the pad back, and said, "You write them down if you don't think you can remember them." She pointed up at one of the cameras, and added, "Or you can check your video. That's been real handy for you, so far, huh?"

Then, counting on her fingers as she went, she began reciting names. "There was Diane Short, George Sweeny, Susan Parsons and her brother Todd. Tim Landry, Dave Kilgore ..." She continued until she used up all her fingers and started over with her thumb, again. "And

Aaron, of course. But he probably doesn't count as a witness because he's on your suspect list, too, right? If you need their phone numbers, I'm sure you can get them."

Jackie recognized every one of the names from Aaron's and Jessica's phone records. That didn't make her feel good, but it didn't mean her theory was completely wrong, either. It could be a very elaborate alibi scheme.

Just then Jackie's phone vibrated. She looked and saw a text from Marcia. "Roof rack checks out."

"Message from your County DA friend watching all this?" Jessica said. "Did she go out and look at my truck?" Without waiting for an answer she got up, and said, "I'm done, Hall. Unless you're going to charge me with something, I'd like to leave."

"You can go," Jackie said as she stood up. "But don't go too far. I might have some more questions after I talk to your friends."

"You mean like don't leave town?" Jessica said sarcastically. "Or what? You'll arrest me?"

"Yes. You have an outstanding bench warrant from Haverhill District Court for failure-to-appear on an excessive-speed violation," Jackie said. "I suggest you get in touch with them Monday and see if you can get that straightened out. If you get pulled over, the next cop might not be as benevolent as I am."

After walking Jessica out, Jackie went back to her office where Marcia had vacated her chair and was once again on the other side of the desk.

"Well, that blows more holes in our theories than there are bullet holes in that barn door we've been drawing targets on," Marcia said. "It's a good thing they're in chalk so they're easy to erase."

"It certainly didn't do much to support them," Jackie said dropping into her chair. "But I do want to talk to at least some of those people from the party. What if Aaron wasn't with Jessica at Pamela's like I imagined, but stayed at the party while Jessica left to do the deed? He could have covered for her for the half-hour or so in case anyone was looking for her."

"Possible, I guess," Marcia said. "But I can tell you without much doubt that the roof rack on her SUV hasn't been off in a long time.

There's dirt in the corners around all the brackets, and the heads of the screws are all filled with dirt, too. I think they take an Allen wrench, but I don't know that you could get one *in* any of them."

"Could it have been smeared with mud after being taken off and put back on?" Jackie suggested. "If they set up this party just as an alibi, that wouldn't be a stretch."

"It looked pretty authentic to me," Marcia said, thinking that Jackie might be a little too reluctant to let go of her theory in light of pretty overwhelming anti-evidence. "You want me to start calling their friends from the party? See what they have to say? We have all of their numbers from Aaron and Jessica's phone records."

"Yeah, let's do that," Jackie said, her own confidence in her theory wavering more than Marcia realized. She took a sip of her coffee, and added, "You take Aaron's list; I'll take Jessica's." From the taskbar on her computer screen, she clicked on a tab to bring Jessica's list back up but selected the wrong one, and the last video she had watched from the Timmons' doorbell cam filled the screen, instead.

With the slimmest of expectations, she went back to the clip of Jessica arriving at the house and played it one more time to see if there was any chance of picking out even one digit from its license plate.

She clicked forward through the video one frame at a time. At first, the detail of the plate was washed out by the brightness of the vehicle's own brake lights. Then, just as the driver took their foot off the brake, reducing the glare, a car passing from right to left between the SUV and the camera blocked what might have been a useable view of the plate. Jackie kept stepping forward until the car was past and the back of the Explorer came back into view, but the car's taillights—perfectly aligned with the height of the SUV's license plate—washed out the last glimpse of it before it was obscured by the shrubbery.

She went to the next video, of Jessica leaving, which began with a car driving past left to right, again, and triggering the camera. She stopped the playback when the car disappeared off the left of the screen and the backup and taillights of the SUV came into view. Again, the plate was washed out by the Explorer's own lights.

Frustrated, Jackie played the frames back and forth a couple of times and even used the playback program's editing menu to zoom in on the license plate area in one of the images. Nothing the least bit legible showed up.

Unable to click forward or back while zoomed in, she went to full screen and advanced a frame at a time watching for a useful change in the image quality of the plate.

There was little if any change in the license plate, but in one of the frames—and only one— there was a red reflection from above and to the left of the plate. It would have been little more than a tiny red flick next to the taillight when the video was played at full speed and would be easy to miss altogether ... which they had. Intrigued, she zoomed in.

"Holy shit!" she said.

Marcia was opening a copy of Aaron's phone list on her laptop while Jackie was viewing the videos, and had no idea that was even what she was looking at. "What? What's the matter?" she asked.

"Come here and look at this," Jackie said.

As she came around the desk, Jackie zoomed out to full-screen and backed the video up a few seconds. With Marcia looking over her shoulder, she said, "This is the clip of the SUV leaving the Fletcher house." She used the cursor to indicate the spot, and added, "Watch right here. You're looking for a little red reflection. It's going to be fast—just one frame."

She hit play, and they were both able to catch the brief flash this time, now that they knew where to look. She stopped the clip and as she stepped back through the frames, Marcia asked, "What is it?"

"Watch," Jackie said as she zoomed in on the reflection. When it half filled the screen, she asked, "Do you see it, yet?"

"It's pretty fuzzy blown up that much, but it kind of looks like a capital letter B."

"Capital letter R," Jackie corrected her. "As in *Rowley*. That's the ghost-graphic on the back of our unmarked cruiser. You almost can't see them at all until a light hits them just right. The taillights of the car that passed a few seconds earlier must have aligned perfectly for that one frame."

"*Your unmarked cruiser?*" Marcia repeated. "Are you sure this is the Jessica-leaving clip?"

"Positive," Jackie replied. "And you know who was driving that cruiser that night?"

"Oh, shit!" Marcia said. "Scott Lain?"

"Exactly," Jackie answered. "Suddenly he goes from a curiously missing person to a fugitive suspect."

"Wow! We weren't even drawing our targets on the right barn!" Marcia said.

"Yeah. And it explains all sorts of stuff, doesn't it?" Jackie added. "His disappearance, for one, but why he offered to clean up after Harry left for the hospital that night, and why he took so many crime-scene photos of a *non*-crime scene. He wanted to make sure there was no trace of him having been there earlier."

"It would seem to be a much better explanation of why he didn't tell you about his affair with Mrs. Fletcher," Marcia offered.

"Absolutely!" Jackie agreed. "And he sure got to the scene quickly when the 911 call came in. He must have been parked down the road waiting."

"Crap!" Jackie said as another thought struck her. "I'll bet that's what the un-cited and unreported DUI stop was all about. He must have let her *buy* her way out of the ticket by promising to have sex with him, again."

"Or he could have blackmailed her to the same end," Marcia suggested. "Subtle difference, but he'd be charged differently, one versus the other."

"If he killed her—even accidentally in the throes of kinky, *consensual* BDSM passion—and then staged it to look like she drowned, he's got a lot bigger problems to worry about than accepting a bribe versus blackmailing someone," Jackie said.

She picked up her desk phone and pushed the button for the dispatch board. "Hi, Helen. I need you to put out an update on that BOLO we have for Scott Lain. He's now a person-of-interest in the Pamela Fletcher homicide investigation, which I'll explain later. Along with our cars, open it up to all of Mass. and all the neighboring states. Thanks. Oh, and can you patch me through to Kyle, please?"

While Jackie waited to be connected with Kyle in his patrol car, Marcia said, "We still have the very confusing bit about Mr. Fletcher returning and leaving after Officer Lain left and before the 911 call."

"I know," Jackie said. "But I think we can find Harry pretty much any time we want to talk to him. Scott has a history of trying to take his own life. I'm more worried about him now than before. I want to go over to Scott's house and look around; see if there's any clue to where he might have gone."

"Did you say that Aaron was supposed to come in today, too?" Marcia asked.

"Crud! Yes, he is," Jackie replied. "I'll call him and ask if we can reschedule."

Jackie's phone rang and she lifted it before the first ring finished. "Hall, here," she said. "Kyle?"

"Hi. Helen said you wanted to talk to me?" he replied.

"I want you to meet me at Scott Lain's house," Jackie said. "How long until you can be there?"

"I'm at the east end; I just turned around at the train station," he answered. "So, fifteen minutes or so?"

"Okay, thanks. I'll see you there and I'll explain then."

## Chapter 26
### Saturday, July 17, 2021

Three minutes after hanging up with Kyle, Jackie and Marcia were pulling out onto Haverhill St. in Jackie's Jeep.

"I don't know how the hell I missed that," Jackie said as she drove. "I even *told* you that the roofline of the truck was just like our cruisers, and it still didn't tumble that it *could* be one."

"Well, we had been kind of led to believe that Jessica might have had something to do with it," Marcia said. "And it *is* a bit of a stretch to imagine that one of your officers could have been involved in committing a homicide,"

"But look at all the flags I missed ... or ignored," Jackie replied. "It really should have started to click with the DUI thing. Damn!"

Shifting away from the blame-game that Jackie was playing with herself, Marcia said, "So, it was probably Mrs. Fletcher who opened the garage door for him to pull in, but who would have closed it when he left? Presumably, she was dead by then."

Jackie thought for a moment, replaying the video in her head. "He pushed the button on the outside keypad," she said, almost triumphantly. "Remember in that clip, we see the light from the garage as the door opens, then we see the backup lights and tails flickering through the bushes. But then they stop for a few seconds before they come into view. That would leave the truck halfway in the garage. He could have reached out the window, pressed the *enter* button on the keypad, then kept moving as the door came down."

"Pressing *enter* closes the door?" Marcia said. "I thought you needed the code."

"Not on the openers that *I've* used," Jackie replied. "You only need the code to *open* the door. As far as I know, that's how they all work."

"Interesting. I'll have to try that on mine; that would be much more convenient," Marcia said. "So, do you actually know that the Fletcher's keypad is located window-high on the left side of the door?"

"No, but I'll bet a buck that it is," she replied. "And it would be easy to get the truck close enough that he didn't need to get out."

Suddenly a new thought struck her, and she said, "Holy crap! I'll bet that's where he scraped the fender of the truck! It's a lot wider than Harry's Toyota; he must have run into something going in or out of the garage!"

They arrived at Scott's, and Kyle pulled in behind them before they were out of the Jeep.

"Hi, Kyle," Jackie said as he approached. "I think you've met Marcia Grieves, right?"

"I've seen her around the station," he replied. He extended his hand, and said, "Nice to meet you."

"Likewise," she said as they shook.

Turning to Jackie, he said, "So, what's up?"

"We've discovered some evidence—circumstantial—that Scott could be somehow linked to Pamela Fletcher's murder."

"Jesus!" Kyle replied.

"To say the least. So, I want to go inside and see if there's anything that can tell us where he might have gone. When you did the well-check before, did you pick a lock?"

"Yeah. The back door," Kyle replied.

"No alarm or anything?"

"Yeah, and it went off," Kyle said. "The company apparently called his cell and he didn't answer, so they called Rowley PD to report a possible break-in. Dispatch told them I was already here, and they shut it off from their end."

They followed the pathway around the side of the house to the small back patio, and Kyle went to work on the lock, again. As he worked the pick, slipping the tumblers one by one, Marcia said, "Listen. Do you hear something? It sounds like a car is running. Is that the garage?" she asked pointing to a window on the back wall of the house.

"Yeah," Kyle said. "But it was empty when I checked before."

They all moved toward the window, and the now-unmistakable sound grew louder.

"Crap!" Jackie exclaimed as they all took off with the same thought; *stop him before he drives away*. Both Jackie's Jeep and the cruiser were in the driveway, but there was probably room for a determined person to maneuver around them across the lawn.

When they got to the front, they were surprised to see the garage door still closed. Kyle went to the right side of the door and had his hand on his weapon, ready to shoot out Scott's tires if necessary. Jackie and Marcia stood at the left side—the driver's side—to rush in and implore him to stop as he backed out.

They waited for the door to open. Ten seconds ... twenty seconds ... thirty seconds. But it never moved.

They looked at one another confused, then Jackie said suddenly, "Shit! He's trying to kill himself!" To Kyle, she said, "Stay here in case he does leave." She then ran back around the garage with Marcia right behind.

Jackie used the butt of her gun to break one of the panes of glass in the backdoor, then reached in to turn the deadbolt. "Crap!" she said when she didn't feel a lever on the inside. "It's keyed from both sides!"

She took a few steps back, then ran at the door, hitting it with her shoulder and hip. More glass shattered, and the door moved a half-inch as the wooden frame around the deadbolt cracked. She hit it again, and the wood splintered letting the door fly open.

She and Marcia ran through the kitchen toward the garage. Jackie flung the door open and they were met with the overpowering smell of diesel exhaust.

She quickly found the light switch, flipped it, and said, "Find the door opener!"

They searched the wall around the door but there was no button. Jackie looked at the ceiling and saw that there was no motor or mechanism attached to the overhead door. She ran to the back of Scott's truck, twisted the handle, and yanked up on the door. It moved easily, assisted by its big springs, and soon Kyle came into sight.

When Jackie turned back around, Marcia was opening the driver-side door of the truck while shouting through the open window, "Scott! Scott! Wake up!" But he didn't move, and when she got the door open she grabbed his arm to shake him, and he began to fall out of the truck.

"Oh, shit!" Marcia cried as Scott tumbled at her. She put her arms around him to catch him, but his weight was more than she expected and she ended up stumbling backward with him falling on her.

Jackie arrived just in time to prevent his dead weight from knocking Marcia to the floor. Together, they managed to get him out of the truck and lying on the cement. It was only then that they realized that he was rigid with rigor mortis and remained frozen in his seated position lying on his side.

Realizing she had just been embracing a dead body—the first she had ever encountered—Marcia gagged, threw her arm across her mouth, and ran for the open door. A moment later Jackie heard her retching and mumbling, "Oh, God!"

Jackie put her fingers on Scott's neck to feel for a pulse, but feeling the temperature of his flesh, and seeing his stiffness, she knew it was pointless.

"Oh, Scotty, what have you done?" she lamented as she knelt beside him and slowly shook her head.

After a few moments, she got up and reached in to turn off the truck. "Kyle, will you get the county ME on his way out here, please," she said to him as he stood behind her. "Then stay out here and keep any curious folks out, if you would. Marcia and I will go check the house for a suicide note or something. I didn't see anything in the truck."

She went outside and found Marcia leaning against the garage wall, spitting and trying to get the foul taste out of her mouth. She handed Marcia the handkerchief from her back pocket, and said, "I've got some water in the Jeep. I'll go get it."

"God, Jackie, I am really sorry about that," Marcia said. "It's just … it was … he was so *heavy*! And … and so *stiff*!" She quickly turned away and fought back another heave.

Jackie patted her on the back, and said, "Just breathe deep. I'll be right back with that water."

When Jackie returned Marcia rinsed her mouth and spit several times before actually swallowing any water. "You might have guessed that was my first encounter with a real live dead person," she said. "I think I've watched too many zombie movies."

"It's never easy, but it's even tougher when you know the person," Jackie said. "Come on; let's go in the house and see if he left a note or something.

Inside, on the kitchen table, was a typed, single sheet of paper with Scott's signature at the bottom.

Without touching it, they both read it to themselves.

July 17, 2021

To All Concerned,

I am very sorry for the hurt I have caused everyone. I cannot go on with the guilt and shame any longer, so I have decided to end my life.

Before that, though, I feel I must cleanse my soul and make sure that no one else is forced to take the blame for what I have done.

I killed Pamela Fletcher. It was an accident, but nevertheless, I am responsible and solely responsible.

On the night of July 1, 2021, I had pulled Pamela over on Rt. 1 heading south toward her home. I had observed her leaving a private residence where I suspected a party had taken place and I expected that she would have been drinking.

During the stop, I could tell from her breath and her slurred speech that she was undoubtedly over the DUI limit, but I told her that I would let her go if she agreed to have sex with me, again (We had a previous brief affair in October of 2020.) She agreed and I followed her home. Harry and his daughter, Jessica, were there so we agreed to meet on Thursday night, July 8.

During our sexual activities that night I pinched off the veins in her neck just as she began her orgasm. She had asked me to do this on our previous occasions, and it seemed to increase her pleasure and had no ill effects afterward.

As in the previous times, she lost consciousness as her orgasm peaked. This time, though, I must have held her neck too long or pinched too hard, and she did not come to right away when I let go. When she didn't wake up after a minute I tried to revive her, but nothing worked. That is when I panicked and came up with the bathtub idea to make it look like an accident.

I carried her body to the tub and hit her head against the edge to make it look like she fell. Then I let the tub fill. When there was enough water, I held her face under and pushed on her back several times to get her to inhale some water so it would look like she drowned.

I then cleaned up and left and waited nearby for the 911 call when Harry got home so I would be first on the scene.

I am very very sorry that Harry or anyone else has been suspected of killing Pamela. I expected the case to be closed quickly as an accident.

May God have mercy on my soul.
Scott Lain

"Signed, sealed, and delivered," Marcia said sadly. "It's too bad he thought that was the only way out."

"Mmm," Jackie agreed, but with little enthusiasm.

"What?" Marcia asked.

"Something doesn't feel right," she replied.

"About the note?"

"Among other things," Jackie replied. "I don't have it straight in my head, yet, but something seems off. I need to let it incubate for a while. Can you go out to the Jeep? In the back, behind the passenger seat, there's a black Pelican case; it's an evidence kit. Can you bring it in, please? I want to look around until the coroner gets here."

As Marcia went out through the open garage, Jackie pulled a pair of always-present surgical gloves from her back pocket and stretched them on.

She went to the refrigerator and opening the door by pulling on its edge, not the handle, she looked inside. It was about what she would expect for a guy living alone. It looked a lot like hers, as a matter of fact, except that there were *not* two bottles of white wine and there *were* nine bottles of Corona arranged on one of the shelves.

She picked up the half-gallon of milk, which was half empty, and looked at the date. It was set to expire tomorrow, so he could have bought it Wednesday, the day he first called in sick. Also anytime after that or a few days before; it really didn't tell her much. She opened it and sniffed; it was still good.

She took out her phone, snapped a few pictures of the inside of the fridge, then closed the door.

Thinking about the beers—nine out of a possible twelve?—she looked around for a wastebasket. She found it in a tall pantry cupboard on the other side of the sink. Among the usual household trash, she found the three empty bottles. But they were not all on top as if he had drunk them all while contemplating his suicide. They were layered with other trash like he had drunk them on consecutive days.

Jackie took her notepad and her pen from her shirt pocket and as she wrote a note to herself to check Scott's credit card activity, Marcia came back with the evidence kit.

"Kyle said the coroner should be here in twenty minutes, or so," she told Jackie as she set the case on the kitchen counter.

"Perfect," Jackie said as she flipped the latches on the industrial case. Inside was a neatly-packed amalgamation of CSI equipment and supplies. There were evidence bags, crime-scene tape, tamper-proof seals, gloves, sterile swabs, fingerprint powder and brushes, print-lifting tape, and much more.

Jackie took one of the large, plastic evidence bags and slipped the suicide note inside. She then sealed it and dated and initialed the outside.

Next, she put the three empty beer bottles in separate bags, which she marked *top, middle,* and *bottom* for the order in which she found them in the trash. As Marcia watched, Jackie said, "I want to check these for prints to see if Scott was drinking alone."

The house was small—perfectly suited for a single guy—so it didn't take very long for Marcia and Jackie to look through the rest of the rooms. In what would have been a small dining room when the house was built a hundred-plus years ago, Scott had set up a sparse office.

On one wall stood a tall bookcase. The middle shelf contained family pictures and mementos. The top was all crime books ranging from the textbooks he had used to become an officer, to works about actual crimes, to pure-fiction who-dun-its. All of Harry's novels were there. She slid one out to see if it was signed. It was not.

His desk was old, but nothing like a valuable antique or anything. He had probably picked it up at a thrift store or a local tag sale. On it were assorted bills and flyers as if he'd gotten his mail out of the mailbox, but not sorted through it. There was a yellow legal pad to one side, and with gloved hands, Jackie picked up and flipped through the pages.

In the middle of the desk was his closed laptop. Jackie opened it and then used the eraser end of a pencil to press the power button. Twenty seconds later, a screen came up asking for a password.

She pressed the enter key and a message came up indicating the wrong password had been used. "Yeah, that would have been too easy if it just opened for us," Jackie said.

"You think Carol can get into it?" Marcia asked.

"We're going to find out," Jackie answered. She stepped back and took a few pictures of the room before putting *Police Evidence* stickers on both the laptop and the printer, then filling in the date and initialing them.

They heard another vehicle and looked out the window to see the Essex County Medical Examiner's van pull into the driveway.

By the time Marcia and Jackie got to the garage, the two men, each carrying what looked like a large plastic toolbox, were just entering through the big open door.

"Hi, I'm Chief Hall," Jackie said extending her hand. "This is Marcia Grieves with the Essex County DA's Office; that's Officer Kyle Hopkins with Rowley PD."

"Michael Hanover," the older man said as he shook hands with Jackie. "This is Frank Dale. What have you got for us?"

"Apparent suicide from exhaust asphyxiation," Jackie said. "When we found him half an hour ago, the truck was running and both garage doors were closed. The only window is actually covered with plywood."

"Is that where you found him?" he asked looking at the body in its frozen sitting posture on the floor.

"No," Marcia answered. "He fell out—almost on top of me—when I opened the door." She then needed to take a couple of deep stomach-settling breaths, again.

Hanover walked over to Scott, set his case down, and pulled on a pair of gloves from his pocket. With Scott lying on his side Hanover made a cursory examination of his front, back, and right side, then he nodded to his assistant and they rolled him over onto his back so he could look at his left side. Hanover then took out a flashlight and looked in Scott's mouth, up his nose, at his eyes, and in his ears.

He knelt down next to the body, opened his case, and took out a tablet. As it booted up, he handed his assistant a blue-tooth thermometer. Setting the tablet on the man's unmoving chest, he pulled Scott's shirttails out of his pants unfastened the last few buttons, and laid the shirt open.

With a scalpel from his case, he made a half-inch incision at the base of Scott's sternum, and then inserted a long-probe thermometer into the opening, pushing it deep into Scott's liver.

A few seconds later the tablet beeped that it had recorded the temperatures of the air and of Scott's body.

Hanover handed Frank his thermometer to clean and put away, then tapped the tablet to input more data, such as whether the body was clothed, its height and weight, whether it was outdoors, if it was dry, and if it was lying on cold ground. That data would all be used to compute an approximate time of death.

"This is giving me eight to fourteen hours as a time of death," Hanover said as he stood up. "Does that fit with what you know?"

"We don't know much," Jackie said. "He's been out of contact for three days, but there's a suicide note dated today."

"Well, between the tablet's calcs and the rigor, I'd say that early today would fit," Hanover said. "But it'll be up to the ME to fill in all the blanks after the autopsy."

By that time, Frank had unrolled a body-bag next to Scott, and he and Hanover lifted him into it and zipped it up.

As Hanover and Frank lugged the body to the van, Jackie said to Kyle, "Will you secure the scene, please? Close everything up, tape-seal the back door, you know what to do. I want to hold onto everything until we get the autopsy report."

"You see something wrong, Chief?" he asked.

"Just being overly cautious, probably," she replied.

To Marcia, she said, "Let's go get the stuff from inside and head back to the station. I've got a very unpleasant call to make to Scott's mother."

In the Jeep, Jackie took out her phone and called Harry. "Hi. Jackie," he answered. "How are you?"

"Doing well, Harry," she lied. "Hey, can I get you to come down to the station today? There's something I'd like you to take a look at and hopefully clarify for me."

"Sure. When?" he answered.

"Right after lunch? Say one o'clock?"

"Can we make it earlier? I've got something at one-fifteen."

"How about noon?" Jackie replied.

"See you then," he agreed.

As they drove back to the station, Marcia said, "So tell me what you're thinking. Put some bullet holes in all these targets we have. You don't seem to like the note; tell me about that."

"Well, for one thing—at least to me—it's too long on the explanation of how he went about killing Pamela and too short on why he feels so guilty about it that he felt he needed to kill himself. It's more like a report than a suicide note."

"I see your point," Marcia said, "but maybe that was his soul-purging. Making sure you understood how and why the accident took place would allow you to forgive him."

"That's another point," Jackie said. "It sounds like it was written to *me*. He never says goodbye to his mother or even alludes that he has one. I've talked to her, and I think they're closer than that."

"So, what's with the printer?" Marcia asked, crooking her thumb to the unit sitting on top of everything behind the seats. "His laptop I get; you want to see if the note's on it, but why do you want his printer?"

"That follows another problem I have with the note," Jackie answered. "It was written on a computer and then just printed and signed. That's not unheard of for a suicide note, but it's pretty uncommon, and I happen to know it's out of character for Scott.

"When I found out he'd withheld the fact that he'd been a CNM partner with Pamela I gave him an assignment to write a report on why that was a problem to make sure he *understood* why it was."

Marcia quipped, "Probably more effective than making him write *I will not withhold information* a hundred times on the chalkboard."

"It's another Booker-ism," Jackie said, "and it's quite effective. But anyway, that legal pad that we took from his desk has that report written out in longhand. And that's not something I told him to do. I expected a typewritten report."

"Maybe that's his draft and he was *going* to type it," Marcia offered more as a devil's-advocate reply than a serious argument.

"His drafts with cross-outs, scribbles, and notes are on the two pages preceding the report, which is nice, neat, and even signed."

Suddenly, Jackie snapped her fingers as a light bulb came on for her. "I'll bet you a buck that the signature on the report and on the note are *identical*! I'll bet it was traced!"

"That should be easy to prove or disprove," Marcia said. "Just hold the two up to the light. Which still doesn't explain the printer."

"Sorry. So, back in the day, the FBI could tell if a specific typewriter was used to write a ransom note or something," Jackie began. "Tiny differences in the letters they struck made them as individual as fingerprints. I'm not sure if the State lab—or the FBI if it came to that—can do the same with an inkjet printer or not. But if they can, and if we find the note wasn't printed on Scott's printer, it's one more darned good indicator that something is amiss. And then if it could be matched to a suspect's printer you'd have some pretty damning evidence."

"I like the way you think, Sherlock," Marcia said. "So, who's at the top of your suspect list if Scott *was* murdered?"

"I think we've circled back to Harry," Jackie answered. "He still has motive, means, and opportunity for his wife's death, so let's say for the moment that he's guilty of that. It didn't get swept away as an accident, as he'd hoped, and with his lies and with us copying his computer, he knows he's in the spotlight.

"He told us himself that Scott and Pamela had an intimate history that included rough sex, and maybe Pamela even told him about the DUI stop where Scott let her off out of the goodness of his heart and fond memories. So, using a few real seeds and his fertile murder/mystery imagination Harry comes up with the confession in the note, kills Scott, and stages another death scene."

"Interesting," Marcia said. "And the fact that he had once told Scott not to see Pamela anymore means he probably didn't like him very much, and that would just add to his frame-somebody-else motive."

"We'll have to see if the ME can narrow the time of death for Scott," Jackie said, "to see if Harry had the *opportunity* to go along with his motives. I'm going to be really anxious to see the cause of death, too. How do you get someone to sit in their truck long enough to be overcome by exhaust fumes? I wish now that I'd looked at his wrists for signs he might have been tied up."

"So, how do you think he would have known that Scott was with his wife last Thursday night, so he could frame him for her murder?" Marcia said. "I mean, he'd *have* to know that for sure, otherwise the whole confession thing would fall apart if you had a record of him giving a ticket or something right when Mrs. Fletcher was being killed. *We* know because we've seen the Timmons' video clips, but he hasn't."

Jackie pondered that for a moment, then, as puzzle pieces fit together in a different arrangement, she said, "Oh! Maybe I have the DUI thing wrong. What if Scott really *did* blackmail Pamela into having sex again, and Harry found out about it? He overheard something or maybe saw Scott driving toward his house right after he left, so he turned around and followed him there. Then he saw him drive right into the garage!" Jackie was getting more excited about her new theory as things dovetailed in her head.

She went on, "We know he has that software on his phone to control the house lights and doors and stuff because that's how he unlocked the deadbolt on the front door when the EMTs showed up. So he watches his phone, and when he sees the garage door open and close, he knows Scott is gone and sees his golden opportunity to get rid of Pamela. He makes some excuse to leave Megan for half an hour, or so, goes home and kills her."

"But why stage it as an accident if he was going to frame Scott for her murder?" Marcia asked.

"Hmm. Maybe Scott was the backup," Jackie offered. "If everyone believed it was an accident, then case closed, and so much the better. But if not—which is how it turned out—he had a fallback plan that would essentially kill the second bird with the same stone."

As Jackie pulled into the station driveway, she said, "Oh, I can't wait to talk to Harry!"

## Chapter 27

**Saturday, July 17, 2021**

In her office, Jackie made the call to Scott's mother. "Hello, Mrs. Lain. This is Chief Hall from the Rowley Police. We spoke earlier."

"Yes?" the woman replied in a very wary tone.

"I'm so sorry to have to tell you, but we found Scott earlier this morning, and it appears that he took his own life. I'm very, very sorry for your loss."

"Oh, my God," Mrs. Lain said heavily. "How … how did he do it? Pills?"

"He sat in his truck while it was running in his garage," Jackie answered. "Carbon monoxide poisoning. It would be completely painless."

The woman let out a long sigh, and then said, "Well, thank you for calling and telling me, Chief. What should I do now? How do I claim the body?"

"Mrs. Lain, I'm going to connect you with one of our volunteers here who can help you through all that. Again, I'm very, very sorry. Please hold on."

Jackie put the woman on hold, then called Crystal and explained what was going on, letting her pick up the call herself.

Marcia was standing in her doorway when she finished, and said, "I have the Timmons videos on my laptop to show Mr. Fletcher when he gets here. You want me to sit in, or observe from out here, again?"

"Inside with me," Jackie said. "I don't want him thinking this is remotely off the record and just between him and me."

"Speaking of laptops," Marcia went on, "do you want me to call Carol and have her come look at Scott's?"

"I was just about to do that myself," Jackie answered.

"Hi, Carol. It's Jackie. How are you?" she said when the phone was answered.

"Do you want to hear about how I might have broken my pinky finger in a kitchen drawer?" Carol replied.

Jackie chuckled, and said, "It's not actually what I called about, but since you brought it up, are you okay?"

"It doesn't appear to be life-threatening, but I have it taped to my ring finger just in case ... and to build sympathy ... which isn't working with Neil. But enough about me. What's up? You have more cyber-sleuthing? I still have my bullet and the use of most of my digits."

"I do, as a matter of fact," Jackie said. "I have a laptop I need to look at, but it's passworded. You have a way of getting past that?"

"There's a couple, actually, but it means taking the computer apart. Are you okay with that?"

"Whatever it takes," Jackie replied. "When can you be here?"

"I'll have Neil drive me out, so ten or fifteen minutes. Does that work?"

"Perfect! Thanks!"

When Carol arrived, she set up in Marcia's temporary office again, and Jackie brought in the laptop. "Can I ask whose it is?" she asked.

"Scott Lain's," Jackie told her.

"Oh!" she said. "I just heard that Kyle Hopkins found him in his truck with the motor running in his garage. Is that true?"

"Unfortunately," Jackie said, not even bothering to ask how the word got out so quickly; it was a small town. "So, do you think you can get into it?"

"Probably," she answered as she took a set of screwdrivers from her tool kit. "I'll have to open Marcia's computer as well as the laptop, is that okay?"

"*My* computer?" Marcia said.

"Well, technically the department's computer that's assigned to you," she corrected with a smile.

"Sure. Go ahead," Jackie said. "But why?"

"I'll take the drive out of the laptop and hook it up inside Marcia's, so I can image it to another external e-drive I brought. Then I can examine the new image. Unless there's full disk encryption I should be able to just read the files on the new image, bypassing the operating system where the password is."

"And if it's encrypted?" Marcia asked.

"Well, let's just cross our fingers that it's not," Carol answered.

At ten minutes to twelve, Harry arrived and Jackie had him shown into the interview room. She and Marcia watched him on the monitor in Jackie's office for several minutes. He didn't appear at all nervous, although he did look at his watch a couple of times, and his phone once.

"Hi Harry, thanks for coming down," Jackie said as she entered the room. "You remember Marcia Grieves, right?"

He stood up, and said, "Of course; nice to see you, again." To Jackie, he said, "No problem. What's up? What can I help you with?"

As they all sat down, Jackie said, "First of all, have you heard yet that Scott Lain was found dead this morning?"

Harry's brow furrowed, and he said, "Found dead? How? What happened?"

The surprised reaction seemed genuine to both Jackie and Marcia. Or maybe he was just a very good actor.

"Apparent suicide," Jackie said.

"Oh, God. What did he do? I mean how?"

"I can't release any details until after I contact his next of kin," Jackie lied.

"That makes sense, I guess," Harry said. "Do you know why? I assume he must have left a note if you know it's a suicide."

"We went through his house and his belongings, and haven't found anything," Jackie answered, watching him closely for a reaction to that lie.

Nothing.

"Wow," Harry said shaking his head in apparent shock at the news. But after a few moments of thought, he looked at Jackie, and said, "Hey! Do you suppose it had something to do with Pamela? Could he have been the one who killed her and his guilt caught up with him?"

"That seems like kind of a leap," Jackie said in mock surprise. "Why would you think *Scott* killed Pamela?"

"Well, you already know that he'd been one of her CNM partners last year, sometime," he said. "and that when I accidentally found out I told her to break it off with him because I think he's a weaselly little creep. She told me that she did."

"Hardly motive for murder," Jackie said.

"What if he didn't like being told no? What if he came to the house that night to either convince her or somehow *force* her to have sex with him again? Maybe he had something to blackmail her with." He thought for a moment, and then added, "I'll bet that's it! That's why he waited so long; he had to wait until he had something on her."

"Did she ever mention that he was stalking her after she told him it was over?" Jackie asked. "Or that he'd made any threats?"

"No," Harry said, "but that wouldn't be surprising. Pamela was no pushover; she would have felt she could handle him without me getting involved. And she knew how much I hated the little prick."

"You *hated* him? Why?" Jackie asked. "It shouldn't be jealousy because he slept with your wife. Not unless you feel the same way about all her other CNM partners."

"No, that wasn't it. It was just the way he threw his weight around when he was in that uniform and carrying a gun and all of his cop-gear," Harry said. "Typical wanna-be bad-ass."

Suspicious that that was a little generic to foster real hatred, Jackie asked, "Was there some specific incident between you and him?"

Harry blew out a deep breath, and said, "Not long after I told Pamela to break it off with him, he pulled me over for going like eleven over the speed limit. I tried to talk my way out of it, and said, 'Hey come on; I let you screw my wife; you can let this go, can't you?' Well, he went ballistic! He made me get out of the car and even *handcuffed* me. He told me he was going to haul me in for reckless driving or endangerment or something. He was being a typical Mr. Authority bully. Lucky for me, he got a call on his radio that he was needed somewhere, so he took the cuffs off me and let me go ... but not until *after* he gave me the speeding ticket."

"I hope you're telling me the truth, Harry," Jackie said. "Because that traffic stop is pretty easy for me to check."

"Why the hell would I lie about it?" he said.

"Because there's something going on here that you're not telling us about," she replied. "And you have a history of lying to me."

"What? *What's* going on? I'm being straight with you, Jackie, I swear. I explained why I lied those other times."

"Why did you return home at 8:38 the night that Pamela died, stay for twenty-one minutes, then leave to return later at 9:30?" Jackie asked with the aggressiveness in her tone intentionally ratcheted up a notch. "What were you doing there, and why didn't you tell me?"

"*What?* What are you talking about? I didn't go home that night until when I found Pamela in the bathtub. Who told you I went home?"

"Nobody told us," Jackie said. "You were caught on Michael and Mary Alice Timmons' security camera. We've seen it for ourselves."

"I didn't even know they *had* a security camera," Harry said.

"Obviously," Marcia said almost under her breath as she opened her laptop. She turned it so he could see it, and reached around to tap the space-bar to start the clip.

"You pull into the driveway at 8:38," Jackie narrated without needing to see the video that she had memorized by then. "The next clip will show you backing out onto the street, and driving away twenty-one minutes later. Now, would you like to trade your denial in for an explanation?"

"No," he answered, "because I wasn't there that night until I came home and found her at 9:30. How do you know this video is even from that night?"

"We've authenticated it, Harry," Jackie said. "It's from the Thursday night that Pamela died."

"Well, then it's not my car," he said. "If that was me, wouldn't I have pulled into the garage? Look, there's probably a dozen people in town with a white Toyota like that and ten thousand in the state. Doesn't your boyfriend drive one?"

"You're saying that's *Jeff's* car?" Jackie said incredulously.

"No! I'm saying it's not *mine*!" he answered. "I don't know what else to tell you. *I was not there!* ... I couldn't have been if I wanted to."

"What do you mean, *couldn't have been*?"

"I was asleep," he answered flatly. "It's a quirk of my narcolepsy. Technically, it's called Bromfield Syndrome Cataplexy. Intense and prolonged physical exertion, when stopped abruptly—like having intercourse and then a climax—knocks me out. Within twenty seconds of my orgasm, I'm unconscious. It's one of the issues that Pamela and I had that led us to CNM. She felt the need to cuddle after sex, and as she put it, 'Cuddling with a cadaver isn't very much fun.'"

Surprised by this new information, it took Jackie a moment to process it, but then she said, "How long does it last? Your unconsciousness?"

"It seems to depend on how intense the sex and the orgasm are," he replied. "I've been out for anywhere from ten minutes to three-quarters of an hour."

"And this happened to you that Thursday night?" Jackie asked.

"You can ask Megan," he said. "She calls it my one-and-done syndrome. She usually takes a shower while I'm out."

"So, if it didn't last long this time, you *could* have slipped out while she was in the shower and she wouldn't have known you were gone," Marcia said.

"No, Ms. Grieves," he said in the condescending tone that he seemed to reserve for her. "It takes ten minutes to get to my house from hers; add your twenty-one minutes I was supposedly there, then another ten to get back, and you're at forty-one minutes. If I had woke up the moment she turned the shower on, she would have been out, dressed, and looking for me long before I could get back."

Jackie exhaled deeply, and said, "Well, that is new information, Harry. I wish you'd shared it with me earlier."

"Until now, I couldn't see how it would make a difference," he replied. "And it's a little embarrassing."

"Is there anything *else* we should know?" Jackie asked.

"Well, again, I can't think how it could mean anything," he replied, "but throwing all my cards on the table, it doesn't happen if I masturbate. Apparently, that doesn't use enough whole-body energy, or something. Oh, and I can give you the number of my neurologist, Dr. Oldham, if you'd like. He can verify that I'm telling you the truth."

"If you wouldn't mind," Jackie said, sliding a pad and pen toward him.

As he wrote, he asked, "So, am I free to go, now?"

"Yes. And thanks for coming in, Harry, but please stop dropping these surprises on me." Jackie replied.

After walking him out, Jackie returned to the interview room where Marcia was looking at the Timmons' videos, yet again.

"Do you believe him?" Marcia asked.

"Based on his past record, not enough," Jackie said. "I'm going to send that recording to Suzan and see what *she* thinks."

"If it wasn't his car it *would* kind of explain why it was left out in the driveway rather than pulling in and hiding it in the garage," Marcia said. Pointing to an image frozen on the laptop screen, she went on, "These are the frames when the driver gets out of the car." She clicked through a dozen frames, and then said, "You really can't tell who that is. We assumed it was Mr. Fletcher because we assumed it was his car. If we're wrong about one, we're wrong about the other."

"It's a long-shot, but I'll ask Paul, up front, to check the RMV database and see what kind of car Aaron drives," Jackie said.

"I'll check on that for any of her CNM partners who don't have airtight alibis," Marcia said.

They stepped into Marcia's office, and Jackie asked Carol, "How's it going?"

"Fortunately, it's not a very big hard drive," she answered. "The progress bar says two minutes and thirty seconds left. Is there something specific you want to look for when it's done?"

"There is," Jackie said and went to make a photocopy of the suicide note. When she returned, the copying was complete and Carol was waiting. Jackie said, "Can you do a search for the phrase *cleanse my soul*?" To Marcia, she said, "I can't imagine his using that in any other document."

Ten seconds later, Carol said, "I have one hit. It's a Word doc named SN.doc. You want me to open it?" As she spoke, she right-clicked the file name, opening a menu of options. At the bottom, she clicked on *Properties*. Before Jackie had a chance to answer, Carol said, "I don't know if it means anything, but it doesn't look like this file was written on this computer."

"How do you know?" Marcia asked.

"The date the file was *created* is yesterday, but the date it was last *modified* is three days ago," Carol said,

"What do you mean?" Jackie said. "You can't modify a file that hasn't been created."

"The *Created* date is when the file first appeared on this computer," Carol said. "That means it was written somewhere else, and copied onto this drive."

"Would saving the file with a new name on the same computer do the same thing?" Jackie asked.

"No. That would give it a new Created date *and* a new Modified date, which would be the same."

"How about renaming the file in its directory without opening it?" Jackie asked.

"Nope. That would keep everything the same," Carol said. "The only way that I'm aware to get the Created date *after* the Modified date is to copy and paste the whole file. So, is that a good or a bad thing, here?"

"Good because it verifies my hunch," Jackie said, "but bad because now we don't know who wrote the note."

Carol put together the fact that she was working on Scott Lain's computer, the *cleanse my soul* phrase she had searched for, and the *SN* name of the file, and asked, "Is this Scott Lain's suicide note?"

Jackie replied, "You're getting good at this, Watson."

"Thank you," Carol said with a smile. "That's a big promotion from Barney."

Jackie laughed and patted her on the back. "Thanks for keeping your sense of humor; you know you're loved. And thanks for coming in and doing this for us. In answer to your earlier question; no, don't open the file. But leave it there, so *we* can. I need to keep the contents on a strict need-to-know basis for now."

"No problem," she said as she started putting her tools away. "Call me if you want me to search whatever computer you think this came from."

Jackie and Marcia looked at each other, and Jackie said to Carol, "Don't leave; we'll be right back."

In her office, Jackie said to Marcia, "Do you think you can work your string-pulling magic and maybe get Scott's autopsy prioritized with the ME?"

"You don't think he suffocated in his truck?"

"Well, if the note is suspicious, so is the death," Jackie said. "I'm not totally convinced that Harry is telling us the truth—at least not all of it. It's a little hard to imagine that Harry dropped in to visit Scott and conveniently stumbled onto his already-dead body in his garage and then concocted the suicide note to make a frame-up work. If Harry wrote that note, he almost certainly had a hand in Scott's death, and since we now know the note wasn't written on Scott's computer, that just reinforces my belief that Harry wrote it."

Marcia looked at her watch and then said, "My father always plays golf Saturday afternoons. I'll call him a little later."

"Good," Jackie said. "Right now, I think we should go over to Harry's and have Carol do the same search on his computers. She cloned the drives on Wednesday, but she says the note was last modified on Thursday. Do you have the search warrant with you?"

"Yup. For any device capable of the creation, storage, or transmission of electronic data," she answered. "So it covers computers, phones, jump-drives, CDs, and even floppy discs. I also have one for the whole premises for anything that could relate to the death of Mrs. Fletcher."

"That second one's a pretty broad brush," Jackie said. "Nice job getting a judge to sign it."

"You're the one who taught the course," Marcia said.

"Well, if I didn't give you a gold star then, you get one now."

"I can do the searches on Mr. Fletcher's computers, myself, you know," Marcia said.

"I do, but if it comes to it, I'd want Carol on the stand as an expert witness for all of this," Jackie said. "Continuity would be important."

She then sat down at her desk, and said, "Give me just a few minutes to send the recordings of Harry's and Jessica's interviews off to Suzan, and I'll be ready to go."

## Chapter 28

**Saturday, July 17, 2021**

On the drive to Harry's in Marcia's car, Carol asked, "What if he's not home when we get there?"

Marcia answered, "We have a warrant to enter and search the premises. He doesn't need to be there, or even give us permission to enter."

When they arrived, Jessica's truck was in the driveway. "Oh fun," Jackie said.

Walking past it, she looked at the roof rack, and saw that Marcia's observations were dead on; the rack had not been off the truck in a very long time.

At the door, Harry did permit them to enter.

"More witch hunting, Hall?" Jessica said when Jackie told Harry that they wanted to take another look at his computer. "Just stumbling through the dark hoping you'll trip over something you can construe as incriminating?"

Jackie shut her up, when she replied, "Have you talked with the folks at the Haverhill District Court, yet?"

Jessica glared at her, then said goodbye to her father, and left.

"What *are* you looking for?" Harry asked after Jessica left. "Does this have something to do with Lain's death? You think it wasn't a suicide and that I killed him?"

"We're awaiting autopsy results," Jackie answered. "And frankly, I'd like to prove that you *couldn't* have had anything to do with it," she lied. "I'd like for Carol to find that you were hard at work on your next novel during his time of death."

"I was at Pamela's funeral—along with you—Friday," he replied. "Isn't that when you said Scott died?"

"As I mentioned, the autopsy report isn't in, yet," Jackie said. "I don't have an exact time of death, yet."

"Whatever," he replied, obviously unconvinced.

With Harry's permission to search his and Pamela's desktop computers, as well as his laptop, he gave Carol the passwords, so her searches went much faster.

While Carol worked with the computers, Jackie went to the garage to check for paint scrapes on anything, and Marcia stayed with Harry in the kitchen.

To break the awkward silence, Marcia said to Harry, "I've read a couple of your books, now. They're quite good; very detailed. You must do an awful lot of research."

He looked at her a little suspiciously, wondering if she was trying to draw something out of him that, in his daughter's words, she could *construe as incriminating*. "I do," he finally answered. "The problem is I can't retain it all. I have the memory of an old 386 computer in a terabyte world."

"I feel like you have a real gift for writing dialogue," she went on in genuine praise. "It reads very fluently; like you're actually hearing the people talking. That builds the characters in such a natural way for me. I come to feel like I actually know them."

"Thank you," he said, feeling a bit less wary. "I write what the voices in my head tell me to write," he added with a smile. Immediately regretting having said that, he added, "That's a joke, Ms. Grieves. I don't really hear voices in my head telling me to do things."

In the garage, Jackie found what she was looking for almost immediately. It was a two-car garage with a large portion of the house built above it. As a result, a heavy wood beam spanned the area, and a steel column was used as a mid-point support for the beam.

On the side of the grey-painted column, Jackie saw streaks of black paint, and a fragment of what she was sure was the decal from the fender of the cruiser.

She took several photos, and then, coming prepared, she took a plastic bag from her pocket, and using her pocket knife, she scraped some of the black paint, the grey paint, and the decal into the bag.

There was now zero doubt in her mind that Scott had been here that night. What was not so clear is what he had done in that twenty-six minutes. Had he had sex with Pamela and left her alive and well, after which someone in a white Toyota arrived, killed her, and staged the accident? If Harry was telling the truth about his cataplexy—and she was going to check—and if it wasn't him, who the hell *would* it be? And why would they do it?

She called the station, asked for Paul, and was told that the only car registered in Aaron's name was a red 2018 Kia Sorrento, effectively crossing him off the list.

Half an hour later, they were leaving with nothing more than a few paint chips that verified something that Jackie felt she already knew.

In the car, Carol explained, "I searched all three computers and every memory device I could find in his and Pamela's office for the *cleanse my soul* phrase, and for SN.doc. I looked for deleted copies, and I even checked for a backup file. That would have been named *Backup of SN.wbk*, so he could have overlooked deleting it. Nothing.

"Then I looked at any file that had been created since we cloned the drives, and none of them were even remotely close. I really don't think that file originated on any of those computers. Of course, that's not to say he might not have used a computer at work or even a tablet we don't know about. Oh, and about proving he was working on a new novel during the time of death," she added, "I don't think so. There weren't that many new or modified files since I cloned the drives, and none that would have taken very long to write."

"Yeah, that was kind of a con, anyway," Jackie said. "I didn't want him to get his guard up too much."

"I don't think it worked," Marcia said.

"Me either," Jackie agreed.

From the back seat, Carol continued, "But anyway, when I was searching Harry and Pamela's USB drives, it occurred to me that if Scott—for some unknown reason—had written that note on a memory stick, and then copied it to his hard drive—again, for whatever reason—it would show the Created date coming *after* the Modified date, even though it was all done on the same computer. Could Scott have had some other storage devices?"

"That's an interesting point, Watson," Jackie said. "We really didn't look very hard for anything like that. We had the note and his laptop, and that seemed like enough."

After dropping Carol off at home, Jackie asked Marcia, "You have time to go back out to Scott's and look around for a memory stick with me?"

"If you can manage that without me," Marcia said as she drove back to the station, "I have in-laws coming in this evening, and I really need to get home."

"Is that a good or a bad thing?" Jackie asked. "Because I could write you a note to get you excused if you need it."

Marcia laughed, and replied, "Thanks, but they're actually really fun. I think they like me more than their son."

# *Chapter 29*

**Saturday, July 17, 2021**

When Jackie arrived at Scott's, she parked the Jeep outside the police tape and walked around back with her crime-scene kit.

Cardboard had been taped over the missing windows of the broken back door, and it had been pulled closed and sealed with a tamper-evident police sticker between the frame and the door. She initialed the sticker, then wrote the date and time before slitting it with her pocket knife. She then donned a pair of gloves and went inside.

She set the kit on the kitchen counter and went to Scott's office. In a drawer of the desk, she found half a dozen different memory sticks in a Ziploc bag, and another six CDs with the word "backup" and various dates written on them. She put everything into an evidence bag. She searched the rest of the office but didn't find any other storage devices.

Taking the crime-scene kit, she went out into the garage, which was illuminated only by a four-foot fluorescent work light above a wooden bench where she set the kit. She used her LED flashlight to look Scott's truck over more closely than she had earlier, checking the interior, especially, for any signs of a struggle or of a second person. Nothing seemed out of place or unusual.

She decided to dust the inside handle of the passenger door to see if the most recent passenger might be able to be identified. To her surprise, there were no fingerprints, at all. Either no one had gotten out of the passenger side using the handle since the last time the truck was cleaned—which didn't seem recently—or someone had wiped the handle down. She dusted the outside handle with the same result, and then checked the driver's side, and found those handles perfectly clean, too. That pretty much removed all doubt for her that she was looking at another staged suicide scene.

Knowing there was another tamper-evident seal on the garage door, she didn't open it from inside, but instead walked out through the back door and around to the front. When she looked at the gravel driveway where several other cars—including hers—had been recently, she knew it would be pointless to try to identify the tire marks of the car that Scott's murderer must have driven.

Then, once more, she began to ponder how the killer—whether it was Harry or someone else—could have gotten Scott to sit still in his truck long enough to be overcome by the exhaust fumes. Again, she kicked herself for not having looked closer at the body for signs that he had been restrained somehow, or maybe knocked unconscious. She thought about that for a while, and then, impatient as always, she took out her phone and called the Medical Examiner's office in Boston.

"Hi, this is Chief Hall with the Rowley Police Department," she introduced when the call was answered. "Can you tell me if you received the body of one Scott Lain earlier today? He would have been transported by the Essex County ME."

After a transfer, a wait, and a repetition of her request, she was told that they had the body.

"I'm investigating his death; I'd like to come in and take a look at it. Is that okay?" she asked.

"Sure," the young-sounding man said. "Bring ID and ask for Kevin Hoyle. That's me."

"Thanks, Kevin. I'll see you in forty-five minutes, or so," she said then went back inside to pack up.

When Kevin, the weekend-duty diener, pulled Scott's drawer open, Jackie was a little surprised to see him lying flat, rather than in the sitting position, which is how she had last seen him. "Has the rigor passed already," she asked, thinking that would indicate an earlier time of death.

"No," Kevin answered. "After we photographed him, we forced his knees and hips so he'd fit in here more easily."

She looked closely at both of his wrists and his ankles, and was surprised and a little disappointed to not find any sign that he had been restrained. She had been imagining seeing marks from his own handcuffs.

Because his head had been slumped forward—chin on chest—when rigor mortis set in, it was now raised up off of the drawer, and Jackie looked all around it for signs that he had been struck by something. Again, she came up empty.

"Is it okay if I look at his eyes?" she asked Kevin.

"Sure," he said and reached over to pull back his eyelids with his gloved hands. As Jackie leaned over and inspected the lifeless eyes, he said, "Looking for petechial hemorrhaging?"

"Yes. But I don't see any," she answered.

"How'd he die?" Kevin asked. "Do you know?"

"Well, we found him in a closed garage in his truck with the motor running, so suicide by carbon monoxide poisoning would be the obvious answer, but there are other things that give me doubt."

Kevin said, "His skin color looks about right for that." Then, he leaned down and took a sniff of Scott's shirt. "Was the truck a diesel? I caught that smell when I opened the drawer."

"Yes," Jackie said. "Does that make a difference?"

"If he died from monoxide poisoning," Kevin said, "it almost certainly wasn't a suicide. And if it was a suicide, it almost certainly wasn't by inhaling the exhaust fumes from his truck."

"You have my undivided attention," she said. "Can you elaborate?"

"Well, I'm not an ME or anything, so I can't speak to this guy's actual cause of death, but I do know a lot about ways to die."

"And you can't die from breathing diesel exhaust fumes?" Jackie asked a bit skeptical.

"You can, but it's a long, agonizing process, compared to gasoline exhaust. It's counterintuitive considering how smelly diesel fumes are, but they contain very little carbon monoxide, and that's what kills you when you inhale auto exhaust.

"However, even that small amount of CO—carbon monoxide—in diesel *will* kill you, but unless you're restrained, you probably won't let it. The CO coming out of a modern diesel is less than point-oh-five percent. The CO-2—carbon dioxide—is more than seven percent, so a hundred and forty times more *di*-oxide than *mon*-oxide. By comparison, that ratio of dioxide to monoxide is about ten to one in a gasoline engine, and a diesel engine produces about one-twenty-eighth the carbon monoxide that a gas engine does."

"Okay," Jackie said, not seeing a connection, yet.

"Now, we get into human physiology and evolution," he went on. "You know that burning feeling you get in your lungs when you hold your breath as long as you can? That's CO-2 build-up. The CO-2 comes out of your blood and fills your lungs, and receptors detect it and increase the burning feeling as the concentration level rises. It's evolution's way of telling you *keep breathing, stupid.*

"But there are no receptors in your lungs for CO, because our prehistoric ancestors rarely would have encountered carbon monoxide unless they stood too close to their fire inhaling the smoke, in which case they probably died, and quickly cleaned up that bit of the gene pool.

"Anyway, the upshot is that the concentration of CO-2 in the garage from diesel exhaust would be causing your lungs to burn so much that you'd want to hurl yourself through a window long before the CO had a chance to kill you. It's the opposite with gasoline exhaust. The carbon monoxide will sneak up on you and put you to sleep long before the CO-2 starts burning your lungs."

"Spoken like you've had some experience with this," Jackie said.

"I just got done teaching an OSHA course on the dangers of enclosed spaces," he replied with a grin.

"Well, it's very enlightening," Jackie said. "I never knew that."

"Somewhat uncommon knowledge that is obviously not possessed by whoever set up your friend here to look like he took his own life," Kevin said.

Walking Jackie to the door, Kevin asked, "So, are you the detective who figured out our guy, Jerome Carlson, was a serial killer?"

"I was," she said. "Did you know him?"

"No. It was all over shortly before I started. I'm actually his replacement," he replied. "But boy, I used to hear stories back then. He was quite a piece of work, making sure his victims got brought in here so he could watch their autopsies. Wow!"

"The stuff nightmares are made of," she said.

On the drive home, a call came in over the Jeep's speakers. "Hall here," she answered.

"Hi, Jackie. This is Suzan Engles. Is this a good time to talk?"

"I'm grinding slowly through Boston traffic," she replied, "so, sure. I thought it might be lighter on Saturday, but I don't think this morass of cars ever changes. You should see this mess!"

"I'm afraid I can't empathize," Suzan replied. "It's not a big problem from the back seat with your eyes closed."

"Sorry," Jackie said, easily forgetting that Suzan was blind.

"Don't be. Being chauffeured is kind of nice," she replied. "And I've learned some pretty interesting cuss words in all different languages from taxi drivers over the years. But of course, traffic and cussing is not why I called. I got a chance to listen to your recordings. First of all, my condolences on the death of your Officer Lain. That has to be hard to deal with. I was sorry to hear about that."

"Thank you," Jackie said. "The call to his mother was tough. We're still trying to figure out what exactly happened. Could you tell if Harry was telling me the truth?"

"I'm afraid not. When I listen to an actor in a movie or reading an audiobook there's usually a very distinct—and understandable—rehearsed quality to their speech. I rarely get a sense that they believe what they're saying. That's the tone and inflection I get from your Mr. Fletcher; well-rehearsed.

"Now, *you*, on the other hand ..." she added, and let the sentence hang.

"Me?" Jackie replied.

"Yeah. The bit about not finding a suicide note, among other things," Suzan said. "You were looking for a surprised reaction from him, weren't you? Like that he knew there *was* a note. I don't know what his face may have told you, but his voice didn't give anything away."

"You're right," Jackie said. "That *was* a lie; we did find a note at the scene, but I didn't get any indication that he knew it, either."

"The other recording, of Jessica, was interesting to listen to," Suzan said. "I don't think she likes you very much," she added with a little laugh. "But I do think she was being honest with you in her own aggressive way."

"Yeah, some other things we checked backed up what she was saying," Jackie replied.

"Well, I have to run," Suzan said. "Let me know if there's anything else I can help with."

"Thanks for the quick response, Suzan," Jackie said. "Make sure to send me your bill."

"It's already in your inbox," Suzan replied with a chuckle. "Good luck with your case."

Once Jackie made it a mile or two north of the Tobin Bridge and outside the city proper, the traffic thinned to where she could think about the case, and not just survival.

She believed that Scott's and Pamela's deaths had to be connected, although without the details in the suicide note—which she was sure was fake—there would really be nothing to tie the two together. If the person who killed Pamela had murdered Scott to make the case go away, they made a serious mistake in writing the note.

When they had found him dead in his truck with the motor running, the first thing that came to Jackie's mind was that he had killed himself because he was responsible—accidental or otherwise—for Pamela's death, and he knew he was going to be caught and couldn't face the consequences.

The note made her suspect exactly the opposite. Her conversation at the morgue just now with Kevin convinced her that his death was not a suicide, which meant that his "death-bed confession" was bogus, too. She felt sure that figuring out who killed either Scott *or* Pamela would solve both murders.

Who were still out there as suspects?

Jessica and/or Aaron were still on the list, although not as near the top as she once had them. They seemed to have an alibi with the party during the time Pamela died. She still needed to check with their friends on that, though.

Scott was still on the list for Pamela, but the phony suicide note muddied that up. The note was almost certainly written by whoever killed Pamela to pin the blame on Scott, and by someone who knew about that un-cited DUI stop.

Once again, that brought her around to Harry. They had not found a copy of the suicide note on any of his computers, but as Carol pointed out, there could be others they hadn't checked. And although Suzan couldn't say that Harry was lying about not going home the night Pamela died, that was why she and real polygraphs were not allowed in court; they could be fooled.

After parking at the station, as Jackie walked past the front tire of her Jeep, something caught her eye and she did a double-take to see the head of a nail flush against the rubber.

"Oh, crud!" she said as she stepped in for a closer look, surprised—and thankful—that the tire hadn't gone flat on the drive to or from Boston.

Then she noticed why; it was a stone wedged in the tread, not a nail. Relieved, she pried it out with the screwdriver-blade of her pocket knife, and then went inside.

She checked her email, forwarding Suzan's invoice for payment, and deleting half the others. She took the stack of papers from her inbox and began leafing through it, sorting by importance. It was all chief-work that needed to get done, but she also wanted to force herself down a different path for a while to let all the facts, suspicions, and guesses of the case—now *two* cases—incubate.

With the sun not setting until well after eight, this time of year, it was still light when Jackie headed for home at seven.

Approaching her Jeep, her eyes happened to fall on the stone she had dug out of her tire tread, and she stopped and stared at it for a moment. The incubation had paid off; she suddenly saw it as more than just a stone.

She bent down and picked it up looking at it closely. She wondered if her tire could have picked up the stone from Scott's driveway. It was sharp-edged—which probably meant it was freshly crushed—and it was similar in color. If *her* tire could have picked up a stone from parking there, could his killer's car, as well? She remembered that one of the things they used to tie up the Holly McCray case was the branch of a small bush caught in the frame under the car the killer used.

She drove to Scott's house, parked on the street, and walked onto the gravel. She had noticed it before, and just not thought much about it, but she could see clearly, now, that the rock looked fairly new; maybe brought in after the spring thaw and rains to make the old dirt driveway less likely to turn into a mud pit when driven over.

She bent down and picked up a small handful of the stones. They varied in size, both larger and smaller than the one from her tire—now in her pocket. She dropped the handful of rocks into an evidence bag and went back to her Jeep.

She drove home and found Jeff's car parked in her driveway. He was not in it, so she assumed he had walked around the side and was probably relaxing in the backyard. Although their relationship was progressing, it had not gotten to the point where she had given him a key, and she had re-hidden the spare he'd used before.

She pulled on a pair of gloves and quickly wiped her hands over all four of Jeff's tires, feeling for any rocks wedged in the treads. On the right-rear, she felt something, and her heart nearly stopped. But when she dug it out, it was a nearly-white peddle; nothing like the rocks that made up Scott's driveway. Nevertheless, she put it in her pocket.

While she certainly hadn't *expected* to find any rocks from Scott's driveway in Jeff's tires, she couldn't very well cross his white Toyota off the list without checking, either. Due diligence.

She pulled off the gloves and went inside.

## Chapter 30

**Sunday, July 18, 2021**

During the unplanned and very romantic night with Jeff, Jackie managed to completely let go of any thoughts of Pamela or Scott. Only after the leisurely breakfast on the back patio did the cases begin to percolate to the surface again. It was a respite that Jackie desperately needed.

After Jeff left around 10:30, Jackie called Marcia.

"Hi. How was your dinner with the in-laws last night?" Jackie asked.

"Even better than expected," Marcia replied. "My parents dropped in for dessert, and we ended up playing charades. We had a lot of fun! How about you?

"No drop-in company, thankfully. Just a quiet, intimate night with Jeff," Jackie answered.

"Nice! You needed that!" Marcia said. "But speaking of drop-ins, aside from the advantage of my father being really bad at charades—we played guys against the girls—there was another benefit to him showing up. I got to ask him, in person, about getting Scott's autopsy moved up. He made a call, right then, and didn't hang up until he had a promise for at least a preliminary report by noon, today."

"Oh, that's awesome!" Jackie said. "I'm sure that didn't make some people at the morgue very happy, but *I'm* ecstatic!"

"So, did you find any other memory devices at Scott's?" Marcia asked.

"Some USB sticks and some CDs," she replied. "I'm going to look through them, but I'll probably have Carol look at them, too, in case there's anything that's been deleted.

"But after I found them," Jackie went on, "I decided to process Scott's truck a bit to see if there was any evidence of a second person being in it." She then told her about the door handles and the interior being wiped down.

"Well, that's interesting," Marcia said. "Who details their truck to commit suicide in it?"

"Exactly! So, then I got thinking about how you get somebody to sit still in their vehicle long enough to at least pass out from carbon monoxide poisoning. While I was kicking myself for not having looked more closely at Scott's body for signs of struggle or restraint, I called the morgue in Boston, then drove in to look at him."

"Oh! You have all the fun!" Marcia said facetiously. "I'm glad I missed it."

Jackie laughed, and went on, "So, there were no marks to indicate he'd been tied up, and no petechial hemorrhaging in his eyes indicating he'd been strangled or smothered into submission."

"So, a waste of a drive into Boston, which I know you so enjoy," Marcia said.

"It might have been, except for the diener who teaches OSHA courses on safety." She then related Kevin's dissertation on carbon *di*-oxide versus carbon *mon*-oxide, the cleanliness of diesel exhaust, and human evolution."

"Wow!" Marcia said. "So, now we know for sure it wasn't a suicide, but what we *don't* know is the actual cause of death. I'm even more glad now that my folks dropped in last night for lemon meringue pie and coffee."

"You had *lemon meringue pie*?" Jackie said. "Was there any left over? That is my all-time favorite!"

Marcia laughed, and said, "I'll go put a do-not-eat-under-penalty-of-law sticker on it in the fridge."

"Thank you!" Jackie said. "Were you planning on coming in today? Because I have something I'd like to pursue, but it's a two-person act. The pie would be a nice bonus, of course."

"How is after lunch? Say, 1:00-ish?" Marcia replied.

"Perfect!'

"So, can you share what my part of your act is?"

Jackie then explained about finding the rock in her tire, matching it to Scott's driveway, and her idea of checking the tires of any suspect white Toyotas—like Harry's—that they could come up with. She told her she'd already checked Jeff's.

"Wow! That's a long shot," Marcia said. "The tread has to be the right width and depth to hold a stone, and then it has to stay there while driving around who-knows-where without getting flung out to crack somebody's windshield ... painful experience talking there."

"I agree a hundred percent," Jackie replied, "and I have a chip in my windshield to remind me. But, long though it may be, it *is* a shot—longer ones have paid off."

"And assuming you're talking about checking Mr. Fletcher's tires first, what do you need my help with?" Marcia asked.

"I don't want him to know we're doing it," Jackie answered. "So, one of us needs to be a distraction while the other checks. I don't want to tip our hand that we still think he could have been involved in Scott's death. That could give him the opportunity to cover other evidence if there is any."

"*Not* finding a matching rock in his tire wouldn't exonerate his vehicle, of course," Marcia pointed out.

"True, but *finding* one would give us probable cause to get a warrant for the rest of the car, which the warrant for his house doesn't cover," Jackie said.

"I didn't think I could get the judge to sign it if I included the car," Marcia replied a bit defensively. "We had no reason to think the car was involved at that point."

"I'm not being critical," Jackie said. "I agree. If you'd asked for the car, too, he'd probably have sent it back to you for amendment. So, anyway, are you in?"

"See you around 1:00," she answered.

"If the autopsy report beats you, I'll wait to open it," Jackie said.

# *Chapter 31*

### Sunday, July 18, 2021

In her office, Jackie looked at the directories and file names on Scott's memory sticks and CDs. Based on the dates, she guessed they were back-ups or items that he had transferred from an old computer to his newer laptop—there was nothing within four months. Being overly cautious, however, she didn't open any of the files, preferring to let Carol check the sticks and CDs for malware, first.

Marcia arrived at five minutes to one and brought the piece of pie into Jackie's office. "You want this here, or in the fridge?" she asked.

Jackie laughed, and said, "Yeah, right!" as she held out her hands. "I skipped dessert at lunch anticipating this." She looked at the fat slice of plastic-wrap-covered pie, and added, "Oh, yes! That looks amazing! It looks homemade. Did you make it?"

Marcia laughed, and as she sat down opposite Jackie, she said, "My mother-in-law. I can cook reasonably well, but I don't bake. That's a whole 'nother set of skills."

As Jackie pealed the wrap off the pie, she told Marcia, "Bring your chair around to this side. The autopsy report has been sitting in my email for an hour."

While Marcia pulled her chair around, Jackie took a fork and paper napkin from her desk drawer.

"Seriously?" Marcia said. "You're going to eat while you read an autopsy?"

"Maybe not the pictures," Jackie said. "But, hey! Come on; it's lemon meringue pie!"

While there *were* photographs attached of tissue samples and microscopic enlargements of cells, the text told them everything they needed to know, although not what they expected to see. The mechanism of death was "Blood concentration of COHb (carboxyhemoglobin) of 46.6% being incompatible with life." The cause of death was "Carbon monoxide poisoning possibly by means of inhalation of vehicle exhaust fumes." The manner of death was listed as "Undetermined."

The undetermined manner of death was further explained: "Outward appearances at the scene where the deceased was found would indicate suicide, but the vehicle in which the body was found was diesel-powered, making passive self-asphyxiation by means of its exhaust unlikely, although not physically impossible. Further investigation by the police is required to better determine a cause of death."

In the section that described the external examination, the ME specifically noted that there were no outward signs of an altercation or struggle, and no indication that the deceased had been restrained in any way. He also noted that there were four parallel shallow lacerations on his back, starting atop the left scapula and extending approximately eight centimeters downward. Healing of the lacerations suggested the cuts were approximately seven to ten days old, and therefore of no significance with regard to the death. The marks were determined to be, "consistent with minor wounds inflicted by fingernails."

"That's not nearly as much help as I'd hoped," Jackie commented after swallowing a mouthful of pie. "Maybe he killed himself and maybe he was murdered. Maybe he died in his truck in his garage or maybe he died in someone else's car somewhere else."

"Well, at least the scratches on his back tie him to Mrs. Fletcher's murder," Marcia said.

"Even that's ambiguous," Jackie said. "Unless the DNA from her fingernails proves otherwise, I'll grant you that the scratches probably put the two of them together within a day on either side of her death. But being on his back where they are it doesn't seem like they'd be defensive wounds. If she was trying to stop him from strangling her, they should be on his face or chest or arms or neck. These would seem to be marks of passion."

"I'm guessing that if I drew blood on my husband's back in the throes of passion the magic of the moment would be over," Marcia said with a little laugh.

Jackie laughed, and said, "Yeah. Seriously different strokes for different folks there!"

"So, what now?" Marcia asked.

Scraping the last crumbs of flaky crust from the plate, Jackie said, "Well, at the risk of offending an overworked ME, and of drawing a target around a hole, I'm going to call Scott's death a homicide. And even though we can't tie the suicide note to him directly," she sent on, "I still think Harry is the most likely person to have written it." She picked up her desk phone and dialed Harry's number.

"Hi, Harry," she said when he answered. "Hey, I really hate to keep bugging you, but can I get you to drop by the station again this afternoon?"

"What now, Colombo?" he replied.

She chuckled, and said, "Yeah, it is getting a little like that. I'm sorry, but the more I think about your theory that Scott Lain killed Pamela and then killed himself, the more it makes sense. I have a spreadsheet timeline of the night that Pamela died, and I'd like to go over it in detail with you to make sure I have it right. Then I can fit that together with what I know about Scott's activities that night, and see if things add up."

"Okay," he said, only a little less exasperated. "Half hour?"

"Perfect, Harry. Thanks!"

When she hung up, Marcia asked, "Do you really have a spreadsheet timeline of that night? Or was that a bluff to get him here?"

"No, I have it," Jackie answered. She navigated through the case folder and opened an Excel file. "I needed to do this to visualize it and to make sure all the ducks fit in the row and in the right order."

| ACTION | MINS | FROM | TO |
|---|---|---|---|
| Dinner (6:30 PM) | 30 | 6:30 PM | 7:00 PM |
| Clean Up | 30 | 7:00 PM | 7:30 PM |
| Movie: FRWL | 120 | 7:30 PM | 9:30 PM |
| Pamela on Computer | 30 | 7:30 PM | 8:00 PM |
| Pamela Goes Upstairs | 5 | 8:00 PM | 8:05 PM |
| Pamela Draws Bath | 20 | 8:05 PM | 8:25 PM |
| Pamela Slips in Bath | 1 | 8:25 PM | 8:26 PM |
| Pamela Drowns | 4 | 8:26 PM | 8:30 PM |
| Harry Finds Pamela | 1 | 9:30 PM | 9:31 PM |

With the first several lines of the spreadsheet showing, Jackie explained, "I have the action on the left, then how many minutes it took based on what Harry told me or what seemed logical. I input the 6:30 as a start time, but after that, it automatically updates the *From* and *To* columns if I change the number of minutes. She then demonstrated by changing *Clean Up* from 30 minutes to 60 minutes.

"I am impressed!" Marcia said. "Is this something they taught at the police academy?"

"No. I had a boyfriend in college who was borderline OCD when it came to being on time. Even worse than I am. He had a spreadsheet like this for his classes, assignments, lectures, everything. If he was going to take a trip he made one with departure and arrival times, the time to get to the airport, time to get through security, and time to get his luggage on the other end. I once accused him of having one somewhere for our love-making sessions. He denied it, but I still wonder."

Marcia laughed, but looking at the screen, she said, "That shows Mr. Fletcher watching the James Bond movie. We know that's not correct by his own admission."

"No," Jackie said. "This is my original that I put together before we knew he was lying about that. I have several other iterations saved that show Harry looking for the phantom MG, that show him with Megan, that have Jessica showing up and Harry coming and going based on the Timmons' videos, and showing Scott in the mix."

"Interesting," Marcia said. "If and when this goes to trial, the DA is going to love all that! So, which one are you going to show Mr. Fletcher?"

"The one with Scott killing Pamela," Jackie answered. "But I think I'm going to make a couple of tweaks to it to give Harry a chance to add his input and correct my *mistakes*. While I'm doing that, why don't you move your car around back so Harry won't know you're here and wonder why you're not with me in the interview room. I want his guard down as low as possible. While I'm with him, you can go out and check his tires for rocks."

Twenty minutes later, Jackie got a call from up front telling her that Harry Fletcher and Aaron Delaney were there to see her.

Jackie looked out her window and saw Aaron's red Kia in the parking lot. "Crap!" she said to Marcia. "Apparently, Harry rode over with Aaron. His car's probably still at home in the garage."

"Do you have a plan-B?" Marcia asked.

Jackie thought for a few moments and then said, "Yes. While I keep them busy here, you go over to Harry's, go inside, and check his tires there. We still have the warrant, so we don't need his permission or to even tell him."

"How do I get in?" Marcia asked. "I don't know how to pick a lock."

Jackie thought for another moment, and then said, "I'll have dispatch send Kyle to meet you over there."

"What if he has an alarm?" Marcia asked.

"I don't think he does," Jackie replied. "I didn't see a keypad anywhere in the house when I was there before."

"But doesn't he have a home automation app on his phone? Don't those send a message that a door's being opened?"

"You're a regular negative-Nancy today, aren't you?" Jackie said. "You're probably right, though." After another few seconds of thought, she went on, "Try going in through the garage side door. There's a pretty good chance that he won't have sprung for remote-control locks on every door in the house. Most people just put them on the front door."

"Pretty good chance?"

"Okay. I'll get him to turn his phone off just to be sure," Jackie said. "If he finds out he finds out. What you're doing isn't illegal; you have a warrant. I just don't want to tip our hand, is all."

After asking dispatch to send Kyle to Harry's right away, Jackie went to the front lobby to greet Harry and Aaron while Marcia went out the back door.

"Hi," Jackie said. "Thank you both for coming in, but I wasn't expecting you together."

"Aaron was at the house when you called," Harry explained, "and he said you wanted to talk to him, too, so we figured we'd kill two birds with one stone."

Aaron added, "That's okay, isn't it?"

"It's just awkward, is all," Jackie said. "I can really only talk with one of you at a time about the case. We always have to be careful about *cross-pollinating* witnesses, so to speak. You understand."

"I guess," Harry said to Jackie. To Aaron, he added, "So much for killing two birds." Back to Jackie, he asked, "So, which of us first?"

She answered by saying to Aaron, "If you don't mind sitting tight for a little while, I'd like to talk to Harry first. Can I get you some water? A soda? Coffee?"

"Water'd be good, thank you," he replied.

She led Harry to the interview room, and then said, "I'll be right back. I need to have somebody get Aaron that water. Oh, and can you turn off your phone while we're in here, please?"

"Turn off my phone? Why? I didn't have to the other times I was in here?"

"Yeah," Jackie said, feigning a bit of embarrassment, "That's my fault. It's actually department policy, but we've gotten kind of lax about it. We had an incident in here yesterday that drove home the point of *why* it's a policy, though."

Harry just shrugged as he took his phone from his pocket. Jackie was glad he didn't ask anything about the incident, because she hadn't made up the details, yet.

Jackie stepped into the dispatch room and motioned Sharon over where she was sure Aaron could see them through the glass at the front. "Will you get Aaron a bottle of water, please?" she asked. "And then keep an eye on him. If he leaves, shoot me a text on my cell." She was going to draw her time with Harry out as long as she could, and she was concerned that Aaron might get bored in the lobby and maybe drive back to Harry's to wait. It was only about seven or eight minutes away.

Back in the interview room, having added as much time as she could, Jackie said to Harry before she sat down, "I'm sorry; I offered Aaron something to drink, but not you. Can I get you anything?"

"No. I'm fine," he said, with just a hint of impatience.

"Okay. Well let me just grab my coffee, and what it is I want you to look at with me. I'll be right back," she said and left the room.

It was several minutes before Jackie returned, and when she did, Harry said, "Where was your coffee? The Agawam?"

"Sorry," she lied. "I did have to freshen it, and then the printer was out of paper." She sat down and slid a printout of her spreadsheet in front of Harry, and said, "Anyway, this is a timeline that I put together of the night that Pamela died. Based on the times from the Timmons' videos, and what you've told me, I think I have things pretty much in order, but these things I have highlighted yellow I'm not sure about; they're more educated guesses. I hoped that bouncing this back and forth with you, we could iron out the wrinkles I still have left."

As he read down the list, Jackie explained—in long detail—what she had been thinking as she had created each entry.

At Harry's house, Marcia had to wait an excruciating three minutes for Kyle to arrive. They went to the side of the garage, and after stretching on his gloves he began his work on the door's deadbolt.

After half a minute of applying a little turning pressure on his lever while he flicked the plungers with the pick, he said to Marcia, "I don't think this lock's had a key in it in a year. It's really stiff. I'm going to need to spray it."

She waited with forced patience as he went to the cruiser and then came back. As he squirted some WD-40 into the lock, she said, "You always carry that with you in the car?"

"Actually, yes," he answered. "Along with it being good for things like this, it can dry out the ignition wires on a car if it goes through a puddle and gets all shorted out."

It took another full minute for him to finally feel all the tumblers slip into place and for the cylinder to start turning. As he worked, he said, "This one is being a real SOB. I can usually get a lock open in twenty seconds."

With the deadbolt finally pulled back, Kyle turned the knob to open the door, but it didn't turn. "Damn! The knob is locked, too!" he said.

"Oh, you've got to be shitting me!" Marcia said as she looked at her watch. She then added, "Pardon my French."

Kyle squirted the knob's lock and went to work on it. After another half-minute, the lock turned, and Kyle finally opened the door.

"Shit!" Marcia said as she stepped inside. "His car's not *here*!"

"I could have told you that," Kyle said. "I didn't know that's why you wanted to get inside. I saw it in Knowlesies' parking lot on my way here. Probably there for an oil change or something."

"Shit!" Marcia repeated. That explained why Aaron had given Mr. Fletcher a ride to the station.

Leaving, Marcia turned the finger-knob on the inside of the door handle to lock it as they went out, but left the deadbolt unlocked, not wanting to waste any more time picking it again to re-lock it.

With Kyle in the lead with his lights flashing and several applications of siren, the two drove as fast as possible to Knowles' gas station.

As they pulled in, one of the mechanics was just getting into Harry's car to move it into the service bay. Kyle pulled in front of it and Marcia pulled in behind. Bill got out and looked between the two with a questioning expression, finally settling on Kyle.

"Hi, Bill," Kyle said, getting out of the cruiser. "Sorry for the dramatics." Pointing at Marcia as she approached pulling on her rubber gloves, he added, "This is Marcia Grieves with the Essex County DA's Office. She needs to check something on Harry's car."

"Essex County DA?" Bill repeated. "What's she looking for?"

"Frankly, she hasn't told me," Kyle said. "I'm just the facilitator."

As they watched, Marcia ran her hands over each of the tires of Harry's car. Three times she stopped to take pictures on her phone. Finally, she stood up, pulled the gloves off her hands inside-out, and stuffed them into her pocket. She opened up the text app on her phone, tapped Jackie's cell number, and began typing.

In the interview room, Jackie was running out of questions and different hypotheses that she could discuss with Harry when her phone vibrated.

"Sorry," she said to Harry as she tapped the screen. "I told them not to interrupt unless it was important."

"So much for department policy," he said.

"That applies to the interviewee, not the interviewer," she said as she read Marcia's text.

Car at Knowles. Long story. Three rocks in his tires. They look like the ones you showed me.

Jackie quickly tapped in her reply:

Impound car. Start warrant ASAP. THX!!

"Sorry," Jackie repeated to Harry as she put her phone away. "So, you think we have this pretty well organized?" she said pointing to her spreadsheet with cross-outs and notes scribbled all over it.

"Short of being able to hear Scott's and Pamela's versions of the events, I don't know how we could get any more detail into it," he said, obviously tired of going over and over it.

Knowing that she didn't need to give Kyle and Marcia any extra time to get out of Harry's, now, when she led Harry back out to the lobby, she said to Aaron, "I appreciate you coming in with Harry, and I'm really sorry to have made you wait all this time, but something's come up and I need to leave. Can I call you and reschedule again?"

"Yeah, sure," he said as he got to his feet. "I'm not leaving town."

"Thanks!" Jackie said as she wondered if that was in reference to her warning to Jessica.

She went back to the interview room, got the marked-up spreadsheet—which really added nothing to her own theories—went to her office, and closed out of the open programs on her computer. As she turned to leave, she looked out the window and saw Aaron's car stopped at the end of the department's driveway. She could see Harry in the passenger seat with his phone to his ear.

The car sat for a long time, then its backup lights came on, and it started coming into the parking area backward.

"Crud!" Jackie said under her breath, guessing what had probably just happened. She considered rushing out the back while Harry came in the front, but she knew that would only postpone the inevitable.

She waited in her office until Sharon called her to tell her that Harry had come back and was asking for her ... and that he seemed upset.

When she opened the door to the lobby, Harry said, "What the fuck's going on, Jackie? I just called Knowles to see if my car was ready, and Bill told me that Kyle Hopkins and your Ms. Grieves are there, and they *impounded* it! What the fuck?"

"It's been deemed material evidence in the investigation into the death of Scott Lain," Jackie said.

"*Material evidence?* What the hell are you talking about? What has my car got to do with that Lain's suicide?"

"There's evidence that your car was at Scott's house in the not too distant past, Harry," Jackie replied. "You told me when we were working on the spreadsheet that you didn't know where Scott even lived. Something's not adding up, and I need to figure out what."

"Jesus!" he said as he shook his head. "First you think I killed Pamela, and now you think I killed Lain. I think you have a serial-killer fixation, Hall!"

Although she probably had enough to hold him as a suspect in Scott's death, she certainly didn't have enough to arrest him, so she said, "Nobody's accusing you of *any* killing, Harry. I'm sorry, but I have to follow where the evidence leads. I'll do whatever I can to get your car processed as quickly as possible. If it ..."

"Processed? What do you mean processed?" he interrupted her.

"We'll need to have the State Police Crime Lab go through it to see if they can further substantiate that the car was really at Scott's and possibly when, and of course to see if there's any indication that Scott was ever in the car."

"*In* the car? Why the hell would he have been in my car? I told you I hated the little prick. Do you think I gave him a ride home after he screwed Pamela? Or maybe you think he'd have gotten in my car with me so I could drive him home to his suicide."

"I'm sorry, Harry," Jackie said. "I'll keep you posted on the progress." She then turned and went back inside.

When Jackie arrived at Knowles', Harry's car was just being pulled up onto the flat tilting bed of a tow truck for the hour and a half ride out to Sudbury where the State Police Crime Lab was located.

As they watched, she said to Marcia, "Do you think you can get your father to pull more strings for us?"

"I already called him," she replied. "He said he'd make a couple of calls."

"Perfect!" Jackie said.

## *Chapter 32*
### Monday, July 19, 2021

Fortunately for Jackie, Monday proved to be a busy day with the normal chief-of-police stuff that took no holiday just because she was focused on a case. It allowed the day to go by quickly while they waited for any news from the crime lab.

Marcia, too, kept busy after coming into her Rowley office after lunch by contacting the people on Jessica's and Aaron's lists. Unless there was a very well-orchestrated symphony of lies, both of the kids were at the party where they said they were when Pamela was killed.

Around three in the afternoon, Marcia received a call on her cell phone from the ME's Office in Boston.

"Hello, Ms. Grieves, this is Diane Crane. I'm a DNA tech with the Office of the Chief Medical Examiner in Boston. I was told to contact you regarding the tissue samples recovered from Pamela Fletcher's fingernails."

"Oh, yes. Thank you. Did you find a match?" Marcia asked.

"We've completed the DNA profile and have run a search of the CODIS database, but no matches were found," Diane answered. "We'll keep the profile on record, and perform a periodic re-search."

"No match?" Marcia replied, obviously surprised. "Do you know if it was checked against a Scott Lain?"

"Oh, I'd have no idea," the woman said. "There are millions of profiles in CODIS, and they don't have names associated with them, anyway. If there was a match, we'd have been put in touch with the agency that provided that profile through NDIS to get a name."

"Can I *request* that it be checked against Scott Lain?" Marcia asked. "He was brought into your facility in Boston Saturday afternoon. We received his autopsy report yesterday."

Marcia could hear a keyboard being tapped, and then Diane said, "Here he is. His DNA work is in queue. It's probably a couple of weeks out. Until it's done and gets uploaded to CODIS, there's nothing we have to match against. Sorry."

After hanging up, Marcia thought about asking her father to get involved in pushing Scott's DNA work to the front of the line. She finally decided that where things stood with the investigation it was probably unimportant. A match would only prove that Pamela had made the scratches, not whether they were passionate or defensive. Besides, both parties were now dead, anyway.

At a little after four, Jackie had a call put through to her from the State Police Lab in Sudbury.

"Hi, Chief Hall. BJ Peters here. You probably don't remember me, but I worked on your serial killer case a few years ago. How have you been?"

"Hi, BJ," Jackie replied. "Sure I remember you. You came up with the idea of doing DNA testing on the piece of shrubbery stuck under the perpetrator's car. Nice to hear from you, again. Do you have news on the car we sent out to you yesterday?"

"I do," he replied, "but I have a question, first. How in the world did you get Sunday overtime authorized for a team to process this thing?"

"Friends in high places," she replied. "I'm working with an investigator from the Essex County DA's Office, whose father happens to be Attorney General Santori."

"That'll do it," he said. "So, anyway, we recovered a few useable fingerprints from the steering wheel and other places on the driver's side, but there were also a lot that were smudged, like someone had been driving while wearing gloves. The good ones all appear to be from the same person.

"But there were *no* prints on the passenger side. The door handles—inside and out—the seatbelt, the window buttons, everything appears to have been wiped down."

"Interesting," Jackie said, thinking about her own dusting of Scott's truck with similar results.

"But we did find a couple of hairs between the passenger headrest and the seatback, up on top," BJ went on. "Per your other investigator's heads-up, we got fingerprints, a blood sample, and hair samples of your Scott Lain sent over from the morgue, and the hairs look like a solid match. No follicles, so we can't run a DNA, but I think they're plenty for you to say that Lain was in that car and not driving it. Add to that the fact that he *miraculously* didn't touch anything while he was in the car, and I think you have foul play on your hands.

"Do you have a set of prints for the owner of the car?" he continued. "We could check those against what we collected from the driver's side."

"I don't," she replied. "He's never been arrested that I'm aware of. But thank you, BJ! I really appreciate the quick work and the call."

"No problem," he said. "I appreciate the OT. It's going to make my next fishing vacation a little nicer. Hey, keep me posted on how the case goes, okay?"

"Will do!"

After hanging up, she called Marcia in and explained what BJ had just told her.

"So, do we bring Mr. Fletcher in for more questioning?" Marcia asked.

Jackie looked at her watch, and said, "He's probably still at work. Let's drive over and wait down the street for him to get home. I'm a little afraid that if I call him and ask him to come in he might figure out that we found something in the car and he could take off."

Jackie and Marcia sat in Marcia's less-conspicuous car in the Timmons' driveway across the street while a patrol officer, Bill French, waited down the street and around the corner to be called up by Jackie.

At twenty past five, with Jackie's coffee from Burwell Beans long gone, Harry pulled into his driveway driving Pamela's silver Hyundai sedan. He stopped momentarily as the garage door went up, then pulled inside and the door closed behind him. Jackie called Bill on the radio, and Marcia drove across the street pulling into the driveway and stopping.

When Harry answered the front door, he looked at Jackie through the screen door, and said, "Now what?" As he spoke, Paul pulled across his driveway in the cruiser and stopped. "Seriously?" Harry added. "The cavalry?"

"Harry, I need you to come down to the station with us," Jackie said.

"Am I under arrest?" he asked.

"No. But there's some pretty serious questions that need answers," she replied.

"And if I refuse?" he said.

"*Then* you're under arrest," she answered. "That's how serious these questions are, Harry."

"Fine," he said with exaggerated resignation. "Let me turn off the microwave."

"Okay if I come in with you?" she asked.

"What? You think I'm going to go get a gun or something?"

"It's department policy, Harry," she said. "You wouldn't want me to have to put myself on report, would you?" she added trying to lighten the moment a bit.

"Whatever," he said as he pushed the screen door open.

With Harry in the back of the cruiser and Jackie in the passenger seat, Marcia followed them back to the station.

In the interview room, Jackie and Marcia sat opposite Harry. Harry appeared more annoyed than nervous.

"The reason your car was impounded, Harry," Jackie began, "is that we found stones embedded in the treads of your tires that match the gravel in Scott Lain's driveway, and you told me you didn't even know where he lived."

"You're shitting me," he said. "Did he pave his driveway with crushed Italian marble? It's dirt for Christ's sake! It's what the earth is made of! It could have come from anywhere!"

"It's not quite Italian-marble unique, but it's not common roadside dirt, either," Jackie said. "We found the receipt, and it's a granite that's quarried in New Hampshire, and crushed and screened in Ipswich by Miles River Sand and Gravel to a certain size to let a driveway drain. They put his driveway in just this spring, so the stones haven't weathered very much."

"And nobody else anywhere in eastern Mass. has it?" Harry said. "No other houses? No shops? No parking lots? Look, I don't know what else to tell you; I have never been to Scott Lain's house, and still don't know where it's even located."

"Well, the stones were just the probable-cause that allowed us to send your car to the State Police Crime Lab for processing, Harry," Jackie said, watching closely for a nervous reaction.

There was none. Instead, he said, "Yeah, you told me that. But I still don't know what the hell you expected them to find."

"They found two hairs that match Scott Lain's stuck to the passenger headrest," Jackie said. "That means Scott was in your car, and it means that you're lying to me ... again."

"Impossible!" Harry said. "Scott Lain's never even been *near* my car except when he pulled me over and harassed me that time, and that was on the *driver's* side. He's sure as hell has never been *in* the car!"

"That would seem to mean that someone else gave him a ride in your car," Marcia said a bit sarcastically. "Who might that be, Mr. Fletcher? Your wife? Your Kids?"

"As convenient as it might be to agree with that, Ms. Grieves," he replied in a matching tone, "they don't know how to drive my car. It's a stick-shift. Almost nobody knows how to use a clutch, anymore. The only person who ..."

Harry suddenly stopped talking. Jackie and Marcia watched him as his eyes darted back and forth as he was apparently recalling and processing something. As he mentally scrutinized whatever it was, his mouth fell slightly agape.

Finally, he said in a slow, incredulous tone, "Holy fucking hell." Still staring blankly at nothing, he stated. "It's Megan! It all fits! It's fucking *Megan*!"

"What fits, Harry?" Jackie said. "What are you talking about?"

"How could I have been so fucking stupid?" he said to himself, clearly still thinking about what was streaming through his mind. Then, as if coming out of a trance, he focused on Jackie, again, and said, "*Megan!* It *has* to be! If somebody killed Scott, it must have been Megan. And if that's true, then it has to tie back to Pamela, too. Motive, means, and opportunity; they're all there!"

"What makes you think that, Harry?" Jackie asked.

He took a long, deep breath, and then began, "The motive is that Megan wanted me to divorce Pamela and marry her. She said that because Pamela and I were doing the CNM thing, it was proof that we didn't belong together. I wasn't interested in leaving Pamela, though; hell that's the whole *point* of CNM; that we were *completely* compatible in every other way. But I pretended to be considering it because I thought if I told Megan that it was never going to happen, she'd break it off with me. Of the CNM partners I've had, she gets my foot-thing better than anyone."

"Where's the opportunity?" Marcia asked, skeptically. "How could Megan have killed your wife without you knowing it? You told us that you and she were together the night she died. Ms. Hope was your alibi that *you* couldn't have committed the murder, now, you're saying *she* did, but without your knowledge."

"My narcolepsy; or more correctly the BSC," he replied immediately, apparently having already fit that piece of the puzzle into its place. "We had a pretty physical—and unusually long—episode of sex that night. She must have been trying to wear me out, knowing I'd be unconscious for a long time afterward ... which I was. So, the car in your videos *is* mine, it's just not me driving it." He then snapped his fingers as another point clicked into place for him. "And that would explain why it stayed in the driveway. The built-in button on the mirror doesn't work—it needs to be reprogrammed or something—I have to use my phone app to open and close the garage door, which Megan wouldn't have known." Another piece tumbled, and he added, "But that would be how she got into the house! She *did* know I used the phone for the front door lock! She obviously took my phone along with my car while I was asleep."

"Which explains Mr. Lain's hair in your car, how?" Marcia asked, still dubious.

He thought again for several moments and then said, "I don't know. She had the *opportunity* to have him in my car, but I can't think of a *motive* to do that."

"How did she have the opportunity to have him in your car?" Jackie asked.

"That's what made all this click for me," he replied. "She had my car most of the day Friday. Neither of us felt it was appropriate for her to be at the funeral, and I didn't need it, so she borrowed it to drive down to Plymouth for something. Her car is an old Prius and she said she didn't trust it to make it down there and back; something about a weak battery. I don't know why she would have met with Scott or how that would even connect with his suicide, though." Suddenly, he looked up at Jackie, and said, "Wait! The whole reason I'm here is that you don't think it *was* a suicide, do you? How exactly did he die? Could Megan have staged that death, too?"

"We're not releasing the cause of death, yet," Jackie said. "Do you happen to know if Megan and Scott were friends?"

"I think they knew each other, but I don't believe they were friends, now that you mention it," he replied. "I had told her about finding out that Scott was Pamela's CNM partner a while back, and she made some comment about him being a slimy little prick." He thought for a few moments and then said, "I wonder if he could have figured out that Megan was involved in Pamela's death and he was blackmailing her. Maybe he was on patrol and saw her coming or going from the house, then put two and two together after Pamela's death was ruled a homicide. Or, maybe when he was there after I called 9-1-1 he discovered something at the scene that he connected to her. You said he stayed to clean things up for me, didn't you? Hell, it could even have been both of those things combined."

With the advantage of knowing that Scott had been inside Harry's house long before Harry called 9-1-1, and knowing the contents of the note found at Scott's, Jackie was sure that Harry was slightly off base with his guesses, but she found the blackmail aspect intriguing. That would certainly be motive for Megan to want to kill Scott. She would get rid of that threat to her, and by concocting the suicide note confession it would end the investigation into Pamela's death, too. Win, win.

Jackie nudged Marcia and then said to Harry, "We'll be right back. Can I get you anything?"

"Can I take a pee break?" he asked.

"Oh, sure, of course," Jackie said. She showed him to the restroom, and then she and Marcia went to Jackie's office and closed the door.

"What do you think?" Jackie asked. "Truth or lies?"

"I started out disbelieving him," she answered, "but more and more of what he said was making sense."

"What we need is Megan's computer," Jackie said. "If we could find the original of the note on it, that would tie a lot of this together."

Back in the interview room, Jackie said to Harry, "We have reason to believe that there may be evidence on Megan's computer that can link some of these things together, but until now, we haven't had enough probable cause to get a warrant for it. But we think that between the circumstantial evidence we have and a sworn statement from you, we probably do have enough. Are you willing to write and sign a statement for us, attesting to what we've just talked about?"

"Of course! Absolutely!" he said. "But there may be an even simpler and faster way. What if I can come up with a way to borrow Megan's laptop for an hour or so? If she gave me permission to take it, then wouldn't it be covered under the warrant you have for *my* property since it's in my possession?"

"Ooo!" Marcia said. "That would be skating on some pretty thin legal ice. If she was arrested, and I were her defense attorney, I'd sure as hell challenge that. And if the ... if what we think might be on her computer got tossed, we'd have nothing."

"Thanks for the offer," Jackie said. "but I think will stick with the tried and true warrant application process." To Marcia, she added, "If you'd get started on that, please." To Harry, she said, "I'll bring my laptop in for you to write your statement about what you just told us. Run the highpoints and the phrasing by Marcia so all the bases are covered and there are no contradictions."

# Chapter 33

**Monday, July 19, 2021**

When Harry got home, he poured himself a scotch and then called Megan.

"Hey! How are you?" Harry said when she answered her phone. "Are you off tonight? You feel like getting together? I have something you might be interested in."

"Yes, you do!" she answered, turning his phrase into a double entendre.

He laughed, and said, "Yes! There is that, too! Boy, I've missed you!"

"Me, too!" she said. "I was just thinking about calling *you*, as a matter of fact."

"Your place? Six-thirty, or so?" he said.

"Sounds great!" she replied. "See you a little later."

"I love you!" he said.

"I love you, too, baby!" she replied.

When Harry arrived, Megan was still in her EMT uniform—which she knew he loved. She threw her arms around him, kissed him hard, and then said, "God, I've missed you! Has it really only been a week and a half?"

"Eleven days, but who's counting?" he replied and gave her another kiss.

She rubbed her hand across the front of his pants, and said, "You said you had something *else* besides this that I might be interested in?"

He put his hands on her butt and pulled her close, while saying, "I spent some time today with Chief Hall and her County DA side-kick."

"Ooo! A ménage à trios?" she replied. "Was it good for you?"

He laughed, and said, "In this case, talking with them was probably far more satisfying than sex would have been. They asked me a bunch of questions about Scott Lain, but the upshot of the whole thing is that they've apparently bought his suicide and the note, hook, line, and sinker. Hall said they're going to close out both Pamela's and Lain's investigations in a day or two."

She kissed him, again, and said, "Oh, you are a plot-writing frigging genius! How is it your books aren't on bestseller lists all over the place?"

"Hey, I'll trade that notoriety for being rid of Pamela and being able to be with you, all day long," he replied. "Her insurance pay-outs should make up for the lack of royalties, just fine."

Another kiss, and she said with a put-on pout, "I suppose we'll have to keep sneaking around for a year or so for the sake of *respectability*."

He held her tightly, and said, "I'd call that a small price to pay for having our whole lives together, future Mrs. Fletcher."

She chuckled, and said, "I like the sound of that!" Taking him by the hand, she said, "Come on; I can't wait for you to take my shoes off and work your magic on my feet."

"One thing, first," he said as he walked toward the stove, still holding her right hand in his left. From the set in the big wooden block on the counter, he slid out the long carving knife, and while the question was still forming in Megan's brain, he spun, pulled her toward him, and drove the blade into her chest and through her heart.

Her eyes and mouth sprung open at the shock and the pain, and as she stumbled backward, she mumbled, "What ... why?" and then collapsed onto the floor.

Harry just looked down at her. She wasn't dead, yet, but it would only be a minute, or so.

He took a pair of rubber gloves from his pocket, stretched them on as he stepped over her, and then walked to the bathroom, just off the kitchen.


A few minutes later, he came back into the kitchen and returned to the knife block on the counter. As he looked down at Megan, trying to determine if she was still breathing, he took the chef's knife from the set.

Holding the knife backward in his right hand—with the point of the blade toward himself and the sharp edge facing down—he placed the edge on top of his left forearm, then drew it down and across, cutting deeply into the muscle.

"*Shee-it!*" he cried out through clenched teeth. He knew the cut was going to hurt but had mis-guessed how much ... by a lot.

He steadied himself against the island and blinked away the tears that involuntarily filled his eyes. After ten or fifteen seconds, and with his teeth still gritted against the pain, he knelt down, put the handle of the knife into Megan's motionless hand, and wrapped her fingers around it. He then stood back up with the knife, and making sure not to disturb the fingerprints he had just made, he held it by the blade between the thumb and finger of his left hand right where the blade met the handle. He then placed the palm of his right hand against the far end of the handle.

Carefully, he positioned the point against his chest below his right shoulder where he knew there was nothing vital, and with one hard, quick shove, he drove it in.

"*Fuck!*" he growled as he collapsed to one knee. Steadying himself with a gloved hand on the island, he let the knife slip from its two-inch deep wound and fall to the floor.

He lifted himself back to his feet, peeled off the gloves, and then, dripping blood, he walked back to the guest bathroom.

First, he flushed his gloves down the toilet, and then he took a washcloth and put it inside his blood-soaked shirt against his chest wound. Finally, he wrapped a towel tightly around his arm. Only then did he take out his phone.

"9-1-1, what is your emergency," Gail answered.

"This is Harry Fletcher. I need an ambulance; I've been stabbed." He paused a fraction of a second, and added, "I ... I think Megan Hope may be dead."

"Oh, God, Harry! Where are you?"

He gave her Megan's address, and then said weakly, "Please hurry." Intentionally leaving the call connected, he then sat down on the floor, leaned against the vanity, and waited to be discovered by the first-responders.

# Chapter 34

## Monday, July 19, 2021

Jackie was home and washing her supper dishes when she got the call from Gail about Harry.

"Oh, my God! Did he say what happened?" Jackie asked as he grabbed her keys and her radio, and rushed out the door.

"No," Gail answered. "He sounded pretty weak, and then he just stopped talking. The call is still connected, though, and I think I can hear him breathing."

"God!" Jackie said as she swung up into her Jeep and started it. A moment later the call switched to the Jeep's speakers, and Jackie asked, "Who's in route?"

"Engine three, and both Kyle and Gary. Kyle should almost be there. American Ambulance responded that they have two units on the way."

"Okay. I'm going to call Marcia," Jackie said. "If there are any updates, call me on my radio."

Jackie turned on her hidden red and blue flashing lights and flipped a switch that redirected her horn button to a siren under the hood.

"Hi, Jackie. What's up?" Marcia answered her phone.

"Harry just called 9-1-1 and said that he'd been stabbed and that he thought Megan was dead. He's at Megan's, and I'm heading there now."

"Holy shit! What happened?"

"Nobody seems to know, yet," Jackie replied after a double blip of her siren. "Apparently, he passed out while he was talking to Gail."

"You want me to come up there?"

"I thought you'd probably want to," Jackie said.

"Hell, yes! Let me get a bra on, and I'm on the way."

When Jackie pulled into Megan's apartment complex one of the ambulances was just leaving with lights flashing and siren wailing. The other ambulance sat still in the parking lot, but with its lights blinking, as well.

A number of the other residents were naturally standing around in groups of two, three, and four, watching the commotion. As she made her way to the unit's door, a man called out, "Hey, Jackie! What's going on? Somebody said Megan was hurt."

"I don't know, yet, Charlie," she answered as she hurried inside. She then took the stairs two at a time to Megan's second-floor apartment.

She reached the top of the stairs just as two EMTs were guiding their empty gurney down the hall.

She looked between the man and the woman, and said, "No chance?"

"Sorry, Chief," the woman said. "There was nothing we could do for her by the time we arrived. The male's been transported to Anna Jaques, though. Cut on the left arm and a stab wound in the chest. I didn't hear any fluid in his lung, so he must have gotten lucky. It doesn't look life-threatening."

"Thanks," Jackie said. "Was the guy conscious when he left?"

"Yes. Though I'm not sure I'd call him alert," she said. "Probably a combination of blood loss and trauma."

Inside, Kyle was taking photographs with the department's digital SLR camera. "Hi, Chief," he said when he saw her. "Pretty gruesome, huh? The EMTs said there was no chance for her, so they just worked on Harry." He pointed, and added, "We found him in the bathroom on the floor, covered in blood."

"Did he say anything about what happened here?" she asked.

"No," Kyle said. "I think he was just barely conscious."

Jackie looked down at Megan lying on the floor in a pool of fresh blood. Her eyes were open and eerily staring upward at nothing, suggesting that she died pretty quickly.

A kitchen knife was buried—nearly to its handle—in her chest. It was just to the left of her sternum, and from its location, Jackie was quite sure it had passed straight through her heart.

She turned and found a wooden block on the counter filled with knives with the same style of handle. There were *two* empty slots, however. She looked down and quickly noticed the other knife lying on the floor between Megan's legs. There was definitely blood on it—presumably Harry's.

That was the chef's knife from the set, meaning that based on the size of the other empty slot in the block, the one in Megan's chest was most likely the carving knife—narrower and longer.

She squatted down to look more closely at the knife in Megan's chest and noticed that although there was an inch or so of blade showing, it too was smeared with blood. She wondered if the knife had been driven all the way through her chest and back, and when she hit the floor, it pushed it part of the way back out.

She stood up, and said to Kyle, "Wait until the ME gets here before you move anything, but then make sure to bag the knife between her legs. We'll want to check that for prints."

"What about the one in her chest?" he asked.

"Let the ME remove it, but bag it, too."

She then took out her phone and snapped several of her own photos to be able to show Marcia later on. Taking photos as she went, she stepped around Megan's blood, and the drips of what she assumed was Harry's blood leading down the short hallway and into the bathroom. From the teardrop shapes of the drops, it was easy to tell which direction he was heading.

In the bathroom, there was blood on the floor, on the face of the vanity cabinet, on the vanity's counter, and in the sink. Also on the floor was a blood-soaked towel and washcloth along with scattered EMT waste. To them, she realized, this was a place where they were trying to save a person's life, not a crime scene.

On the top of the toilet tank, she saw a bloody cell phone, but there was no blood around it on the white porcelain. She called out, "Hey, Kyle, do we know who moved the phone in here?"

"That was me, Chief," he said. "I found it on the floor right next to Harry, so I put it on the toilet to get it out of the EMTs' way. Oh, and it was still connected to Gail, so I ended the call, too. Is that okay?"

"No problem," she said. "Remember to bag it and take it to the station with everything else."

While picturing how the blood got in all the various places, she called Marcia.

"Hi. Are you on your way, yet?"

"I'm coming up on the Rowley exit off I-95," Marcia replied.

"Well, don't take it," Jackie told her. "Keep going to Newburyport. I'm leaving here now to go to the hospital where they took Harry. It's called the Anna Jaques; can you map it?"

"As soon as we hang up," she replied.

"Okay, see you there in a little while; you might actually beat me."

Jackie put her phone away and stepped delicately back out into the kitchen, where she told Kyle, "You've got the scene. I'm going to the hospital to check on Harry. If the ME tells you anything that's not completely obvious, here, call me on my radio."

## Chapter 35

**Monday, July 19, 2021**

Marcia had indeed beat her to the hospital, but only by a minute or so.

"So, do you know any more about what happened?" Marcia asked as Jackie approached.

"Well, I haven't seen or talked to Harry, yet, but from the scene at Megan's and the EMTs' description of Harry's wounds, I'm guessing there was an altercation between Megan and Harry where she tried to stab him with a chef's knife, but he managed to stab her better—right through the heart—with her carving knife. Both of the knives came from a block on the counter, so they were weapons of opportunity for both of them."

"What the hell was he even doing there?" Marcia asked as they walked inside. "He knew we were getting a warrant to search her place. What did he expect to accomplish by talking with her?"

"Yeah," Jackie said, "I got nothin' on that one."

Ten minutes later, they were talking with the ER doctor who had attended Harry.

"He has a deep laceration in his left forearm, but it was a clean cut, and sutured easily. He apparently got lucky with the puncture wound in his chest, too, because it hit him to the right of his right lung and below his subclavian vein and artery. He said he was attacked by a woman with a kitchen knife. I assume that's what you're here to talk to him about, but from my experience, his wounds seem consistent with his story."

"Thank you, Doctor," Jackie said. "Can we talk to him now?"

"Give us ten minutes," he said. "We're moving him to recovery. We'll want to watch him for a half-hour, or so, then he'll be free to go. You can talk to him while he's waiting. I'll have somebody come get you when he's settled in."

While they waited, Jackie showed Marcia the photos she had taken at Megan's.

"Yikes!" Marcia said when she saw the picture of the knife sticking out of Megan's chest. "That must have damn near gone all the way through her!"

"Yeah. I didn't want to move her before the ME got there, but I'm pretty sure it did."

Swishing through the pictures, Marcia said, "So, then he goes into the bathroom to get something to stop his bleeding, calls 9-1-1, and collapses on the floor."

"Everything but why he was there in the first place makes sense," Jackie said.

A few minutes later, they were brought back to the recovery area and shown to Harry's curtained-off bed. He was sitting upright on top of the sheets. He was wearing his pants, which were stained with blood, but he wore a hospital johnny in place of his shirt. Jackie assumed it had been cut off to get to his chest wound by either the EMTs or the ER staff.

"Hi," Harry said in a resigned tone.

"Hi, Harry," Jackie replied. "The doctor said you're going to be okay. I'm glad for that, but what the hell were you *doing* at Megan's, and what the hell happened while you were there?"

"Screwing up monumentally," he answered.

"I'd agree with *that* assessment," Jackie said. As she spoke, she took out her phone and opened the voice-recorder app. She tapped *record*, and said, "It is Monday, July 19, 2021. This is Chief Jacquelyn Hall. With me are Marcia Grieves and Harry Fletcher. Are both of you aware that this conversation is being recorded?"

"Yes," Marcia answered.

"Yeah," Harry said, having been through this before.

"So, tell me what happened tonight, Harry," Jackie said as she set the phone on the bed beside him.

"It started around six o'clock or so when Megan called me and wanted to get together. We hadn't seen each other since the night that Pamela died. Obviously—and in retrospect—I should have just said no, but I was afraid she might get suspicious that we had figured things out if I said I didn't want to see her."

"Your books are full of people making up excuses, Mr. Fletcher," Marcia said. "Somebody's always lying to someone. You couldn't make one up to placate Megan?"

"It can take me hours of writing and rewriting, sometimes, to get my character's fabrications to work," he replied. "I'm not very good at *spontaneous* fiction."

He went on, "But it's interesting that you bring up my writing because it was a plot element that I'd written for a story that inspired me to go talk with her."

"Which book?" Marcia asked.

"I didn't use it in anything that's been published," he said. "I took those two characters and the story in a different direction, so it ended up on the cutting-room floor. It would have been ..."

"Harry, tell us about you and Megan tonight," Jackie said, getting him back on track.

"Sorry," he said. "So, the plot—imagined and real—involved secretly recording a conversation to get a confession.

"I started my phone's recorder just before I walked into her apartment, hoping I was going to be able to get her to say something incriminating about killing Pamela. I got the impression that you felt there was something on Megan's computer to connect her to Lain's death, but there was really nothing that tied her to my wife's murder."

"And how did you plan to get her to confess while you recorded it?" Marcia asked.

"The same way the character did in my story," he replied, "By proposing marriage."

"And she said no with the point of a knife?" Marcia said.

"Actually, she said yes," Harry replied. "The knife came later."

"Go on, Harry," Jackie said giving Marcia a quick *stop interrupting* look.

"Oh, and you can verify all this on my phone, which I assume must still be at Megan's because they told me it didn't arrive with me," he said.

"We have it," Jackie said. "Is there a password to open it?"

He told her what it was, and then went on, "So, anyway Megan and I met like nothing was amiss, and we kissed and hugged for a little bit, then I told her that I had figured out that it had to have been she who had killed Pamela, but that once I got over the shock of that, I could see it was the greatest act of love imaginable. I told her that we needed to hold off some appropriate mourning period, but that I couldn't wait to marry her as soon as possible.

"She was a little surprised that I'd figured it out, but she chalked it up to my mystery writing," Harry went on. "But she was thrilled that I was *happy* about it, and she immediately said yes to the proposal."

"Since she didn't *deny* killing Pamela," he continued, "I figured that was *sort* of a confession, but probably not enough. You would need her to actually *state* that she had killed her, or say something that only the killer could know.

"I asked her how she had known when Pamela's CNM partner for the night had left, so she could take my car over and kill her while I slept. She said that she knew who the partner was and that he had called her. I asked if it was Scott Lain, and she just smiled at me. Then I asked if he had left her tied up or something so she could kill her without a struggle. She answered, '*She was dead when I got there.*' So, then I asked her how in the world she had gotten Lain to kill her, and she told me that she had something pretty big to blackmail him with."

"It must have been *huge* to get someone to commit murder for you," Jackie commented. "Did she say what it was?"

"No. I didn't get a chance to ask her that," he replied. "But what I did ask her was, '*So, if Scott killed Pamela on your orders, I see why you had to get rid of that loose end, but why did you leave and go to my place right after he left the house?*'"

"Well, that was my open-mouth-insert-foot moment. She looked at me suspiciously, and said, '*Hold on a minute. How could you have known I took your car and went over there? You were out cold after I fucked your brains out. What the fuck is going on, Harry?*'"

"As I said," he went on, "I'm not very good at think-on-my-feet lies, and while I was stammering, she shouted, '*You son of a bitch! You're trying to set me up! Are you wearing a fucking wire or something?*' That's when she grabbed the knife from the block on the counter and came at me."

He pointed to the bandage on his arm and went on, "I managed to deflect her first slash, and push her off balance. I grabbed for a knife, myself, just to keep her at bay and try to calm her down, but she came right at me, again." He pulled the johnny down off his shoulder to show his other bandage, and said, "I think we stabbed each other at the same time. I deflected *her* knife, but she basically charged right into *mine*. It wasn't until she fell over on the floor that I realized where and how deep she'd been stabbed."

"I went to the bathroom to try to stop my own bleeding and I called 9-1-1. I remember feeling dizzy and weak, and the next thing I knew there was a paramedic putting an oxygen mask on my face."

"Did you check Megan for a pulse or anything?" Jackie asked.

"I think I was probably going to after I called 9-1-1, but as I said, I passed out."

"All right," Jackie said. "What you've said, what we know, and what I saw at Megan's all pretty well match up. I suspect the DA will call this self-defense, but I'd like to have you come to the station sometime after they let you go here. Maybe tomorrow? I'll have somebody transcribe what you just told us, and you can sign it. Is that okay with you?"

"Not too early," he said. "I'm probably going to want to sleep in."

"Sure, sure. That's fine," she replied. "In fact, how about after lunch?"

"Even better. One o'clock?" he said.

"I'll have your statement ready."

As they walked out of the hospital, Jackie asked Marcia, "So, what do you think?"

"I'm not sure if he's an incredibly good shot, or if he just drew targets around a whole barn full of bullet holes," she replied. "Everything fits, all the loose ends are neatly tied, and two cases are closed."

"Then you think he's lying?" Jackie asked.

"Not about anything I could put my finger on," Marcia replied, "but when you shake the pieces out of the box and the jigsaw puzzle falls together all by itself, you should probably be a little skeptical."

"Nice analogy," Jackie said. "Chief Booker would like you. But I agree. I'm not sure what he's lying about, or why, but something doesn't feel right. Can you be on the courthouse steps in the morning and get that warrant for Megan's place signed? With the addition of a death and an assault having taken place in the subject's apartment, it should sail through."

"I'll amend it tonight, and be there waiting in the morning," Marcia said.

"Call me while the judge's signature is drying," Jackie said. "I'll be parked in front of Megan's building to go in and get her computer as soon as I hear from you. Then I'll ask Carol to come in and search it for the suicide note. But I'm also going to ask her to re-search Harry's drive for that plot that he said he wrote and didn't use."

## Chapter 36

**Monday, July 19, 2021**

As Jackie drove home, all she could think about was that plot outline that Harry had told them about. She looked at her watch, and although it was pushing 9:30, she decided to give Carol a call.

"Hi, Carol. It's Jackie," she said she answered. "I know it's late, so if you're getting ready for bed or anything, tell me and I'll call back in the morning."

"Oh, you're funny," Carol said. "Even if I was already *in* bed, there's no way I could sleep after a cryptic call like that. What's going on? Is this about Megan Hope? I heard she got stabbed. Is she all right?"

"You have a good grapevine," Jackie said. "And no, she's not all right. She died at the scene."

"Oh, my God! What happened? Do you know who did it?"

"This is strictly privileged information, Carol; no repeating it to *anyone*, understood?"

"Understood loud and clear!" Carol replied.

"It was Harry Fletcher," Jackie said.

"*What*? Harry? Why?"

"That's what I'm trying to piece together," Jackie said. "Did you delete that bootleg copy of Harry's drive that you had on your computer like you told me you were going to?"

There was a longish pause, and Carol answered, "Oops. And I was just thinking about having my bullet made into a necklace. I swear, Jackie, that I *meant* to delete it, honest. It just kept slipping my mind ... which is becoming increasingly easy to do. I'll go do it, right now, while you're on the phone with me. Hold on."

"Hang onto your bullet, Barney," Jackie replied. "Your slippery memory is a good thing in this case. I'd like you to do a search on his drive for me if it won't interrupt your sleep cycle too much. It can wait until morning, otherwise."

"Lying there *thinking* about it would interrupt my sleep *more*," Carol said. "What do you need searched?"

"I'm looking for a piece of a story that he wrote, but that he apparently never put into a book. So, it could be in a normal file, or it could be a deleted file."

"Do you have some words or phrases for me?" Carol asked as she walked to the kitchen to find a pad and pen.

"Let's try *proposal … marriage … confrontation … record*—which will also give us *recorder, recording,* and *recorded … double cross*—with and without a hyphen … *set up*—also with and without hyphen … and *self defense*—again, plus and minus the hyphen. I don't know for sure that any of those will be in the file, but I think they're good guesses to start with based on the story that he told Marcia and me."

"Do you have a timeframe for when the file was created?" Carol asked. "How big it might be? Those things could narrow the search."

"No on both counts," Jackie said. "Sorry."

"No problem," Carol replied. "I'll get on it right now."

"Call me on my cell if you find anything," Jackie said.

"How late is too late?" Carol asked.

"With all this churning through my head, I don't expect to get much if any sleep tonight," Jackie replied. "But let's both pull the plug at eleven-ish, so we're not complete zombies tomorrow."

"What time is good for a wake-up call in the morning?" Carol queried.

"Let's pick up at six," Jackie answered. "Are you up then?"

"I'll be on my second cup of coffee," she answered.

At the station, Jackie went to the evidence locker and looked at the items that had been brought back from Megan's.

In separate bags, there were the two knives. She noted that the longer, narrower carving knife was easily long enough to have gone through an average-size person. Other bags contained a blood-soaked towel and washcloth. The last contained Harry's cell phone.

She desperately wanted to listen to the recording of the altercation Harry had told them about, but she knew that although the phone was legally recovered from the crime scene, that fact didn't give her authorization to examine its contents. Only a warrant or explicit permission from the phone's owner would do that. He had given her his password so that could be seen as *tacit* permission to view what was on the phone, but she didn't want to play any legal word-games.

She went to her office and copied the recording of Harry's hospital interview into the case folder. She then wrote a note for Sharon to begin transcribing it as soon as she got in. And if she finished it, to transcribe his earlier interview there in the station.

Next, she linked both of the recordings in an email to Suzan, asking for her opinion of his truthfulness, and then finally she put on her headphones and listened to Harry's last in-station interview, hoping to see if she could figure out what was causing her unsure feelings. As she listened she made notes on her pad.

When Harry mentioned his narcolepsy as the reason that he didn't know that Megan had left to kill Pamela, it reminded her that she had forgotten to check out the particular syndrome that he said he had. She needed to flip back through her previous notes to find its name.

Her Google search for *Bromfield Syndrome Cataplexy* returned no matches. Truncating to *Bromfield Syndrome* brought up a book written by Richard Bromfield, titled, *Doing Therapy with Children and Adolescents with Asperger Syndrome*. She made a new note to ask Carol if the phrase was used anywhere on Harry's drive.

She finished listening to the station recording, but with nothing leaping out as being out of place or contradictory. Then she listened to the recovery-room recording, hoping that it was a discrepancy between the two that she was subconsciously picking up on. Again, nothing jumped out. And maybe that's what it was; as Marcia had noted, *the puzzle pieces fit together almost too easily*. If someone had been scripting it all, it wouldn't have fit together any better.

She looked in the direction of the evidence locker. She could easily take Harry's phone from the bag, listen to the recording from Megan's, put it back, and pretend it was all fresh to her after Marcia got the warrant. That would not be just *skating* on thin legal ice, though; it would be jumping up and down on it.

Jackie was closing files and folders and getting ready to head home when her cell phone rang with a call from Carol.

"Hi, Jackie. I struck pay-dirt!" Carol said. "I wrote a batch routine to search for files with any of those words you gave me, and one popped up with all seven of them. That was pretty good guessing on your part!"

"Excellent work, Watson!" Jackie said. "Do you know when the file was written?"

"It was created a little more than two years ago," she answered. "Last modified about four months after that."

"Can you tell when it was last opened? Last read?" Jackie asked, wondering if Harry would have wanted to read it to refresh his memory before acting the scenario out in front of Megan.

"No. The timestamp only updates if he made changes and saved it," Carol said. "There *is* an *Accessed* date in the properties, but it's always the same as the *Modified* date. I never have figured out what the difference is supposed to be."

"Can you send a copy of the file to me?" Jackie asked.

"It's attached to an email and waiting for me to hit send," she replied. "And ... it's off!"

"Thank you. Now, I have another search for you, but this can wait until morning," Jackie said. "I was talking to Harry about his narcolepsy, and ..."

"Wait! *Harry* has narcolepsy, too?" Carol said.

"Oh, that's right, I didn't tell you that," Jackie said and explained that Harry had been doing the searches that Carol found on Pamela's computer. "So, anyway, he mentioned a condition he has that's called Bromfield Syndrome Cataplexy. I Googled it, but can't find anything about it. Can you search his drive and see if there's anything there? Actually, search any kind of cataplexy. Bromfield is what I have written down, but I won't swear that I heard him correctly."

"You did," Carol said. "It's actually in his book that he gave to me the other day. I only remember because that's the name of the street where I grew up in Newburyport ... Bromfield Street. not Cataplexy Street. I looked it up, too, and it's apparently something he made up for the story because I couldn't find anything, either."

"Really? How did he describe the condition in the book?"

"The character who has this syndrome apparently always falls asleep after vigorous exercise—like having wild sex with a prostitute—which he does, and she robs him and steals his car. That happens in the first couple chapters, and the story is about him tracking her down—he's kind of an amateur sleuth."

"Well done, Watson!" Jackie said. "You had the search completed before I asked for it!"

"All in a night's work!" Carol said. "With my bullet in jeopardy, I knew I couldn't let you down. But, if that's all you have for now, I think I'm going to *call* it a night."

"Good idea," Jackie said. "And thanks, again. I'm going to look at that file you just sent, and then I'm going to head home, too. I'll call you in the morning if I come up with anything else."

The aborted storyline from Harry's drive told a similar story of trying to trick a confession out of a lover. Only the crime had been a robbery, and the trick had been successful. Somewhat incongruously, the meeting then evolved into a graphically-described sex scene.

Jackie skimmed through the steamy part until the woman discovered the man's hidden recorder in his shirt, after which she stabbed him with a knife from the kitchen.

He described in some detail the knife entering the guy's chest between the second and third ribs of his left side, puncturing his left lung, slicing through his left atrium, and cutting his mitral valve in two. It even mentioned that the woman had intentionally turned the knife sideways before thrusting it into her lover's chest, to make sure it didn't strike a rib and impede its progress. Jackie remembered that the knife sticking out of Megan's chest was sideways, as well.

She took one last, longing look in the direction of the evidence locker, and then shut down her computer for the night.

# Chapter 37

**Tuesday, July 20, 2021**

Jackie was at the station before 6:30 the next morning and was antsy to listen to Harry's recording of his altercation with Megan. But she knew that judges didn't work on the same schedule as the police and that she would likely be waiting until after 9:00, and maybe after 10:00 before she heard for Marcia on the warrant.

While going through her chiefly duties, Sharon put through a call from Marcia at just after 8:00.

"Guess what I have in my hand?" Marcia said when Jackie answered.

"The warrant? You're kidding! How did you do that so early? Did you get your father to yank some more strings?"

"Nope. I worked my own connections," Marcia replied with no small degree of pride. "I was looking through my list of district court judges, deciding where I should take the application, and noticed that Judge Barbra J. Hopkinson had been assigned to the Newburyport District Court. She taught a course that I took in college, and because of some direct help she was giving me, I happen to have her personal phone number.

"I took the huge risk of waking her up early and called her this morning. Fortunately, she's an early riser, and when I explained that my warrant request involved the killing of a police officer, she told me to come right over to her house, which happens to be about ten or twelve miles from you. She lives on Plum Island. So, I will see you, warrant in hand, in about ten minutes."

"How specific were you in the application?" Jackie asked. "Is it going to cover Harry's phone?"

"It covers anything at the crime scene that could relate to the deaths of Megan, Scott, or Mrs. Fletcher," Marcia replied. "His phone certainly falls under that umbrella."

"Another gold star! I'll send someone, right now, for blueberry muffins," Jackie said. "Great work!"

Deciding that it was not a good idea to handle evidence crusted with dried blood while eating, Jackie sequestered a muffin in her office, and then she and Marcia went into the interview room with Harry's phone.

With the room's recorder running, Jackie removed the phone from the bag, and with gloved hands pressed the power-on button. Nothing happened.

"Crud!" Jackie said. "Kyle said he ended Harry's 9-1-1 call, but apparently he didn't turn off the phone." She looked at the phone's socket, and added, "I have a cord for this. What say we give it a muffin's worth of charge, and try again?"

In her office with washed hands and a fresh cup of coffee, Jackie divided the muffin while explaining the searches that she had asked Carol to make on Harry's drive the night before. Marcia assumed that Carol must have come into the station, and Jackie didn't correct her. That Carol had a bootleg copy of the drive on her computer at home was another patch of legal thin ice to be avoided.

"So, he was apparently telling the truth about the secret-recording, kill-or-be-killed storyline he said he wrote," Marcia said and then took a bite of muffin-top. She closed her eyes, and commented, "Oh, Lord! That is so good! I didn't have any breakfast."

"You eat the top first?" Jackie said. "I save that for last."

"If I get called away and have to leave half of it behind, it's going to be the bottom half," Marcia replied.

At that moment, Jackie's desk phone rang, and Marcia added, "See? See?"

Jackie cleared the muffin from her mouth with a sip of coffee, and answered the phone, "Hi, Sharon."

"Hi, Jackie. I have Suzan Engles on the line."

"Oh, yes. Put her through, please."

"Hall, here," Jackie said. "Hi, Suzan. Thanks for getting back to me so quickly. I have Marcia Grieves here with me. Is it okay if I put you on speaker?"

"Sure. Go ahead."

Jackie pushed a button, and Marcia said, "Hello, Suzan. Chief Hall has told me a lot about you. It's nice to finally sort of meet."

"Likewise," Suzan said. "Jackie has told me good things about you, and it's my job to know she wasn't lying."

"But the real question is," Jackie replied, "was *Harry* lying in those interviews?"

"Once again he has me stumped," Suzan answered. "No clear signs of deception, but none of honesty, either. For instance, in your interrogation-room recording when it suddenly occurred to him that this Megan person was responsible for killing his wife, I didn't pick up that he was lying, but I don't think he was surprised, either. At least it didn't come through in his voice. I got the impression he knew he was going to say that, he just wasn't sure when."

"Wow!" Marcia said. "He's a damned good actor, then."

"Or something," Suzan replied, not sure whether Jackie would have shared her non-professional psychopath assessment with Marcia.

"What about the hospital recording?" Jackie asked. "Did you get a chance to listen to that one?"

"That one *really* came through as rehearsed," Suzan said. "He mentioned that he had written a storyline that he acted out with this Megan, but I got the impression he had written out his conversation with you, as well. Almost nothing seemed spontaneous, except from you two."

"Well, again, thanks for getting back to me so quickly," Jackie said. "I guess we'll …"

"Oh, I almost forgot," Suzan interrupted. "He mentioned making a recording of his interaction with this Megan; have you listened to that one, yet? Are you going to be sending it to me? As I told you before, this guy fascinates me."

"We wanted to get a warrant for his phone and there was a dead battery issue," Jackie said. "We're going to listen to it as soon as we're done here. I'll definitely send it to you."

After hanging up, Jackie broke off a piece of her muffin—the top, this time—and just before popping it into her mouth, she said, "Let's go see how his battery is doing."

The charge was only up to twelve percent, but it was plenty to get the phone to come on. Jackie left it plugged in as she tapped in Harry's password, then swished through several screens to find his recording app.

The most recent recording was date-stamped, "2021_07_19_18_38_21."

"There it is. Yesterday at 6:38 p.m.," Marcia said. She then added, "Oh, wait a minute. Look. It shows it's only eighteen seconds long. How can *that* be?"

Jackie tapped the play button, and they heard Harry's voice, in almost a whisper and obviously very close to the microphone saying, "This is Harry Fletcher. It is July nineteenth, twenty-twenty-one at six-thirty-eight in the evening. I am about to enter Megan Hope's apartment." They then heard a knock, followed by a shuffle of clothes, and then the recording ended.

"Oh! You have got to be sh ... kidding me!" Jackie said, shifting from the expletive that sprung to mind as she remembered she was being recorded by the room's system.

"He must have hit the button a second time when he put the phone in his pocket," Marcia said.

"That's one explanation," Jackie said. Using quote-fingers, she went on, "The other is that he *accidentally* ended the recording intentionally so there would be only his word for what actually happened. And I'm getting less convinced all the time that we can take his word for *anything*."

Putting the phone back in its evidence bag, Jackie said, "Let's go get Megan's computer. Maybe we'll have more luck with that."

At Megan's apartment, Jackie initialed the evidence-seal on the door, slit it, and they went inside. The kitchen was just the way that Jackie remembered it, with the exception of there not being a body on the floor. The pool of blood was still there, only somewhat darker as it was almost completely dry now. The managers of the complex would not be allowed to have a biohazard clean-up service come in until the police released the scene.

Jackie pointed out to Marcia where Megan's body was lying, the knife block on the counter, and the trail of blood to the bathroom. The bathroom looked pretty much the way Marcia had expected, based on Mr. Fletcher's description.

They walked into the living room across from the bathroom, where a flat-screen TV was sitting on a small bookcase. The bookcase had one shelf of books that included all of Harry's published works, an EMT tech manual, a book on backpacking in Europe, a copy of *Bicycle Repair for Dummies*, and a dozen back issues of a bicycling magazine.

Across from the TV was a three-person sofa with a small table at each end. In front of the sofa was a coffee table with a shelf under it that held a small stack of *Earth First!: The Journal of Ecological Resistance* magazines.

One of the two bedrooms had a neatly-made double bed and a couple of matching dressers. In one corner was a desk and office chair. Lying across the desk was a charger cord of a type that would connect to a laptop, but there was no laptop.

"Why can't anything be easy?" Jackie sighed.

"Could one of your officers have taken it as evidence when they were here yesterday?" Marcia asked.

"They sure as hell shouldn't have," Jackie answered. "And it's not in the evidence locker with the other things."

"Mr. Fletcher?" Marcia suggested. "He knew we were going to come here for it. He even offered to come and get it himself, remember? If he's telling the truth about coming here to trick a confession out of Megan, could he have done something with it? Hidden it so she couldn't get rid of it in case his plan failed? ... in some other way than it did."

"What if he's *not* telling the truth?" Jackie said. "Could there be something on there that he doesn't want us to see? Which could be the real reason that he offered to come get it for us."

"But either way, what could he have done with it?" she asked as she thought. "It doesn't seem likely he could have left with it, put it in his car, and then come back without Megan noticing and becoming darned suspicious. And if he did take it—*to preserve the evidence for us*—why wouldn't he have told us at the hospital that he had the computer?"

"Well, there's no blood in here," Marcia said, "so he didn't come get it *after* he got stabbed and cut. Did he hide it somewhere when Megan was in the bathroom or something?"

"Again, why didn't he tell us?" Jackie said.

"I'm guessing that if I had just been cut and stabbed by a lover, then was forced to stab him through the chest and watch him die, that detail could have slipped my mind," Marcia said playing her now-usual devil's advocate role.

"Okay, I'll give you that. We'll leave a question mark next to motive," Jackie said. "Let's look around."

They opened drawers, looked under the bed, checked the closet, and opened the computer bag they found there, all with no success. In the bottom of a dresser drawer, under some sweaters, they found half a dozen spiral-bound notebooks. Marcia and Jackie each flipped through one, and discovered they were personal journals, obviously written by Megan.

With some excitement, Jackie said, "That one was on the top. What's the last date in it?"

About halfway through the notebook, the writing stopped with the entry for July 11, 2002. "Why do you think she suddenly stopped writing?" Marcia asked. "What she wrote doesn't indicate anything unusual; just day-in-the-life stuff."

"I'll bet it's because she continued her journaling on her computer," Jackie said. "Hello twenty-first century."

"And if she's kept up with it, that might make it all the more important for Mr. Fletcher to get his hands on her computer!" Marcia added.

Lifting the stack of notebooks from the drawer, Jackie said, "These are all from long before she moved to Rowley, but I'm going to take them anyway. I'm curious about how detailed she got with her day-in-the-life stuff. That might give an indication of how worried Harry might be if he knew."

Continuing their search, Marcia went into the second bedroom that had a single-bed pushed into one corner, and was otherwise used for storage of a bicycle, and assorted backpacking and camping gear. There wasn't even a dresser.

After the search of the second bedroom, Marcia went back and began scrutinizing the living room more closely.

Meanwhile, Jackie went back into the kitchen. She opened all of the cupboards and even checked the refrigerator, the freezer, and the oven.

Marcia looked behind the TV and the bookcase, under and behind the sofa, and between and under its cushions.

Walking out to the kitchen past the bloody bath, something caught the corner of Marcia's eye, and she stopped and did a double-take.

"Bingo!" she called out to Jackie.

"What? Where?" Jackie said as she hurried over.

Marcia pointed to the magazine rack next to the toilet. A black laptop stood on its end next to a variety of magazines.

"Hidden in plain sight?" Jackie said as she entered the bathroom, carefully avoiding the blood splatter. She knelt down and looked at it closely for any traces of blood, then lifted it out and lowered it into the evidence bag that Marcia was holding open.

"I'd have at least put it *behind* the magazines if I was hiding it," Marcia said. "That's a little too much in plain sight. I'm thinking that maybe Megan was a person who *used her time efficiently*. I know I've taken my laptop into the bathroom with me before."

"I'll give you that one, too," Jackie said. "It *didn't* look very well hidden." She then added, "Would you go get the power supply? We don't know how long it's been sitting there, and I don't want a replay of Harry's dead phone-battery episode.

While Marcia retrieved the power supply, Jackie called Carol.

"Hi, Carol. Can I get you to come to the station, right away?" she said. "I have another laptop that I'd like you to crack."

"Um, how about an hour?" Carol replied. "I'm at a client's right now and waist-deep in the middle of alligators."

"Okay," Jackie said, "as soon as you can make it. Thanks."

## Chapter 38

**Tuesday, July 20, 2021**

At the station Jackie plugged the power supply into Megan's laptop and turned it on, pressing the button with the eraser-end of a pencil. While it booted up, she plugged a spare keyboard into one of its USB ports. Depending on what they found on the system, she might want to dust the computer's keys for fingerprints.

The screen came to life with a screen-saver photo of a castle somewhere, with the date and time superimposed across the bottom. Jackie tapped the Enter key on her keyboard. The screen-saver went out of focus and a small circular photo of a person on a mountain bike appeared. Below the photo was "Megan Hope" and below that was a box requesting a password. With fingers crossed, Jackie pressed the Enter key, again.

A message popped up that read, "The password is incorrect. Try again." with an "OK" box below it. Again she pressed Enter, and the password box came back, but with "Password hint: House Pet" underneath it this time.

Taking a wildly hopeful leap, Jackie typed "House Pet" into the box. When it returned the same incorrect password message, Jackie said, "Why should our luck suddenly turn, now? This is obviously a job for Watson."

While they waited for Carol, Marcia listened to the recordings of their interviews with Harry, as Jackie had done, but she didn't pick up on any obvious contradiction or cues that he was lying about anything, either.

She then logged onto Harry's cloned drive and began randomly looking around, not even knowing what she hoped to find.

At about quarter past ten, Carol arrived, and quickly set up in Marcia's office. She soon had Megan's laptop disassembled, its hard drive connected to Marcia's computer, and was imaging it to the external e-drive. As the program ran, she asked, "What are we looking for?" of Marcia and Jackie who were standing behind her.

"The same thing as on Scott's laptop," Jackie said, "his suicide note. Can you run the same search for *cleanse my soul*?"

Carol looked at the progress bar, and said, "In eighteen minutes and thirty seconds."

With a fresh cup of coffee, Jackie was back in the doorway seventeen minutes later. As soon as the progress bar disappeared and *Finished* popped up, Carol opened her DOS routine and made the search. A second later, the screen showed the addresses of two files that contained the words *cleanse my soul*.

"When were they written?" Jackie asked.

Carol opened the properties on the newer file, and said, "SN.doc—which is the same name as the file on Scott's drive—was last modified three days ago, on Wednesday—which, again, is the same as Scott's file. But this one was *created* at exactly the same time. What that tells me is that it's a *save-as* file. It's probably a duplicate of this other one—they're both the exact same size—just saved with a different document name."

"And the other one?" Jackie asked.

Carol right-clicked the other file, and said, "SSN.doc was created on Wednesday, too, but about four hours before SN. It was last modified fourteen minutes before SN was created."

Marcia said, "You think SSN was the draft and when she felt she had it right, she saved it with a new file name for some reason?"

"Maybe SSN meant *Scott's Suicide Note*," Carol suggested, "which wouldn't make much sense if he was supposed to have written it."

"What time was it written?" Jackie asked.

Carol looked, and said, "Created on Wednesday, July 14, 2021, 1:01:19 PM. Modified on Wednesday, July 14, 2021, 3:52:03 PM."

"That's before Scott called in sick that day," Jackie said. "Could she have told him to lie low and then hid him out at her place, all the while knowing she was going to kill him but waiting for the right time?"

"And being able to borrow Harry's car on Friday provided that right time," Marcia continued the speculation.

"Oh!" Jackie said as another thought occurred to her. "What if she needed Harry's car to asphyxiate Scott? As a nature-lover or in her capacity as an EMT, could she have known the bit about how clean—monoxide-wise—diesels can be? And maybe her Prius was too clean to kill, too?"

"What the heck are you guys talking about?" Carol asked.

Marcia and Jackie exchanged a glance, suddenly remembering that Carol was not privy to all the details of the case.

Jackie pantomimed zipping her lips, and said to Carol, "Right?"

Carol pretended to lock her lips and throw away the key.

"Okay," Jackie began. "Scott didn't die from breathing the exhaust from his truck. It's a diesel, and they put out almost no carbon monoxide. These two copies of his *alleged* suicide note on Megan's computer—especially with the dates and times you found—pretty well link Megan to Scott's death. She had access to Harry's car, which we know was at Scott's house at some point, and the State Crime Lab recovered Scott's hairs from the car, so we know he was in it."

"Holy crap!" Carol said.

"To say the least," Jackie agreed. "Are you going to be able to keep that a secret?"

Carol went uncharacteristically serious, and said, "Yes, Jackie. Absolutely. What else do you want me to do with her computer? Is there anything else you need from Scott's drive?"

"We think Megan was probably keeping a personal journal on her computer," Jackie said. "See if you can find it. It could be called something simple like *Journal*, but it could be something obscure, too, so it wouldn't be obvious to anyone if she lost her computer or had it stolen."

"Or seized by the police after she was killed," Carol added.

"Or that," Jackie said. "While you do that, Carol, Marcia will you read through some of her written journal entries and see if maybe there's some phrasing that she used often that Carol can plug into her word-search routine? I've got something I want to check out. I'll be back in a few minutes."

# Chapter 39

**Tuesday, July 20, 2021**

Jackie left the station and walked across the parking lot to the fire station, next door. She found Chief Broderick in his office and knocked on the open door.

"Hi, Jackie!" he said. "Come in, come in! Have a seat."

"Thanks, Jim," she said. "I wanted to express my condolences about Megan. That was quite a shock to all of us who knew her, but I imagine you folks over here even more so."

"Boy, it sure was," he replied. "Have you figured out what happened, yet? Did Harry Fletcher really stab her through the chest?"

"He's admitted it," she said. "He says it was self-defense, and he has the wounds to back it up."

"So, *she* attacked *him*?" he said in obvious disbelief. "What the hell for?"

"That's what I'm trying to figure out, and part of why I'm here," she answered. "She normally worked the day shift, right?"

"Yeah," he said. "Second and third shifts are on an on-call basis. She does sometimes take those calls, too. Or *did*, I should say."

"Would it be possible for me to see her duty log for the past week or so?" Jackie asked.

"Sure," he said. "Can I ask why?"

"I'm trying to corroborate some things that Harry told me," she replied, hoping that would placate him. From his expression, it didn't look like it was going to, but a call came into the station at that moment, and he apparently decided that that had priority.

He made a few entries into his computer and then turned the screen so she could see it. "There you go," he said as he got up. "Do me a favor and hit the close button when you're done looking. And keep me posted, will you?"

"Sure thing, Jim. Thanks," she said. "Good luck with your call. Be safe."

Back in the station, Jackie stepped into Marcia's office doorway, and said to Marcia and Carol, "So, if Scott didn't write his own suicide note, and Megan didn't write it, who do you think *might* have authored it?"

"What makes you think it wasn't Megan?" Marcia asked.

"Because she was helping to extricate a person from a mangled car while the note was being written," Jackie replied. "I just looked at her call log over at the fire station. She was on duty all day, and on the scene of that crash when the note was being saved on her computer with a new file name."

"Mr. Fletcher," Marcia stated.

"And he and Megan had to have been in on it together," Jackie said. "She couldn't have written the note because she was miles away at a crash scene—and not likely to have her laptop with her—and he couldn't have killed Scott because he was at Pamela's funeral service surrounded by relatives and friends, including me."

Carol's eyes went wide, her mouth fell open, and her hand flew up to her throat. "*Holy shit!*" she said, then quickly moved her hand to her mouth, and added, "Oops! That wasn't supposed to be out loud. Sorry."

"So what the hell caused a knife fight to break out between them?" Marcia asked. "Could Mr. Fletcher have gone over there to do pretty much what he said, and record a confession so we'd go after her alone?"

"Doubtful," Jackie said. "If he turned on her and set her up, then he'd have to expect that she'd respond in kind."

"Jesus! Then he went to Megan's *planning* to kill her to get rid of that loose end," Marcia said. "Only she managed to fight back, and she was the one on the defense, not him."

"I think you could make a strong argument for that," Jackie said.

"But why would either of them—or both of them—want to kill *Scott*?" Carol asked. "What did *he* do?"

"We think that Megan may have murdered Pamela," Jackie explained. "And somehow, Scott figured it out and he was blackmailing her."

"Pardon my French in advance," Carol said, "but, again, *holy shit!*" Then, as something else about that clicked, she added, "Wait, wait, wait! If Harry and Megan killed Scott because Scott was blackmailing

Megan over killing Pamela, then Harry must have known that Megan killed Pamela! *Double holy shit!*"

"It's all circumstantial evidence," Jackie said, "but it sure points in that direction. The timestamp of Scott's suicide note on Megan's computer means that she *couldn't* have written it, but it doesn't mean that Harry *did*. The DA would need a lot more than that to be willing to file charges. Did you happen to find Megan's journal?"

"No," Carol answered. "But with an asterisk. You were right that Megan re-uses certain phrases in her entries; Marcia found a few for me to try. But surprisingly, none of them popped up in anything that would resemble a journal. So, then I tried searching for dates written in every way we could think of. July four, twenty-twenty-one, Four July twenty-one, seven four twenty-one, on and on, ad nauseam. Again, nothing.

"That sounds like a no," Jackie said. "What's the asterisk?"

"It may be here, but hidden," Carol replied. "While I was scrolling through folders, I came across one called Hinder. It didn't mean anything to me so I just kept going, looking for the obvious *Journal*.

"When that came up empty I went back and started looking inside each folder, thinking maybe she named it something *not* obvious. Inside the Hinder folder were a couple of .dll files, a .dat file, and a couple of .exe files, along with two sub-folders, one for images, and the other for languages."

"I'm assuming that's more of a smoking gun for you than it is for me," Jackie said.

"What it means is that Hinder is an executable program located in that folder. So I did an online search for Hinder, and it turns out that it's a program to make file folders and everything that's in them invisible to a search. There's another program called *Hidden Folders* that I've installed on a client's shared computer so that each person who had access to the system had their own personal and private locker, so to speak. And don't ask me how it works, by the way; that's a few levels above my programming pay-grade.

"So, anyway, I executed the program and it naturally opened with a box asking for a password ... which we naturally don't have. I made a couple of guesses, but stopped because it said, '*Warning: 4 attempts left before lock-out.*' And that's where we are at the moment."

"So, you managed to get around the password to get into the drive," Jackie said. "That won't work for this Hinder program?"

"Nope. Without going into sleep-inducing detail, this version of Windows uses one style of permission-protocols, while an executable file would use something altogether different. They typically have no backdoor unless it's something quirky that the programmer built in for his own convenience."

"I'm hoping that you wouldn't be telling us all this unless you had a solution," Jackie said.

"I think I do, and I found it just as you got here," Carol replied. "So, I don't know what your memory is like—you're young, yet—but I have a Word doc on my computer where I keep all of my assorted passwords. It has its own password to get into, of course, but that's only one that I have to remember when I forget one of the myriad others."

"I do have a password cheat-sheet," Jackie agreed.

"Oh! That's hilarious!" Carol said. "That's just what Megan called hers! It's an Excel file named PWcheat. At least I assume that's what I think it is; I haven't gotten into it, yet. Another password roadblock."

"But you have a workaround for it?" Jackie asked.

"There's a program called Puppy Linux that I can download to a USB drive," Carol began, "and when I boot the system through it, it will totally ignore all the Windows-set password permissions. That's because the Linux permission-protocol is completely different than Windows, and …"

"Carol, I trust you," Jackie interrupted her. She looked at her watch, and went on, "It's quarter of twelve; Harry is due here at one; do you think we can be reading journal entries before then?"

"Unless Megan throws even more roadblocks in the way—like writing in hieroglyphics—then yes," she answered.

"Good! I'll get pizza ordered in," Jackie said. "What do you want to drink?"

"I'm guessing chardonnay is off the table," Carol replied, "so diet Coke, for me."

"I'll give you a rain-check on the chardonnay, and will happily join you with a glass of cab when this is over," Jackie said.

While Carol went back to work on Megan's computer, Jackie and Marcia went into Jackie's office and started reading through Megan's hand-written journals. Marcia started with the earliest ones and read forward as Jackie started with the last one and went backward in time.

Jackie began to see that if there was a common theme to Megan's journal entries, it was probably promiscuity. Sex wasn't all she ever talked about, but it was rare for two entries to go by without some mention of it, even if it was how much she was missing it.

After swallowing a bite of her pizza, Marcia commented, "I don't know if she changed as she got older, but Megan was a bit of a wild-child in her teens ... and a bitch, too. She talks about liking to tease the boys at school, and several entries talk about changing her clothes in her bedroom with the shades open, and walking around naked, knowing the boy next door was watching. Up to that point, I'm thinking she's an exhibitionist—she's all excited when she realizes he's masturbating while watching. But then she writes about telling her parents about the Peeping Tom pervert next door and getting him arrested. She thinks it's funny as hell when he gets convicted of being a sexual predator even though she had set him up."

"You're kidding," Jackie said. "Does she mention the kid's name?"

Marcia flipped back a page, and said, "Rick. Why? Does he show up again, later?"

"Does she say what eventually happened to him?" Jackie asked.

"Only that the family moved away a little while after, and a couple of old farts moved in," Marcia said. "Why?"

"Holy crap! She's talking about *Scott Lain*! She has to be!" Jackie said. "His given name is Richard; Richard Scott Lain. And that's the exact story that his mother told me when I contacted her trying to locate him. She didn't mention the girl's name though. Holy crap!"

"So, could this be the big thing that Megan was blackmailing Scott with?" Marcia said. "His sexually deviant past?"

"He hadn't disclosed that prior arrest and conviction on his application to the department, probably because he believed it would have killed it immediately. I wonder if Megan may have figured that out or guessed it somehow and been holding it over him."

"Your department here seems a little more thorough than that," Marcia said. "How could you have missed an arrest and conviction in a background check even if he hadn't disclosed it?"

"According to his mother, he was a minor and completed the court-ordered counseling, so the conviction was probably expunged when he turned eighteen," Jackie said. "It wouldn't show up in a normal background check; we would have to have requested special access to juvenile records, which we had no reason to do."

"*Would* it have killed his application if you'd known?" Marcia asked.

Jackie thought for a moment, and answered, "I don't know. A sexual predator conviction is pretty serious, but knowing what you just read in there about his accuser makes it sound more like teenage hormones reacting to a manipulative nymphet than predation. The more important question is would *he* have believed it could get him fired and maybe prosecuted for making false statements if Megan came to us? If he did believe that, it would be pretty strong blackmail material on Megan's part."

"But strong enough to get him to commit murder?" Marcia said.

Jackie thought for a moment and then said, "So, maybe he was pissed off at Pamela for blowing him off with her no-means-no text, so it didn't take that great of a shove. Plus, maybe he saw Pamela's murder—or more correctly, the *conspiracy* to murder Pamela—as his own blackmail ammunition. Harry told us that Megan said the killer—presumably Scott—called her right after the deed was done and that she drove over there, which the Timmons' videos verify. What if that was a trap on his part so he was able to get some proof that Megan was there with the dead body and then left without reporting it? That could easily support a claim of conspiracy against her if he wanted to raise it."

"Oh! He could have hidden his phone in the Fletcher's bathroom somewhere and taken video!" Marcia suggested, quickly warming to the idea. "Then when he responded to the 9-1-1 call, he retrieved it during his clean-up!"

"With Pamela's murder being planned well in advance, he could even have bought a tiny spy-cam someplace," Jackie agreed. "So, all of a sudden, Scott and Megan are in a blackmail Mexican standoff. You tell on me, and I tell on you. If one of us goes down, we both do."

"And Megan pulled her trigger first," Marcia added.

"What we know certainly does appear to make sense this way, but once again we have a nice round target drawn neatly around a bullet hole," Jackie said. "A tantalizing theory supported by supposition, unsubstantiated testimony, and circumstantial evidence."

"And where does Mr. Fletcher fit?" Marcia wondered.

"If he's telling the truth about what happened with Megan, then he's the unsuspecting husband of the victim," Jackie said.

"And if not, he's the third in a three-way conspiracy," Marcia added, "in which the other two are dead. Wasn't it Sherlock Holmes who said, '*Three may keep a secret if two of them are dead*?'"

"That was Ben Franklin," Jackie corrected, and added, "But it holds true nonetheless." She suddenly stopped talking and flipped back a couple of pages in the notebook she was reading. She scanned, then flipped a few more, and scanned again.

She looked up at Marcia, and asked, "Did she use the adverb *nonetheless* anywhere in what you've read, so far?"

"Doesn't ring a bell," Marcia said, "but I wasn't looking for it. Is that significant? You want me to check?"

"She's used it twice in the entries I've read," Jackie said. She slid a pad and pen across to Marcia, and said, "Write it for me. Nonetheless."

Marcia did, and then slid the pad back with a curious look.

"That's the way I was taught to write it; as one word," Jackie said. "But Megan writes it out as three words. None the less."

"Which is significant, how?"

Without answering, Jackie pushed the pad back, and said, "Write, *I cannot tell a lie*."

Again, she complied, and again slid the pad back with a questioning look. "What's up, Jackie?" she asked.

"One word!" Jackie said looking at the pad. "Megan writes cannot as two words. I've seen that maybe half a dozen times in here."

"Still wondering about that significance," Marcia said.

Jackie opened up a manila folder on her desk, slid out the photocopy of Scott's suicide note, and looked it over. She picked up a pencil, circled two words, and handed the note to Marcia.

"*Nonetheless* and *cannot*; both spelled as one word," Jackie said. "Add this to the timeframe thing, and that tells me that Megan *certainly* didn't write that note."

"Mr. Fletcher, again!" Marcia said.

"Motive, means, and opportunity," Jackie said. "The motive was to frame Scott for Pamela's death to get that investigation to stop. He's a writer of fiction, so he certainly has the means, and Megan probably gave him access to her laptop to write it, which is the opportunity. The only thing lacking would be his fingerprints on the keyboard, but I'll bet anything he wiped it clean when he was done. We'll only find Megan's prints when we dust it."

"I wonder how Carol is doing with her hidden files quest," Jackie said as she pushed her chair back. "If Megan was as open in recent journal entries as she was in these, I can easily imagine her rambling about Pamela, Harry, and Scott."

## Chapter 40

**Tuesday, July 20, 2021**

"How's it going?" Jackie asked as she and Marcia stepped up behind Carol.

Carol held up a finger as she chewed and swallowed, and then said, "Your timing is impeccable. I just got her password cheat-sheet open."

On the screen was a three-column list with file or program names in the left column, their passwords in the middle, and user-names—if there was one—at the right.

Carol scrolled down and they all looked for the word *Journal* in the left column. It wasn't there.

"I don't see *Diary*, either," Carol said as she scrolled back up the list. "Well, poop!" she said. "Maybe she felt she could commit that one password to memory."

"Is *Log* there?" Jackie suggested, trying to think of other synonyms for journal. "Or *memoir*?"

"Nope," Carol said after scrolling down. She then said, "But look at this." She moved the cursor over the column of passwords, and said, "Look how many are nearly the same. I tell my clients not to use the same password for everything because if somebody hacks it they have access to your whole digital world.

"But this is a common type of compromise that people use. She uses this six-digit number—which probably has some significance to her—and her name spelled backward; *nagem*. Then she adds a three-letter abbreviation for the file or program—always in upper case—followed by a plus sign. That would satisfy the classic requirement for upper and lower case, at least one letter and one number, and a special character."

"I think you're onto something, Watson!" Jackie said as she looked at the password for TikTok, which was *461975nagemTIK+*, and for her PayPal account, which was *461975nagemPAY+*.

Carol went back to the Hinder folder, double-clicked the .exe file, and soon had the password box open, again. It still showed the 4-attempt warning below the box. "Rats," Carol said. "I was hoping it would have reset while it was shut down for a half-hour." She typed *461975nagem* into the box—which showed up as asterisks—and as she hovered her fingers above the keyboard, she asked, "So, what do we want to use as the abbreviation? Choose wisely!"

"Let's start with the obvious," Marcia said. "Try J-O-U for journal."

Carol typed it in with the plus sign and a box opened with the message, "Wrong Password! Please enter the correct Password!" A 3-attempt warning also displayed. She clicked the OK and the password box reappeared with a 3-attempt warning.

"Strike one," Carol said. "How about D-I-A for diary?"

"Go for it," the others agreed.

The wrong-password and warning box—now at 2—popped up, again, and Carol said, "Swing and a miss! Strike two! Your turn at the plate, Chief."

"Hold on a second," Jackie said as she took out her phone. "Let me look for synonyms for *journal*."

Carol looked over her shoulder at Marcia, and said, "And that's why she's the chief."

Looking at her phone, Jackie said, "Well, that's not too helpful," and then read off several of the twenty words that showed up, including *Periodical, Digest, Chronicle,* and *Diary.*

She then tried synonyms for *diary*, which returned only half the suggestions, including *History, Log,* and *Record.*

While Jackie was looking up synonyms and deciding what to try, Carol was looking at the password spreadsheet open in front of her. At the bottom of the page, her eyes fell on the *Sheet1, Sheet2,* and *Sheet3* tabs that new spreadsheets always created. She clicked on *Sheet2,* and a blank worksheet appeared. She clicked *Sheet3,* and an *almost* blank worksheet opened. It contained one line.

"Well, look-it here!" Carol said. "One file and password all alone under its own tab. Like maybe someone didn't want it found easily?"

They all looked at the name of the file in the left column. "Mead?" Marcia read. "What the heck is that?"

"Oh, my God," Jackie said. "We'd have guessed a hundred years and not hit that. It's the manufacturer's name on the cover of all of her hard-copy journals. Wow!" She patted Carol on the back, and said, "Nice work, Watson!"

"And the password doesn't fit the pattern, so we'd have been locked out in three shots even if we had guessed Mead," Carol said. The password was "6175513612+Mh."

"I wonder if that's Megan's phone number when she was a kid," Jackie said. "The 615 would have been the area code for all of eastern Mass. back then, and I remember the 551 from when I called Scott's mother in Waltham, and we know that Megan lived right next door."

"Really?" Carol said. "Next door? *How* do we know that?"

"It's part of how we think Megan might have been blackmailing Scott," Jackie said. "I'll explain it later, but for now, let's try the password."

Carol typed the number into the password box while Marcia and Jackie crossed their fingers.

A new box opened up showing the names of two files and one folder at the left, and the word "Hidden" next to each at the right.

"Yay!" Carol cheered while tapping a little dance with her feet. "Success!"

One file was an .ini file and the other carried a .dll extension. "Those would be part of the program, which the program keeps hidden so you don't know the program is there hiding things." She selected the folder named, "Mead," with a single click, and a button became highlighted that read, "Unhide."

"The moment of truth!" Carol said, and clicked the button. The word *Hidden* was replaced by *Visible*.

"Be still my heart!" she said as she went back to the parent directory. There sat a new folder named "Mead" that had not been there before.

"Well done!" Jackie said.

Carol double-clicked the folder and a series of .doc files appeared. Each had a year as its filename. They started with *2012.doc* and continued to *2021.doc*.

"Bingo!" Marcia said triumphantly. "Boy, even if it wasn't hidden you'd never guess that a folder named *Mead* was going to contain personal journal entries."

"Open 2021," Jackie said as her excitement grew. "We'll go back and look at the others later, but I'm anxious to see what she's written in the past couple of weeks."

The Word document began with a date—1/1/21—on its own line, followed by a short paragraph of text. It was followed by a blank line and then the next day's date and that day's journal entry.

"Go to July eighth; the day Pamela died," Jackie said.

7/8/21

Well, it's finally done although numb-nuts almost screwed it up and I had to go and put her in the tub. And of all nights for me to get called to fill in at the station! It was damned weird pretending to try to revive a person I had made sure was dead an hour earlier. It was hard for me to not give Harry a wink or something, but I was afraid of how he might have reacted if he knew it wasn't really an accident. I will tell him someday ... maybe.

"Holy crap!" Marcia said. "Guns don't get much smokier than that!"

"No they don't," Jackie agreed "Carol, go to July sixteen. The day of Pamela's funeral and the day that Scott died."

7/16/21

It's a good thing I didn't go to the funeral today; my big smile might have been inappropriate. LOL! It would also have meant that I couldn't have used Harry's car to get rid of Ricky. I sure hope he appreciates all I'm doing so that he and I can be together. It sucks not having been with him for more than ten minutes since Pamela's "accident" but he's afraid of what would people say. I say fuck 'em!

"Wait! Who's Ricky?" Carol said.

Jackie and Marcia looked at each other, and Jackie said, "Okay, one more secret out of the bag."

To Carol, she said, "You told me once that you'd seen stuff on people's computers that you didn't even want to remember, much less repeat. Well, this is one of those things. Richard is Scott Lain's real first name. He and Megan lived next door to each other in their teens. She set him up to get arrested for deviant sexual behavior for masturbating while watching her get undressed when she left her shades open so that he *would* watch her. And we think she could have been using that to blackmail him since he never disclosed it on his police application."

"Wow!" Carol said. "I never thought that Megan was exactly warm and fuzzy, but that's so cold she'd make you look forward to January to get warm. And a serving of *wow!* on him, too."

Back to business, Jackie asked, "What was the day that the suicide note was created?"

"The fourteenth," Carol answered, and before Jackie even asked, she was jumping to the new date.

7/14/21

Fun day at work! Some guy wrapped his car around a pole and we got to use the jaws of life to get him out. Blood freaking everywhere! I bet he loses his right arm.

Ricky is making me nervous. He says Hall's been talking to him about Pamela and I don't think he's going to be able to hold his shit together much longer. I think it's time that he goes away. He's got enough weird crap in his past that his suicide will be totally believable.

"This is the day that Scott called in sick for his night shift, and then he wasn't heard from again," Jackie said. "What's the timestamp on this journal entry?" she asked.

"There is none," Carol said. "It's just a piece of the whole *2021.doc*. There's no way to tell when a *part* of it was written."

"Crap! I was hoping to see if this was written before or after the suicide note," Jackie replied.

"What would that tell you?" Carol asked.

"Well, I think we've pretty much concluded that Harry wrote Scott's suicide note," Jackie explained her thoughts. "Which we know was written in the middle of the day when Megan was having fun with the jaws of life. So, if she does her journaling in the evening—as it appears from other entries—then her statement, '*I think it's time that he goes away*,' would be out of order. The decision to kill him should have come *before* the note to make it look like suicide was written, right?"

"I'm still not sure what that's telling you," Carol said.

"Okay, this is a little convoluted," Jackie said to both of them, "but here goes. Harry and Megan decide that they want to get rid of Pamela. But Harry knows from his own writing how hard it is to get away with the perfect murder, so they probably just pillow-talk about it, enjoying the *if-only* fantasy. But the more they fantasize, the more they want it to become a reality.

"Enter *Ricky* Scott Lain. If we go back through Megan's journal entries we may find when they crossed paths here in Rowley, which I'm guessing will be *after* he became Pamela's CNM partner. That would be a serendipitous set of events for Megan and Harry because Megan has something to blackmail Scott with, and he has a history of intimate contact with Pamela."

Carol interrupted, "Um, I hate to keep sounding like I'm completely in the dark, but Scott-slash-Ricky had *a history of intimate contact with Pamela*? And what's a CNM partner?"

"Yes, they had an affair sometime last year," Jackie said. "If you're sure you want to know, I'll explain it all later."

"Okay. Maybe not. Sorry for the interruption."

"So, anyway," Jackie went on, "Harry and Megan come up with the bathtub accident scenario, which, if everybody buys it; great! But again, from his own writing, Harry knows how hard it is to fake a perfect fatal accident, so in case the authorities do get suspicious, they decide to use Scott as the fall guy. My guess is that they planned to get rid of him regardless of whether he was able to *hold his shit together* or not. Loose ends are the death of conspiracies.

"I could only guess on how they got Scott to drop out of sight—maybe it will be in the journal—but I think that somehow they convinced him that we suspected him—possibly because of his history with Pamela plus his sexual-predator conviction—and Megan agreed to let him hide out at her place while they all figured out what to do ... but more importantly so that Harry and Megan had control of him.

"Pamela's funeral was the perfect storm of opportunities to get rid of him. Harry was going to have an airtight alibi surrounded by friends and family and even me; Megan was off duty and had access to Harry's car and was supposedly on the road to Plymouth and back; and virtually everyone who knew Pamela and Harry was congregated at Pamela's services, so no one who knew him would have noticed if his car was still in town.

"Again, I don't know how she might have done it, but I think she must have asphyxiated Scott in Harry's car somehow."

"She could have used her camping heater," Marcia suggested. "I saw one in her extra bedroom—probably right where Scott was sleeping."

"A camping heater?" Carol repeated. "How would that work? We have one of those; I thought they were safe."

"Typically, they are," Marcia replied, "and I only know this because of a product-tampering case that I helped to investigate when I first got to the County DA's office." She then explained what the person had done to make the heater burn inefficiently and give off high amounts of carbon monoxide. "She killed her grandmother and her grandfather, and then sued the manufacturer for ten million dollars. She's serving two consecutive life sentences."

"I remember that story on the news!" Carol said. "That was you, huh?"

"We need to go back over there, and get that heater," Jackie said. "But I like your theory better than mine. Getting him to sit still in Harry's car while she ran a vacuum cleaner hose from the exhaust to the window might have been a little difficult. In her house she could have waited for him to fall asleep—and there was alcohol in his system to help that—and then cranked the A/C and lit the heater. The A/C might even have helped to drown the noise those heaters usually make."

318

Continuing her rundown, Jackie went on, "So, Megan puts Scott's body in Harry's car, and drives him to his house, accidentally leaving his hairs on the headrest. She puts him in his truck, starts it up, then copies the suicide note to his laptop. She prints it out, traces his signature from the pad that by dumb luck is sitting right there, and leaves the note on the kitchen table. She then drives off with Scott's driveway rocks stuck in Harry's tires."

"I like this picture better than her knowing he wouldn't die from his truck exhaust," Marcia said. "Even for a tree-hugger that seemed a little too arcane for her to know."

"I agree," Jackie said. "Your heater idea is much more logical." She then said, "Carol, will you do a search for *can not*, two words. Search the whole *Mead* folder."

A few seconds later, the entry for January 7, 2012 was on the screen with "can not" highlighted.

"Do *Find Next*," Jackie said.

February 28, 2012 popped up.

"Keep going," Jackie said. "Let's see how often she uses that."

They stopped counting by the time they reached the end of 2014, but Carol kept tapping the Find Next button, jumping from entry to entry, year after year. When she reached the end, she said, "Looks like she uses *can not* maybe a dozen times in an average year. Does that tell you something?"

"Maybe," Jackie said. "Now do the same search with *cannot* as one word."

The entry from July 9, the day after Pamela died, appeared.

7/9/21

Harry says they want to do an autopsy! I specifically told Ricky to knock her out and put her in the tub. I cannot believe that he had to play his BDSM games and choke her while he fucked her. Moron! I hope it was good for him because it's sure fucked things up for me! Poor Harry! As the husband, he's going to be at the top of their suspect list. He didn't do it, so I hope the truth will set him free.

"Are there any more?" Jackie asked.

Carol hit Find Next, and a message popped up saying that Word had finished searching the document. "Afraid not," she answered.

"It may only be a sample of one, but to me, it says *Harry was here*. I think maybe he got into Megan's journal somehow and edited out any references to himself. He may have been playing the odds that she wouldn't go back and re-read any of her own entries."

"How would he even have known Megan had a journal? The whole folder was hidden," Carol said.

"I don't know," Jackie replied, then asked, "So, when you close out of a file or folder that *had* been hidden, does it automatically get hidden again?"

"No. You have to open the program back up, select what you want to hide, and click the *Set to Hide* button."

Jackie thought for a moment and then said, "What if something interrupted her while she was writing? She could have saved and closed the document, but not had the time to hide it, and forgot to go back and do it later. Maybe it was sitting there when she let Harry use her laptop to write the suicide note."

Marcia pointed out, "But that would only give him access to entries written up to that date. If he edited future ones to delete himself and set Megan up, he'd need future access, right? Carol, is there any way to get the password from the log-in screen if the program is sitting there open and running?"

"Not unless it was written by the worst programmer in the history of password protection," she replied. "But if the Hinder dialog box was showing on the screen because Megan hadn't closed out of it, that would have told Harry that her journal was normally hidden. I'd be willing to bet a nickel that he installed a keylogger program at that point to capture her keystrokes and figured out her password from there. And the reason I'd bet my hard-earned nickel—which I would only do on a sure thing—is that his amateur sleuth in the book I'm reading did exactly that to track down his nemesis."

"If he installed one, can you tell if it's still there?" Marcia asked. "Or *had been* there?"

"If he follows his character's lead," she replied, "it won't be. He deleted it as soon as he got what he was looking for. But let's take a look at the browsing history and see if he—or someone—went searching for one."

Carol navigated to the browser's *Show Full History* screen and typed "keylogger" into the search window. Half a second later, the screen displayed eight searches, all for "free keylogger," and all on July 14 between 2:18 and 2:32 p.m.

"That works for me," Marcia said. "We know Megan couldn't have made those searches."

"So, is all this enough to make an arrest?" Carol asked.

"Let's look at one more entry," Jackie said. "Is there one for yesterday? The day Megan died?"

Carol did a *Find* for 7/19/21 and the entry appeared.

7/19/21

For a day that started out like crap, it looks like it's going to end on an up-note. Harry's coming over! I'm looking forward to fucking, of course, but he said he had something for me, and I think it might be a ring! We'll have to wait some God-awful mourning period, but all this will finally pay off in the end. Maybe I'll tell him that Pamela's death was my wedding gift to him; to us. Maybe not. We'll see.

"That fits with what he told us at the hospital," Marcia said. "But if he was rewriting her entries that would make sense."

"Carol, what's the time-stamp on this document?" Jackie asked. "The last time it was modified and saved?"

She went back to the Mead folder and pulled up the properties for the 2021.doc file. The *Modified* line read: "July 19, 2021, 6:52:21 PM."

"Harry started his recording at 6:38," Marcia said. "I remember because I did the mental-math to convert it from military time. So that's fourteen minutes after he got there."

Jackie picked up the phone and called Gail at the dispatch desk. "Hi, Gail. Can you tell me what time the 9-1-1 call from Harry Fletcher came in last night?" There was a several-second pause, and Jackie said, "Perfect. Thank you."

As she set the phone in its cradle, she said to the others, "Seven o'clock and thirteen seconds. So, that's eight minutes after Megan's final journal entry was last saved. I'm thinking that he stabbed Megan—and not in self-defense—went and made the final edit to her journal, then went back to the kitchen, gave himself his defensive wounds, and called 9-1-1."

"I hate to keep repeating myself," Carol said, "But, *holy shit!* So, is that enough probable cause to arrest him?"

"Annoyingly, it's still all circumstantial," Jackie said. "The gun is lying there in plain sight, but it's not smoking." She looked at her watch, and said, "Harry should be here in fifteen minutes or so. Let's sit down and outline what we have. Maybe we can rattle him if we present it as fact and not supposition."

Carol said, "This sounds like it's getting above my pay grade, anyway, but if you don't need me for that, I have a client with a quickly-approaching deadline who desperately needs my support."

# *Chapter 41*

**Tuesday, July 20, 2021**

"Thanks for coming in, Harry," Jackie said when she met him in the station lobby. "How are you feeling? Still sore, I'll bet."

"And still stupid," he said. "I can't believe I thought that was going to work like it did in my story. I guess life doesn't imitate art as much as I'd hoped."

In the interview room, Jackie started by saying, "We listened to the recording on your phone of the altercation you had with Megan."

She watched him closely for a reaction, but there was none. Instead, he said, "Oh, good. Were you able to hear us both okay? In my pocket, I wasn't sure it was going to pick her up."

"We never heard her voice, at all," Jackie said. "The recording is only eighteen seconds long."

"*What?* No! How can that be?" he said in very convincing surprise. "I started it right outside her door and stated my name and the date and the time. Then I put it ... Shit! I'll bet I hit the record button a second time when I put the phone in my shirt pocket. Shit!"

"Yeah," Jackie said. "That's what we came up with, too ... sort of."

"What do you mean, *sort of*?" Harry asked.

"We do think you tapped the button a second time," she replied, "but it wasn't an accident."

"What are you talking about? Why would I do that?"

"So there wouldn't be any record of what *actually* happened between you and Megan."

"What I told you happened is the absolute truth," he said. He held up his bandaged arm, and asked, "Do you think I did this to myself?"

"Actually, yes, Harry, we do."

"*What?* Where did you come up with something like that?"

"Lots of little pieces of evidence, Harry, but they all point in the same direction; right at you," Jackie answered.

"What evidence? What are you talking about?"

"Well, we're going to start with how many times you've lied to me. Some you've admitted to, others we've proven by other means."

"For instance?" he said in a challenging tone.

"Your *Bromfield Syndrome Cataplexy*," Jackie replied. "It doesn't exist. There's no record of anything like it anywhere on the Internet. The only place it exists is in one of your novels."

"Oh, that," he said, "You're right. I did make that up. But there's nothing nefarious about claiming to have it. A bit self-serving, but not nefarious.

"Without delving deeply into your sex lives," he went on, "have you ever made love and then had your partner want to roll over and nod off? Well, that isn't a lack of interest in you, it's a biological reaction to a chemical-cocktail released immediately after ejaculation. The hormone prolactin, along with a couple of chemicals whose names I don't recall, and a bit of melatonin for good measure conspire to put your man to sleep so he can *get ready for another go*.

"*Oddly*," he went on making quote fingers, "most women don't find that nod-off to be very romantic. They are, however, nearly always sympathetic to a medical condition. It's the mothering instinct; you can't help it.

"I invented Bromfield years ago because I needed it as part of a storyline in a novel. It was a detriment to my fictional character—he ended up getting robbed by a hooker—but I saw its potential in reality, and I began explaining to my lovers that I had this BSC, for short, and what was going to happen to me after we made love. Not only did they not get angry when I wanted to go to sleep, but they also tucked me in and turned out the lights. And the longer I slept, the better they felt about themselves for having *worn me out*. Everybody wins."

Trying to fight back the irritation at his smug manipulation of women in general, Jackie said, "You gave me the name of your neurologist to verify your condition; that was a bluff? You were depending on my *motherly instinct* buying into it—like your partners?"

Harry smiled, and replied, "Dr. Oldham actually helped me to create the syndrome when I was working on the book. When I told him later on how effective it was in getting a nice post-coital nap, he actually began to *prescribe* it to some of his other male patients. I think he may have *contracted* it himself. If you'd called, I believe he would have verified that BSC is real and that I have it."

Set back on her heels slightly that he had such a ready explanation for what she had envisioned as the exposure of a lie that would set *him* on his heels, she had to take a moment to re-gather her thoughts before going on.

"When did Megan first tell you that she knew Scott Lain from before either of them moved to Rowley?" she finally asked. It was a rather desperate shot that he would fall into the guess-stated-as-fact trap and it didn't work.

"I *didn't* know that," he said. "When Megan and I were together we didn't spend our time talking about things like that." He then sat waiting patiently waiting for Jackie's next volley. It irritated the hell out of her.

Mentally scrambling to come up with a *gotcha*, Jackie slid a pad and pen across the table to Harry, and said, "Would you write, *I cannot tell a lie*, for me, please?"

"Cursive or block letters?" he asked as he picked up the pen.

"Cursive, please," she said, guessing that he probably thought she was looking for a sample of his handwriting. She wondered if he was going to try to disguise it, somehow, and although that meant nothing to her, she added, "Would you write it three times, please?" to reinforce that erroneous guess.

When he slid the pad back across, she showed it to Marcia, and then said to Harry, "The mistake you made when you changed the entries in Megan's journal on her computer is that you wrote the word *cannot* as one word—just as you've done here. Megan always wrote it as two words."

"Megan kept a journal?" he said ignoring the one-word, two-word thing. "I didn't know that. Did she mention me in it?"

"She did. Numerous times," Jackie said, running a bluff.

Calling it, he replied, "Did she write about her obsession with wanting to marry me?"

"She wrote of your pillow-talk about how to get rid of Pamela and collect her insurance money," Jackie said, doubling-down on the bluff.

He looked her in the eyes, and replied, "Fantasy ... on someone's part." He sat back and relaxed, and said, "So, are you accusing me of being involved in my wife's murder, somehow?"

"By your own admission, you had motive, means, and opportunity," Jackie replied. "We have a small mountain of real and circumstantial evidence that you conspired with Megan Hope and Scott Lain to murder Pamela, and then you and Megan got rid of Scott. Binding up all the loose ends, you then murdered Megan and staged it to look like self-defense."

He leaned forward, put his arms on the table with his wrists together, and said, "Then you should probably arrest me ... if you think you could make any of your fantasy evidence stick." He paused a moment, and added, "If not, I think I'm going to go home, now."

## *Chapter 42*
**Tuesday, July 20, 2021**

"Well, *that* sure as hell didn't go as planned," Jackie said as she and Marcia walked to her office after Harry left.

"Is he that good at lying," Marcia replied, "or are we that far off base?"

"*I'm* convinced that we're right," Jackie said. "The problem would be to convince a DA that this could be prosecuted and then to convince a jury that Harry is guilty. Everything is targets around bullet holes."

"You want to start looking through Megan's journal entries?" Marcia asked. "On the off chance that Mr. Fletcher missed something?"

"I don't have any better ideas," Jackie replied. "But he sure seems to have covered all of his tracks. Even if we found an entry where she named him he'd claim it was her wishful thinking or something. Damn, this is frustrating!"

They went back into Marcia's office where Megan's laptop drive was still connected to Marcia's computer. Marcia sat down and opened the Mead folder.

"Copy and send me the files for the last five years," Jackie said. "I think that's about how long Megan had been in town."

In her own office, Jackie did a search for the name Ricky and made an immediate hit in September of 2020. The journal entry read:

9/4/20

Finally sold that piece of crap bike! Now I have the money and room for a new one with tires that will survive the trails.

Met an old "friend" today. Ricky Lain! He's been working next door as a town cop! He goes by Scott now so I didn't even know. He pulled me over for speeding and when he saw who I was he nearly shit! LOL! I asked if Hall knew he was a convicted sex fiend and I knew from his face that she didn't. Not only did he not give me the ticket, I now have my hooks in him for any future violations! Sometimes life is just fun!

The next entry with his name was from March of 2021.

**3/7/21**

Bought a Prius today. Old but great gas mileage! Hope the battery holds out.

Ran the light at 133 & 1 and who should be at the Agawam but Ricky! He didn't know it was my new car and pulled me over. I pretended to play nice this time, and I pulled my shirt down under my naked boobs as he walked up. I thought he was going to swallow his tongue when he looked in at me! LOL! I told him if he let me go he could follow me to my place and I'd give him a blowjob. He did, and he lasted all of a minute. LOL! I hope it was good for him because I managed to snap a couple of pictures to prove that he "forced" me to have sex with him to get out of a ticket. I haven't sprung that twist on him yet ... he thinks we're the best of friends, now. Moron!

Jackie was certainly seeing a side of Megan that she never would have suspected. She clicked Find Next, and the journal entry from June 9 came up.

**6/9/21**

Busy day at work! Two car crashes and some idiot getting his hand crushed between his boat and his trailer down at Perley's.

Ricky responded to the boat call, as well, and he asked me if I wanted to get together again so he could "return the favor" I'd done for him. When we got here later, I suggested he put his handcuffs on me and "take" me. He loved it! Of course I had my phone on the dresser taking video. If I say so myself, my damsel-in-distress acting was damn good! I <u>own</u> that stupid little shit, now! Perfect for Hsrry's plot.

"Wow!" Jackie said out loud. She then let her eyes settle on *Perfect for Harry's plot.* Harry's plot to kill Pamela?

But if Harry had gone through Megan's journal to purge any connection to himself—probably searching for his name rather than reading every entry—why hadn't he found this instance? She looked at his name again and saw that it was misspelled. Megan must have accidentally hit the *s* rather than the adjacent *a* on the keyboard and not noticed it.

She was about to click Find Next, again, when her desk phone rang. "I have Carol Soucy on the line," Sharon told her. "She says it's urgent."

"Hi, Carol. What's up?" Jackie said when the call was switched over.

"Is Harry still there?" she asked.

"No. He left a few minutes ago still sticking to his I-don't-know-what-you're-talking-about story," she replied.

"Well, you might want to get him back," Carol said, "because I found something that will refresh his memory. Is Marcia with you? She'll want to hear this, too."

A few moments later, Jackie said, "Marcia's here and you're on speaker, Carol. Talk to us."

"Okay, so when I got home after helping my client," she began, "I decided to look at my copy of Harry's drive to see if maybe he had a folder-hiding program on it, too, where he might be hiding a master outline of this real-life story. From the way you two were explaining it, it seems way too complex to keep in your head."

"You have a copy of Mr. Fletcher's computer drive at your house?" Marcia said.

"Oh, I ... um ..."

"That's on me," Jackie said to Marcia. "I'll explain later. Carol, go on, please."

"So, well, anyway, I didn't find anything," Carol continued. "But that doesn't mean it was *never* there, I did the same kind of Internet history-search that I did on Megan's laptop, and saw that he had been looking for *free folder hiding software* back in November of last year."

"But no way to know if he ever installed it?" Jackie asked.

"This only tells me what he searched for, not if he downloaded it," Carol said. "Your State Police Lab might be able to drill down that deep, but I can't. Maybe you could get records from the software companies, even. But the good news is that that won't be necessary.

"So, I remembered that Harry had been using Pamela's computer for a week or so while I was fixing his back around February. You remember that's why I thought *she* had narcolepsy when it was really him. So, I got to wondering if he had been creating an outline of this reality murder plot, would he have copied it to Pamela's system so he could keep working on it while his computer was out of commission? Turns out, the answer is yes."

"Watson, you're my hero!" Jackie said.

"It also turns out that he had installed a copy of Hinder on Pamela's computer to keep her from stumbling upon his plot while they were both using the same system. He must have forgotten to delete it when he got his own computer back.

"I went back to *his* drive and found a password cheat-sheet, and his Hinder password was sitting there. It wasn't even quasi-hidden on another sheet like Megan's"

"And there *was* an outline on her computer?" Marcia asked excitedly.

"Yup! Of course, you guys are the experts in that, but I'd sure think what's written there, along with everything else you were talking about, would be enough to get your arrest warrant for him. Oh, and when I said I thought Megan was cold; well, she's a balmy breeze compared to Harry. He is cryogenic!"

"When was the outline created?" Marcia asked. "How long was he planning this?"

"I looked at my records, and it was created while I had *his* computer here putting in a motherboard and doing overdue updates," Carol replied. "There's no way of knowing when he first saved the file on his own computer; like the note on Scott's laptop, it got a new created date when it was copied to Pamela's system. But, also like the note, the modified date was earlier than the created date. That was Friday, November 6, 2020."

"So, at *least* nine months," Jackie said.

"Why would he have copied it to his wife's computer and not his own laptop?" Marcia asked.

"His laptop is old, nearly full, and was a piece of junk when it was new," Carol answered. "I've told him to get a new one and I'll transfer all his files."

"Okay, that makes sense. But then why go to the bother of copying the outline to his wife's computer—and adding the file-hiding software—if he wasn't going to add to it or revise it?"

"I wondered that, too," Jackie said. "What if he felt the need to get it off his system before Carol took it? Maybe he thought he'd be working on it, but then didn't get to it."

"Which might tend to explain why it's still there," Marcia said. "If he never went back to work on it, maybe he forgot that it *was* there."

"Be all of that as it may, fantastic work, Carol!" Jackie said. "Can you send me the file right now?"

"I just hit Send," Carol replied.

# Chapter 43

**Tuesday, July 20, 2021**

Marcia moved around to the other side of Jackie's desk so they could both see her monitor. After a few clicks, Harry's outline was on the screen.

1. How
    - 1.1 Home accident
        - 1.1.1 Fall
            - * Hits head
            - * Broken neck
            - * Basement stairs?
            - * Garage? Slip on oil?
        - 1.1.2 Choking
            - * Hard to fake!
        - 1.1.3 Fire/burns
            - * Want to keep house!
        - 1.1.4 Drowning
            - * Fall in tub
        - 1.1.5 Poisoning
            - * Accidental overdose? Of what?
            - * Always leaves traces!
    - 1.2 Fall down basement stairs
        - 1.2.1 2,521 deaths from falls on stairs in 2020
        - 1.2.2 Trip or push
        - 1.2.3 Hit head on floor
            - * Hit her on head first (hair/blood transfer!)
        - 1.2.4 Broken neck from fall

* Break her neck first (must be snapped back not twisted!)

1.3 Fall in garage

    1.3.1 6,000 deaths from falls per year

    1.3.2 Spill oil while working on lawn mower

    1.3.3 Trip her

    1.3.4 Push head into floor (must be done with one hit!) (hair/blood transfer!)

1.4 Choking

    1.4.1 1,000 deaths per year

    1.4.2 Push meat into throat during sleep (sure to wake up!) (evidence of struggle until she passes out!)

1.5 Fire/burns

    1.5.1 No

1.6 Drowning

    1.6.1 341 times in 2020

    1.6.2 Falls in tub then drowns

        * Hit her on head first (hair/blood transfer!) (must be water in lungs!)

        * Watching movie while Pam is in bath (volume up so didn't hear water running!) (motive, means, and opportunity!) (top of suspect list!)

1.7 Poisoning

    1.7.1 5,000 lives per year

    1.7.2 Research her meds for interactions

    1.7.3 Force OD by putting in drink/food (will she notice taste!) (illogical accident!)

2) Back-up plan if "accident" is questioned

    2.1 Her lover will be prime suspect

        2.1.1 Get Scott to reengage w/Pamela?

            * Can Megan facilitate that?

* She has something on him. What?

2.2 Could fake Scott's suicide with confession in note.

"Holy shit!" Marcia said. "That's more than enough smoke for *two* guns! Mrs. Fletcher's *and* Scott's"

"It confirms some of our guesses, and fills in some blanks," Jackie added. "He must have updated this a lot more after February, but as a first draft this certainly works for us."

"And Carol was right about cryogenic!" Marcia said. "He obviously researched all the common household accidents and how many people died every year from each type. Then he *spitballed* how each one could be used to kill his wife before apparently settling on drowning."

"He even adds parenthetical warnings to himself about possible pitfalls," Jackie added. Pointing, she went on, "He talks about getting Scott to *reengage* with Pamela so he can use him as the scapegoat. He even talks about the faked suicide and the note. But he stopped updating this copy in February." Jackie minimized the screen with the outline to show the page of Megan's journal that she had been looking at when Carol called. She pointed out the typo of Harry's name, and that it was probably why Harry hadn't found and purged it.

Marcia read it, and said, "Jesus! Talk about a viper! Wow! And the '*Perfect for Harry's plot.*' line ties directly to the outline in my opinion."

"And where she says, '*I own that stupid little shit, now!*' I'll bet that's how she got him to actually commit the murder," Jackie added. "She had her hook into him like a marlin gaff."

"Only he screwed it up," she went on. "Maybe he thought strangling and drowning would look the same. So Megan—and maybe Harry too—had to go over and straighten things out."

Jackie went back to her email and forwarded Harry's outline to Marcia. As she clicked, she said, "Can you call your judge friend, and see if she'll grant you an emergency audience to sign an arrest warrant for Harry? I don't want to waste any time. It suddenly occurred to Carol that this piece of outline could have been on Pamela's computer; there's no reason that that might not pop into his head, too. I don't want him destroying her drive even though we've cloned it. That's a whole can of legal worms I'd prefer not to have to untangle."

Four minutes later, Marcia was in the passenger seat of a Rowley cruiser and heading for Newburyport District Court with lights flashing and siren wailing.

# Chapter 44

**Tuesday, July 20, 2021**

Fourteen minutes after she left, Marcia called Jackie, and said, "It's signed and we're on the way back."

"Excellent!" Jackie replied. "Tell Paul to go directly to Harry's. I'll meet you there."

Ten minutes later Jackie was parked around the corner from Harry's street, and when she saw the cruiser coming up behind her, she pulled out. She pulled into Harry's driveway and Paul parked across the driveway behind her.

When Harry came to the door, he looked out at the cruiser with its lights flashing, and said, "Again? If you had telephoned, I'd have come to the station on my own. I don't need a ride."

"Would you mind stepping outside, here, Harry?" Jackie said.

He opened the screen door and as he stepped out onto the landing, he asked, "What's going on, Jackie? You're way too serious."

"Turn around and put your hands behind you, Harry," she replied. "You're under arrest for the murder of your wife, Pamela Fletcher. You have the right to remain silent ..." When she finished his Miranda rights, she asked, "Do you understand these rights as they've been explained to you?"

"Yes. And you've got to be shitting me," he said. "You're arresting me based on that circumstantial crap you were telling me about earlier? I thought you were smarter than that."

"That and the partial outline of Pamela's murder plot that you left hidden on her computer," Jackie replied. "It was plenty to get a judge to sign an arrest warrant."

He stood there silently, facing away from Jackie and Marcia for a few moments, then, looking back over his shoulder, he said, "So, Carol, huh? She's a bit too clever for my good, apparently. Damned sloppy housekeeping on my part. I forgot completely that I'd even copied it over there. If I'd remembered, I'd have made sure it was flushed when they requested an autopsy ... long before you had Carol clone it."

Paul put Harry in the back of the cruiser, and Jackie told him, "Book him and leave him in the holding cell until I get there. I shouldn't be long. Let him call his lawyer if he asks."

With Marcia in the passenger seat of the Jeep, Jackie drove off toward the center of town.

## Chapter 45

**Tuesday, July 20, 2021**

As she drove, Jackie called Carol's cell phone through the Jeep's speakers.

"Hi, Carol," Jackie said when she answered. "I'm just calling to see if you're home. I have something I want to drop off for you."

"Did I leave my sunglasses at the station?" she said. "I haven't been able to find the darned things all afternoon."

"Afraid that's not it," Jackie said. "We should be there in about ten minutes. Marcia is with me."

Carol invited the two women in, and with Neil in the kitchen, too, Jackie told her, "I wanted you to be the first to know that we just placed Harry under arrest for the murder of his wife."

Even though she had been deeply involved in the investigation, it still shocked her, and she inhaled sharply and put her hand to her chest. "Oh, my God!" she said. "So, did he actually admit it?"

"The next best thing," Jackie said. "He didn't try to deny it. He acknowledged that he had forgotten his murder-plot outline on Pamela's computer, and referred to you as *a bit too clever for his good* for having discovered it.

"So, for your invaluable services in solving the case," Jackie said as she took an item from her pants pocket, "You are hereby granted the first-ever *Dr. Watson Award* for civilian sleuthing above and beyond the call of duty." As she spoke, she handed her a brass-rimmed magnifying glass with a polished wood handle. "To go along with your bullet," she added.

Both Jackie and Marcia shook her hand, and with a big smile, she showed her trophy to Neil.

"Nice!" he said. "Congratulations! So, do you think you'll be able to find your sunglasses with that?"

## Chapter 46

**Tuesday, July 20, 2021**

As they drove back to the station, Harry said from the backseat of the cruiser, "I guess I should have known better, huh? You'd think with all the crime novels I've written—in which the killer never gets away with it—that I'd have known there'd be a loose end somewhere. I have to give Hall a lot of credit; she's more tenacious than I expected. I underestimated her."

"She's a good chief," was all that Paul offered in reply.

They pulled around behind the police station, and Paul tapped a number into a small keypad on the dash. The big garage door of the sally port rolled up, and he pulled inside. He then pushed a single button and the door rolled down behind the cruiser, securing it, Paul, and Harry inside the garage bay. Only then did Paul get out.

Paul helped Harry out of the backseat, led him to the door leading into the station, and holding him by the handcuffs with one hand, unlocked the door with his other. He clipped the keyring onto his belt as he led Harry to the booking area.

Paul took the cuffs off Harry, and as he rubbed his wrists, Harry said, "Can I go pee before we get started with all this?"

Paul pointed to the holding cell, and said, "You'll have to go in there. The restroom's not in a secure part of the building."

Harry shrugged, and said, "Department policy, huh?" He went inside the holding cell with its painted cement-block walls, its unpadded bench, and lidless stainless steel toilet. He stood in front of the toilet, pulled down his fly, and then looking down, he said loudly, "Oh, seriously? Paul, come here. Do you really expect me to piss on this?"

Paul came in and asked, "Piss on what?" as he looked into the stainless bowl.

Harry brought his elbow up as hard and fast as he could and hit Paul in the throat. Choking, Paul staggered back, and Harry followed him and hit him across the jaw with all of his might. Paul's head snapped around, jarring his brain inside his skull, and after seeing a brilliant flash of white light, he dropped to the floor unconscious.

Harry pulled his keys from the clip on his belt and took the weapon from his holster.

At the door to the sally port, Harry had to try three different keys before the deadbolt would turn and let him out. He started toward the garage door to find the button to open it, but when he saw the ten-digit keypad next to the door he knew better than to even try.

He got into the cruiser, started it, and quickly pulled forward as far as possible. Shifting into reverse, he pushed the accelerator to the floor and the cruiser roared backward, crashing into the door, ripping it from its guide rollers.

As the truck went out under the mangled door, the light-bar on the roof was ripped off and flung down across the windshield, held on by only its wires.

Harry shifted into drive and was speeding out of the parking lot as Sharon and Kyle rushed to the back of the building to see what all the noise was.

## Chapter 47

**Tuesday, July 20, 2021**

"So, do you think we'll be able to make a case for Mr. Fletcher being involved in Scott's death?" Marcia asked as she and Jackie drove back to the station. "He does mention faking his suicide and the note in his outline."

"Possible, but probably a real long-shot," Jackie replied. "And I don't see much hope of going after him for Megan's murder, at all. That's all circumstantial and speculation."

Just then Jackie's radio blared, "Dispatch to Chief Hall. Do you copy?"

She lifted it from the cup holder, and replied, "Go for Hall."

"Chief, Harry just broke out! He knocked Paul out, stole the cruiser, and crashed out through the sally port door. He went east on 133 when he left here. And he has Paul's sidearm."

"Jesus! Is Paul okay?" she replied.

"I think so. He's awake but he can't talk. We think Harry hit him in the throat. The EMTs are with him now. An ambulance is on the way."

"Jesus!" Jackie repeated.

Suddenly, Marcia hollered, "Look out! Look out!" as she pointed out the windshield.

Coming at them was a Rowley cruiser with its light-bar hanging from the roof by wires, and passing a car in their lane.

Jackie swerved off the road, hitting a mailbox with her right mirror while the whipping light-bar hit and shattered her left one.

She skidded to a stop, handed the radio to Marcia, and as she cranked the wheel all the way to the left, she said, "Tell them we're in pursuit eastbound on 133 headed toward 1A. Request all possible assistance."

With her fights flashing and the siren blaring, she pulled out and accelerated after Harry.

Harry was hemmed in by a truck going the speed limit and a long line of oncoming traffic, and Jackie was able to gain on him. But as she approached from behind, a small opening in the line of traffic beside him appeared, and he darted between a car and a truck, coming out on the other side of the road. He roared across driveways and lawns and took out mailboxes and planters, and finally made it back onto the road beyond the line of traffic and far away from Jackie.

Laying on the siren to get the traffic to part, Jackie suddenly said, "Oh, shit! I wonder if he's going after Carol! Use your phone and call her!"

"I don't have her number!" Marcia said. "Can't we use the speakers?"

"There's too much noise with the siren; it'll cut in and out," Jackie said as she took the corner onto Bradford St., very fast.

"Where's your phone?" Marcia asked.

"In my pocket!" and she twisted herself to be able to get it out while steering with one hand. She almost dropped it handing it to Marcia, and said, "She'll be in the contacts. It's sorted by first names."

"Hi, Jackie," Carol answered. "The mystery of my sunglasses is solved! I forgot ..."

"Carol, this is Marcia! Fletcher broke out of the station and we think he's on his way there! We're only a minute behind him; do you have a safe room or something?"

"A safe room? This isn't tornado alley," Carol said. "All we have is closets."

"Well, get in the basement and barricade the door or something," Marcia said. "We'll be there in a couple minutes."

"Oh, wait!" Carol said, "The cavalry's here. A cruiser just pulled into the driveway. You had me really worried there for a minute."

"If the light-bar's busted off the roof that's Fletcher! Run and hide, Carol! We'll be right there!"

# Chapter 48

**Tuesday, July 20, 2021**

Harry slid out of the cruiser, and as he walked quickly toward the house he pulled the slide back on Paul's Glock, making sure there was a round in the chamber and the weapon was cocked. Harry didn't own a gun, but having written about this one, he knew that it had no external safety; just a little mechanism built into the trigger.

He glanced at the two cars in the driveway; both Carol's and Neil's presumably. He had no beef with Neil, and in fact, rather liked him, but he'd be extendible if he wanted to play the hero husband.

Although Harry knew where Carol lived from when he dropped off his computer to be fixed, he had never been inside the house. But from the pathway that led to the garage, he could tell where the backdoor would be.

He walked along the side of the house, around the end of an extension to the main house that he guessed contained the kitchen. With the gun at his side, he walked across the back patio, up the few steps, and tried the door. The handle turned, but it was deadbolted. He was a little surprised at that; this was Rowley and it was the back door. Had they seen him pull up and seen the gun in his hand? No matter.

He used the butt of the gun to shatter the windowpane next to the deadbolt, and reached in. There was no knob on the other end, however; it was keyed from both sides. Again, no matter.

He stepped back as far as he could on the landing and then drove himself at the door, hitting it with his hip and his arm held tightly against his side. He heard to crack of wood and he could see that the door had moved a bit. He took a second charge at it, the frame splintered, and the door flung open.

So much for the element of surprise if he ever had one.

With the gun held in front of him, Harry scanned the kitchen. At one end there was a door with a big frosted-glass window with the word, "Pantry" etched into it. He walked toward it, stealing frequent glances toward the other end of the kitchen, and listening intently.

He turned the knob slowly and then pulled the door in quickly, throwing it open and making it bang against the cabinets behind it. When he pulled, he stepped to the side in case someone was ready to jump out at him, and he listened closely for a scream or a gasp from within. Silence.

He looked in the pantry, and satisfied that it was empty, he put the gun in his waistband and walked over to the big kitchen table. He pushed a couple of chairs aside and then shoved the table against the closed side door where he came in. This wouldn't stop anyone from getting out that way, but it would slow them down and allow him to hear it while he searched the rest of the house.

Gun in hand once more, he walked into the living room. It was a big, open area, and looked like it had been remodeled more recently than the rest of the house. Great place for parties, but no place to hide.

At the far end was a door, partially ajar. He looked in from a short distance, even peering through the crack at the hinge side of the door to make sure no one was behind it.

Inside the room was a desk with two big flat-screen monitors on it. A laptop computer sat closed on the desk, and a big PC stood on the floor under it. It was obviously Carol's office, and Harry was tempted to put bullets through her computers and screens. He decided against it and continued his search.

Again he put the gun in his waistband, and he pushed the sofa around and up against the front door.

Directly opposite the door—running half the length of the wall—was a stairway with an open railing that led up to the second story. Below the stairs was a door that Harry was sure opened onto the basement steps. Beside that door was another that could have been almost anything; closet; bathroom; bedroom; junk room; whatever.

He decided to check the rest of the house before the cellar, and he walked over and picked up a tall floor lamp from beside an overstuffed chair and gave it a tug, ripping its plug from the wall. He carried the lamp to the basement door and leaned it precariously against the doorknob. If anyone tried to sneak out of the cellar he would hear the clatter as it fell.

As he had done with the pantry, he turned the knob of the other door slowly and then flung it open. It looked like a catch-all room, although it had probably been a bedroom at one point in the history of the house. He scanned it quickly and then, using the barrel of the gun, pushed open one of the sliding doors of the closet. It was obviously where they kept their winter coats, and there was no room for a person.

He left the room, closing the door behind him, and headed for the stairs. He went up making no pretense of being quiet. When he got to the top, he stopped and listened for any noise from below. He heard nothing.

***

After finally working free of the traffic clog on 133, Jackie flew across Bradford St., past Hardy's Auto Body, made the right turn onto Wethersfield St., and then came to a screeching halt. A big, ten-wheeled dump truck, its bed tilted up in the air, totally blocked the road as two workers metered gravel into an open trench on the side of the road.

Jackie had completely forgotten about the roadside construction going on here since last Friday.

To the right, the front end of the truck was only a few feet from a telephone pole, and to the left was the open trench, so Jackie spun the Jeep in a u-turn, going up on the sidewalk, and then sped back down Bradford St. forced to backtrack and take a longer route through the center of town to reach Carol's.

***

At the top of the stairs was a short corridor that extended left and right from where he stood. There was one door to his left, which was slightly ajar so he could see it was the master bedroom. Straight ahead was a closed door that he guessed was the upstairs bath. On his right, the corridor was longer, and had a door on either side of it, probably opening into bedrooms. One door was wide open, the other about halfway.

He chose to try the bathroom first, and once again, he opened the door noisily, but this time stood directly in it with the gun out in front in both hands. He stepped in and flipped open the linen closet door, but a magician's contortionist assistant couldn't have fit in it. He moved in deeper and with the barrel of the gun he swished back the shower curtain. Empty.

He decided to check the master bedroom next because he would be able to see the top of the stairs while in there, in case anyone darted from one of the other rooms. While making frequent glances out the doorway, he checked under the bed and in the closet.

He left and pulled the door closed. He went to the bedroom on the right and again looked behind the door before he went in. He looked under the bed and was about to open the closet door when he heard a squeak from below him in Carol's office.

*Shit!* Distracted by wanting to shoot her computers he hadn't checked the closet in there! *Shit! Shit! Shit!*

As he ran from the bedroom he heard running in the living room, and as he came down the corridor he caught a glimpse through the railing of legs going past down below. He fired a shot that nicked one of the balusters and punched a hole in the oak floor a foot and a half behind Carol.

As she ran, Carol threw the leaning floor lamp out into the floor in a useless attempt to slow down her pursuer.

Harry took the stairs two at a time and used the newel cap at the bottom to spin himself around and in the direction of the kitchen.

Heading for the kitchen door and escape, Carol yelled, "*Shit!*" when she saw the table pushed against it. She tried to pull it back, but when she heard Harry's feet hit the living room floor, she gave up and yelling "*Neil!*" at the top of her lungs, she ran into the pantry, pulling the door closed behind her.

Harry entered the kitchen just in time to see the door close.

"Brilliant place to hide, Soucy!" he said, loudly. "You must have learned that from watching teenager horror movies."

He leveled the gun at the pantry door and pulled the trigger. The bullet went through the tempered glass, and it exploded into thousands of tiny pieces.

"*Neil!*" Carol screamed, again from her crouched spot in the corner of the pantry, her hands clapped tightly over her ears.

Outside, Jackie slid the Jeep to a stop in the front yard, and she and Marcia were out as the dust was still catching up to them.

In the kitchen, Harry moved his aim a couple of feet along the pantry wall and fired again. He knew she wasn't there; he just wanted to terrorize her. He aimed another couple feet to the right and fired once more.

"Oh, shit!" Jackie yelled as she ran toward the back of the house where the shots came from. "Marcia, stay down!"

Jackie could see Harry through the kitchen window. He was facing away toward the far end of the kitchen, and although she couldn't see it, from the posture of his upper body she was sure he was aiming a gun out in front of himself.

She raised her weapon and took aim although he was a terrible target. From her spot in the driveway, she could only see him from the shoulders up, he was in profile, and he was moving. Making the shot worse, the bullet would have to go through a screen and a double-pane window.

Suddenly, she caught some motion that made her hold her shot.

Harry's ears were ringing from the three shots he had fired in the confinement of the kitchen, so he didn't hear Neil come up out of the cellar or creep up behind him. He *did* catch the sound of the swish of air as Neil swung the long-handle shovel at his head, however.

Reacting to the sound, Harry spun and only by accident happened to move just enough so that the point of the shovel's blade glanced across his right cheek, leaving a deep scratch, but then sliced into his ear, cutting it nearly in two.

"*Son of a bitch!*" Harry yelled and blindly fired his gun in Neil's direction as he brought his left hand up to grab his ear.

The shot missed, but as Neil brought the shovel back for another swing, Harry quickly stepped back, turned to squarely face his attacker, and although his right eye was watering badly he brought his gun up for a much more controlled point-blank aim.

The window behind Harry suddenly shattered and he felt the searing pain of a 9mm slug rip into his shoulder, tearing through flesh and shattering bone. His gun fired one more time—the bullet pinging off of the shovel's blade—but the recoil caused it to jump for his weakened grip.

Clutching his shoulder, Harry spun to look out through the broken window and directly into the barrel of Jackie's Glock twenty feet away. As he focused on her determined face behind the gun, his eyes rolled back in his head and he fell over. First onto the counter, and then off onto the floor.

Neil dropped his shovel, picked up Harry's gun, and then stepped through the blown-out door of the pantry. He turned to see his wife crouched in the corner in as small of a ball as she could get herself. "Are you okay?" he asked as he crouched down with her. "He didn't hit you, did he?"

"No," she answered on a long breath that she didn't even know she'd been holding. "I guess he couldn't hit a trembling target."

She reached out to him to be helped to her feet, but a crunch of glass caused Neil to spin around and find Harry stepping quickly through the door with a carving knife in his good left hand.

Neil instinctively raised the gun and aimed at the middle of Harry's chest.

Harry stopped momentarily when he saw the gun. He knew he had dropped it, but he didn't know that Neil had picked it up. But when he didn't pull the trigger right away, Harry guessed that Neil was one of those people who just couldn't take another human life, and he resumed his advance.

Harry was half right; Neil *didn't* want to kill him. Instead he lowered his aim and put a bullet through Harry's left knee from three feet away. It blew his knee cap into a hundred fragments and ripped away a golf ball-size chunk of his lower femur.

Harry bellowed, dropped the knife, and collapsed sideway, bringing a couple of shelves and a dozen cans down onto himself.

There was another crunch of glass, and Neil and Carol looked up to see Jackie looking around the door with her Glock out in front of her.

"Is everyone okay?" she asked, seeing all three people on the floor, but training her gun on Harry.

"*We're* okay," Carol said as she looked at the destruction in front of her. "But my pantry's pretty well wrecked!" She looked up at Jackie, and added, "I can put the repairs on my expense report, right?"

## *Epilogue*

**Harry Fletcher** was arraigned remotely from his hospital bed after undergoing surgery on his left knee. He has been charged with the first-degree murder of his wife, Pamela; with assault with a deadly weapon and the attempted murder of Carol Soucy; with the assault of a police officer; with theft of police property; with willful destruction of police property; with illegal possession of a firearm; and with conspiracy to commit murder in the case of Scott Lain. No charges have been filed with regards to the death of Megan Hope as there is insufficient physical evidence to dispute his continued claim of self-defense. A date for Harry Fletcher's trial will be set after his knee replacement surgery. He is currently incarcerated in the Lemuel Shattuck Hospital Correctional Unit in Jamaica Plain.

**Megan Hope**: When they read through all of Megan's journal entries they found many episodes of sexually deviant behavior, and several other instances of blackmail. A group of entries from her hard-copy journals alluded to another homicide when she was young. The info was forwarded to the Waltham Police for investigation and closed a decades-old unsolved case. Electronic journal entries made it clear that Megan had hatched the idea of Pamela's DUI stop to force her to get together with Scott one more time, thereby setting him up as the scapegoat.

**Marcia Grieves** continues to work for the Essex County District Attorney's Office, and is part of the team that will prosecute Harry Fletcher. Marcia and Jackie continue to be close friends.

**Jackie Hall** remains Chief of Police in Rowley and is prepared to testify when Harry Fletcher's trial begins. She continues to date Jeff Holder and has given him a key to her front door. They enjoy frequent sleepovers.

**Carol Soucy** continues her IT work for numerous local clients, including the Rowley Police and other town agencies. Neil and her kids have encouraged her to retire, but she claims that her interaction with her clients and with solving their problems is what keeps her going. She is excited and nervous to testify at Harry Fletcher's trial.

**Neil Soucy** had Carol's bullet gold plated and made into a necklace as a Christmas gift.

## *Acknowledgements:*

I would like to thank the following people for allowing me to use their real names to add authenticity to this work of fiction.

(In order of appearance)

*Susan (Hardy) Belle*: Rowley native and current resident. Author's close neighbor while growing up. Daughter of Bob Hardy, Rowley's first Chief of Police.

*Carol (Larson) Soucy*: Current Rowley resident. Author's Newburyport High School classmate and IT wizard. *Neil* is her remarkably patient husband.

*Mary Alice (Berger) Timmons*: Rowley native and current resident. Grade school and high school classmate. *Ray* is her husband.

*Fred & Brice Hardy*: Rowley natives and current residents. Father-son owners of Hardy's Auto Body in Rowley. Fred is Chief Bob Hardy's nephew.

*Barbra J. (Parsons) Hopkinson*: Author's Newburyport High School classmate. Co-author of "A Butterfly's Journey; Healing Grief After the Loss of a Child." She is a certified Grief Recovery Specialist and founder & CEO of the non-profit "A Butterfly's Journey."